She screwed up. She broke protocol. She saved a life. Grim Reaper Margo Petrov may have resurrected a drowned surfer on the brink of death, but she isn't earning any awards or receiving employee of the month from Corporate; she's under more scrutiny from the Grim governing body than ever before. Since she has a massive secret that could spell disaster if revealed, she sure as hell doesn't want to be in the spotlight, in any form.

Margo vows to keep her head down and stay out of trouble, reaping her quota of spirits lest she cause more problems for herself and the woman she saved with an illegal blood bond. She certainly shouldn't be opening doors to the Fae lands or offering her neck to an Empusa woman suffering from bloodlust, but Margo's laundry list of bad decisions keeps growing. With the threat of becoming decommissioned by Corporate looming in her periphery, Margo stumbles deeper into the politics of her people and soon realizes their intentions are far worse than she initially thought.

GRIMMER INTENTIONS

Tales from the Grim, Book Two

Jodi Hutchins

A NineStar Press Publication

Published by NineStar Press
P.O. Box 91792,
Albuquerque, New Mexico, 87199 USA.
www.ninestarpress.com

Grimmer Intentions

Printed in the USA
First Edition
December, 2019

Print ISBN: 978-1-951057-77-0

Also available in eBook, ISBN: 978-1-951057-71-8

Warning: This book contains sexually explicit content, which may only be suitable for mature readers, references to death and dying, including that of children, childhood trauma, grief, blood, abandonment, hate/racism toward a specific group of preternatural creatures, and references to cancer.

To Scotty (3/7/91—3/13/19), who brightened the world with every single one of his smiles.

Chapter One

TEN YEARS EARLIER

"Margo, calm down. You can't go killing someone just because they pissed you off."

Margo Petrov pumped her arms, increasing her speed as she cut across the dead grass of the front lawn, though her initial fury had settled to a low broil. The cold metal of the baseball bat against her palm was soothing but not calming enough to ease the rage completely.

The sound of Luis's sneakers pounding the asphalt behind her indicated he'd finally caught up. "I'm not going to kill them," she grumbled.

Luis snorted. "Okay, well, when you storm out of your apartment, yelling, 'I'm going to fucking kill 'em, Luis,' I think I can safely assume you're going to kill someone."

She stopped abruptly, causing Luis to run into her chest as she turned to face him. "Fine," she said, tossing the bat into the bushes lining the sidewalk. She grabbed his shoulders, lowering her gaze to his. "Nobody fucks with my brother without consequence. Nobody," she said, shaking him slightly to emphasize her seriousness.

Headlights from a passing car gleamed in his wide brown-eyed gaze as he nodded.

"Besides"—she started, as she dropped her hands from him, quirking an eyebrow—"I just want to know if they're afraid of the dark." She'd been livid when Luis told her the resident group of asshats from their high school decided to give Luis hell on his way back from the library.

Without further discussion, Margo continued down the cracked sidewalks of downtown Philadelphia.

"They still hang out at the bowling alley on Daly Ave?"

Luis huffed a discontented sigh, eliciting a grin from Margo. "Dude come on. Think about this for a second; do you really want to risk another arrest? You're almost eighteen, and you could be charged as an adult."

He had a point, and she admitted that to herself, but she continued down the sidewalk anyway, cutting across the street, her feet displacing loose black asphalt pebbles on the worn roadway. "Yeah, but they need to leave you the hell alone. This is getting ridiculous." For years, she and her brother experienced taunting for their otherness, Luis taking the brunt end most times. The basketball team tormented Luis for merely existing; however, Margo guessed they blamed their mocking on his differences. They needed a good scare, using a bit of magic, the otherness his tormentors weren't aware of. She wanted to scare them so bad they'd piss themselves. If all else failed, she'd just beat the shit out of them.

Luis gave a shrug of nonchalance, something she instantly recognized as her brother's passive language, which furthered the desire to teach the perpetrators a lesson. Instead of digging into his dismissal, she turned and continued her way toward downtown.

Luis followed.

The streets were busy even though rush hour had ended a few hours prior. Cars zipped past, a stray honk resounding a few blocks away, voices rising in a cacophonous argument. The late-night city sounds were laden with a warning, hinting at the kind of night bad things happened, stirring a deep foreboding in the air around them.

Luis jabbed her in the ribs, ripping Margo from her eerie thoughts. "Hey, do you see that?" He pointed to LOVE Park on the opposite side of the crosswalk. Standing beside the water fountain was a child, their head turning from side to side in rapid succession. Luis was clearly pointing to the small person; however, the iridescent shift of air around the child indicated to Margo they weren't alive.

Before meeting Luis, she agreed with the titles given to her—weirdo, crazy, psychic—the names condensing her down to a freak who could see ghosts with the only person to possibly believe her long dead. Of course, she'd been ecstatic to find kinship in another, to prove at least to herself she wasn't crazy. That is until Luis stopped for every spirit in sight with their Sally-sob story. "Yeah, I see them, and no, we don't have time."

Luis scoffed just as the light turned, and he hurried across the street without waiting for Margo.

She rushed after him, forgoing her planned scare tactics on the basketball team in hopes she'd convince him to leave well enough alone.

They approached the park's edge, Luis carefully watching the child. Luckily, the park held no other visitors, alive or dead. "We have to help her," he whispered before he stuck his lower lip out.

She rolled her eyes. "They aren't stray puppies, Luis. We can't help every single one of them."

Brows cinching, he met her gaze with an icy stare. "Maybe this is why we can see them, to help them move on."

Though reluctant to admit it, she'd come to the very same conclusion herself a long time ago. With no way of knowing why they could guide ghostly apparitions to the other side, she couldn't come up with a better reason herself. She glanced over at the redheaded girl and sighed. "Fine, but we need to be quick, and I still want to find those idiots so I can mess up their night."

They cut through the grass, making their way to the child cowering beside the placid pool in a few strides. Years before, Margo had visited LOVE Park with a foster family; she couldn't remember who they were as the names and faces all meshed together, but she recalled the beautiful water spilling from the fountain, countless skateboarders cruising the sidewalks, and scents of French fries and hot dogs wafting from the closest wheeled food cart. The atmosphere was one Margo wanted to stay in forever. During the night with a cold winter chill in the air, though, she wanted nothing more than to get the hell out of there. They approached the spirit, Margo shoving her hands into her pockets. The child dipped her head as if downcast, her crimson ringlets shielding her face.

Luis knelt, head tilting to the side to catch her gaze. "Hi, there, kiddo. Are you lost?"

Margo stayed back and observed her brother at work. If this were an occupation, he was made for it. His soft voice and calm demeanor combined with his eager desire to help others and the sometimes nauseating greater-good complex slated him perfectly with helping spirits cross over. When they first met, neither had a clue they shared such a monumental power. The discovery of their mutual energy was happenstance; Luis saw a spirit in their foster home, as did Margo, and they helped them move on to the other side, wherever the shimmering doorway led the person.

The origins of their talents differed; Margo drew hers from instinct, the budding energy filling her after losing the closest thing she had to a parent as a child, aiding her foster mother to the other side shortly after her death. Luis experienced a similar situation after a death in the church his foster family attended when he was six. The only difference between them was Margo's extra ability.

The child's face lifted, the light catching the faint glittery aura around her. "My mommy told me to stay here and not move a muscle. Sisie ran into the park and Mommy had to catch her. They ran over there," she said, pointing in the direction of the deserted park. "I saw this coin in the water, and it was so pretty, so I climbed into the fountain to get it. I heard mommy calling me, and I was scared she would be really, really mad so I tried to jump out, but I slipped." She glanced at Margo, her face disconcerted. "I think I hit my head."

The back of the child's head opened on a massive wound, blood glaring and glistening. Margo bit back her gasp. She pretended she was used to seeing the morbid displays some ghosts showcased from their deaths, but in reality, a wave of nausea rocked into her each time. She turned to Luis again, listening to their conversation. A shiver ran through Margo, and she shook her head.

"I bet that hurt," Luis said, seemingly unphased. He took the ghost's hand in his own. "Why are you still here?"

With a scrunch of her nose, the little girl shrugged. "I dun know. Mommy told me not to move, so I have to stay here till she gets back."

A car slowed as it drove by the park, and Margo yanked her hood over her head. This was a bad idea. Most times, the two were discreet when they aided souls in abandoned buildings, graveyards, or at least indoors, fearful of curious passersby potentially calling them crazy or calling the police. She didn't want someone assuming their presence in the park at such a late hour was suspicious. "Luis, hurry up."

He ignored her, his full attention on the child. "I think it's okay for you to go. I think just this once she wouldn't get mad at you for leaving this spot." His warm smile eased even Margo's anxiety. Only slightly.

"Are you sure? Mommy told me not to talk to strangers or go with them." She kicked the ground, tilting her head so her hair concealed her face again.

Margo cleared her throat. "Smart mom. Thing is, you aren't of this world anymore, kid. I think when you hit your head things changed for you."

A glare crested Luis's face before he looked at the child again. "Did your mommy ever tell you about life and death?"

Grass filled the cracks in the cement of the sidewalk, and the little girl kicked the blades with her dirty tennis shoe. "When my fish died, we flushed it down the toilet." She peered up at Luis so fast her hair whipped her in the face, and her forehead creased dramatically. "You're not going to flush me down the toilet, are you?"

He chuckled. "No, we aren't going to flush you. So, you know you aren't alive anymore?"

She pursed her lips and nodded.

"We want to help you to the other side." He jerked his thumb in a vague gesture behind them.

"What's that?" the girl asked.

"Luis, we don't have time—"

He raised his hand to silence Margo. "We aren't sure. All we know is that it's better than waiting here for your mommy who isn't going to come."

The hair on the back of Margo's neck stiffened under her hood, and she turned around. A light fog had begun to roll in, lingering between the scant trees. Luis and the child continued their conversation, but Margo tuned them out. Somebody was watching them. How she knew this, she wasn't sure, but someone or something was among the trees, and she didn't want to find out what was lurking back there. "Luis."

He was smiling when she turned back to them. "She's ready to go." Iridescent light flickered at his fingertips.

Margo rubbed her hands together, casting a glance over her shoulder. "All righty, I think we should move this little shindig somewhere we're not, you know, right out in the open." Before she could continue with her warning, Luis began to form the portal on the ledge of the fountain, which in Margo's mind was a little too morbid for her liking.

Despite her own feelings on the portal formation, the little girl glanced up, her face alight in the glowing doorway, eyes widened and mouth ajar. "So pretty!" she squealed.

Margo and Luis lifted their hands in unison, their teamwork flawless from helping so many spirits over together. If she had to guess, the little girl had to have been their seventh crossover just that month. Margo conducted a handful on her own as a child, the very first being a foster mother who'd nearly adopted her before her unexpected illness and death.

The child clambered onto the ledge of the fountain, her head wound visible again as she faced the portal forming. The portal shuddered to a stop. Tentatively, the little girl touched the doorway with her finger, the movement sending out ripples to the edges. "Can I...can I go?"

"It's all yours," he answered. "We made this just for you."

A thin shadow crept back into Margo's periphery, and she dared a glance behind them. Nothing was there save the same trees, mist coiling around their bare limbs.

The child swung her arms from side to side. "Thanks."

Margo turned around just in time to see her disappear into the shimmering surface of the portal.

Luis clasped Margo on the back and chuckled with a glance at his watch. "See? She didn't take us more than twenty minutes, and now she's off to...what, heaven?"

She snorted. "Brother, you know my own views on what lays beyond that door." She didn't judge his beliefs, but his didn't mingle with her own views, or lack thereof. To Margo, the spirits didn't go to a big beautiful beyond like he believed, though she refused to rain on his positive outlook of the afterlife. She wiped sweat from her brow. Opening a portal wasn't as hard as it had been when she was younger, but the act still brought on mild fatigue, something akin to how she felt after a double shift at the gas station. "Now, let's get the fuck out of here."

They needed to move, and fast. The creeping sensation plagued her, and she was unsure who or what had watched them open the portal. From experience she'd become aware that, although extremely rare, she and Luis weren't the only individuals in the world who could see spirits and the rest of the sometimes-sickening things they'd witnessed. Before she'd turned seven, she'd seen a monster—a real, true to form monster—a ravenous sharp-toothed beast in the sewers at the end of town. Red eyes glared at her. Clawed hands reached for her. Saliva dripped from their gnarled mouth. The moment was all too comic-book-worthy in Margo's opinion.

"Can't we share a tiny moment of pride for helping her? I mean, how long do you think she's been standing there waiting for her mom, knowing she was dead? You should be happy she's off to whatever afterlife she earned," he rambled, bringing Margo back into the world.

Luis's smile was infectious, and Margo found herself grinning as she noticed the unsettling sensation had ceased. "Fine, fine. I'm in a better mood than I was before we communed with the dead, but now I'm hungry. Let's steal some doughnuts from the Tastykake factory."

Mist gathered below the streetlights, hanging loosely a foot above the ground, the effect causing the red hand to glow at the crosswalk. Margo tapped her foot on the sidewalk, and the shadows from her movements danced on the white cement. She stopped. Faint footfalls piqued her attention, and she glanced back.

Her smile faltered. "Someone watched us open the portal, and now they're following us."

"What?" Luis whispered. He started to turn his head, but Margo stopped him.

"Don't look."

"Who do you think it is?"

"More like what," she whispered. The white walk sign appeared. "I don't know. Come on." She slipped her arm around his elbow and steered him down a different street. A dark-suited figure followed them, proving her original assumption correct.

Her heart hammered in her chest as she picked up speed, and Luis kept up with her. The footsteps grew closer, causing her to bite her lip. Not only were they walking into a really bad part of town, but their stalker was also making progress, their footsteps echoing louder off the brick and plywood-covered windows.

"Hey, you," a voice echoed off the abandoned buildings lining the street.

Margo turned her head toward the voice. The person's shadow dragged over the damp asphalt, the tail of their suit jacket lifting as they advanced. Scoffing, Margo turned and looped her arm under Luis's once again. "Let's get out of here."

"Wait!" the stalker yelled.

Luis quickened his pace next to her as their follower's footfalls grew closer. "Margo, they're chasing us."

"No shit," Margo breathed. She yanked him down an alleyway, the stench of rotting food in the dumpster barely perceivable as they ran. Thoughts raced through her head. *Had he seen what they'd done in the park? No, no one ever noticed before, how would they now?* An average person would've written them off as a couple of kids on shrooms talking to a hallucination, or they would've simply called the police on them, not chase them through the worst streets of Philly. A chain-link fence stretched out between the brick buildings and the two halted, effectively cornered.

"Would you two slow down?" Their assailant's voice was gruff and winded as they spoke.

Margo turned, ready to fight the stranger. "What the fuck do you want?"

He wasn't much taller than Margo, his russet skin dark in the scant lighting of the alleyway. A gold wristwatch glistened in what little light was shed by the bare incandescent bulb from the flickering streetlight above them. Bent at the waist, he heaved shallow breaths as he spoke, "I don't run often, and you two are very fast."

Luis puffed out his chest, his shoulder bumping Margo's. "Yeah? Well, you'd probably run, too, if you had some weirdo chasing you down in the middle of the night."

A chuckle filled the alleyway, haunting as it reverberated off the walls. "Isn't that what one would come to expect when they're walking in this neighborhood at almost one in the morning?"

Margo took a step forward, fists clenched at her sides. In her periphery, spilled light stirred and slithered, moving from the shadows hidden in the grout of the wet bricks, soaking in the anger permeating from her. Her skin chilled in anticipation.

The man raised both of his hands in surrender. "Look, I'm here to help you. If you'd give me a second to offer an explanation before you two go all macho on me, maybe we could get somewhere." He couldn't have been much older than the two of them, perhaps mid-to-late twenties, but his attire screamed affluence, and his words were tinged faintly with an accent.

Margo didn't trust him. "Help us with what?" she snapped.

He dropped his hands, blinking in a thoughtful manner. "I've been watching you two for a few months now, and there's something I need to share with you."

Luis snorted and took a step back. "You've been stalking us?"

"Not specifically. I've admired your work from afar."

"That's basically the same damn thing," Luis remarked.

"What the hell are you talking about?" Margo played dumb, knowing damn well his reference pertained to them opening portals. What good would it do to admit to opening the portal? Who was this dude, and what kind of consequences could they face? Her questions were muted by a primal fear and the need to protect not only herself but her brother.

Margo drew a deep breath, succumbing to the familiar sensations. She flicked her wrist and the light abandoned the shadows, the various shards mixing as they crawled toward her, becoming a glowing mass. She reached her arm to the ground and closed her eyes. The mass wrapped around her fingers, coiled up her arms like a frigid snake, twisting and tightening until icy power thrummed through her. Her arms glowed in a vibrant incandescence, subduing the chilled pain. "Back off," she growled.

Luis sidled up beside her—evidently aware of her intentions—and touched her shoulder, whispering, "Margo, don't." She shrugged him off, her gaze set on the man before them. The power she held over light was one Luis didn't possess, fueling his apprehension of its use along with the cost Margo endured in the form of bone-deep weariness.

The man gasped, stumbling over a crushed can as he stepped backward. "I didn't expect this." He appeared amused, his eyes ablaze, perhaps even awestruck, rather than fearful. The sight infuriated her, and she shed the light like a pair of frozen gloves. The glowing mass recoiled, dispersing sporadically to the darkened locations from which it came.

"Let's go," she said, tugging Luis's arm. She steered them around the stranger, whose gaze was still glued to the light as it resumed its original positions.

Margo and Luis headed to the opening of the alleyway, the street beyond as still and barren as the dark depths behind them.

The stranger cleared his throat and pitched his voice louder. "Haven't you ever wondered why you're able to see the macabre of the world when no one else can?" Margo bit her lip at the question. How had the man known enough to follow them in the first place? "What you did with that little girl—it's who you are."

Cautiously, Margo looked at the man, *really* looked at him. Light glinted off his dark-rimmed glasses, and his slight smile was warm, welcoming even. He met her gaze, undeterred from her menacing stance.

"He's...he's like us," Luis murmured.

She crossed her arms over her chest and muttered, "Even if he is, he could be dangerous."

As they stood staring at each other, a police cruiser slowed as it rounded the corner, heading toward them. "We need to leave right now," she grumbled, inclining her head toward the cruiser. From an outsider looking in, Margo figured their little gathering in the neighborhood appeared all too similar to an impromptu drug deal. "Come on," she said before heading down the street. Luis followed, as well as their newly acquired shadow. She'd fallen on the tactic of using her light conjuring to protect them and possibly freak the man out, and as the man continued to follow them through the city streets, she realized her plan had backfired.

Though the cop car slowed as it passed them, the vehicle continued to the traffic light and turned left away from them. Margo let out a long sigh, thankful for avoiding the law. She talked up her arrogance a bit too much, but she was truly terrified of being arrested so close to eighteen.

They continued around the corner in the direction leading back to the park where they'd aided the child's spirit. The shady buildings around them were gradually replaced with closed shops, a couple all-night minimarts, and bars. After a few blocks, she admitted to herself their follower wasn't going to leave them alone. She wasn't sure she wanted him to. "Would you get the hell away from us?"

He chuckled. "Not until you give me a moment to explain."

"Maybe we should hear him out," Luis whispered.

The glow of a late-night diner shined in Margo's eyes as they passed the windows, causing her to squint at the peeling white paint on the sign. "Let me buy you some dinner," the man offered.

As if on cue, Margo's stomach growled. Payday from the gas station she worked at wasn't for another day and a half, and Margo's depleted pantry caused her to answer without preamble. "Deal." Letting the weirdo explain why he thought he knew anything about them was worth a free meal. Plus, she needed to know how he knew what they could do.

The trio walked into the Denny's knockoff restaurant, stale coffee and maple syrup eliciting a second, louder growl from Margo's stomach. They were seated by the window; Luis and Margo in the same booth, and the man on the other side.

The dark stranger tossed a messenger bag on the seat beside him and then tented his fingers together on the table between them, glancing from Luis to Margo. "Let's start with names. I know you're Margo and Luis. I'm Brent Caspian."

A waiter stopped by their table and took their orders. When he left, the man named Brent took a tin from his messenger bag and opened it in the middle of the table. An unfamiliar aroma wafted from the muffins within the tin, a spicy, biting scent making Margo's mouth water. Brent offered the tin to them with one hand, taking a muffin in the other before biting a piece off. "Want one? These help with the crash."

The crash? Could he mean the fatigue washing over them after opening a portal? "No." Though the muffins smelled good, she was not about to take food from a stranger, especially one who admitted to stalking them. Margo leaned back against the booth and crossed her arms, the cracked plastic seat groaning under her weight.

How dare this dude hunt them down and act as if they were good friends? Margo chewed the inside of her cheek as she glared at him, finally saying, "So, you admit to being a stalker?"

Grinning, Brent shook his head. "I wouldn't call myself a stalker, more of an investigator trying to locate specific individuals."

"Is that supposed to mean something to us?" Luis asked. "What kind of individuals?"

"Psychopomps. What you did with the child in the park—how often do you do this sort of thing?"

Luis glanced at Margo, face questioning, and looked back to Brent. "A few times a week. How do you know what we did?"

"As I said, I'm an investigator searching for individuals who possess the same qualities as me and the rest of the Grim."

Luis leaned forward, intrigue clear on his face. "The Grim?"

"Yes, a subset of preternatural people who aid the recently deceased and the lingering through the veil to the other side. The Grim is all of us collectively, but individually, it's just Grim: you're a Grim, I'm a Grim, we're all Grim."

A smile broke across Luis's face as he turned to glance at Margo. She clenched her jaw, drawing a sharp breath through her nose. All this time, she'd ignored the internal intuition that they belonged somewhere, shoving the juvenile idealistic notion deep in her mind. But now, she couldn't deny it.

"If you'll let me, I'd like to show you the world you've missed out on."

Chapter Two

PRESENT DAY

Ash splintered from the cigarette pinched between Margo Petrov's fingers, fluttering to the ground as she pondered what dead soul she'd be stuck with tonight. Dusk stained the sky with indigo clouds, covering the city of Somers Point like an umbrella. Over the churning bay lay Ocean City, New Jersey, her home. The twinkling lights of the Ferris wheel jutted over the skyline despite the late season, mingling with the gentle fog rolling in. Margo's leather jacket did little to ease the chilled air coming off the water as she took a deep drag.

The dock she stood on bobbed in the rippling wake of a boat. She pulled another cigarette from the smashed pack in her back pocket and brought it to her lips, cupping the still smoldering butt to the fresh one as it lit. She really ought to quit, but with the recent events, Margo decided the time wasn't right but knew no time would be right. Lifting her foot, she stubbed the butt out with the toe of her boot and tossed it in the closest waste bin. Smoke coiled out of her mouth as she leaned against the pillar, closing her eyes briefly.

"I'm glad to see you're still breathing," a familiar voice said from behind her.

Margo gazed up as her brother bounded down the wooden stairs and onto the floating dock. "You saw me last night. Pretty sure I was breathing then too," she said through the smoke.

The sharp breeze drifting off the bay ruffled his mussed black hair and caused his blue scrub pants to billow around him. "Yeah, but I had the lingering thought the Board would change their mind last minute, and you'd end up dismembered and scattered around the Tristate area."

Margo snorted, smoke flooding from her nose as she laughed. "I don't think they'd be that disorganized, and I'm sure they have a fancy policy in place if they made the decision to off a Grim." She pinched the filter as she took another drag. "No, they haven't changed their minds. Yet."

Sloshing water sputtered onto the wooden planks by her feet as the bay rippled in the wake of another small boat drifting into dock for the evening. Although fall was leisurely creeping in, the day had been warm, warranting several residents of the seaside town to take their boats out onto the ocean before the cold fully set in. Luis ambled up beside Margo. "I hate to sound cliché, and Sam seems like a nice person and all, but no good deed goes unpunished."

Margo pulled another drag and shook her head. "Yeah, see what I get for being nice? If I'd just stayed being an asshole, I could've avoided all this." Saving the surfer who'd washed ashore with a blood bond wasn't a mistake; what *was* a mistake was getting caught by the pretentious upper management of the Grim. Unlike the rest of the world, psychopomps in America—better known as the Grim—were overseen by a group of officials who treated the process of reaping spirits as they would a business transaction. Once a soul was released from a body or a death was reported, the individual was added to a large queue if not aided to the other side immediately.

Luis bumped her with his elbow. "You did a good thing. When have we ever had control over what happens? You took control of the situation. So, what? I mean, I know it probably wasn't the smartest thing you've ever done, and that's saying a lot for you, but—"

"Shut up," Margo said though her grin betrayed her seriousness. Control. The one thing Margo and Luis both lacked most of their childhoods, from the clothes they wore to what home they'd be placed in next. Adulthood and their subsequent knowledge of their underlying heritage hadn't brought much relief to this, but at least they belonged somewhere. "Where are we finding this spirit?"

"Hold on a second." He held up a finger, glaring at her. "I'm not done. You did a good thing, but I warned you. When you asked me to translate that book for you, I was under the assumption it was for hypothetical reasons. Come to think of it, you said that's what it was for."

Glancing at the cherry of her cigarette, Margo sighed. The old book about otherworldly creatures she'd found on eBay intrigued her, the description hinting to information on a less than common preternatural race she belonged to but held little knowledge of. She didn't mean to use the information Luis translated to utilize necromancy to save someone's life. "My bad. It's not like I was planning on using any of the crap in there." *And Sam wasn't supposed to turn into a Grim.*

"You're just lucky I was so proficient in Latin when I was in high school. At least one of us paid attention in class." He quirked an eyebrow at her. "I still don't know how you got away with all of this. Not that I'm complaining because I didn't want anything bad to happen to you."

Frankly, she couldn't believe it herself, but she wasn't going to tell him that. The truth was, she knew her boss, Brent, had more to do with saving her than anything she'd said to the Board. "What can I say? I was extremely persuasive and had them fawning over my words." Margo fanned herself, perpetuating her faux haughtiness before dropping the act. "Like I told you last night, Brent worked magic and convinced the Board to reconsider, but now I owe him a favor."

"You may be off the hook with Corporate for now, but what if they find out what you are?" Luis's voice was a whisper on the wind. "Is she like you?"

Ever since she'd made the rash decision to save the surfer girl, Margo worried about the implications imposed from the blood bond. Yes, the process saved Sam, but at what cost? Her life, for one thing, as now she stood under the watchful eyes of Corporate, who waited patiently for her to make the wrong move.

The pretentious code of conduct Corporate upheld regarding the full-blooded status of a member of the Grim was not only obnoxious but dangerous to anyone who didn't fall into that category, including those made Grim via blood bond. If Corporate were to discover Margo wasn't wholly Grim, not only would she suffer, Sam would instantly lose any leniency given to her. "Fuck, I hope not," she muttered, gazing out over the bay. "Don't we have somewhere to be?"

Luis glanced down at his watch. "Crap, you're right. We've got to go."

The two climbed the rickety stairs onto solid ground and started toward the sidewalk. The coastal town was bombarded by tourists during the summer as much as Ocean City was but lacked the usual busyness on Friday night, the chill of autumn heavy in the air despite the warmth of the day. As they approached the stoplight, her brother pressed his palm hard against the crosswalk button.

They weren't blood, but they were siblings. Margo had turned thirteen when she was placed in the same foster home as Luis. The shy kid of twelve immediately sidled up to her when she thwarted a bully on the playground a few days after they started school together, and if not for her intervention, the bully would've left Luis with far more than a few superficial bruises. Foster care was rough, and Margo clung to their friendship, a friendship that swiftly turned into kinship. Margo didn't believe in destiny, but she did find the circumstances odd when they discovered they could both see spirits and open portals to the other side.

"I really appreciate the help," Luis said. The light changed, and Margo followed Luis through the crosswalk, glad their conversation finally deviated from her.

"No worries. I don't mind helping you out."

"The last thing I need when they're still all pissed about what you did is them nagging on me for not getting a newbie to cross over in time."

Margo rolled her eyes. "Does the Board really get on you for something you have no control over?" While Margo's focus was a strict set of reluctant spirits based upon a list provided by Corporate, Luis's specialty was the freshly dead.

"Nah, I doubt they'd nag me for one, but he's my responsibility. I've got to get him to cross over."

Margo chuckled as she clasped Luis on his shoulder. "Any spirit you can't get to pass on right away comes to me anyway, right? But, yeah, I bet upper management would be thrilled to hear I'm helping you against protocol." Ruling the affairs of Grim Reapers as if it were comparable to the inner workings of a standard business caused the already difficult task to become stressful, laden with policies, procedures, and protocol the members of the Grim had to follow. Margo saw it all as a bunch of bullshit.

"Thrilled isn't the word I'd use." Headlights spilled over them as a car sped by, heading toward the bridge. Their footfalls were muffled by the noises of the city, cars driving past them, and shouts from the bars. Though the sun had recently set, bar patrons were already becoming rowdy on the sidewalk.

A buzzing in Margo's pocket caught her attention. A text message from a strange number.

This is Jackie. Hope it's okay I stole your number from Brent. I think I might have lost something in your car last night and was wondering if you found anything.

Margo texted her back.

What are you looking for?

"Who're you texting?" Luis asked, nosing up behind Margo. She shied away from him, laughing.

"None ya."

A purple stone. Amethyst, actually. If you find it, can you drop it by my place?

A stone? Ah, the necklace. Every time Margo saw Jacqueline, the vibrant purple gem was present. Though they'd only interacted with each other a handful of times at Brent's in passing, Margo had seen her enough to know which stone she meant. Margo's gaze always lingered on the gorgeous necklace around Jacqueline's neck. She'd half thought to ask about it but didn't, not after she accidentally called the woman a vampire on their first meeting years before. Though Margo's question had been in earnest curiosity rather than facetious or insulting, the mistaken identity caused Jacqueline to despise her and nearly earned Margo a scar on her shin from Jacqueline's steel-toe boot. *Oh well.*

"Jackie, as in Jacqueline, the Empusa, who kicked you so hard in the leg, you bled all over the floor of my car?" Luis questioned, chin resting on her shoulder, obviously having read the whole conversation. She shrugged him off, sidestepping away from him.

Yeah, I'll bring it by if I can find it.

Margo tried to avoid the pointed stare from Luis, his mischievous grin wide and taunting. "Do you have a thing for her? I'm surprised. I thought she hated you."

Without looking up from her phone, Margo said, "Yeah, she does hate me." Margo felt his eyes on her, and she held back the scowl she wanted to throw his way. "Where's this dude we've got to convince?"

Luis threw her an impish smile. "No, we're having this conversation. Since when have you two been a thing?"

Scoffing, Margo pulled her cigarettes from her back pocket. "We're not a *thing.* I gave her a ride home last night after Sam and I got back from our near-death experience with the Board. She's texting me because she lost a stupid stone." Her cheeks flamed a deep crimson as she lit the cigarette and inhaled. He shot her a quizzical gaze, and she figured he saw the truth in her embarrassment. With the cigarette dangling from her parted lips, she said, "Doesn't matter anyway—she loathes my very existence."

He quirked an eyebrow at her, smirking. "I'm sure the feeling is mutual."

They walked in silence down the street until they came upon a bus stop. Luis ducked beneath the roof of the sheltered stop before sitting down on the bench. The enclosure didn't prevent the cold gust of wind from ruffling Margo's hair, and the bench chilled her as she sat. Her brother's comment was anything but true; she didn't know enough about Jacqueline to loathe her or like her, and she expected she would've done the same thing in Jacqueline's position, probably worse than a kick.

"Are we meeting this spirit here?"

Luis shook his head and leaned on the side of the enclosure. "No, he'll be on the bus. He's been on the bus since the day he died—his soul never made it to the hospital with his body."

She kicked her feet out in front of her. "What happened to him?" Tilting her head, she blew her smoke sideways to avoid Luis's face or any other innocent pedestrians.

"He came in a few weeks ago as a gnarly trauma patient. The ED doc pronounced him dead upon arrival. He rides the same bus that killed him."

She could never understand how Luis stayed in his line of work. His job helped with reaping the recently departed within the hospital and anywhere else he was assigned. As if he were on the frontlines of their never-ending battle, Luis aided new spirits across to their afterlives, and if he failed, they were turfed to Margo or another Grim nearby who would then help the spirit with their unfinished business. How did she ever become so lucky?

"Shouldn't be too hard, huh?"

"I hope not. And I'm not done talking about Jacqueline. She's pretty cute, and after you two get over the whole vampire versus Empusa thing, I bet you two would hit it off well." The distinction between the two paranormal creatures was extremely different, but at the time Margo hadn't a clue. Empusae required blood to survive similar to vampires, yes, but that was where their comparable traits ended.

Vampires weren't natural entities. They fed off the most vulnerable in society, were quite rare, and were more like parasitic animals than cognizant beings while Empusae were more aligned with other living, breathing preternatural individuals with wants, desires, and most importantly, a conscience. *Not something they teach you in grade school.*

"All right, that's enough. We've got shit to do." She gestured to the bus as its tires squealed to a halt in front of them, sick of her brother's matchmaking attempts. Margo tossed her unfinished cigarette to the ground and stomped it out as the doors opened to the vehicle. The two bounded onto the bus, depositing the required fare into the box beside the driver. The bus was empty save two commuters in the front, both in varying states of intoxication and laughter. Margo and Luis headed to the back of the bus, avoiding the two individuals. It was only eight o'clock at night, but Margo expected at least a sprinkling of drunk people on the city bus.

At the end of the vehicle sat an older man, his back hunched and scraggly blond hair cropped close to his head. As the two approached, he looked up and cursed softly. "Oh, not you again." He shook his head, nose crinkled in disgust. "I told you, I've got places to go."

Luis eased down onto the bus seat. "Where're you heading, Mel?"

Noting the questionable qualities of the fabric upholstery, Margo continued to stand, opting to grab hold of the handle jutting from the ceiling of the bus rather than sit beside Luis.

"I'm heading to work, not that it's any of your business." Mel turned his head toward the window and muttered, "Weirdo."

Margo grinned at her best friend. "Hey, Mel?"

The ghost tilted his head at Margo's voice. "What?"

"The name's Margo. You notice anything unusual lately?"

Shifting in his seat, Mel pursed his lips, face contorting as he appeared to consider her question. "As a matter of fact, yes, I have. Aside from your buddy here."

"Like what?" Margo pried.

"You think you know someone. I've been playing poker with the same group of guys for years. Years! I missed my game last month, and now they're acting like I'm chop suey."

"What happened?"

The bus halted as a handful of passengers climbed on. Mel stayed quiet until the vehicle was in motion again.

"I show up for our game last night, and none of them talked to me. They acted like I wasn't even in the same room with them." His voice rose an octave. None of the other bus patrons gave any notice to his upset, silent on their human senses.

"Mel," Margo said softly.

He clapped his hands together. "Teach me to miss a night. You know, I've been playing poker with these jerks for fifteen years. Fifteen years!"

"Mel."

"And now they're going to start cheating? They didn't even look at me. I only missed one night!"

"Mel!" Margo bellowed.

"What?"

"Dude, you're dead. Luis has been trying to tell you since the day you died. You were hit by this bus." Margo indicated to the filthy seats.

Mel shook his head, gazing down at himself. "No, that's not true." He looked back up at Margo. "This can't be true."

"Tell me this: What did you do today? Can you remember being home or with your family this morning or last night?"

He blinked rapidly, and his nose flared while he thought. "I can't remember. The last time I saw Cheryl was..." he trailed off, turning to the window. "Monday morning. The dog got out, and I went running after him, right into... Oh, my."

Pity etched Luis's face. "Yeah. Right into the road, chasing after your dog. Your dog ran off into the woods, but the bus hit you."

"Oh, my God," Mel whispered. The spirit sank to the seat of the bus, eyes watery and jaw slack.

Luis leaned forward. "I'm sorry. We just want to help you move on to the other side."

With great restraint she didn't know she possessed, Margo kept from rolling her eyes. No wonder Luis couldn't get him to move on. He was too soft, too kind, but Margo couldn't expect less from her brother; the kindness he naturally held made him a compassionate nurse and an even better Grim.

"No point in wasting more time around here," Margo said.

"This makes so much sense." Mel threw his hands in the air. "But, where do I go now? What happens to my family?"

Margo yanked the pull string, initiating a soft pinging sound. The bus slowed at the next corner. "Wherever you're supposed to go. We don't know where. Come on." When the bus stopped, Margo headed to the rear exit and ushered the spirit down the stairs. She lit a cigarette and surveyed the area. Conveniently, they disembarked on a quiet residential street, absent from any curious bystanders.

"I don't understand how this happened," Mel said.

Margo grew impatient with the spirit. "You ran into the road, you got hit by a bus, and you died. These things happen every day, all over the world. You're dead. The sooner you accept this, the sooner you can move on."

His Adam's apple bobbed as he swallowed the truth in Margo's words. "Very well." Power swelled within her as light condensed between her fingers.

Her brother mirrored her action, the two lifting their hands to throw the light and create an amorphous portal.

"Damn," Mel whispered. The glassy air in front of them shimmered, a translucent veil swaying in an invisible breeze. He glanced back at Margo, expression uncertain. "Am I supposed to walk through there?"

"Yeah, right through the funky light," Margo said.

With long strides, the spirit stepped into the portal and disappeared.

"And you thought this would be hard." Margo tried to tease, but her tone fell flat. Her crappy mood seemed to be lingering effects brought on by her close call with death, not to mention the very real possibility of the Board finding out she had muddled blood coursing through her veins. She stubbed the cigarette out on the sidewalk, sweeping away the ash with her foot as if it would scatter her worries along with it.

"Don't you wish you could do something different with your life than this?" The rhetorical question came out with more emotion than Margo intended.

Luis shrugged as he pushed his hands in the pockets of his hoodie. "I mean, yeah. There are times I wish we didn't have to do this." He shook his head and glanced over at her. "But, who else would? If it weren't for us, they wouldn't have a way to get to the other side, and they'd be wandering around here watching their families move on and grow old until they died themselves. What kind of existence is that?"

"When did you become so philosophical?"

"I always have been. You just never pay much attention to detail. Besides, I find it incredible to help a patient cross over when I've been taking care of them. That kind of thing makes this so much different. I can help people on a whole other level."

"Don't get me wrong—I do like helping these people move on, but sometimes..." Margo trailed off, the fleeting explanation lost. Her brother seamlessly turned her somber question into an optimistic stance, leaving her dubious.

He stopped, his expression sad. "I get it. You feel helpless."

"Yeah," she agreed. They stood in the quiet street for longer than Margo found comfortable.

Finally, Luis spoke first. "Is that why you saved Sam?"

Margo nodded slowly. "I didn't know she'd turn into a fucking Grim." The statement was the truth; when she saved Sam, she was under the assumption the blood bond would only save Sam's life, not turn her into a psychopomp. *Hopefully, nothing more either.*

"How's work been going?"

Margo shrugged and shoved her hands into her pockets. "Not a whole lot going on. I hope it picks up soon, but I'm not holding my breath." The fall and winter were always slow for her work. Not many people needed a handyman during the fall unless it was to board up their windows to prevent damage during the peak in hurricane season or to take their summer awnings off. Luckily, she'd had a busy enough summer to keep herself afloat.

Luis nodded, glanced at the ground, then back at Margo. "Are you planning to take off again?"

Margo looked away from his accusatory glare. Leaving hadn't worked in the past when she needed to escape her problems but perhaps this time would be different. So much more was at stake—Margo's life, Sam's life, Brent's reputation. If she left, her debt to Brent wouldn't be an issue. Plus, how could the Board discover she was more than she let on if she wasn't around? She found leaving quite tempting. *Third time's a charm, eh?* "The thought has crossed my mind."

She met his gaze and more silence passed between them. "Although I wouldn't blame you, please don't do that again," he whispered.

Margo said nothing.

Luis peered at his watch and huffed a loud sigh. "I've really got to head to work, or I'll end up being late. Thanks again for your help."

"Duh, why wouldn't I help you?"

He shrugged. "I don't know. Sometimes you're a little testy."

Margo shot him a wicked smirk before they went separate ways at the intersection. Testy was an understatement, and they both knew it.

Chapter Three

JACKIE HAYES SEARCHED the faces of her students, taking in the subtle hints of tears lining the cheeks of many: some with their heads bowed, others making direct eye contact. "Though I'm sure most of you have already heard from friends, family, or social media, Anthony McKinney passed away over the weekend. I know he told us all what was going on, and for lack of a better phrase, we expected this, but his passing has been hard for us in the faculty as I'm sure it has been on all of you." The news had come early in the morning, a call from the principal, informing each teacher the student had passed away after a lifelong battle with cancer.

A few black dreads slipped free from the clip at the back of her hair, falling into her face, and Jackie pushed them back impatiently. "For the next few weeks, a group of grief counselors will be available by drop-in and appointment to help us all process this difficult time, and I encourage you to sign up." She cleared her throat, absently shuffling a few sheets of paper on her desk before she broke the silence drowning the room. "Now, today is free art, so go wild. Do whatever you want, no restraints, any medium; I want to see what you can come up with."

A student rose, then another, and then they all moved around the room, gathering supplies, talking quietly as they began on their individual projects. She watched a few students hog the acrylic paint, others going for colored pencils, while some favored the pastels. She was simply grateful to have her students engaged in something, anything, after the speech she'd given.

For the first time since she began teaching, Jackie had lost a student. Two years prior, she'd met the energetic teen—so full of life and a passion for art that almost surpassed Jackie's own. As his skill and determination for perfection grew with each day in her classroom, Anthony had become her focus. When he came back from summer vacation with the news of his diagnosis, Jackie nearly crumbled in front of him, but she forced her composure, offering him as much encouragement as she could to fight through it. He had been plagued by cancer early in his childhood but had been in remission for years. When the cancer resurfaced, it came back full force, taking over his body, poisoning him from the inside out.

She looked over the six rectangular tables arranged in front of her desk, noting the piece Anthony had been working on last week was still resting upon the easel by his workstation. She crossed the room, most of her fifteen students too engrossed in their own work to take notice as she plucked the painting from the stand and returned to the front. The canvas was heavy, its size closely resembling that of a small coffee table instead of a piece of artwork, and she heaved the painting onto the lip of the dry-erase board. She took a step back to appreciate the quality.

No, she wasn't simply appreciating quality, though it was a beautiful piece. She was experiencing the pain, the trauma portrayed behind the subtle picture.

A dreary city street, slanted rain cascading down over a lone park bench, and barren trees on either side signified the barren hope filling the artist's heart. The monochromatic image held varying shades of blues and teals, which no doubt set the melancholy mood; however, the depth of emotion seeping from the dark hues tugged at Jackie's chest, causing her physical pain. She was no stranger to the visceral response art could provoke—she embraced such work from her students, but Anthony's work set the bar far higher than the tone of angst within other student's work. She knew where the lack of hope stemmed from, but this didn't take away from the awestruck state the painting elicited.

Jackie dabbed her eyes on the loose sleeve of her sweater as she read the title: *Traffic Stop*. The image depicted in the work could've been any city, deep in the darkest streets, a seedy location where families once lived now in ruin.

Class went by faster than Jackie anticipated, and when the bell rang, her students went to work putting away the art supplies before they all hurried through the door. An hour of solitude while the students took their lunch. Jackie usually spent the time grading art or working on her own current projects, but the desire wasn't there. She surveyed her empty classroom, the painted portraits dangling from the rope going one side of the room to the other, landscapes and abstract pieces lining the walls in lieu of famous artists. Jackie would rather display the work of her current and past students than any famous artist like many other instructors.

A knock on the door brought her attention to the front of the room. Her close friend and colleague, Lauren, stepped through, raising a coffee mug in one hand. "Hey. Brought you some tea." Her brown hair hung over her shoulder in a delicate braid, and her lips lifted in a sympathetic smile.

Jackie reigned in her despondence and grinned, taking the offered cup. "What's up, stranger? I figured you'd call in a substitute so you could spend more time with Sam."

A blush rose to Lauren's cheeks at the mention of her girlfriend, the vivid crimson matching the painted flowers displayed on the far side of the room. "Just because I wanted to stay home doesn't mean I could. Besides, Sam's supposed to start some training with Brent today. That's his name, right?"

"Yep. He's a good guy and not nearly as arrogant as Margo." Jackie hopped onto the ledge of her desk. She'd come to know Brent Caspian, the local ethnobotanist and Grim, by knowing the right people, and she valued their friendship.

Lauren threw her head back and laughed. "Thank God."

Jackie chuckled along, agreeing with the assessment. Margo had to be the worst Grim she'd ever met. Thinking of Margo, Jackie brought her hand to her neck, though grasped at nothing, reminding her that her necklace was still missing. The amethyst wasn't a magic cure, but it calmed her thoughts in times of stress. She'd lost the stone the night Margo gave her a ride home from Sam's after Margo and Sam nearly lost their lives because of Margo's reckless behavior—the same reckless behavior that saved Sam's life at the cusp of death.

Jackie didn't really know much about Margo, which was Margo's own fault given her arrogance and brusque way of talking to people. The only thing Jackie had learned from the snarky woman was her disdain for rules and a perpetual grumpiness that bled into every interaction they had, however fleeting those were.

Although only three days had gone by, it felt as if much more time had passed since she'd shared the awkward car ride with Margo.

"Do you think it'll get easier for Sam?" Lauren's question was quiet.

Jackie raised the cup and breathed in the aroma of chamomile, the scent not as soothing as it should have been. "What do you mean?" She took a sip before she placed the cup beside her on the desk, a wave of guilt washing over her as she looked at her friend. Back in college, Jackie had met Lauren in the education program, and the two became close friends over a short span of time. As the years passed, their friendship only grew stronger, though Jackie never planned to tell Lauren she was an Empusa.

Well, things had changed. A lot. After Lauren discovered her girlfriend was brought back to life by a Grim Reaper and subsequently turned into one herself, she figured Sam was making the whole thing up. Jackie convinced Lauren she was telling the truth, by delving into the reality surrounding her own preternatural state of existence, something Jackie had never intended to do, but she'd found the disclosure necessary for Lauren to believe Sam.

Lauren leaned closer, dropping her voice, as if a passing student or teacher would hear them even though they were in Jackie's vacant classroom. "The helping souls thing."

"I don't know as much about reaping as Margo and Brent because I'm not a Grim, and honestly, I try to stay out of all that crap, but I've heard it can be hard. I'm sure Sam will learn a lot of helpful info from Brent." Jackie avoided her gaze, concern drawing her brows together.

She wasn't ready to talk freely about the paranormal with her very human friend.

Lauren nodded, seemingly content with her answer and presumably picking up on Jackie's unease. "We're going to do the mitosis project together again this year, right?" Ah, a better topic. Back to the normal stuff. Lauren hadn't brought up Jackie's confession since the day she'd told her what she was, and Jackie wasn't too upset about that. The project she brought up had been something they'd worked on the year before—a merging of art and science for one large project. The two chatted through various mundane aspects of the project, and Jackie was grateful for the reprieve from the topic of the paranormal.

Part of Jackie was glad for the exposure, happy to finally have her best friend know the reality of her life—she didn't see herself as straying too far from the norm; everyone has their secrets—hers simply involved blood and survival—the two intrinsically linked. The other more insecure part of her worried Lauren would never quite adjust to Jackie's differences.

The rest of the day went by without issue, aside from the dreary fall rain pattering against the windows. After her last group of students exited the room, Jackie moved to the back of the class. A large pile of paintbrushes sat soaking in the deep sink, and she turned the water on to rinse them. Blue swirled through the water cascading from the faucet, bending and bowing with the current. Frosty air pressed against her back, running over her shoulders and tickling the wispy hairs at the base of her neck.

"Hey, Ms. Hayes." The familiar chilled voice came from behind her.

Jackie dropped the brushes in the deep sink and faced the spirit of her dead student. Her lip trembled, but she kept her cool. This wasn't the first time she'd seen a ghost, though it was the first occasion she'd known the person while they were still alive.

"Anthony, what are you doing here?" The sunshine filtering in through the window drenched his face in gold. He looked younger, his sallow cheeks full, and green eyes brighter than they had been last week only a few days before his death.

He shook his head as he walked between the tables, staring up at the string of artwork hanging from the ceiling, raising his hand to touch their edges, face serene but brow creased. "Is this a rhetorical question like why are we all here?" he chuckled. "I didn't think you'd be able to hear or see me. No one else can." He glanced down at himself before looking up at her. "You've always been different to me—I guess maybe somehow I just knew you'd be able to see me," he said, lips lifting in a melancholy smile.

"Have you seen your family?"

"Yeah, I saw them already, but I can't stand to be around them. They're all so sad, and I know why, but they knew this was coming. There's no way they've been thinking I'd live through this. I wish they would've spent more time accepting that I was dying instead of trying to get me to fight. This isn't fair." He sighed; the sound akin to a tuft of icy air against warm glass. "I wish they wouldn't have wasted so much time." The hurt and anger etched into his features was evidence of his pain.

"Anthony, I'm sure they did their best. They loved you so much, and you have every right to be mad. Anger is a valuable step in the grieving process."

He chuckled without humor. "I'm the one who died, not the other way around. Why should I be grieving? They're the ones who lost me. What are they going to do now? I was their whole life, and now they have nothing."

"You should be grieving the loss of your own life." Her voice was a whisper to her ears, tinged with unshed tears. She couldn't, wouldn't cry in front of him. He'd undoubtedly seen enough mourning from his family and friends.

His shoulders rose in a shrug. "I only came here to tell you to take that home," he said, pointing to his latest artwork.

"Don't you think your mom will want it?"

"No, she has enough depressing artwork of mine. She doesn't need the last thing I painted floating around in some box in the attic."

Laughter drifted in through the cracked classroom door and Jackie turned. When she looked back to where Anthony had been standing, the artwork in her empty classroom was the only thing staring back at her. She wiped her cheek with the sleeve of her sweater before gathering her bag and grade book. She'd be mad, too, mad at fate, mad at the way things worked, and she was. He was too young, too kind, too...everything. Too big for this world. When she left her classroom for the day, Jackie snatched the painting from the ledge of the dry-erase board and tucked it beneath her arm before heading home.

THE SPLIT-LEVEL home at the end of the street hugged the boardwalk, and the wind whipped her hair into her face as she climbed out of her car. She gathered her work bag and Anthony's painting. Torrents of air whistled through the dune grass sprinkling the sand around the narrow staircase, and the wind tugged at the framed painting as she hurried up the steps. Instead of going through the main part of her house, she went directly upstairs to her workspace. The scents of lavender and cinnamon met her as she walked through the door. After tossing her bag on the chair right inside the door, she paused, then heaved the painting onto her solid oak table in the middle of the room.

The first decision she made when she purchased the split-level duplex years before was to designate a level strictly for her art. With the upper floor offering more natural light, she deemed the space her studio. Seldom did she put anything on the walls surrounding her workspace. Downstairs, there wasn't a blank patch of wall, but upstairs, she needed the wood-paneled walls to stay blank to—as cliché as it made her feel to say—allow her creativity to flow. She held the painting up. His last painting. The last thing he created was in her hands. *He'll never create again.*

Five minutes passed, and she finally decided to put the painting on the wall opposite her bay window overlooking the ocean directly where the sun would illuminate the beauty each morning.

Then, she paced. Although clouds rapidly approached from the east, the lingering afternoon sun threw rays of orange over her hardwood floor, warming Jackie as she moved. She ran her hand over the back of the suede chaise as she passed, thrummed her fingers over her worktable, brushed her palm across the frayed velvet of her couch, and finally stopped when she stood in front of her shelf of art supplies. The unease was brought on not only by the death of her student but the continued silence from her close friend, Roz.

Their friendship wasn't as strong as Jackie and Lauren's, but she was a vital friend. The problem was, Roz's fondness of rules and regulations lined up well with Margo's—viewing them as unnecessary and leaving without notice when she saw fit. Her last hiatus to visit her parents overseas, pushing two months, seemed to be her longest disappearance yet, especially with no word to Jackie or Jackie's sibling. Of course, Jackie had tried to reach out to her more times than she was willing to admit, going as far as contacting her mother with no word.

She grabbed a blank canvas, her still wet oil paint palate, and a handful of brushes before she clambered atop the wooden table, tucking her legs beneath herself. Running a hand over the canvas, she closed her eyes. This is what she needed; the quiet peace of creating regardless of the medium. She opened her eyes and grabbed a brush, unsure what would come of her need to create. Her muse chose red, which she found unusual because her creations ranged in various hues, mostly muted and subtle colors, rarely ever warm. The deep crimson seeped into the taut fabric as she dragged the brush across. Jackie scrunched her nose, pulling the brush swiftly up, then dropping it to the table with a clatter as a pang filled her chest.

Duh, she thought as the pain took her breath away, the sudden ravenous hunger encompassing her ribs, potent and unyielding. When the sensation subsided briefly, she hopped off the table and hurried to the far side of her studio. The elixir she purchased from Brent lengthened the time between feedings and, combined with sufficient blood stored in her refrigerator, kept her beast at bay.

The small refrigerator upstairs held her month's supply of blood and the elixir she bought from him. With a mastery of crafting exotic and irreplaceable potions and elixirs, Brent charged Jackie a miniscule fee for the liquid that kept her from turning into a monster if she didn't take blood every three to four days. Even still, she required blood once a month, so she kept at least four pints of donated blood alongside the elixir she needed weekly. To her family, the system seemed flawed, complicated, and unnecessary if willing to take blood from a living person, but to Jackie, it was her way of life and had been for some time.

The fridge sat under the counter and was no bigger than a microwave but almost as vital to her life as the breath she took. As she knelt beside it and opened the door, she realized with horror that no cool air emanated from the appliance nor did the light turn on. Four bags of blood were positioned on the shelf, and when she touched the top bag, the surface was as warm as the rest of her home. "Oh, crap," she said, checking the other bags to find they too were room temperature as were the six dark elixir jars. Nausea cascaded over her, stirring turmoil in her stomach. She gripped the countertop and closed her eyes, pleading for the discomfort to pass.

"Shit," she muttered as the sickness gently ebbed away. Crouching again, she peered around the back of the fridge. The plug lay in tatters on the floor, tiny teeth marks at the severed end of the cord along with tufts of fur and a burrow hole in her wall. Sitting back on the floor, she shook her head. *Now what?* she wondered, chewing the inside of her cheek to stave off her mild panic.

Her mother and father were too accustomed to living the way they did and neither of them found it as repulsive as Jackie did, nor did her sibling, Ezra. This, Jackie mused, had to do with their lack of the unusual side effects she experienced. The taste and the act didn't bother her; she enjoyed the level of comfort she experienced within herself after a feeding. However, drinking blood directly from the source also brought on an unpleasant experience for Jackie: strings of conscious, and sometimes, unconscious thoughts pouring into her own mind. Striations of people's innermost thoughts weren't what she was interested in.

Not only was it a breach of privacy, she also didn't want to see what was lingering in the crevices of someone's thoughts. The things she saw always ended up being their most guarded secrets, the bits of information people consciously tried to shield, which ultimately led to the thought coming to the forefront of one's brain. Jackie found it funny how things worked this way, not ha-ha funny either. The most recent time she took blood from another didn't end so well.

Too bad I can't control fire like Dad or get premonitions by touching people like Ezra and Mom. Jackie rolled her eyes at herself as she picked up her phone. Brent answered on the second ring. "Hey, Jackie, how are you?"

They spoke for a few minutes, mulling over perfunctory details of their lives before Jackie inquired about the elixir. "Would brewing up another batch take long?"

"Didn't you just stop by about a week ago for some?"

Jackie chuckled softly. "I had a little bit of trouble with the fridge I keep it in." She glanced down at the jar in her hand, swirling the liquid around. "Do you think I'd be okay to take it if it warmed up?" She placed the jar down.

"How warmed up are we talking?" Brent asked skeptically.

Jackie chewed her lip, picking dried paint from the surface of her work table. "Well, I'm not sure but definitely room temperature."

Brent sighed into the phone. "I can't say for certain if it'll work the same. Exposure to higher temperatures could degrade the properties of the synthetic myoglobin. I'm unsure of the half-life on this particular elixir, but I *do* know it won't hurt you to take if that's what you're asking."

"Yeah, that's what I'm asking." As much as she worried to take the warm elixir, she also feared the repercussions if she didn't without having blood on hand. She stared at the small jar, the dark liquid appearing sinister in the shadows. Nothing else kept the bloodlust abated. Nothing other than blood. Butters, her orange cat, jumped onto the counter, sensing her upset and ramming his furry head against her arm, but his action did little to soothe her trepidation.

"I'll put a call out for the ingredients I need because I don't have any reserves right now, but I'll try to get you another batch in a few days. Think you can manage?"

She popped the lid from the top with a satisfying thud. As she brought the container to her lips, the pungent odor washed over her. "Yeah, I should be fine. Thanks, Brent."

"I'm on it. Oh, and I've been meaning to ask, have you heard from Roz?"

Jackie closed her eyes and sighed. "No, I haven't. I'll send her mom another email."

They said goodbye, and Jackie placed her phone on the counter.

She took a deep breath and brought the jar to her mouth. The elixir burned, the liquid thick and noxious as it flowed down her throat. She gagged slightly but continued to knock it back. *Can't this crap taste sweet like honey instead of motor oil and acid?* she wondered, noting that the elixir tasted just as bad warm as it did cold. A fire began in her chest, wisps of heat scratching her ribs, stretching her muscles, scalding her very essence. Each breath seared through her lungs, her insides a cauldron set alight. Although the elixir held in the beast, wrangled in her bloodlust, it didn't fully sate her.

Her cat meowed at her, tilting his head to the side as he stared at her with warm amber eyes. "Don't look at me like that. If it weren't for you and your brother's horrible hunting skills, I wouldn't be in this predicament." Butters chuffed at her before he jumped to the floor and walked off.

Chapter Four

"GREAT," MARGO WHISPERED as she glanced down at the name. The edge of the index card she held fluttered in the heat flowing through the vents of her car.

She looked up at the high school, an eerie glow shining in the predawn hour that Tuesday morning. Reaping the soul of a reluctant spirit was challenging, but the difficulty was tenfold when it was a young person. The car idled as did her mind. She'd taken yesterday off to catch up on the sleep she'd missed Sunday night. After leaving Luis in Somers Point, she'd hurried to the next location, a rundown bar by the bridge with fraying for-sale signs in the gravel parking lot. She couldn't complain much; the soul had been willing to leave. With a few laps around the building while lamenting about an early death and a simple goodbye to their whole life's work, they'd gone through the portal without a fight or any hesitation, though she'd been exhausted the day after.

Focusing on the task at hand, Margo scanned the name again. Anthony, a teenager who'd died the week before. She shifted the car into park and turned the engine off. Taking a deep breath that did nothing to settle her unease, she got out of the car and headed to the outskirts of the campus. Her edginess sparked by her meeting with the Board hadn't diminished, lingering into her daily thoughts with an additional burden of worry. She didn't want to be under constant scrutiny with those asshats watching every move she made and every soul she helped or didn't.

The buildings were dimmed, her path only brightened by the scant rays falling from the streetlights dotting the parking lot. A tall figure stood by the fence of the football field, their back to Margo, and their form throwing a wilted shadow over the turf. The incandescence around their body spoke of their true form, signaling to Margo this was the spirit in question—his aura, for lack of a better word. Even from the distance, she could tell this one would be difficult.

A difficult spirit is just what I need. She rolled her eyes at her own sarcasm before eventually ambling up to him. "Hey."

The teen watched her. He glanced behind him and then side to side before meeting Margo's gaze again. "Why are you talking to me?"

"Because I'm here to help you; you know, move on."

He scrunched his brows further yet. "Move on where?"

Margo sighed. "Let's start with the basics. You know you're dead, right?" The teen nodded, his face somber. "Okay, good." Throwing her hands into her pockets, Margo fished out a cigarette and her lighter. "How'd ya die, kid?" Smoke billowed from her mouth as she put her lighter back.

He picked at his cuticles. "Cancer."

"Cancer?"

He offered her a nod. "When I was nine, I was diagnosed with an osteosarcoma. At first, I didn't know what it meant—like, what kid would?"

"That must've sucked," Margo said before taking another drag.

"Yeah, it did. My childhood went from kicking a ball around the backyard with my friends to being stuck in the hospital for months. Things got better; I went into remission, started feeling good, like a normal kid." A smile teased the corner of his mouth as he reminisced, but it swiftly morphed into a frown. "But then it came back, full force, and there wasn't a treatment. That's what got me in the end."

He couldn't have been older than sixteen; at least, that's how he appeared to Margo. "I'm sorry, dude."

The teen dropped his gaze to the ground, sniffling. "I just wanted to graduate, go to art school, and make a name for myself. My parents were always so encouraging in everything I did, especially when I sucked at it, like math," he chuckled, raising his head high to meet Margo's gaze with his watery green eyes. "I thought I'd have more time to make them have something to be really proud of me for."

"I'm sure they were proud of you, no matter what. Your life couldn't have been easy with the shit you went through."

Anthony shoved his hands into the pockets of his jeans, looking down. "I know you probably hear this a lot, but—" He paused and met Margo's gaze again. "—this isn't fair. I'm not done."

She blew out a sigh laced with smoke before she put the cigarette out in the grass. "I know, but you *are* done, kid. There's not a damn thing I can do about it either. You died last week. It's over."

"No." He shook his head, disheveling his brown hair. "Can't you talk to the big guy?"

Margo exhaled. "There is no big guy. As cliché as this sounds, it's way out of my hands. I know this is shitty."

"You don't understand. I didn't get a childhood. I don't consider being in and out of hospitals until I was twelve a childhood! And then after I get so close to finishing high school and making my parent's suffering worthwhile, I fucking die. It's not fair!" Anthony threw his hands in the air and took off into the field of grass.

Nothing she could say would alleviate the hurt his soul was experiencing. Encouraging him to accept his death seemed wrong; the circumstances *weren't* fair, but regardless, she had a job to do, and she'd be damned if she didn't finish her work. She trailed him through the opening in the fence, the dew-coated grass dampening the legs of her jeans as she hurried to catch up to him. She could see him a little clearer now; black paint splattered his white T-shirt and jeans, some paint even coating his arm and fingers in vibrant hues.

He didn't appear to be sick, but Margo had grown to accept the differences spirits took on, as opposed to how they truly appeared before, during, or after death. Some maintained their grotesque injuries from death, a testament to the knowledge they were, in fact, dead, while others took on a younger, perhaps healthier, version of themselves.

"Anthony."

Instead of answering Margo, he closed his eyes. The sky took on a soft glow from dawn's impending approach, and the light illuminated his cherub features left from childhood as he poised his face upward.

"Anthony, I'm sorry. I'm not going to tell you some bullshit lie like it's God's will because it isn't. You were born with shitty genes that caused you to be riddled with cancer, and this *isn't* fair." She watched him, wanting to see how her words fell around him. He kept his eyes closed as she continued. "But you're dead. Your body is in the ground. No amount of sulking, pleading, and denial is going to change that. I wish I could do something about it because you deserve to have a full life. You're just a goddamn kid."

Anthony finally dropped his head and opened his eyes, staring off in the distance. "I don't want to go."

"I know, but you can't hang around here watching your family mourn your death and your friends get older. You'll grow more and more envious and miserable when you could be starting a new life."

He peered at Margo, face alight. "What? I'll get another shot?"

Margo nodded. "Yeah. When you're ready, you'll get to start new. You know about reincarnation?" When he nodded, she continued. "What determines where you go is karma. You've had a rough life, kid, and I think your next one will be much different from this, but I don't know, and you won't know until you go on."

A car drove into the parking lot behind the high school, and Margo worried someone might see her. Gathering the pulsing energy from within, as if engulfing an invisible cloak around her body, she threw a deception around herself. The last thing she needed was attention on herself from human law enforcement while she was still on the probationary period imposed by the Board.

"I want another chance, but I'm going to miss my parents."

"They already miss you, and you're done here."

His lip quivered, and his voice trembled. "This isn't fair."

"I know." She swallowed back her own tears, fighting to keep a strong hold on her emotions. It wasn't fair. None of this was fair.

A silence stretched over the space between them as Anthony contemplated Margo's words. The telltale signs were there, and she knew it was only a matter of time until she could open his portal. Her palms warmed, and she smiled as the sensation flickered to life within her. She lifted her hands, splaying her fingers outward. A faint crackling sounded around them as the portal formed in front of Anthony, bright and pulsating on the backdrop of the dull gray of the high school. "I *really* don't want to go."

"You don't want to stay here."

His hair ruffled in the gentle breeze coming from the doorway and tears slipped down his face. "Fine." He walked to the portal. The energy pulsed through her as he stepped into the door, vanishing as the tendrils of otherworldly color yanked him forward.

Kids were always the hardest for her to encourage to move on, their lives usually cut short in a violent manner. For Anthony, it was prolonged, furthering the difficulty. *Poor kid*, she thought as she lit a cigarette and meandered over to the curb lining the parking lot. A few cars had pulled in since she initially arrived, and she kept her façade up, not quite ready to walk back to her car. Easing down on the curb, she let herself crack slightly.

Margo sniffed and pulled her hood over her fingers to dab the tears forming in her eyes. She hated to cry. The sharp reality of her life had begun to fall around her, wedging a small hole in her wall of control, leaving her frustrated. The Board nearly decided to kill her for saving Sam, and if they knew she wasn't wholly Grim, they would've without consideration. The blood that ran in her veins was far from the pure standard they wanted to upkeep in their strict policy, and with her luck, they'd use this as an example for why their policy was to stay in place.

She knew saving Sam was a risk, not only because of the potential death caused by the blood bond or the lingering threat of the Board offing her but the fear of her other lineage making it to the surface. How could she have been so fucking stupid?

Margo and Luis weren't raised as normal Grim children, but she could tell from the way Brent and the other members of the Grim she'd met that not one individual enjoyed the pointless regulations set in place by the upper management. Good thing she wouldn't have to deal with them when she left. She just needed to figure out when was the best time to take off.

Her phone chimed in her pocket, and she sighed heavily when she noticed the sender was Brent. Part of her was hoping for a boring job to fulfill. Repairing a hole in someone's wall or weatherproofing windows was exactly what she needed to distract her from the uncertainty her life held.

I'd love to meet for breakfast this morning to discuss the terms of your debt.

Margo pinched her nose, forcing a deep breath. Jackie warned Margo she was indebted to Brent, but what the hell could he want from her? Anything of monetary value he could get from Collin or obtain on his own. He made out well enough with his moonlighting business: selling odd elixirs, tonics, and specialty beverages to the other ethereal creatures in the area. She formulated her response, sans the usual pinch of sarcasm.

Can you just tell me what you want and get it over with?

The light crested over the horizon as the sun grew closer to rising, a beautiful sight that should've warmed Margo's chilled state; however, the melancholy mood surrounding her didn't abate. A tear slid down her face as she lit another cigarette. She blew the smoke out and hunched forward slightly, placing her hands on her knees. Her phone buzzed again, and she straightened.

Meet me for breakfast. My treat.

Oh, like food was still the way to her heart? A subsequent text gave her a diner location and time, though, she wasn't sure she would be meeting anyone.

If I leave town right *now, maybe they'll leave Sam the hell alone,* she thought. If Corporate hadn't found Roz yet, surely Margo could evade them long enough to make it out of the states; however, if they did catch up to her, she'd be in deep shit. She stood, brushing a hand over her jeans as she headed to her car. Luis would be pissed at her if she left without saying goodbye again, but he'd forgive her; he had before.

She stuffed her phone back into the pocket of her jacket without making a decision and sighed. Brent told her and Luis in the beginning that their life's work could be tolerable at best somedays. She couldn't say she wasn't warned, but it wasn't as if she had a choice. Throwing a cautious gaze around, Margo noted she was alone and let the deception fade. *Don't want to freak anyone out with a driverless car.*

A royal blue SUV that Margo recognized as Jacqueline's car pulled into the parking lot. When the vehicle stopped, sure enough, Jacqueline emerged from the driver's side with a large rectangular satchel, wrangling the strap over her shoulder as she shut the door. She pushed her dreads over her shoulder, where the dark strands stood out against her bright sweater, and she started toward the campus grounds.

Although Margo was a few yards away from her, Jacqueline turned when she noticed her and started toward her, prompting Margo to hastily wipe the dampness from her face. Jacqueline's sharp facial features were softened in the dim dawn light though the strange lure Margo associated with her remained. She wondered if the attraction was similar to a vampire's enthrallment, something Jacqueline threw off innately rather than with purpose. Whatever the reason, when Jacqueline made eye contact with her, an odd flutter in Margo's chest forced her to look down.

"Margo?"

Without lifting her head, Margo offered her a lazy wave. "What's up, Jacqueline?"

"Jackie is fine, you know." Jackie's voice grew closer as she approached Margo.

Margo gazed ahead, nodding. "Okay, Jackie."

"What are you doing here?" Though the words themselves appeared accusatory, her voice only held curiosity. Much to her dismay, Jackie watched her expectantly from only a few feet away. Margo swallowed back the tears threatening to fall and leaned against her car casually. She didn't dislike the woman; shockingly, it was quite the opposite—not that she wanted to admit this to even herself. Plus, if she spoke, she wasn't sure she'd be able to keep the tears back.

She cleared her throat and picked at her cuticles. "Daily grind and all that shit."

"A spirit?" Jackie stepped close to Margo.

Margo nodded again, looking up just as Jackie glanced down at the clasp on her satchel. She stole a glance at Jackie, taking in her beautifully angular nose, sculpted jawline, and lush lips before she turned her attention back to her own fingers.

Jackie kicked her foot up onto the curb and fiddled with the zipper on her knee-high boot as she sighed. "Let me guess: Anthony?" Her long dreadlocks cascaded down her back, fastened behind her head in a hairclip the shape of an octopus, the tentacles struggling to keep her wild hair secured.

"Yeah, how'd you know?" Margo asked, surprised Jackie knew the teen she'd just helped.

"He's been a student of mine for the last two years. He did some exceptional work, and I already wrote him a letter of recommendation for the Philadelphia Art Institute." Jackie sighed, face falling. The stray light from the nearest streetlamp reflected the fresh dampness in her eyes. "It's horrible what happened to him." She turned to Margo.

A car pulled into the parking lot, followed by a second, and then a third. The darkened sky had begun to lighten substantially, the clouds a tinged magenta as the sun rose over the buildings. A few individuals, presumably teachers by their attire, waved Jackie a hello. When they were on their way to the entrance to the high school, Jackie caught Margo's gaze. "Did he move on?" Her sadness softened her words to a mere whisper.

Pride bubbled in Margo's chest and she nodded. "Yeah, he did. He didn't want to at first, but yeah, he moved on. I hope his next life treats him better than the last." Fresh tears formed in her eyes, and she stifled a grumble.

Jackie put a hand on Margo's shoulder. "It's okay to cry, Margo," she murmured.

Margo lit the cigarette, and when she chuckled, smoke poured from her mouth. "Who said I was crying?" She met Jackie's gaze, her own unwavering. "I got smoke in my eyes." *Why is she being nice to me?*

"You know, you wouldn't get smoke in your eyes if you'd quit." Jackie's playful tone caught Margo off guard, and she tilted her head.

The cigarette dangling from Margo's mouth bobbed as she spoke. "What doesn't kill you makes you stronger, right?"

Jackie shook her head. "You trying to quicken the process?"

"Two packs a day isn't going to kill me any faster than anything else in the world. I know it's a horrible habit, but it gets me through the day."

"At what cost?"

Margo glanced at her, perplexed. "Why are you being so nice to me? You hate me."

Jackie pushed herself from Margo's car, dangling her satchel over her shoulder. She crossed her arms over her chest defensively. "I don't hate you—I hate your chronic piss-poor attitude."

"Do you blame me?"

Jackie turned her head, the muscles in her jaw tightening.

Before she could stop herself, Margo continued, "You'd have a shitty attitude, too, if your job was convincing angry spirits to pass on when they feel their time isn't done. Do you think Anthony was ready to go?" She knew her words were cruel and immediately regretted her question even before Jackie scowled at her. They stared at each other for a long while, a challenge hanging densely in the early morning air. Jackie's nostrils flared, the tiny movement quickening Margo's heartbeat.

Finally, Jackie was the first to break the stare by looking down at her phone. "I've got to get going. Class starts in twenty minutes."

Margo nodded. "I've got a meeting anyway," she said, unlocking her car door.

The parking lot began to fill with cars, faculty, and students alike flooding toward the building. Jackie touched her arm. "Wait, Margo. Have you seen my necklace?"

Shaking her head, Margo stubbed the cigarette out with the bottom of her shoe. "Nah, but I'll look again."

"Thanks. I'll see you around," Jackie said. With the hand she'd touched Margo with, she offered her a short wave as she headed toward the building.

Margo tried to keep herself from watching Jackie walk into the building but turned anyway. Jackie was staring at her, their gazes meeting. Margo snapped her head around, a slight heat rising to her cheeks sending a fury of irritation through her.

Once in her car, she gripped the steering wheel and cursed. The teen really got to her—the feeling only exacerbated from Jackie pointing out the obvious, and everything leading up to that point. Yeah, helping Anthony to pass on caused her to cry, but she didn't need to be psychoanalyzed.

She started the car and pulled out of the parking lot, heading to the diner where Brent would be waiting for her.

THE CROWDED RESTAURANT dining room caused Margo to shift in discomfort because there were far too many voices echoing around the space at eight in the morning for her liking. After leaving the high school, she'd barely made it in time to meet Brent at the mom-and-pop diner downtown.

"Thanks for meeting me here." Brent pushed his glasses up his nose, the silver frames contrasting against his russet skin and dark beard. His hazel gaze met Margo's as he brought a glass of water to his mouth.

She tipped her head in his direction. Nothing good came from owing anyone, as far as Margo was concerned. Steam lifted from the white cup of coffee in her hands and she brought it to her mouth.

Brent watched her carefully. The unfathomable expression on his face led her to believe the debt she owed him would not be an easy feat. After swallowing almost half of the hot fluid, she cleared her throat. "Let's cut the shit. What do you want? I know this isn't going to be your run-of-the-mill debts. Not money, not anything I can hand you, so what is it?"

"Your power of observation is astounding," he said, looking down as a smirk formed on his lips. "I need a favor."

She leaned back in her chair, finishing off her coffee before she spoke. "Yeah? What kind of favor?"

He lifted his head. "I want you to use your specific talent to help me open a door to Fae lands, specifically to Prince Jael's court."

Margo slammed her cup on the table, causing a patron at a nearby table to shoot her a questioning expression. She knew enough about Fae politics to understand opening a door to their lands without permission was not only dumb but dangerous. *Oh, and the fact he always reminds me and Luis to stay out of people's politics.*

"Are you out of your mind, Brent?"

"Collin asked for a pardon from Queen Demelza for his misfortune of being what he is and was denied. I'm not asking you to join him when he goes but simply to help me find the right direction."

The two Fae kingdoms in the area were different sides of the same coin; Queen Demelza ruled over a portion of the land while her counterpart, Prince Jael, held power over the other. Margo hadn't stepped foot in either, the worlds separated by a veil similar to the one between here and where the spirits went when they passed on, and she didn't long to jump into either.

He had to realize the weight of his favor. Maybe he was simply ignoring the risks involved. She'd become indebted to him once he saved her and Sam from death, but she couldn't put either of them in danger again regardless of the reason.

She crinkled her nose and shook her head. "I'm not risking my ass just so your boyfriend can try to win his way back into the Fae world."

The words didn't appear to phase Brent. He cocked an eyebrow and brought his water to his mouth, his expression neutral. "I don't like to be crass but if it weren't for my doing, you and Sam would've been left in the situation you brought on yourself. It would be a shame if the Board reconsidered their initial decision."

Fear prickled the back of her neck, but she held her glower. "Are you blackmailing me? I never imagined you stooping so low." Her words dripped with venom. They may have had their disagreements, but she never pinned him for one to blackmail. Had she misjudged his character all along? No, the soft smile on his face deterred her from thinking he'd threaten her in such a manner.

She rolled her shoulders as if the motion would banish the restlessness that plagued her since their meeting with the Board. "And why do this all of a sudden?"

He heaved a heavy sigh. "No, Margo, I'm asking a favor. Nothing will come of you if you decline." Shrugging, he lifted his glass to his mouth again before saying, "I'll have to find a different way you can repay me if you don't want to help." He ignored her last question.

"I've never tried to open a portal to either of the Fae lands. What makes you think that'll work?"

His gaze flickered from the table to hers. "There's an existing door in the woods, and all we need to do is access it. I'm sure we're more than capable, my friend."

Margo scoffed and leaned her head closer to him. "What, you think I can warp light to open this door because I'm half..." She didn't speak the rest aloud; she didn't need to. When he first discovered Margo and Luis, he was the one who pinpointed the origin of her mysterious power. Her ability scared him as much as it fascinated him. Encouraging her to manifest her power with the possibility of something going wrong was far from his norm. "What happened to the values of the corporation—the mission statement?" she deadpanned. The Board's golden child was about to partake in something that muddied their self-imposed ethical code with malevolent oil.

He smiled broadly. "We both know how I feel toward their misguided ideations."

"I don't think this is a good idea, Brent. You have no clue what kind of shit we could get into by doing this. If the wrong person sees us, I'm as good as dead." Though tempting, Margo couldn't ditch her own trepidation. She was already in enough trouble, and Brent knew this as well as she did. As she opened her mouth to shoot down his request, a resounding clatter of dishes echoed from the kitchen, and they both turned to search for what caused the commotion. A waiter knelt on the floor, picking up shards of white from a handful of broken plates.

Rays from the sunlight poured over the tiled floor in torrents, tumbling over the reflective surface. Oh, how she longed to pull the light to her, feel the indescribable magic coursing through her very being. The thrill her magic gave her was far beyond the power she experienced when she opened a portal for a spirit. The two manifested much the same way; however, conjuring light stirred a darkness within Margo, prompting her to view the power as inherently evil. Brent's fear, and fascination, with the power stoked this thought. Brent cleared his throat. "I do know, but this isn't for me; this is for Collin. The way Demelza has treated him is unfair. As if his very existence is questionable due to his halfling status. Out of anyone, I should think you'd understand what angst this can bring to someone." His voice ripped her from the thrall of the light bouncing off the floors.

She lifted her head and chewed her lip, meeting Brent's impenetrable gaze. The conversation was beginning to turn her bitter attitude into an abysmal mood. "Using my weakness against me? You're on one today."

"I was making a simple comparison. He'd like to visit his childhood home, to see his mother."

Ah, so it's family, Margo mused. "I was joking."

The bottom of her shoe tapped the tiled floor of the restaurant as she bounced her leg nervously. She wondered why Collin's mother hadn't visited him but bit back the question. For the most part, Margo kept herself from poising questions about Brent's other half, not out of lack of curiosity but to respect his privacy. The Fae, whether they were elves, selkies, pixies, or something else entirely, held a strong belief in secrecy. Brent briefly delved into their history when he first taught Margo and Luis about the various individuals who made up the hidden society of ethereal creatures but skimped on details. Margo didn't even know what Collin was, but now she found herself more than a little inquisitive.

He quirked his eyebrow at her and pursed his lips. "So?"

"When are we doing this?"

"Right now."

Margo laughed, the sound louder than she anticipated. She couldn't deny her curiosity. "All right, let's go."

"BRENT, I KNOW I agreed to help you, but this is making me a little nervous." Margo tripped over yet another gnarled root jutting out of the forest floor. "You didn't tell me this was going to be in the middle of nowhere."

Brent, who calmly walked forward through the dense trees, chuckled.

A droplet of water fell from the leaves above and splashed Margo's forehead, the resulting dampness a lingering indication of the heavy rainfall from the night before. Brent would be stupid to underestimate her apprehension around the use of her magic. Since he informed her of how dangerous it was if she were caught by Corporate, she never used her ability—well, once in a while alone or in front of Luis. Corporate's usual protocol to remove a Grim who possessed heritage that didn't align with their policies was to decommission the individual. From what she'd learned from other Grims, the disturbing process required a powerful mage, one who removed a

Grim's ability to open portals, leaving them cognizant to spirits and other beings but unable to assist any spirits that came to them for guidance to the other side. The thought alone gave Margo chills, or maybe this was due to the sharp gust whipping through the barren branches around her.

"We're about seven miles north of the closest shifter territory, and as far as I know, this area is sanctioned off as old Fae lands, so you won't find anyone wandering around here on purpose," Brent said. He threw a glance over his shoulder at Margo and smiled what she assumed to be his reassuring smile. "Don't back out on me now—we're almost there."

Margo stepped over a shallow stream, her boot kicking loose stones into the water. The air was clean and clear, giving her a small shred of peace. She'd always held a strong respect for the Pine Barrens, and along with this, she held a healthy fear of the dense woods in the middle of New Jersey. The Fae made her nervous, especially Brent's boyfriend, Collin. Though only a halfling, Collin's presence itself exuded a power as copious as the cigarette smoke spilling from her nose.

"Why can't Collin get into the lands on his own?"

"The same reason he's unwelcome; he's a halfling. Getting to Demelza isn't a challenge but we've gone that route without success, or I wouldn't have asked you. Finding a way into Jael's territory is no easy feat, which is where you come in."

"Right, but why here?" Margo knew the strange world was concurrent with their own, some Fae coming and going as they pleased while others stayed on either side indefinitely.

Brent glanced back as he stepped over a mossy fallen log. "This part of the forest is the least inhabited by the Fae so less likely for anyone to interrupt us. The portal here has been out of use for a long time and has some extremely strong bonds to prevent the opening, but that's where you come in. From the research I've conducted, it's my hypothesis your light conjuring is similar enough to theirs that you should be able to open the door just as they do."

His hypothesis? Margo rolled her eyes, betting his plan wouldn't even work. But she had to ask, "What happens if someone catches us?"

"No one will catch us."

"But what if someone does?" she asked again.

He ignored her and continued toward a clearing in front of them. Thick copses of ferns crunched underfoot, sweeping their legs as they continued to a clearing. Collin's ginger hair shone like a beacon in the foliage surrounding him, his emerald-colored polo camouflaging him. The colors of autumn hung around him, drapery stitched in the finest silk thread. Deep-crimson leaves scattered across the floor of the meadow, dappled with canary yellow and a deep coffee tinged the massive tree trunks. The Fae man belonged in the trees, surrounded by the beauty only nature could produce. Margo finally understood why this was so important for Brent to do for him. He glanced up, his fair hair a shade lighter than the leaves falling from the trees in an errant breeze. "Brent. Margo."

She approached the area, dry leaves crunching beneath her boots. "'Sup?"

"Thank you for agreeing to this," Collin bowed his head in her direction, face strained.

Instead of commenting that it appeared she had no choice in the matter, Margo nodded. She held a sliver of pity for the Fae man since she'd learned of his exile from his homeland for being half human. To Margo, his circumstances were worse; at least she hadn't known a loving family and been ripped away from them. She'd rather have had no one to love than to live her life with the pain clearly evident on Collin's face. She wanted to inquire about the details surrounding the incident but feared him too much to pose the question. She figured it was rude anyway.

Collin pointed to a pair of trees, their trunks twisting upward, branches intertwined to the very top. Beneath where the trunks met sat a shallow divot no larger than a miniature doorway, and the darkened space sent goosebumps over Margo's shoulders.

"The portal is right there," Collin said. "I shouldn't be long." Collin turned to Brent, his whisper inaudible. They shared a short kiss before they moved away from each other.

Brent stretched his arms behind him and cracked his knuckles as if prepping for a fight. "Are you ready?"

Margo refrained from grumbling an uncouth remark as she nodded and closed her eyes. Although opening a portal for a soul filled her with energy, the unbridled power that engulfed her when she drew the light from around her was incomparable and worth the draining crash afterward. When she opened her eyes, a patch of light wavered, then another bowed toward her, and another crept over the rough terrain of overlaying leaves. She called to them, summoning the glowing patches to her, ready for the vibrant mass to consume her senses with icy power.

Numerous shards of light lurched toward her, and she touched the ground, allowing them to coil around her wrist, savoring the cold power that bled into her skin. The white light appeared serene, warm, and bright, but once she allowed it to pour over her, the chill always took her breath away. Absently, Margo thought she heard Brent gasp but couldn't be bothered to look in their direction to see if it had been him or Collin.

She rubbed her hands together and grinned. "Okay, let's do this."

Brent joined her by the crook in the tree, the flickering light coming to life in his fingers. Margo's own hand was also doused in light; however, whereas Brent's light twirled around his fingers, Margo's took over her entire hand, encompassing the expanse of skin. Focusing on the empty space between the trees, Margo threw the light forward as Brent toyed with the edges of the forming door. Her fingers burned, singed by the frigidity brought on by the light as if it stole her warmth—and perhaps it did, tucked it away in return for its power.

She fell to her knees, breathless as fatigue washed over her. "Fuck, that felt good," she chuckled, and she rose from the ground, knees damp from the dewy grass and matted leaves. The doorway was black and the sunlight peeking through the dense canopy above reflected off the surface, reminding Margo of slick oil-coated asphalt. How could such power, such light create the image of darkness?

"Wow, that worked," Brent gasped in surprise as he pointed at Margo's arms. "Your hands."

Taking in the state of herself, Margo noted the lingering glow around her fingertips, dripping into a pool of shimmering luminescence at her feet, setting the bright foliage on the ground ablaze in unnatural light. She tried to shake it loose, to brush off the blazing light from her hands with no avail. She shrugged and shoved her hands into her pockets. "Yeah, that's normal." And for the most part, it was as if the light couldn't bear to depart from her, clinging to the warmth. She shivered, more from the thought than the actual chill brought on by using the light.

A fallen log a few feet away appeared inviting, and she walked over to it, ignoring Brent's attention. Her muscles ached, and she flexed her fingers in her pockets, fatigue hanging over her shoulders like a burial shroud. *Or maybe I'm just being dramatic.*

"Thank you, Margo. I shouldn't be long," Collin said. Holding his head high, he stepped through the portal, his body disappearing through the placid pool.

Once he was gone, Brent wandered to the edge of the clearing before he disappeared into the thicket. Minutes passed. She retrieved her pack of cigarettes and lit one. When she brought it to her lips, she noticed the glow had finally receded, marring only the tips of her fingers as if she'd painted her nails a fine metallic white. *Like I'd ever wear nail polish.*

A branch cracked in the direction opposite of Brent's receding footfalls. The hair on the back of her forearms rose, and an unsettling realization surfaced: something was watching her. Margo threw her head back and gaped at the empty woods behind her. Moss coated the tall oak trees and dense evergreens. She held her breath, waiting for movement. A leaf silently fell from above, dancing as it drifted to the forest floor. When nothing happened, she turned back to the crook in the trees and realized her cigarette had burned down to the filter while she searched for the phantom observer that was probably an animal.

Brent trekked back, holding his shirt out to create a pouch. The fabric strained under the dozens of mushrooms he had tucked in front of him. "If I would've known how many amanita phalloides grew out here, I could've brought a basket."

"You're weird," Margo chuckled. "So, why did that work?"

He picked a few dry leaves from his pile of mushrooms. "Your magic is similar to Fae magic. The big difference is where you draw your strength from the around you, Fae pull from within."

Margo stifled a shudder as she lit a fresh cigarette. "Huh, I didn't know that."

"If you'd paid more attention when I taught you and Luis about these things, maybe you would've remembered." His unwavering stare became irritating. "Aside from the obvious reasons, why do you dislike taking advantage of your gift?" he asked.

Margo couldn't help but roll her eyes. "*My gift*? Brent, you're the one who told me not to use it even if my life depended on it." Ash fell from her cigarette and hit her thigh, burning a small hole in her jeans before she flicked it from her lap, noting that her hand had shifted back to her normal pale complexion.

"You aren't wrong," he sighed. "I was only trying to protect you after the initiative passed when most of us didn't think it would move through the Board of Directors. We've been living and reaping fine for the last millennia; I still don't understand why they didn't leave well enough alone."

The initiative he spoke of determined most Grim who held differing bloodlines weren't welcome in the community. Any new Grims born, or who otherwise didn't fit the new standard, were ostracized or worse with Luis and Margo being grandfathered in. Even so, Margo took off, heading for Canada, fearing they'd take away the only identity she had. She didn't get very far.

"The power you hold is incredible and nothing to balk at."

She nodded, not wanting to continue the conversation. "So, what's Collin trying to accomplish by going to see Jael? Does he think he'll offer him an answer different from Demelza?"

Brent cradled a few mushrooms in his palm, studying the fungi as he spoke. "He believes Jael will offer him a pardon, so he can come and go as he pleases. I'm not well versed in the politics of either ruler, but I do know Jael can be rather unpredictable. As for Demelza, Collin expected her reluctance to allow him back in as her beliefs align well with the Board." He sighed loudly as he met her gaze. "He misses the land, his home. It pains me to witness his homesickness, and nothing I say will ease his mind and soften the hurt."

There was a long pause, accentuated by a breeze that rattled the trees. "There's something I've been meaning to ask you about the blood bond..."

Margo blinked at him. "What about it?"

"Well," Brent said as he inspected one of the many mushrooms in his lap, "I asked around, with the utmost respect to the secrecy of this matter, and I discovered a little more information. There isn't much on your people in regard to blood bonds, but what I did come up with leads me to believe Sam is a rarity. By all accounts, you're a rarity."

Your people. The phrase alone nauseated Margo. They weren't *her people.* They'd left her as an infant in the lobby of a generic inner-city hospital with nothing more than a receiving blanket wrapped around her tiny body and her abhorrent name on a slip of paper. They were nothing to her. Not to mention they were completely unheard of in North America. "Yeah? Well, good for Sam. And the Djinn aren't *my people*."

"You shouldn't have been able to resurrect her with a blood bond because of your split heritage; however, you were successful."

Not knowing what to say, Margo shrugged in answer. *This is not a conversation I want to have right now*, she thought as the skin beneath her eye twitched in irritation. If she had it her way, she wouldn't have wanted to know she was anything more than a freak foster kid who could speak to ghosts and play with spilled light.

"Margo, does Sam exhibit any of your, uh, specific attributes?"

The question hung between them. A trio of birds fluttered down from a nearby tree, their chattering quieting as Margo tapped her foot on the forest floor. She'd known the question was bound to be brought up at some point. "No, not even a hint of it, so don't worry. And before you ask, no, I didn't tell her anything." The first bit had been a lie, but she'd been honest with the latter. She had no idea if Sam shared her anomaly, and, frankly, she was too afraid of the potential.

"Good. I didn't notice anything out of the ordinary with her, but I wanted to be sure I hadn't missed something you might've witnessed."

"Nope. She's as normal as a turned Grim could be, not that I've met any others," Margo laughed. She wasn't an idiot and knew why he'd asked; Sam was already a target in Corporate's eyes, someone to watch carefully, to wait for her to slip up. If there was any inkling of her obtaining even a sliver of Margo's Djinni blood, she and Margo wouldn't be given any chance of survival.

Noise stirred at the crook in the trees where Collin had stepped through. The viscous portal shifted, and Collin came tumbling through, falling to the ground. Blood-caked hair stuck to his temples, droplets slipping down his face, but he bore a smile on his lips.

"Collin!" Brent jumped up from his spot on the ground, dumping the mushrooms onto the forest floor as he ran to his boyfriend.

His torn shirt exposed dark bruises spanning his sides, matching the marred skin of his face beneath the blood. Scratch marks etched his pale skin, and his chest heaved as Brent wrapped his jacket around him.

"What the hell happened?" Margo rushed over, narrowly avoiding thick roots protruding from the ground.

Collin lifted his head and offered her a weak smile. "They weren't thrilled to see me. Thought I was the enemy." Pushing up from the ground, Collin allowed Brent to help him stand, and Margo looped her arm around Collin's other side to aid in his efforts. "Hope is not all lost, my friends." Collin laughed crudely.

"What do you mean?" Brent asked, wiping a droplet of blood from Collin's forehead.

"Jael has agreed to consider our proposition, and I should have word by tomorrow morning."

Margo straightened and tightened her hold on Collin, who wavered. "So, there's a chance?"

"Yes, a slim chance but a chance nonetheless."

Somehow, this made the risk of opening the portal worthwhile in Margo's eyes. At least for the moment.

Margo helped Brent half carry Collin the two miles back to the grassy patch, where they'd parked their cars, the trek quicker than she would've expected given Collin's injuries.

They helped him into the passenger seat, Collin grabbing Margo's hand and thanking her in a soft voice.

Brent shut the door, sighing heavily. "The trip must've been pretty rough on him," he said, wrapping his arms around himself. "Traveling to and from can be not only exhausting, but dangerous." He appeared as tired as his other half. "Thank you, Margo."

"Yeah, you're welcome," she said.

Brent walked to the driver's side and got in.

She turned to her own vehicle, smiling briefly. She was glad she hadn't left yet.

Chapter Five

SUNLIGHT THREADED THROUGH the dense gray clouds, sprinkling the rough gravel with specks of light as Jackie drove her car up the driveway to Brent's home early Wednesday morning. Brent and Collin had been together for as long as Jackie had known Brent, which was a long time. Roz had introduced the two when she and Jackie were still in high school when they were both in their early teens.

Jackie's general unease at Roz's continued silence was becoming a distraction. With the added weight of near bloodlust, Jackie was ready to unravel. Roz leaving from time to time without a word wasn't completely unusual; however, the time frame of radio silence from her friend usually didn't last longer than a week. By now, Roz would've touched base with her to assure she was all right.

Roz hadn't always been so flighty. There'd been a shift in her personality roughly six months or so before, a turning point where Roz ceased her usual appearances in Jackie's life, stirred by seemingly nothing. Jackie had asked Roz if she was all right, if something had sparked her avoidance, but Roz deflected, claiming she was simply busy. Jackie hadn't bought her excuse, but now she wondered if Roz's disappearance was brought on by this.

Before leaving the house, Jackie sent another email to Roz's mother, not holding her breath on a response.

Both vehicles were parked in front of the house as Jackie pulled up, gravel crunching beneath the tires of her car. Her mild distress of missing a feeding had swiftly become a gnawing pain blossoming in her gut; a sharp, insatiable hunger, a prelude to the beast within, signaling that the elixir definitely had lost the ability to hold her off longer once it had warmed to room temperature. Her knuckles whitened on the steering wheel, and she forced herself to relax before she turned the engine off. Though fall was settling over the area early, and colorful leaves littered the ground, the ivy around the porch of the house held an emerald so vibrant, the plant seemed to move on its own accord.

She entered the home without knocking, breathing in the familiar scents of oak and potent tea. The soft base of smooth jazz met her, and she followed the uplifting music down the hall.

"Hello," she called out as she grew closer to the large study. Dark wood paneling encased the expansive room, offering a coziness unparallel to anywhere else. She enjoyed their time in the greenhouse, the majestic foliage it offered and the pleasant sense of being surrounded by nature, but she loved the homey study.

Collin was perched against the desk at the far end of the room, head bent over a wilted plant. "Hey, Jackie," he muttered without looking up at her. His red hair hung low, nearly brushing the brown leaves of the plant he held, obscuring his face.

Brent hopped down from the step stool with a leather-bound book under his arm. "Hey, I forgot you were coming today." His brows were furrowed, and he approached Jackie with what she perceived as caution.

"Yeah, like we planned," she said, puzzled as she tossed her bag on the floor next to one of two chairs placed near the desk.

Brent plopped in an armchair and opened the book. "No, that's good. Did you hear anything from Roz's mom?"

Shaking her head, Jackie took the seat opposite Brent, pulling her feet beneath her as she sat. "No, but I did send her yet another email this morning. I'm not new to the whole disappearing act she does once in a while, but this is different. At first, I wasn't worried because I know she can't use her phone over there, but she was supposed to be back by now." Since Roz's last email, Jackie had begun to worry. Her simple trip to Europe to visit her parents could've turned into something more serious. "I've sent Roz tons of emails because her phone is disconnected."

With a soft thud, Brent closed the book. He reached over to the coffee table between them and picked up a teacup. "The Board has officially deemed her missing, and when she is found, if she isn't in any way mangled or mauled, she'll be in quite a deal of trouble with Corporate. They've questioned me on several occasions as to her whereabouts, and I've told them the same thing—she's flighty and she'll turn up eventually."

His nonchalance worried Jackie, but she could see the concern behind it. "If she takes off, she's usually back way sooner. She'll at least shoot me a text to let me know she's all right, but I haven't heard from her in weeks," Jackie said. Her last email from Roz was right before Roz left for the airport to come home. Jackie feared something happened to Roz before she made it to her flight.

"What if she's hurt or worse?" *For all we know, she could've been kidnapped.* A shiver ran over her shoulders. "When do we start thinking about filing a missing person's report with the human police department?"

Brent folded his leg over the other, face tense. "You don't want to do that."

Before Jackie could question him as to why she wouldn't want to, Collin muttered, "Ouch." She glanced over at him. A crimson ribbon of blood trailed down his wrist from a small puncture on his palm. The red hue shone stark against his pale skin, and Jackie gulped down her need.

Brent rose from his chair. "You okay?"

"Yes, I'm fine." Collin held his other hand up to halt Brent's concern. "A thorn jabbed my hand is all." After placing the plant on the table, Collin pushed off the desk and made for the door.

The ache in Jackie erupted into a searing pain throughout her chest and head. She flared her nose, catching the coppery hint of blood as Collin walked past her. Dropping her gaze, Jackie picked at the seam on the worn armchair, desperately trying to smother the drive to devour, to taste blood, to tear flesh with her teeth. She lifted her head at the sound of Brent's voice but couldn't distinguish what he was saying. Though she could see him speaking, the rhythmic pulse of his heartbeat blocked his words. Her gaze moved downward from his face to the thrumming at his neck.

"Jackie."

She blinked and drew a sharp breath. "Yeah?"

"I said there's something I have to tell you." He clutched the heavy book in his lap, jaw tight and lips a thin line. "I don't have any of the elixir made up."

"Huh?"

With a sigh, Brent held up the massive book, long fingers grasping the withered binding. "I've been searching for an alternative to the one I've been making for you, but I'm coming up empty-handed. I haven't been able to obtain the ingredients I need."

"Okay, you've got to spell it out. What does this mean for me?" Thankfully, the pain in her gut waned.

He grimaced as he spoke. "I don't have the ingredients, and I have no reserves."

Jackie brought the heel of her palm to her eyes as the ache spread through her chest again, and the pain forced her to stand. "How long until you have the ingredients you need?" When she lowered her hand, Brent was still watching her.

"I don't know. I apologize, but I think it's going to be quite some time before I'll be able to acquire the necessary plants."

"How long?" Jackie asked. The grandfather clock boomed the top of the hour loudly, and Jackie cringed.

Letting out a long sigh, Brent brought teacup to his lips. "Possibly next year."

"Next year," she repeated slowly. She began to pace, the beast within stirring at the realization she wouldn't have the elixir any time soon. What would she do? How would she survive? What would she become? Her mind raced and she nearly tripped over the lip of the ornate rug beneath her sneakers. "What happened?"

"I made a poor decision, and I'm reaping what I sowed," Brent said.

She glared at him. "What do you mean?" Her voice came out much lower than she anticipated, the darkness from within seeping into her tone.

Brent quirked an eyebrow. "How long has it been since you last fed?"

Too long, Jackie thought. She shook her head and sat on the ledge beside the window, gazing out. Her beast arched within her, pleading to be freed. If she didn't have the elixir soon, she wouldn't be able to abate her hold any longer unless she took blood.

Concern etched Brent's face, but he kept a short distance from her. "Are you okay?"

Jackie closed her eyes, drawing a deep breath. Was she okay? No, not even close. There wasn't any blood left in her refrigerator, and he didn't have anything to help her. The threatening fire from the beast expanded in her gut, and Jackie pinched the bridge of her nose. "I'm fine." Opening her eyes, she found Brent openly studying her.

Brent scoffed. He turned to the desk, ditched his teacup, and filled two tumblers full of amber liquor. "Liar. How long has it been since you fed?" he repeated.

She gazed up at the ceiling and tensed, taking a moment to think about the question. "About a month."

Brent handed her the tumbler of liquor. "You've got to be kidding. A month, Jackie? Do you have any idea how dangerous that is? You could've died." She knew that and regretted hoarding her blood storage. If only she knew she'd lose it. *Talk about horrible timing.* "I have ways of helping besides the elixir, you know."

She did know, but she wasn't interested in a live donor. The thick alcohol burned the whole way down, and she coughed to clear her throat. "Of course, I know how dangerous it is. I'm not an idiot, but I didn't know you'd be empty-handed. I had plenty of blood in the refrigerator until a rat chewed through the damn power cord. I had what you gave me a few weeks ago, and usually, I only have to feed once a month with that. Why can't you get the ingredients you need?"

His jaw tensed, and it was his turn to look away from Jackie. "I tried to bargain a little too hard, and it was not well received."

The bargain gone wrong had possibly set Jackie up to be consumed by her beast, the only alternative to take blood from a person until Ezra came home from their business trip. "Crap." She pinched the bridge of her nose and sighed heavily. "Ezra's my only backup, and they won't be back in town until Tuesday."

"I can help you find someone willing. You can't wander around without feeding, Jacqueline. You'll be a danger to yourself and everyone around—"

"I'm aware," she growled without meaning to. "Sorry. I'm just not comfortable taking that from someone directly."

"Things like this shouldn't happen. You can't be around others until you've taken care of yourself, you know what happens when—"

"Brent!" Jackie whirled around, glaring at him. The beast fumed within her, heat pouring to her fingertips. Brent widened his eyes as he took a step back. "I know. I didn't plan this." She loosened her clenched hands and liquid dripped from her palms, causing Jackie to gaze down. Sharp claws protruded from her fingers, small divots marring her fingers where they unsheathed. She closed her eyes, willing the image to go away. Years had gone by since she'd been this close to losing her control. But, she knew, this wasn't about control. The beast lingering inside had one job: protect her when her own immune system depleted her of oxygen-carrying red-blood cells.

Collin entered the room holding a tray topped with three steaming mugs. "Jacqueline," he began, voice trembling. He turned his attention away from her and glared at his boyfriend. "Don't lie to her, Brent. She deserves to know the truth."

Jackie finally viewed Collin's face for the first time since she'd gotten there, too distracted in her own needs. His cheeks were marred with tiny cuts, peppering his face with red. Bruising lined his eyes, darkening all the way to his hairline. How had she missed his face when she'd walked in? "Collin, what happened to you?"

"It's my fault Brent doesn't have the ingredients." The pained expression relayed the weight of his words. "I stood before Prince Jael to petition dual residence, and my proposal was accepted but not without issue."

Brent exhaled through his nose. "As you can imagine, this led to cascading dominos, hence the lack of the elixir. We pissed off people with valuable resources."

Collin put the tray on a side table and moved closer, putting himself in between Jackie and Brent. Did she pose such a threat? The possibility of her beast breaking free and harming others struck her painfully. "I'm sorry," she croaked. How could she have let herself go this far?

Collin reached his hand toward her, a cautious smile on his face. "Love, let us help you. We can find a willing individual to satisfy your needs."

She shook her head, lowering her hand to retrieve her bag from the armchair. "No, thanks. I've got to go." Brent began to say something, but Jackie ignored him as she rushed to the front door and into the cold air. This wasn't their responsibility. She'd figure something out.

She glanced behind her to see Brent on the porch, arms crossed over his chest. She knew he feared for her safety, but Jackie couldn't stay, couldn't take their offer. She had to have another vial, maybe hidden in the fridge downstairs.

The cold air caused the breathlessness to heighten, and Jackie took shuddering breaths as she ran to her car. *Screw biology,* she thought. Taking blood from a willing individual was easy for almost every other Empusa she knew; however, she couldn't bear to see the images it provoked, especially from a stranger. The blood Ezra brought her from the blood bank didn't cause her the upset or the moral dilemma. She didn't see unwanted memories or thoughts when she consumed it because the blood wasn't coming directly from the source. No heartbeat pumping the blood, no unwanted imagery.

Her tires displaced countless rocks as she drove out of the driveway faster than she should've. If all else failed, she'd have to take Brent up on his offer or find someone else.

Chapter Six

MARGO SLEPT IN late Wednesday, fatigued from her magic use more than she could've anticipated. When she finally woke well after noon, grabbed her first cup of coffee, and sat outside on the chilly balcony overlooking the town, she had three new messages on her phone, all from Brent.

Thank you again for yesterday. Collin's proposal was accepted by Prince Jael.

Also, I apologize for the inconvenience, but I need you to pick up your assistant today and help her with the next charge.

Details on the individual will be forthcoming.

She smiled as she brought the steaming coffee to her mouth. Well, at least their venture hadn't been for naught.

She sent Brent a quick reply.

Cool beans, glad to hear it.

She hadn't seen Sam since the day they shared the same fear of dying within the confines of the small Corporate office up north. She'd tried to keep Sam calm, but the whole time Margo thought they'd both be killed with the unlikely hope they'd spare Sam for being an innocent byproduct of Margo's stupidity. Still, she wondered what changed their minds; how Brent swayed their decision, from a near unanimous "Let's kill them," to a two-to-one "Spare them."

As promised, Brent sent the necessary information on the spirit: a name, location, and date of death through text. Most often, Brent would stop by once a week with a list for Margo and Luis, Luis's always much shorter than hers due to the nature of his work. He helped an uncountable number of spirits along by happenstance, which lightened his assigned load.

Margo sent off a text to Sam.

Guess what Buttercup? You get to work with me today. What time is your shift over?

She sipped her coffee and relaxed back in the plastic beach chair.

Sam texted back. *Three. I have a short day today. What's wrong with Brent?*

Ash fluttered to the floor from Margo's cigarette as she texted Sam back. *I'll explain when we meet up.*

Where?

Margo took the information again, noting the last known location of the ghost was a little flower shop by the boardwalk.

The boardwalk.

Her phone chimed before she had a chance to place it back in her pocket.

Okay, we can meet at the arcade around three-thirty.

Coolio.

She couldn't tell whether the one Brent sent her way was his or Sam's as she wasn't privy of how the Board was treating her or doling out her work. She stood, stubbed out her cigarette, and went into the house. According to the clock, this only gave her about forty minutes to get ready and go out to find one of her own charges. Nope, not enough time. So, instead, she showered, dressed, and headed to the boardwalk.

As she drove, Margo wondered what Collin planned to do with this new freedom. Would he leave Brent forever, or would he simply travel back and forth? Margo recalled the damaged state he was in, the fatigue that instantly washed over him—not unlike the fatigue she succumbed to after using the light—when she and Brent helped him into the car.

Traveling back and forth didn't seem to be a healthy option, but Collin wouldn't leave Brent to stay with his Fae family, would he? Margo pulled into the parking lot of the arcade still pondering the dynamic. Why did she even care so much? Brent and Collin were as much a part of her life as Luis as a constant fixture, so she reasoned this was why she wanted to understand what the new situation would mean. Was his exile the only reason he stayed with Brent for so long? Margo knew this was the cynical part of her brain talking, the part that took over most often, triggered by an instinct to protect herself. She worried about what would happen to Brent if Collin did decide to take off.

None of my business, she thought as she got out of the car. *Not my problem.*

She headed up the stairs to the arcade. The doors were propped open by big boulders, sending out a clamor of noise into the parking lot. People filled the space, kids of varying ages around pinball machines or throwing balls up the Skee-Ball tracks, while others threw basketballs into the tiny hoops or raced cars. Music clashed under the domed ceiling, reverberating into a whirlwind arcade orchestra.

Sam, still in her post-office blues, stood at an air-hockey game, slamming the puck across the table to a teen on the other side, her dark hair pushed back. With a deft movement, the teen blocked the puck and shot it back her way, causing the puck to clatter into the goal. The game ended, the teen mumbling an awkward thank you before scurrying off.

Sam turned to Margo and smiled. "Sorry. I was trying to kill some time before you got here."

"No problem. Let's play a game," Margo said, motioning to the table.

"Why are you stuck with me today instead of Brent?" Sam asked as she fished in her pocket and pulled out a couple of quarters.

Margo crossed her arms and sighed, projecting a feigned annoyance. "Well, Brent's other half is feeling pretty shitty, so he had to stay home and play nursemaid while I get to help you out with this one." Air pushed off the surface of the table again, lifting the puck back up. Sam smacked it toward her. "Who was that?"

Sam blocked Margo's return and hit the puck with a loud clack. "Oh, I don't know."

"Some random kid?"

"Yeah. He looked lonely, so I offered to play a game with him."

Margo slammed the puck past Sam's defenses and into the goal. "That's nice of you," she said sincerely. "How's life treating you?"

Sam shrugged her right shoulder without much effort. "Brent's been helpful in all of the learning with this, but there are so many rules."

"Yeah," Margo chuckled.

Sam frowned, shifting her gaze around before staring at Margo, expression unreadable. "I really can't tell Katie, can I?"

"About being Grim? No."

"Never?"

Margo ushered the puck to her. "Never." Sam had already told her girlfriend; she couldn't tell her sister.

Sighing, Sam hit the puck back to Margo lazily. "I can't ever tell her you saved my life, and that I didn't almost die—I *did* die."

The puck flew across the table toward Margo, and she narrowly diverted it from her goal. "Dude, I know it sucks that you can't tell her, but it's bad enough Lauren knows. You can't go breaking rules by telling people we exist."

"Crap. That's a real rule, huh? I guess I probably shouldn't complain. I just feel like a liar when Katie asks me how I've been since the accident, and I make up a story." Sam's sigh was teeming with melancholy uncertainty, and then there was silence, save the background noise from the arcade and the clanking of the puck. "I guess being a liar is better than being dead."

Margo looked away from her, unsure how to answer. Light streamed in from the windows set high in the ceiling above them, speckling the industrial concrete floor, casting long, billowing shadows. Each ray was distinct in its own way, innocent by itself, but with a flick of her wrist, Margo could call them all to her, strip the room of light to harness the power. This always happened after using her magic; she'd become hyperaware of its presence, thrilled by the energy exuding off light in waves. It wasn't simply the light from the sun; she'd learned years before how to control artificial light, fluorescents and LEDs alike. At that moment, she decided she'd have to test Sam out, to weigh the potential she could possess to contort light. She'd left the woman in the dark enough after the blood bond, and her guilt was nearly palpable.

The air-hockey table deflated of air. "There's our cue we should probably get going."

Margo waited as Sam grabbed her jacket from a bench by the prize counter and they both walked out onto the boardwalk. The sun had begun the slow descent to the horizon, and the rain slowed, leaving a layer of stickiness dense in the air.

"I asked Brent who told Corporate about us, and he didn't have any clue. Who do you think would've said something? Another type of supernatural creature?"

Margo shrugged. "It's possible, but I don't know anyone who would do that to me. I haven't pissed anyone off recently who would want to get me in trouble. The Grim don't interfere with vampires, Empusa don't get into shifter business, and nobody fucks with Fae stuff. We all try to mind our own business."

Hm, she'd technically stepped into Fae business by helping Collin to Jael's territory. Sam didn't need to know that. The question did stir uncertainty in Margo. How *did* Corporate find out about Sam?

"You all mind your own business?" Sam asked. Although Margo was sure it was unintended, Sam's question brimmed with dubiety.

Mist fell from the sky in sheets as they walked north, past the water park closed for the season and the boarded-up restaurants and hole-in-the-wall eateries. A few places remained open throughout the cold season, their glass windows foggy with condensation.

"We generally deal with our own people, but sometimes crap comes up where a larger scale meeting has to happen. A couple of delegates meet in New York every, like, six months or so to go over issues. Nothing serious. Usually useless feuds or sometimes discrepancies. Think United Nations but with shifters, vampires, Fae, and us. In my opinion, they don't really do anything at all. Typical politicians but with magic."

Sam laughed, shaking her head at Margo's comment. "This is still so surreal."

They headed down the nearest stairs onto a street lined with a handful of small shops, most closed for the season.

"If you're in the mood to answer questions, I've got another one for you," Sam muttered with hesitation.

Margo forced a fake sigh and lolled her head to the side to glance at Sam. "Color me surprised."

Sam grinned at the comment. "Why is it that I got the funny in-between, but none of these spirits I've helped crossover do?"

"I thought Brent would've explained this. You weren't officially dead yet, as in your soul was still attached to your body. The in-between usually happens right at what we call the 'cusp of death' before you completely abandon the fleshy confines of your body."

Sam lifted her shoulders in what appeared to be a shiver. "Why do you have to make that sound so icky?"

"Because it is!" Margo laughed as she fished for a cigarette in her pockets and brought one to her lips. Good thing Sam wasn't slated to do any of her reaping in a hospital. "There's a tiny flicker of life still in your body even if there's no chance of survival. Think of it as your soul waiting for your body to make a comeback it isn't going to make."

"I don't get it."

Smoke plumed from her mouth as she spoke. "When you drowned, your body was torn up, your head smashed in—there was no way you were going to survive, but your soul still hung on for one reason or another. That's why this," she said, pointing to herself and then to Sam, "worked. If you had let go of your body, there wouldn't have been anything I could've done to fix that. The blood bond wouldn't have worked. You would've been dead, for good."

Sam looked away, nodding, perhaps satisfied with Margo's explanation or unwilling to continue her line of questioning. Without giving the movement a second thought, Margo wrapped her arm around Sam's shoulders and gave her a small squeeze before letting go.

"Thanks again," Sam muttered.

Gratitude wasn't what Margo had expected or, quite frankly, wanted. "I wasn't fishing for a thank you, kid; I was explaining why things are the way they are." She spotted a shimmering figure a few yards ahead of them and pointed. "Here's our next job."

Rainwater pooled at the edge of the building where the ghost stood with her back to them. The woman could've been in her late forties, her blonde hair streaked with gray and fine lines etching her forehead as she squinted into the window. Pale denim overalls hung from her tired shoulders and when she pulled back from the window to stare at them, Margo noticed a dusting of yellow powder coating the front of the woman's floral blouse under the overalls. Painted in elegant flowing calligraphy across the storefront glass read "Hazel's Floral Shop," with a small message scribbled on a white paper beneath. The spirit turned her back to them again.

"Now"—Margo began in a whisper, touching the back of Sam's arm—"this is where you get to try out being invisible, so we don't get the police called on us for snooping around."

Sam widened her eyes. "You called it a deception. I can do that too?" She appeared much younger than she was, childlike almost, and a renewed pang of guilt engulfed Margo for forcing her into the Grim world.

"Yeah, you're going to have to because we don't want anyone seeing us this close." Margo pointed to the window where the spirit peered in. From where they were standing, Margo could make out the figures of three people gathered around a table inside. "We don't want them seeing us when we go up there and make contact."

Sam nodded slowly. "Okay, how do I do that?"

Margo chuckled. "All you have to do is focus on hiding yourself. You know the feeling you get when you're about to open a portal? That buildup of energy deep in your chest?"

Sam nodded again.

"You take the same energy and will yourself to hide, for your body to be invisible, like, cloak yourself in it." Margo fought the urge to light a cigarette, wanting to be wholly present while Sam tried the new skill.

Rolling her shoulders and closing her eyes, Sam let out a long exhale. After a minute of stillness, a draft lifted the loose strings hanging from Sam's hoodie, and an eerie glow surrounded her skin.

"Nice," Margo said truly impressed. "If I didn't know better, I'd assume you were a born Grim. You're a natural."

Sam blushed as she opened her eyes, staring at Margo with open doubt. "I can't tell if you're being genuinely serious or just a serious smartass."

They crossed the street and approached the spirit with slow, thoughtful steps, Margo giving Sam a gentle nudge with her shoulder. "You need to grow some confidence, kid. Go on, you start this time."

Beyond the thick glass window within the shop stood three adults, one throwing their hands in their air, face contorted and cheeks flaming. The second sat in a chair, arms over his chest with an air of apathy. Condensation layered the glass, obscuring Margo's view of the rest of the room aside from the various boxes stacked on top of one another. The sign above the window proclaimed the store was closed until further notice.

"Look at them," whispered the spirit in a soft Southern drawl. "Just look at them in there arguing over who gets the bigger portion." A green apron dangled over her floral dress, embroidered with bright-white thread stating, Hazel's Flowers.

Sam took the opportunity to sidle up beside the woman. "Portion?"

"Portion of my assets. All they've been doing since I died has been arguing over who runs my business, who sells my home, who gets the car." She laughed crudely as she turned to face Sam and Margo. "My children don't care I'm gone; they care more about what I've left behind for 'em."

Well, there's no mystery to what her unfinished business is. Footsteps in the distance echoed in the periphery of Margo's hearing, and she twisted herself, staring off into the distance. The empty street lay behind her, rainwater dripping down the closed storefront of a fudge shop. An uncanny sensation crept into Margo's skin, and she gazed down the road, turning her head from side to side slowly. Though she could see no one, Margo knew someone was watching them, and the individual wasn't human.

"I'm sorry," Sam offered softly.

The woman shook her head, placing both hands on her hips.

"What do y'all want from me? Most folk I've encountered can't see me or hear me, and that's how things have been since I died. Can't tell you how many times I've tried to give these kids my two cents, and they ignore me, just like they did when I was still alive."

Sam wrung her hands in front of her. "We're here to help you to the other side."

"What, you're the angel of death or something?"

Sam glanced back at Margo nervously.

"Yeah, you could say that," Margo agreed.

The spirit huffed, glancing back through the window. "I don't understand where I went wrong. I gave them everything, put two of them through college. Walter didn't want to go, but I funded his business ventures. I encouraged them to be themselves, to take life by the horns and ride it. And then when I die, they're like this," she said, gesturing to the window with her palm up, shaking her head yet again. "Where did I go wrong?"

The urge to step up to help Sam was strong, but Margo stayed where she was, watching, waiting for Sam to make the next move in this tedious game of chess. The voices on the other side of the glass rose, the seated adult child standing suddenly and pointing accusatorily at their siblings. Although the words were inaudible, and Margo couldn't read lips, the conversation was clearly not going well.

Moving closer to the spirit, Sam placed her hand on the glass, her face genuine. "I don't think you did anything wrong, ma'am."

The woman crossed her arms in front of her in defiance. "I don't care what you think; I'm not going anywhere until I set these kids straight."

"Don't you think that'll be a little hard when they can't see you?" Sam asked in earnest.

"Do you have children?"

Sam shook her head.

"So, you have no idea how hard this is for me," the woman said, and she turned away from Sam and Margo. Sam's face was resigned, yet not defeated.

Margo closed the distance between herself and Sam. "Sometimes you have to remind them they're dead. Even if she wants to make her kids understand how she feels, they never will hear her," she murmured.

Sam cleared her throat, determination upon her features. "You're right, but what will you solve by standing and watching them argue over your stuff? Who knows how long they'll continue to do this? They may not figure any of their differences out until after one of them dies. Do you really want to stand around and be miserable until that happens?"

The woman spun around and glared at Sam, obviously as surprised as Margo was at her words. Her brown gaze was unfathomable until her lower lip trembled slightly. "I got to try, don't I?"

Sam was struggling; that Margo was certain of, but she continued to stay back to give Sam the chance to finish this. "I can't imagine how hard this is for you, no, but I do know it'll only get harder for you when you should be moving on. You deserve peace, regardless of the state your children decide to be in."

The spirit blinked a few times and then turned to look through the window again. The room she gazed into now stood empty, her children having gone somewhere out of sight. She placed her hand on the glass beside Sam's, closed her eyes, and shook her head. "I don't want to stay here anymore," she whispered.

A shift in the air lifted Margo's arm hair and she smiled as she watched light spark between Sam's fingers.

Sam peered at her over her shoulder, and Margo gave her a small nod, which was all Sam needed. She raised her hands and closed her eyes. The portal formed hazily in front of them, directly against the window of the woman's shop: dazzling reds, and opaque teals. The ghost stepped back, hand to her mouth as she stared in awe. "Do I...do we go through this?"

"No, only you can pass through here." Sam reached out and touched the woman's shoulder. "I truly hope you find peace."

"Thank you, honey." The woman gave her a small, pained smile before she turned and lazily walked into the shimmering portal with a slight limp.

Margo was hoping to give Sam more confidence, assuming the charge would be an easy one, but now she worried the job only knocked Sam's confidence down a level. Her gaze was still on the window when the portal disappeared, brows knitted and jaw tight.

Stepping closer, Margo wrapped her arm around Sam's shoulders and said nothing, squeezing her before moving away. "Now, to make the deception go away, you just have to relax. Let it fall off you." Sam took a deep breath and slowly exhaled through her nose, removing the glittering aura. Margo did the same, letting the deception slip from her.

Eventually, Sam began walking down the street toward the staircase to the boardwalk and Margo followed. "I'm sorry. I didn't know—"

"No problem. I think she was good practice," Sam said, cutting Margo's apology off.

Margo took the stairs two at a time until she was in front of Sam. When they reached the top, she grabbed Sam's shoulders and stared at her. "You did good, really good."

Finally, a smile, a real one, broke across Sam's face. "I'm glad," she said. "Now, are we all done for today?"

Margo dropped her hands and continued walking, keeping pace with Sam. "You bet. Go see your girl. I've got some crap I've got to do anyway."

Darkness shifted over the boardwalk as twilight approached. They were nearly to the entrance to the arcade, but Margo hadn't forgotten what she needed to do. Multicolor lights gleamed off the various games at the opening of the arcade, bright and dazzling against the backdrop of impending night. "Hey, Sam." She halted midstep to look back at Margo. "I want you to try something for me."

Perplexed, Sam faced her, taking her hands out of her pockets. "Okay, what do you want me to do?"

Margo jutted her thumb to the colored lights weaving through the dune grass and dumping onto the wooden planks. "I want you to make those lights move."

Sam lifted her dark brows with a smirk, clearly waiting for the punch line. "Yeah? How?"

Instead of answering, Margo yanked her pack of cigarettes from her pocket. Only three sat in the box as she stuck one in her mouth. "Humor me and just try," she said around the cigarette. "Wave your hand over them or something, and maybe they'll come to you." When Sam noted Margo's sincerity, she obeyed, stretching out her hand, reaching for the dancing lights. Nothing. No movement other than the normal dance brought on by the erratic wind. "Focus, just like with the deception and portal opening. Take the energy from inside."

Sam closed her eyes, chest rising as she drew a deep breath. Sweat crested Margo's brow as she waited, uncertain what her experiment would determine.

A minute passed. Sam took a deep breath and rolled her shoulders. Another minute went by. "Okay, I give up," Sam said as she dropped her hands to her sides. "And why did you want me to do that?"

Margo shot her a crooked smile, feigning her jesting. "To see how long you'd try." Despite her fears, Margo's relief was profound. She put her cigarette out and narrowly dodged Sam's punch to her arm.

"You can be such a jerk," Sam said as they walked through the arcade and exited the back door into the parking lot.

"Yeah," Margo began, slowing as she reached the bottom of the staircase to the parking lot. "But you have to admit, at least I don't half ass it."

Sam was still laughing as she headed to her Jeep. Instead of a wave, Sam gave her a thumbs-up and climbed into her vehicle.

Margo had a smile on her face when she got into her own car, allowing herself a minute to relish in the relief. Sam could throw a deception around herself, open portals, see the dead, but she couldn't move light. "Thank fuck," Margo whispered to the empty car. When she went to put her key in the ignition, her hand slipped, and the keychain fell to the floor of her car. She reached down, instantly feeling something cold and hard instead of the keys, and she picked the item up. In her hand sat a deep purple stone, rough and unpolished but still breathtaking. Jackie's necklace, she thought. Tucking the stone into her pocket, she grabbed her phone and sent Jackie a quick text, hoping she'd be home.

Hey, I found your rock, and I'm going to come drop it by right now.

With how important the stone seemed to Jackie, Margo figured she'd want it back as soon as she found it. At least, that's what Margo told herself as she pulled out of the parking lot and headed south. Her impromptu decision to drop by Jackie's house had nothing to do with the fact she was slightly fascinated by the Empusa.

Not a thing.

Chapter Seven

AFTER AN HOUR of meditation, Jackie's hunger was marginally better. She could breathe without her body struggling, the incessant pounding in her head lowered to a dull annoyance, and she managed to stand from the position she'd sat in for the entire duration. If she'd known her refrigerator would be destroyed by little vermin when Brent was without the necessary ingredients, she would've come up with a backup. Less than a month had passed since Ezra gave her the month's supply of blood in the refrigerator. In the right temperature, most blood stayed usable for up to forty to fifty days. Jackie discovered she could push it to an even sixty days before it lost its quality, and if this happened, she ended up having to drink more than usual to feel sated, to be able to breathe with ease.

She knew she should've taken Brent's offer before she left his home. Blood from a stranger meant unwanted thoughts and memories, an option she couldn't take unless she had no other choice. She hardly took blood from Roz anymore when she was around due to the unwanted imagery, though she much preferred the thoughts she'd endured from Roz over a stranger. She had to look around the house one more time.

A thorough hunt of the large refrigerator downstairs proved a waste of time, as did searching the freezer for a wayward bag of blood, not that they froze well anyway.

Resolutely, she went back upstairs to her workspace, hoping an artistic distraction could help calm her.

Just as she reached the upstairs, her body convulsed and she stopped, grasping the edge of the ancient chaise chair in the living room. In through her nose. Out through her mouth. The intensity was poignant, painful, and she couldn't ignore the need. What time was it? If she didn't feed soon, not only would her beast break free, but she could very well die. Cells depleted of oxygen caused her muscles to spasm. Soon, her blood would no longer be able to transport the oxygen throughout her body, and the beast would burst forth, and if she didn't consume blood, she would die in that form. She knew her body took on the terrifying state to protect her from her own self-destructive immune system, but this didn't mean she needed to like it. She hunched over the chair as sweat trickled down her neck, and she clenched her jaw, forcing a breath through her nose.

The pain passed for the moment and she straightened. She wasn't without resources; Brent offered to find her a willing donor. Her reluctance to take blood from anyone kept her from taking his offer. *If only I knew where Roz was, she'd help me.* A soft meow by her feet caused Jackie to open her eyes. Butters tilted his head, chirping at her again. She reached out and scratched him on the head. *Ten more minutes and I'll call Brent.*

The doorbell rang and Butters ran down the narrow staircase to the lower floor to avoid the visitor. She closed her eyes and forced a few more breaths. Brent must've been worried if he came all the way to her house. Maybe he'd found an extra bit of elixir or maybe even a bag of blood in his refrigerator. "I doubt it," Jackie scoffed to herself, but at least she didn't have to break down and call him herself.

When Jackie opened the front door, she took a step back, surprised to see Margo instead of Brent. "Can I help you?" she asked, feigning her calm.

Margo held her hand up, the purple amethyst vibrant against her pale palm. "I finally found it by chance on the floor of my car," she chuckled. Raindrops pelted her open leather jacket and slid down the collar, dampening her shirt beneath when she shifted her position. The tiny stud in Margo's nose glinted in the soft porchlight. "I tried downstairs, but no one answered. Figured maybe you were up here."

Taking the gem from Margo, Jackie smiled. "Thanks. I hang out up here when I'm working." Against her better judgment, Jackie moved to the side, opening the door wider. "Do you want to come in for a cup of tea or something?"

"Sure."

Margo stepped into the living room, then closed the door behind her.

Why would she invite Margo in? Not only did she find the infuriating woman attractive, but her beast also vibrated within her, excited at the prospect of blood. The faint echo of Margo's heartbeat thudded in Jackie's ears, and she cleared her throat to dispel the hypnotizing sound.

"You can sit wherever you want. Let me just get some water boiling." Past Jackie's massive art table in the middle of the room lay her kitchen, or the space that would've been her kitchen but only held the counters and a large sink for cleaning her art supplies. Paint brushes littered the countertops, drying on threadbare towels. Jackie filled her kettle with water and placed it on the single burner hotplate she kept solely for tea. Beside this stood a four-cup coffeepot for the late nights Jackie sometimes spent on the upper floor.

The floorboards creaked a soft melody, and Jackie turned her head. Margo wandered around the art table, fingers softly brushing the latest wooden block Jackie had been working on before she left the house. Margo titled her head, taking in the details of the wooden sparrow. Her blonde hair fell to the side, exposing the fragile skin of her neck and Jackie's heart hammered in her chest. Her messy hair reminded Jackie of the sand dusting her cedar porch each morning; beautifully tawny and unbelievably stubborn. She took a shaky breath, looking away from the other woman. Salvia pooled in her mouth, and she swallowed back her thirst.

No. She couldn't and wouldn't.

She opened the cupboard and a tremor ran through her hand as she retrieved the two mugs, the ceramic clinking together raucously. She leaned over the counter, her breaths shallow and forced as the cups hit the surface. Dizziness washed over her, keeping her eyes closed to stop the vertigo. The wooden planks on the floor groaned loudly and a warm palm rested on Jackie's back.

"Are you okay?" Margo's voice sounded far away, muffled to Jackie's ears. She nodded, squeezing her eyes shut as she fought the beast. *Easy breaths. In and out.* The beast within raged on, and Jackie's skin prickled, fingers searing with pain.

"Jackie?" She opened her eyes to find Margo staring at her, worry lines etching her forehead. "You okay?"

"I'll be fine," she said, forcing the words out in a whisper as she pushed off the counter and took a few steps away from Margo.

Margo moved closer to her. Jackie fought to move away, drawn to her with frightening insistence. "What's going on?"

"Brent hasn't been able to get the ingredients he needs for the elixir." Sweat slipped down her forehead as she battled for control; control that was steadily diminishing. A handful of dried paint brushes sat inside the sink, soaking from the night before. Jackie grabbed them and turned the water on.

"What happens if you don't drink it?"

Jackie scrubbed the thick, dried paint from the brush, the menial task calming her beast briefly. "I have to drink blood." Her eyes stung. She closed them briefly and the action caused the sensation to worsen.

"Right. You're like a...never mind," Margo muttered. Normally, Jackie would've laughed at Margo's misstep, but she couldn't stop the quaking in her muscles, couldn't quiet her beast's raging need to escape. The brushes dropped from her hands, clanking as they hit the bottom of the metal sink. "What happens if you don't do either?"

"Nothing," Jackie breathed.

"No, really, Jackie, what happens? I'm not trying to be rude. I know I made an ass of myself before, but I can't do better unless you educate me on the topic."

Jackie whipped around, jaw tight as she stared Margo down. Margo gasped, shaking her head before the fear disappeared from her face. Blood warmed Jackie's palm and she glanced down at her hands. Her nails had elongated, claws sliding up from the bones in her fingers. The horns on her head pushed through her temples, a pleasantly painful release as they coiled above her head. Her vision was far too crisp, the colors around her too vibrant and sharp in the dim room to be normal. She looked up at Margo, who was still watching her. "I turn into a fucking monster."

Margo held onto her tough exterior and nodded. The only hint of her noticing Jackie's grotesque traits was the crease in her brow, making her eyebrow ring stick out oddly. How the hell could she gaze into the eyes of a monster and show no fear?

"Bite me, then," Margo said. She rolled up the sleeves of her shirt as she waited for Jackie's response, and dark tattoos peeked from under the fabric.

Jackie shook her head dismissively. Oh, she wanted to bite Margo, but no, it wouldn't be right, she told herself. "No, Margo. I couldn't." Could she stop at a *one* simple bite? Keep the beast from harming Margo? She wasn't sure and without her certainty, Jackie couldn't allow herself the luxury. Never had she allowed herself to become so close to the edge of uncontrolled bloodlust.

"Can you bite anyone? Does it matter what type of blood you get?" Margo asked, slightly breathless.

Jackie stared at her. "I haven't bitten a ton of people in my life, but I've never had any issues with Grim blood." Or shifter blood, or Fae blood. "As long as you're not a vampire."

They both chuckled.

"Bite me, then."

"No, Margo, I'll be fine."

"Come on. I owe you." Margo shoved a hand in the pocket of her jeans, producing a small pocketknife. Shaking her short hair to the side, she brought the blade to her collarbone.

"Margo, stop!" Jackie shouted, closing the space between her and Margo. "What the hell are you doing?"

"Repaying my debt. Jackie, you look…" Margo trailed off, perhaps unwilling to describe what Jackie knew to be her beastly appearance—bone white horns at the crown of her head, alabaster eyes in place of her murky brown. "Just take what you need. It doesn't bother me," Margo said.

"Put the knife down."

"Then, let me help you."

Jackie licked her teeth, her mouth salivating at the thought of biting her. "I can use my mouth."

Another shrug as Margo slipped the knife back into her pocket. "Whatever floats your boat, I guess." How could this woman be so nonchalant during such a conversation?

"Are you sure?" Her beast clawed at her insides, the muscles between her shoulders painfully taut.

"Yeah. If it weren't for you, Sam and I would both be dead." Convincing Brent to save them hadn't been difficult at all—he already had a plan in motion when she reached out to him—and Jackie didn't want to take advantage of Margo thinking the opposite. The more pressing matter to Jackie was her fear of what thought or image could possibly unfold if she bit Margo.

"I don't want to hurt you," Jackie pleaded. Although she didn't want to hurt Margo, her true reasons were selfish. What if behind the tough exterior lay an equally devious individual? Jackie didn't want to see what was within Margo, wanted to hold onto the possibility she was more than her attitude, than her bleak outlook on life.

Margo scoffed. "You're not going to hurt me. I owe you. Think of this as repayment." She unzipped her leather jacket, pushing her hair back to expose her long neck.

The soft thrum of her heartbeat against her skin enthralled Jackie. She kept her eyes on the gentle pulse beating visibly under her skin, the sound audible as she took an unconscious step forward. Margo tilted her neck, exuding calm as if Jackie planned to clasp a necklace around her neck rather than bite it. "Margo, if you aren't sure, I can't do—"

"I'm sure. Just do it," Margo whispered, her voice furthering the desire within Jackie.

Tentatively, Jackie touched Margo's skin, pushing back a few stray hairs. She brought her mouth to Margo's neck, piercing the skin with her elongated teeth. Margo took a sharp inhale, her body stiffening briefly. Gripping the table behind Margo, Jackie greedily sucked on the wound, her beast elated as the blood filled her mouth. It thrashed within her, provoking her to take more than she needed from Margo, gulping the liquid down.

Margo arched into Jackie, her body warm and firm. Jackie hadn't expected the vibrancy, Margo's blood thicker, thrumming with magic and uncertainty that shocked her. No stranger to blood from a Grim, Jackie was taken aback by the taste, the viscosity far from anything she'd ever consumed before. Her claws dug into the oak table behind Margo, gouging small holes in the wood as she moved closer to Margo.

Jackie closed her eyes and succumbed to the vision. The image was crisp, and Jackie immediately recognized the surroundings. Although she remembered the occasion differently, Jackie realized it was the day Margo met her. Jackie saw herself, dreads loosely hanging around her brown shoulders beside the wispy blue straps of her sundress. She made eye contact with herself as Margo, her dark eyes warm and radiant. *Is this how she sees me?* she wondered. A thing of beauty. Her mouth was moving in the memory, but Jackie heard nothing. She didn't need to hear anything. She remembered the day clearly. The moment Brent introduced them, a chance meeting while Margo was at Brent's home midday when she'd come by to pick up the elixir. She asked Jackie what she was, and when she explained, Margo assumed she was a vampire, the insulting word infuriating Jackie.

Margo moaned, ripping Jackie back into the present. The noise was akin to throwing dry kindling on the fire burning in Jackie's chest. Letting go of the table, Jackie wrapped her arms around Margo, who tilted her neck even farther, providing her with more space. Jackie threaded her fingers through the hair at the nape of her neck and Jackie groaned, pressing her body harder against Margo, clutching her tighter. Vibrant tendrils of fizzing energy spread through her, filling her with electricity. She saw herself again through Margo's eyes in the dull lighting of Sam's apartment. Jackie wanted more. More of Margo. More of the floating sensation the visions elicited. Nothing could've prepared Jackie for this.

No. She needed to stop. The heat of Margo's touch proved difficult to remove herself from, the challenge increasing as Margo moaned a second time. Jackie pulled back, gasping. She let go of Margo and took a step back. Margo's cheeks were as red as Jackie assumed hers were, coated in blood. Phantom firelight swirled in Margo's irises, muddying the crystal blue like flames over a placid lake. "Margo, what—"

"I need a fucking cigarette," Margo said as she pushed past Jackie and rushed to the front door.

Before Jackie could turn around fully, Margo was already outside. She stood transfixed on the faint outline of Margo's profile through the open door, the screen door distorting her features. The rain had slowed to a gentle trickle, and Margo shielded her lighter from the droplets as she brought it to the tip of her cigarette. Her fingers trembled as she pulled the cigarette away to exhale. A pang of guilt tugged at Jackie's chest, twisted tightly with a wisp of lust. *What the hell is she?* Jackie wondered. Surely, she wasn't just a Grim. There was something more, something richer, powerful, overwhelming. The taste clung to her tongue, and Jackie licked her lips in hopes of catching the electricity anew. The tea kettle whistled loudly from the kitchen, and Jackie hurried to remove it from the hot plate.

After she grabbed a hoodie from the couch, Jackie shrugged into it and stepped outside into the cold, salt-tinged air. "Hey."

Margo drew a deep drag from her cigarette and nodded in Jackie's direction. Her façade was back up, the stoic, unamused expression gracing her once again, but the fingers holding her cigarette still shook as she flicked ash from it. Jackie longed for the look Margo held after she pulled herself from her neck. The soft, vulnerable beauty as she stared back at Jackie, her gaze heated and filled with unspoken desire and flames. What kind of Grim held flickering embers in their eyes like that? "Your horns are gone."

Jackie glanced up, not that she could see her own head, and laughed. "Yeah, they retract afterward."

Margo quirked an eyebrow as she took another drag of her cigarette. "Like cat claws or something?"

"More or less."

A long silence filled the space between them, a short hiatus offered by a dog barking in the distance and the rush of the ocean over the beach. Margo lit another cigarette, much to Jackie's dismay. "Welp, you didn't kill me," Margo noted, the fire gone from her eyes so swiftly,

Jackie wondered if she imagined the red flames entirely. And maybe she had.

Of course, Margo would make light of the situation. Jackie wasn't surprised, and the comment made her smile despite herself. Her steps were lighter, as they always were after taking blood. With the beast dormant, she could breathe, continue to live. The acrid smoke wafted into her face. "Well, if I don't kill you, the cigarettes sure will."

Margo sneered at her, pulling another drag. "I can't die early no matter what I do or how hard I try, barring someone cutting my head off. Perks of being a psychopomp, remember? I get to live a long life until I'm a hundred." The words coiled on a tuft of putrid mist that promptly dissipated in the wind coming off the beach.

"Margo, what are you?" Jackie asked.

Margo scratched her head and glanced away from Jackie, her gaze fixed on the desolate scenery of the darkened beach rather than on Jackie again. *Did my question make her uncomfortable?*

"Nothing you don't already know."

"I just drank your blood, I'm pretty sure knowing what you are aside from being Grim is pertinent information."

"I thought you said it didn't matter where you got the blood from." Shaking her head, Margo turned her attention to Jackie once more. The woman tightened her jaw, and she took in a deep breath before a cruel smirk spread over her lips, her gaze still smoky. "It is I, the one who helps the recently deceased across the river Styx; a true descendent of Thanatos himself."

Jackie crossed her arms over her chest, thrown off by Margo's brief flash of vulnerability and swift rebuff of sarcasm. A gust pushed toward her house, eliciting a shiver. Nonetheless, Jackie continued to pry, certain Margo was deflecting. "Margo, really, I won't tell anyone."

Margo stubbed her cigarette out on the bottom of her shoe and blew the last of the smoke upward. "What do you want to know, Jackie? I'm a Grim who hates their job, plain and simple."

Jackie folded her arms over her chest. She obviously wasn't going to get anywhere. *Margo can't be just a Grim,* Jackie thought. No. Jackie could sense the difference in Margo's blood, the electricity of something far more powerful, and it thrummed through Jackie in that very moment as she turned to her again. "I thought maybe there was something else, but I guess I'm wrong."

Margo peered up at the sky. "I better go."

"Thanks again. I don't think you know how much I appreciate what you did."

"No problem. I owed you one, and now I don't." The clipped edge of Margo's tone was sharpened by her narrowed gaze as she zipped up her jacket. She blinked before she turned and bounded down the stairs without another word.

What the hell just happened? For a second, Jackie felt as if she'd made a connection with the emotionally devoid woman, convinced for a moment Margo would disclose her true nature. Jackie's tongue continued to tingle as she walked back into her house and closed the door behind her.

She crossed the room to the narrow stairwell leading to the lower level of her house, shaking her head at what had transpired as she descended the stairs, her body shivering with the vibrancy in Margo's blood with each inhale. The bottom floor of her home held her living space; a fully operational kitchen, living room elegantly furnished with a modern couch and armchair. Although she didn't spend much time watching television, the wall held a television and beneath it, a stereo system. Jackie grabbed her laptop from the petite kitchen table and eased herself into the armchair, turning on the television for background noise. Just as it were every time she fed, her senses were heightened. Butters padded across the kitchen floor, his nails tapping the tile as he moved, which Jackie heard as if she were lying on the floor next to him.

Not only that, the rush of the ocean resounded through the room, crashing around her, muffled by the walls but clear to her. She closed her eyes, breathing deeply, allowing the noises and scents to engulf her in overstimulation. The bite was uncanny, nothing she'd experienced from any Grim she'd fed off before. No, this was different—so much different. When she opened her eyes again, she turned on her laptop and logged into her email. Nothing from Roz, but, to her elation, a reply from Roz's mother.

Ms. Hayes,

I apologize for the delayed correspondence to your first email. I'm confused—it was my understanding that Rosalind took a new position in Southern California. In fact, I spoke with her briefly on the phone last week, and she seemed well. Perhaps she lost your contact information in the move? She is quite busy with her freelance work as well, so I doubt her lack of response is in malice. I'll let her know you're trying to speak with her the next time she and I talk. Take care,

Kala Darab

"What the hell?" Jackie whispered aloud. She read the email a second time. A third. "What the hell?" she repeated. The details in the email stung. For her childhood friend to say nothing to her upon moving, hurt her initially. Then, she grew angry. Why would Roz leave without telling her? They weren't as close as they had been as teenagers, but they still shared important things together: new jobs, new loves, holidays, definitely something as important as moving across the country. After the anger settled, she began to worry. She withdrew her cell phone from her pocket and called Brent.

"Jackie, are you all right?" Brent asked breathlessly.

"Yeah, I'm fine. Did you know Roz moved to the West Coast?"

"What?"

"I got an email from her mom, who said she moved over to the West Coast for a new position." After a brief silence, she asked him, "Did you know about this?" If he lied to her previously about not knowing where Roz was, she'd be livid.

"No, I had no idea," he said. "Are you sure?"

"Yeah." She read off the email to him from Roz's mother.

"Well, this is news to me," he said. He grumbled something inaudible before clearing his throat. "I'll look into this in the morning. How are you? Do you need anything from me like we discussed earlier? I'm able to find someone for you if—"

"No, I'm okay, thanks. I figured it out." She picked at the sticker on the keyboard of her laptop, wondering why on earth Roz would move without a word. Her feelings were hurt, but she was also disappointed in her friend. Mostly, she was worried. Something wasn't right.

"If you're sure."

"I am."

Brent sighed. "I have a new recipe for an elixir I'd like to try if you're willing."

Jackie smiled, shaking her head, though she knew Brent couldn't see her. "I'll try anything you've got to offer." Anything, including a willing donor if need be because she knew the favor from Margo was unlikely to ever happen again.

Chapter Eight

MUSIC FILLED THE void of the car as Margo drove home from Jackie's house. Although her thoughts were clouded from the boisterous music coming from the stereo, the sounds did nothing to hinder the vivid memories of Jackie's body so close to her own. *And I almost told her what I was.* Few people knew the truth, and now someone who she thought hated her could've had the knowledge just like that. Not her best decision. *Did* Jackie hate her? Now *that* assumption seemed flawed, terribly so. She wouldn't have invited Margo into her home if she hated her; unless she planned to feed from Margo. Empusae couldn't thrall the way vampires did, or could they? Margo knew magic, could feel the stems of it on the air when it grew, none of which she sensed when she offered to let Jackie bite her. She had to stop lying to herself; this wasn't magic.

Though Jackie's face had transformed, thick horns pressing outward from her head, sharp teeth peeking from under her lip when she spoke, Margo wasn't afraid; in fact, she found herself unable to look away, beauty within the seemingly grotesque. The bite hadn't hurt, contrary to what she thought when she offered Jackie her blood. A hint of pain had spread over Margo's neck when Jackie first pierced her skin, but afterward, Margo did not want Jackie to stop.

But, regardless, she still came to the same problem—could Jackie tell what she was based solely from her blood, and if she did, would she tell anyone? Margo gritted her teeth and tightened her grip on the steering wheel. Knowledge was power. Obtaining a secret with the weight of Margo's gave Jackie power over her life. She'd known Jackie was in her head, the strange sensation similar to...shit, nothing comparable. They shared a nostalgic moment of their first meeting vividly displayed in her mind's eye, though, Jackie hadn't breached any deeper.

Margo reached the parking lot of her condo quicker than she anticipated, the entire drive on autopilot. Her skin seemed to buzz with energy from Jackie's bite, the contact alone eliciting a profound feeling of desire. She had to hope Jackie wouldn't say anything to the wrong person if she had discovered what Margo was. If Corporate found out pre-blood bond, they'd simply decommission her, strip her of her ability to open portals, and send her on her way. The blood bond changed everything. They wouldn't hesitate to kill her or Sam.

She parked her car and hurried up the stairs. The second story condo was quiet when she walked into the small entryway. Lights danced across the living room from the large television against the wall, and a dew-coated beer bottle dripped on the surface of the wooden coffee table. She plopped down on the charcoal gray couch, letting the pressure push the air from her lungs, and she kicked her boots loose and tugged off her socks. The soft texture of the carpet beneath her bare feet grounded her after such an otherworldly experience, and she closed her eyes briefly.

She'd gone to Jackie's with the intention of handing her the necklace and going home. *At least I don't owe her anything for helping us.*

"Margo?" Luis's voice called from the kitchen, cutting off Margo's thoughts.

"Yeah, it's me," she said.

"Come in here!"

Margo stood and meandered over to the kitchen around the slight wall dividing the two spaces. The television from the living room glowed across the room, illuminating the empty dining room table. Cold tile shocked Margo's bare soles as she padded into the bright kitchen.

Luis crouched in front of the open refrigerator in boxers and a white T-shirt as Margo rounded the corner. "Why is it we never have any food in the house? All we've got is beer and—" He yanked a bottle of ketchup out to show Margo. "—condiments?"

She shrugged, squeezing in to grab a beer from the top shelf.

"Is that—? Did, did someone bite you?" he asked.

"Get out of the way," she said, smirking.

Instead of listening, Luis grabbed her arm gently as he inspected her neck. "You've got a bite mark? Holy shit, Margo, that is the real deal. Did it hurt?"

She pulled away from him and turned her head as her cheeks heated. "Duh." She tried to avoid his pointed stare, but she could see his wide grin in her periphery as she rose from the floor. Popping open the beer, she finally met his gaze.

His laughter filled the kitchen and he clapped his hands together loudly. "I fucking knew it! Jacqueline, right?"

"Don't," Margo growled.

"Really? Don't get all grumbly with me, dude. I'm happy for you. It's been so long, I thought maybe you'd forgotten about girls or something."

Despite her irritation, Margo grinned and tipped her beer in his direction. "Thanks for the kind words, bro, but all I did was return a favor."

He took a sip from his own fresh beer and shut the fridge. "A favor involving teeth?"

"Yeah," she said. "Just a favor." She could lie to Luis, but she couldn't lie to herself. Margo wanted Jackie to bite her, wanted to feel her mouth against her skin.

One brow drastically quirked, Luis eyeing her suspiciously. He turned back to his task, raiding the cabinets for food.

"Should we order some food since you're obviously starving to death?"

"Are you two a thing now? Did you go all fiery-eyed on her?"

"No, I've already told you that we are not a thing. I'll repeat myself one more time. I returned the favor of her saving me. She needed blood; I obliged. End of fucking story."

The dubious grin spreading across his lips irritated her. "I don't buy that for a second."

She chewed the inside of her lip. "How's that cute nurse treating you?" She digressed, hoping Luis would be more than happy to change the subject and talk about himself.

Luis smirked and looked away, faint color rising to his brown cheeks as he took the bait. "Jesse? I don't think we're going anywhere."

Margo recalled the brief encounter with the nurse once when she dropped Luis off at work, the pointed, almost possessive gaze that was fixated on Luis as if staking claim to him. "I wouldn't be so sure. Have you told them how you feel?"

"They're leaving next week for another traveling gig, so I won't have the chance." He stretched his arms behind his head and shot her a wry grin. "I should've listened to you when you said to make a move. And, wow, is Margo—filed-for-emotional-bankruptcy-in-the-seventh-grade—Petrov talking about *feelings*?"

Margo walked away, yanking her phone from the pocket of her jeans. "Hold on, I might sneeze now that you've mentioned the word," she shouted, holding her free hand under her nose as she fake sneezed. "I'm ordering pizza. What do you want?" She threw herself back on the couch and kicked her feet over the arm.

Luis settled across from her in the matching armchair, the one he *had* to have when they first moved in together when their stipends from Corporate finally kicked in.

The comment on her emotional status hadn't bothered Margo. Spending most of their lives in foster care hardened their experiences, taught them to expect less from the world around them, and, as a consequence, both were rough around the edges. The banter they shared was as important as the times they cried together. Even as close as they were, Margo couldn't tell him she'd nearly told Jackie about herself, or more specifically, Jackie almost saw the truth in her head. The fresh memory of Jackie surrounding her flashed through her mind, and she closed her eyes as if to savor the brief invasion in her brain.

He picked up the remote control, shrugged, and flipped through the channels. "I don't care, as long as you don't get Hawaiian. Pineapple on pizza is a goddamn atrocity."

"All right," Margo said before she ordered their pizza. She ran her fingers through her hair, glad for the distraction from what just transpired at Jackie's house. A faint throb ran over the bite marks with each beat of her heart, which made things harder to ignore; things like how badly she wanted to take Jackie into her arms and let her bite her again.

Once off the phone, Luis turned to her. "Are you going to hang out with your new girlfriend for your birthday?"

Margo glared at him, more for the mention of her impending birthday than Jackie. "No. And I'm done talking about her. She saved Sam and me. I paid back a debt owed. Done."

"Okay, no more Jackie. Got it." Luis threw his arms behind his head. "Here's a safe topic: you never told me how things went with Brent. What did you have to do for him?"

"He had me help him open a portal to Jael's territory. The old door was supposedly disabled, and he thought maybe we could do it if I used my light bending."

Luis sat up, eyes wide. "Like, Jael as in Fae royalty Jael? A portal with your Djinni magic?"

Margo tucked her arms beneath her head as she nodded. "Yeah, surprised the hell out of me too."

"Why'd he want to go to the Fae lands, anyway? Doesn't he have connections?" he asked, puzzled.

"Not for Brent but for Collin. Collin went in front of Jael to ask for permission to enter their lands because he was denied from Queen Demelza. Apparently, Jael is going to let him come over though, so, hooray for him, he can go see his family."

Luis nodded. "Wow. I wonder why Brent didn't mention that to me. He's been kind of distant lately."

"I wouldn't know," Margo said honestly. "All I do know is I feel like I need a fucking vacation." The last two months had left their toll on her, beginning with Roz's disappearance and peaking with the blood bond. She yawned and stretched out on the couch.

"How did you open the portal?"

Margo placed her forearm over her eyes and kicked her feet over the arm of the couch. "I just threw light at the door. Brent said Djinni magic is similar to Fae magic but different."

"That makes sense. They take the light, or darkness, they have inside them, and you take it from whatever is around you. Not all of them can open portals though. I know elves can't and neither can sprites. They're too *good*."

Margo threw her arm from her face and glanced at her brother. "Yeah, Brent said the same thing. What do you mean by good? There aren't good versus evil in the Fae, right? I thought they were all pretty gray."

Luis shrugged. "I don't hang out with them, so I wouldn't know."

Margo covered her face again. She didn't want to talk about the Fae anymore. All she wanted to do was pretend things were normal, or at least as normal as they could be in her and Luis's life. One thing could be laid to rest, she realized with satisfaction. "Sam can't conjure light," she said flatly. "I had her try." The relief rekindled, offering Margo peace for a moment.

The humor had slipped from Luis's face, and he looked everywhere but her face. "What would you have done if she could?"

"Fuck, I don't know." And she was grateful for one less thing to worry about.

Chapter Nine

THE SOFT DRONE of Brent's voice woke her from a dreamless sleep. Margo pushed the blankets off and surveyed her room, darkened by the blackout curtains. Faint light bled from the crack beneath the doorframe, and she listened. Brent's deep tone stopped, and she heard Luis's softer voice pitch in. She realized he must've been dropping off their list of charges. Her head swam from the night before, like the precursor to one hell of a hangover lolling her thoughts to the border of her mind. Jackie's mouth on her skin, breath hot over her neck and hands, no, *claws*, grasping Margo's sides as gently as possible. She knew the memories weren't a dream, but she wasn't quite sure how to process what she'd done, or let happen, rather. Jackie's chilling gaze came to life in Margo's mind, and her cheeks warmed.

With the scant light squeezing under the door, Margo reached around for a sweatshirt, one with a large hood to cover the bite marks. In through the doorway to her bathroom, she switched on the light and stared at herself in the large mirror. The stained redness in the whites of her eyes matched her red flannel pajamas as if she'd been up late drinking the night before, which matched the state she was currently in. On the right side of her neck, visible under a lock of hair, a bitemark nestled in the crook, purpled and gnarled. She sighed, running a finger gently over the tender spot. When Jackie bit her, she'd felt anything but pain. Pleasure, yes. Pain, not really, which sent her in a whirlwind of terror combined with the breach of her privacy as Jackie threaded into her thoughts, the images uncanny and breathtaking. *Okay, the bite did hurt a bit, but so worth it.*

She put the sweatshirt on over her pajamas, tugging the hood over her head. The pragmatic solution to conceal the aching bite on the side of her neck seemed good enough, though she worried Luis would open his mouth or had already. Nothing would happen to Margo if Brent found out about the bite—he wouldn't care, she was in enough shit already—but she didn't want her business spread around further than it needed to be. She headed down the hallway toward the kitchen where their voices lifted again.

Luis leaned against the countertop, a large muffin in his hand sprinkling crumbs over the tiled floor as he brought the food to his mouth. Beside him, Brent was focused, typing away on his cell phone. When he glanced up, he grinned warmly at Margo and pushed his glasses up the bridge of his nose. "Good morning."

"Morning," Margo grumbled. The coffee pot was, thankfully, still on, and she poured herself a large mug with plenty of creamer. With a nod in Luis's general vicinity, she snatched her pack of cigarettes from the counter and walked over to the balcony door.

A mild chill hung in the air as she eased into the weathered beach chair positioned toward the railing. She lit a cigarette and settled back. Thick clouds obscured the midmorning sun and a light rain fell, darkening the edge of the concrete balcony where the awning above didn't shield. When she checked her phone, she was disappointed to see no work calls, but she wasn't surprised. Working under the table as an unlicensed handyman, whose advertising went as far as word of mouth, didn't guarantee her much work to begin with. Summer season usually gave her the most clientele, but with having to turn away countless jobs after picking up Roz's queue of spirits, she expected a fallout. Along with her stipend from Corporate, she had enough to coast by during the off-season. *Or enough to use toward starting a new life somewhere else.*

The sliding glass door opened and closed behind her, but instead of Luis walking around in front of her, Brent joined her outside. He walked to the railing and looked out over the dreary town. "I appreciate your recent flexibility," he said.

Margo stretched two fingers in a lazy peace sign as an answer, sipping her coffee with her free hand. The liquid was strong, and that much she was grateful for. Although she'd had a dreamless sleep, fatigue plagued her from the day before, causing her to wonder what it took out of her for Jackie to take blood. She'd felt fine afterward, albeit a bit shaken by Jackie questioning her.

Brent turned away from the edge and faced her. "That's why I hate to ask you to do this, but—"

Margo cut him off. "Do what?" She hadn't noticed the faint puffiness beneath his eyes while they were inside, hidden from view by his glasses but visible in the dull lighting from the cloud-muddled sun. His usually trimmed beard seemed scraggy, and his clothes were slightly rumpled. Margo tilted her head as she waited for him to continue. A tension swirled around him, pinching his black brows together, a perplexing and stark contrast to his normal demeanor. Brent wasn't himself, and she had a feeling it had everything to do with her actions.

"The Board has decided you're fully capable of picking Sam back up as your assistant, starting today."

She stubbed her cigarette out in the ashtray and sat forward. "Very funny. What's *really* going on?"

"I'm giving you a few extra jobs," he said. When Margo began to protest, he put his hand up to silence her. "You can divvy them up between you and Sam, but you'll have to figure out which ones you think she'll be able to do by herself or help her with them."

She scoffed, nearly spitting her coffee out. "No. Dude, she needs you, not me."

"You should've thought of that when you initiated the blood bond. She's your responsibility regardless of what the Board thinks." His tone held a level of finality she couldn't argue with. It wasn't his fault she'd made the decision in the first place, and he shouldn't have to bear the responsibility.

"All right, fine."

"There are other forces at work here that require my presence, aside from the Grim, or I would continue with Sam's training," he added.

Margo shrugged carelessly, but part of her was curious about what he meant. He wasn't usually so severe, and Margo noticed a definite shift in his demeanor—other things were undoubtedly plaguing him. She assumed his moonlighting dealings had to do with his expected absence and nothing else, remembering what Jackie said about him unable to make the elixir he usually made for her. Not that it was any of her business to begin with.

But how could she know if it was her business or not? She never asked what the repercussions were for helping in the Board's decision to keep Sam and Margo on. Had they given Brent more work due to *her* mess up with Sam, for siding with Margo rather than them? Margo stared at the liquid at the bottom of her coffee cup.

"The Board has decided to test every Grim for their lineage in less than two weeks—a census, they claim," Brent whispered.

Margo's cup slipped from her fingers and coffee splattered to the balcony floor. "What?"

His despondent expression elicited a profound fear deep in her gut. And then he spoke, "The Grand Board met last week and voted to test the blood of each Grim member for their lineage. I think it may have been sparked by Sam's revival, but I'm not certain." Before she could speak, he held up a hand. "I'm working on something to mask your specific markers before this happens, so please don't do anything stupid or suspicious."

Margo said nothing, unsure how to respond. Eventually, she cleared her throat. "Why the hell are they doing this all of a sudden?" Was it her fault? Had Sam's creation prompted this? Her stomach threatened to give her coffee back.

"I'm unsure, but I believe it's been in the works for some time now," Brent muttered. Margo lost the opportunity to question him more when he went back inside.

The fleeting thought to leave everything behind became her solution without her making the conscious decision. Did she have enough money? Staying was an option before, but now she had no choice, and the sooner she left, the better. Putting faith in Brent and his bizarre potions wasn't on her to-do list. She'd taken his help with nothing in return for far too long, and she wouldn't put him or Sam in a perilous position again.

The cup of coffee had survived the tumble to the floor, and she plucked it up as she stood. When she went back inside to grab a second cup, the space was quiet, leaving her to her thoughts until Luis called for her from down the hall. She refilled her coffee and went to his room.

"I need help," Luis said, flinging clothing from his open dresser. Margo walked through the door and sank down on the end of his unmade bed. More shirts flew over his head until he turned, one in each hand. "Which one?"

One white button-up dangled from his left hand while his right held a black sweater, much different than the jeans and T-shirt ensemble he wore most days if he wasn't in his scrubs. "Where're you going—a funeral?"

He scoffed, noting the two shirts with scrutiny. "No, I'm meeting up with Jesse."

"I thought that wasn't happening?"

"I figured I'd throw a coffee date out there as an option before they leave, just in case we wanted to catch up if Jesse comes back this way."

Margo grinned, happy at the prospect of her brother putting himself out there. "Oh, a coffee thing? That sounds fun. I don't like either of those for a 'coffee thing.' What about that cute blue-plaid shirt you have?"

Luis threw his head back with a frustrated grumble before tossing the two options into the pile and moved his search to the closet.

Placing her coffee on his nightstand, Margo sprawled out on his bed. A lump caused her to move and when she reached to remove the lump from beneath her, she pulled out a mongoose stuffed animal. The beady little eyes stared back at her, frayed fabric barely holding onto the little pink nose, and most of the toy's whiskers were long gone. "You still have this thing?" she asked, sitting up on the bed.

"Yeah, why wouldn't I?" he rebuked without turning.

Margo chuckled, remembering when she'd given him the stupid toy. He'd confided in her, only months after they were placed in the same home, telling her his dreams, worries, insecurities, fears. He told her he'd never be as big or as strong as her. After stealing the toy from a shelf at the local grocery store when she was fourteen, Margo made up a story about a mongoose taking down a black bear, telling him no matter how small he was, he could be a badass if he needed to be. And then he came out as himself to her.

"I don't know. This thing has seen better days," she said, placing the toy back on Luis's pillow with a smile on her face.

"I love Vincent. He keeps me company."

"You named a stuffed animal?" Margo asked, picking up the toy again. Though she chuckled at his attachment to the stolen toy, her heart warmed at the realization that he kept it through so many moves: from the last foster home he'd lived in, to their brief stay at Brent and Collin's home, to the various apartments leading up to the condo they now shared.

Luis turned, buttoning up the shirt Margo mentioned. "How about this?"

The blue heightened the striking hazel of his gaze "Nice."

"Thanks." His smile faltered as he finished buttoning. "Did Brent tell you about the census-testing shit?"

Margo nodded and picked up her cup of coffee from the nightstand. "Supposedly, he's going to make me some super fancy potion to make my Djinn disappear. At least in my blood." She wiggled her fingers with her free hand, accentuating her skepticism around Brent's endeavor.

Though Margo tried to lighten the mood, Luis spoke with severity. "I think everything will be okay. If it's not, I may have to jump ship with you. What they're doing isn't right, Margo and—" His phone rang loudly, and he cursed. "I should head out, or I'm going to be late. I'm not done with this conversation, though. I can't be tasked with finding myself a new roommate because Corporate made you run away." Though his words were meant to be funny, his tone lacked any humor. He made no move to leave, his gaze steady on Margo.

They both knew he made more than enough to afford the condo on his own, but she played along. "They can't scare me off that easy, and with your good looks, you'd have no trouble finding a cutie to coexist with," Margo said as she slid off the bed, careful not to slosh any coffee on his blankets. "You go enjoy your *coffee thing*. We can talk about this later."

His frown diminished and he punched her in the shoulder gently. "Okay, fine." With a rushed smile, Luis grabbed his coat and darted out of the room.

The front door slammed before Margo made it to the kitchen. She grabbed her phone and sent Sam a text, telling her to be ready. Rather than the customary seven to fifteen index cards, each containing information for the assigned soul, Margo counted well over twenty-five individuals. She scoffed and stuffed the stack of cards into the pocket of her leather jacket. There was plenty of time to get them all done before the census, especially if she divided them up between herself and Sam. It gave her an opportunity to ensure Sam was ready to work on her own. After getting a refill, she went back outside for more coffee and silent contemplation.

THURSDAY AND FRIDAY went by in a flurry of activity, Margo's jobs seemingly more difficult, but she was happy with the progress Sam was making. She steadily gained confidence with every spirit she aided, and Margo allowed herself the small pride she experienced with Sam's achievements. The progress also helped Margo keep her mind off Jackie.

Late Saturday morning, Margo picked Sam up and they headed off the island to their first location to start the weekend. Smithville was a quaint faux town built to attract tourism. Though Margo had learned the tiny town had once been a real community but was transformed into a tourist destination only a few decades before. The buildings were taken from various historical locations in South Jersey and brought there to set up the weird attraction in hopes of increased revenue. Margo figured it was cute enough with the small windmill and cozy little bridge hanging over the murky water, but the buildings did give her the creeps—she knew spirits weren't the only entities attached to objects such as the houses lining the streets of Smithville. She pulled into a gravel parking lot teeming with cars, people pushing strollers and walkers alike down the sidewalks leading to the cluster of buildings.

Margo circled the lot a dozen times when, finally, Sam pointed out a spot with a long yawn, and Margo snagged it. "You all right? Is Lauren keeping you up all night?"

Sam shook her head. "No, more like nightmares."

Putting the car into park, Margo stared at Sam, concerned. "About what?"

A gentle darkness lay beneath Sam's eyes like the sweeping shadows under a rain cloud, and she turned away from Margo, gazing out the window without answering. "I didn't know we were coming to the art festival."

"Yep." Though she wanted to pry, Margo chose to leave the topic alone.

Margo turned off the engine and climbed out of the car. "Well, we could've put the job on hold, but the guy died a year ago, so I figured we'd better get on it before we lose his location." What she didn't say was she wanted to see if Sam could convince a troubled soul to move on who had been lingering for a longer than average time. The oldest soul Sam opened a portal for was the little boy, which Margo remembered as having roamed the little amusement park for almost ten months before they helped the child cross over.

"Does that happen often—so many months going by without them passing on?" Sam asked, shutting the passenger door and rounding the car to meet Margo.

Margo pursed her lips as she reached for her pack of cigarettes, coming up empty-handed. Scratching the back of her head, she turned to Sam. "Depends. I get a good variety of souls, but depending on the location, you could get someone who's been hanging around for years."

"Years? That's depressing."

Margo chuckled but agreed with a nod. "Yeah, I'd say. The worst part is most of them stay because of other people."

Sam seemed to consider this, her face perplexed as she avoided Margo's attention, leading Margo to wonder if Sam was thinking about her own death if she would've lingered around for her sister Katie or Lauren. After spending as much time as she had with Sam, Margo knew she would've been one of the hardest spirits to help move on if she hadn't taken the deal with her.

They continued down the path until they reached a wooden bridge cresting over a sickly colored stream. Margo kicked a pinecone off the bridge into the tea-brown water below, disturbing the green algae nestled at the stream's bank. The little town did have charm, she knew, but she didn't want to linger around the place; she wanted to find the spirit and get on with her life. She lowered her voice as they passed a family. "This spirit should be around here somewhere. I'm sure it won't take us long to convince them to pass on, but I'm going to let you do the work because I know that's what Brent would want you to do by now. You're kicking ass with these jobs."

Sam smiled at the praise.

The pathway leading from the bridge was lined with various vendors selling crafts, jewelry, soap, and other homemade items. Margo figured reaping the spirit during the event would be easier than any other day where they'd be questioned for wandering around the little town.

"Hey, I didn't know Lauren would be here," Sam said, pointing toward a cluster of art stands. "Oh, she's waving at me."

"Lover boi, we don't have time for you to go say hi to your girlfriend. We've got..." Margo stopped talking because Sam was already trotting off to the stand. Rolling her eyes, Margo hurried after her.

The small setup Sam ran to held various pieces of art. Paintings hung from the bowed ceiling of the white vendor tent, pulled together by thick twine and adorned with tiny price tags. A long table laden with crystals, tiny wooden carvings, and handmade jewelry stood at the front. Behind the table, Lauren and Jackie stood side by side.

Jackie smiled when she saw the two approaching, her dark gaze flashing over Margo. "Hey," Jackie said. Margo slowed as she reached them, shoving her hands in her pockets, wishing she had a cigarette to distract herself from Jackie's stare.

She stepped up to the table, glancing down at the display to avoid Jackie's hauntingly beautiful face. "Hi. These are pretty," she said, touching an intricate design on a small metal necklace.

The metal bracelets around Jackie's wrist clanked together like wind chimes in a breeze as she pushed a stray hair out of her face, and she smiled coyly at Margo. "Thanks. And thank you again for the other night."

Margo shifted awkwardly. "No problem." She tapped her foot on the ground, unsure what to say with Jackie's gaze still firmly on her. The memory of Jackie so close to her, her hands on her body, breath in her ear, blossomed a heat in Margo's cheeks. She turned, staring out toward the lake to keep Jackie from noticing. She heard Sam's hushed conversation with Lauren peaking in a bout of giggling to Margo's left, and she sighed heavily. *Come on, Sam, let's go.*

"What are you two doing here?"

"You know, the daily grind," Margo said. She wanted nothing more than to walk away from the woman in front of her or ask her what she knew, what she saw when she'd bitten her. "What about you?"

Jackie flattened a pile of thin tissue paper on the table. "Selling some of my art. The whole starving-artist thing never really worked out for me, and teachers don't get paid enough to afford the fancy supplies I like." She winked at Margo, a slow, evocative action that left Margo recalling the night at Jackie's house in stark detail. The darkness that flooded Jackie's gaze, how the recessed lights in her living room glittered over the bone-white horns protruding from Jackie's head, perfectly parting her hair, pointed canines resting upon her plump lower lip.

Giggling floated behind Margo from a passing group of children, and she peered over at Sam, who was still chatting with Lauren, their voices inaudible in the noisy midway of the art fair. *Did she see more than what I saw when she bit me?* Margo wondered. "Jackie, I wanted to ask you something."

"Okay," Jackie said.

Margo placed both hands on the table and tried to steady herself. She needed to know what Jackie saw—if she saw anything other than the brief glimpse in her brain. Before Margo could gather the courage to ask, Sam and Lauren moved from the back of the tent, saying their goodbyes. Lauren kissed Sam on the cheek, and Margo had to keep herself from rolling her eyes at the cute display. "Never mind," she said to Jackie.

Glaring at Sam, she said, "Come on, we've got to go."

"Don't forget about game night tonight," Lauren murmured as Sam left her embrace.

Jackie touched Margo's arm, her smile warm. "Margo, you're more than welcome to come too," she said.

Margo chuckled, running her fingers through her hair with her other hand. "Nah, thanks, but I've got plans. I'll make sure Sam won't be late though."

Jackie let her hand fall from Margo with a slow nod.

Margo hooked her arm under Sam's and dragged her away. Silently, Margo cursed herself for not asking Jackie, though their interaction hadn't been without some insight. She deduced by the flirting that Jackie probably hadn't seen anything more, especially not what she was. *She'd be running for the hills if she knew, definitely not touching me.*

The crowds thinned as they approached the small stream-fed lake. Children ran through the neatly trimmed grass, and a band played beneath a white gazebo set beside the water. A lone balloon drifted up in the air above the faux windmill on the shore.

Margo handed the card to Sam. "This guy's name is Dale," she said. Not much information was present but enough to get a gist. Dale Prendergast died from cardiac arrest and was quite reluctant to leave.

"Think this is him?" Sam asked.

Margo looked to where Sam was pointing. A lone person stood by the water's edge, chin jutted out to the pond where a couple paddled an obnoxious swan-shaped boat across the lake. Shimmering incandescence surrounded the man, spanning around his body. "Yep, that's him. We should probably be unseen." Margo took in the people around them, ensuring no one was watching before she wiggled her shoulders, pulling the energy from her chest to cover herself in the deception. Sam watched her in awe until she understood she was supposed to be doing the same. "Nice," Margo said. Sam barely struggled this time, offering Margo a bit of pride in her teaching skills.

"Dale?" Sam called out as they approached him.

The spirit turned his head, looked from side to side and then settled his gaze back on the duo. "Yeah?"

"Hi, Dale, how can we help you?" Sam sidled up beside the man as he continued to sniffle, his gaze set off into the field beside the small lake. Elegant wooden swan-shaped boats drifted over the placid surface of the water, laughter erupting from the closest one to the shoreline. His salt and pepper hair was cut close to his ears, and the navy blue button-up he wore had to be two sizes too large as it hung over his khakis.

He turned toward them, sulking. "Is there anything that *could* help me?"

"We're here to help you move on to the other side."

"And where might that be?"

Sam glanced at Margo, who shrugged. Contrary to what Sam probably believed, Margo knew as much about the other side as she did about biochemistry: not a whole lot. "We don't really know, but I can tell you it's better than sticking around here doing nothing."

The man snorted. "I'm not interested." He faced the water again, clasping his hands behind his back, position stoic.

Sam shot Margo another pitiful expression. Margo rolled her eyes and meandered closer, clearing her throat. "My friend here is new to this, and she's doing her best, so cut her some slack. We want to help you leave this place for good. You don't have to stay here anymore."

The man whipped his head around, face contorted. "What makes you think I *don't* want to stay here?"

"What's keeping you here?" Sam inquired before Margo could answer.

Shaking his head, the man yet again turned away. A gold ring glinted on his left hand as the sun pressed through the clouds. Margo moved closer to him, mirroring his posture. "Where's your spouse?"

"Dead," the man said without preamble.

"Then, you're not staying for them, are you?"

"No."

"Why not go if there isn't anything here for you?"

He glanced at Margo, his lips a thin line. "Can you guarantee I'll see him when I go?"

Margo went to open her mouth but sighed instead. "No, I can't," she finally managed.

"Then, I stand by my original answer. Thank you and have a nice day." He turned on his heels and started down the shoreline. Margo hesitated for a moment before she followed, Sam right behind her.

"Now what?" Sam muttered under her breath. Margo wasn't sure. What could she say to him?

"I don't know. Why don't you give this a try? Ask him about his spouse or something. Get him talking. That's usually a good start," she said, her tone as tender and quiet as she could muster.

Sam smiled but the gesture came out more like a grimace as she quickened her pace to catch up to the spirit. "Hey, can I talk to you for a quick minute?"

The man halted and abruptly turned to face Sam. "What do you want from me?"

"I thought maybe you could tell me a little about your other half."

The spirit shook his head, the dismissive gesture laden with unspoken frustration.

Sam continued to press. "No, I'm serious. What was he like?"

Margo stepped back as Sam worked, wanting to stay back so the kid could do this all on her own.

Hesitation crossed the man's face as he peered up at the sky. "He's been gone seven years now." He clutched his forehead, eyes downcast. "I still don't understand how a stroke could've killed him. He was such a healthy man, strong, determined, went to the gym every single day. Al wouldn't even drink a glass of champagne on New Year's. Convinced me to go vegan a few years after we met."

Sam touched the man's arm. "I'm sorry for your loss."

Tears glistened down his cheeks, and he shook his head. "All I have left are the memories. We married here only three years before he passed. If I go, if I move on, what happens if I don't see him on the other side, and I lose my memories of him? He'll essentially be gone from me forever. In the end, memories of our loved ones are the only things we have left."

Margo moved closer. "We don't know whether or not you'll see him on the other side. You might, you might not," she said softly. "What we do know is you can't stay around here forever holding onto the memory of him. Would he want you to sit around, holding onto his memory when you could be moving forward—maybe finding peace?"

His face twisted into a scowl. "I can't risk losing the only thing I have left of him." He turned and trotted through the damp grass.

"Wow, we're sure on a roll lately," Sam muttered.

Margo thought for a minute as the ghost continued down the slight slope of the green lawn, heading to the clustered shops. He could've easily vanished to wherever his destination was, but he walked the distance as if wanting them to follow. "Come on," she said, hooking her arm under Sam's elbow.

Together, they walked the route the spirit took, right back to the cobblestone pathways zigging and zagging through the rustic town. They were a few paces behind him by the time he stopped in front of a bench shaded beneath a massive willow tree placed in the middle of a small courtyard. People filtered through the area, but no one took notice of them. The tree's vines stirred in the wind as Dale sat impassively.

Sam glanced over at Margo, who shrugged. She knew from experience that some spirits needed time, and perhaps with time, Dale would be more willing to move on. Time seemed to ease the sting of things, lighten the load of burden grief undoubtedly weighed upon the dead. People always spoke of the ones left behind, their pain, sorrow, and mourning but never of the dead themselves.

"Dale," Sam began, sitting down at the opposite side of the bench. "We can't promise you'll see your husband when you cross over, but you can't stay here out of fear."

"Sure, I can," he said stubbornly. A pettiness adorned his face in the soft afternoon light streaming through the willow branches, and his eyes glinted with tears.

Margo bit her lip as the increasingly familiar sensation hit her again: someone's attention focused on her. The hairs on her shoulders rose, and dread increased her heartbeat. This time, she gently craned her neck around, peering up at the sky instead of where the haunting sensation originated from. She let her gaze wander, drifting over to the hobby shop selling art kits and homemade candles. A glimpse of a black trench coat caught her eye. Blonde hair pulled back in a tight ponytail, angular features, and a sharp nose. The woman was watching her, crystal-blue gaze piercing in the autumn sunlight. Margo kept her sight trained on the woman as she touched Sam's back. "I'll be right back," she whispered and took off.

On cue, the woman darted between two wooden-framed shops, the tail of her trench coat fluttering as she ran. "Hey!" Margo yelled as she gained speed, pumping her arms faster to catch up to the woman. The stretch of space through the shops was narrow, the buildings far too close to one another. Margo recoiled as her shoulder caught the edge of a windowsill, tearing a small hole in the fabric of her jacket. She rounded the end of the walkway, stumbling into another courtyard crammed with people. The everchanging cluster of shoppers moved too fast as Margo attempted to scan their faces in search of the watcher but the woman had vanished.

Shit, maybe the point of that was to get Sam alone. Cursing, Margo turned around and swiftly headed back through the buildings.

Sam was still seated beside the ghost, her deception holding strong as Margo ambled up to them, Sam shooting her a questioning quirk of her lips.

"He asked me to marry him, right here under this tree." Dale pressed his hand to the bark as if to invoke the memory over in his mind, closing his eyes.

Margo crossed her arms and watched him as he reminisced. *Why did her face look so familiar?* Margo wondered. *I know her from somewhere.* Surely, she wasn't human; she wouldn't have seen them if she were. Her predatory stare had elicited an instinctual fear within Margo, leading her to believe she was Fae, or perhaps a shifter, which lead her to the question: why the hell would they care enough to follow her anyway?

"We'd been together for a long time by then, dreaming we would get married one day." Dale opened his eyes and looked at them. "See, we never imagined we'd get to, never imagined we'd see marriage equality in our lifetime, let alone become one of the first to wed." He smiled, gazing up as a breeze ruffled the long branches of the willow tree. "I've missed him so much since he passed."

An ache spread in Margo's chest and she sniffled, turning her head sharply to shield her tears. *What the hell is wrong with me lately?* she wondered cynically. *I'm crying at the drop of a fucking hat.*

Sam scooted over on the bench, face toward Dale's. "I'm sorry."

"Why should you be sorry? It was his time," he said, jutting his chin upward, gaze set toward the shops. "I'm aware it's mine but I'm not ready."

Sam glanced at Margo, whispering, "I think we're at a stalemate."

Her mind still whirling from her chase, Margo nodded and attempted to formulate a plan. Dale had a right to refuse—they couldn't force him over—but Margo pondered how much he could've already forgotten since his husband passed. Did he maintain the memories he thought he did or had they began to disintegrate like the wood of a weathered porch?

"What do you remember about him, daily life stuff?" she asked.

A whimsical sort of smile spread across his face as he answered instantly, "He had this unruly patch of hair on the back of his head," he chuckled, "and it never seemed to behave no matter how much product he used to smooth it down. The little tuft was as stubborn as the crabgrass in our walkway."

Margo leaned forward. "What color was his hair?"

Blinking, Dale's mouth opened as if to answer but he snapped it shut.

"Did he wear glasses?" Margo questioned.

Dale's lower lip quivered. "I-I don't remember." His face fell as if stricken by the realization that he couldn't remember such simple qualities of his late husband.

Margo didn't want to push him further, to stab at his pain anymore but she pressed, "What color were his eyes?"

He set his lips in a thin line but kept his gaze steady on Margo's. "You've made your point," he finally whispered.

Placing a hand on his shoulder, Sam said, "You're already forgetting him, Dale. Don't you want to move on with the memories you have still intact?" Why did they have to cause him yet more pain? His teary gaze forced Margo to look away from the hurt she'd stirred within him.

"I'll go," he murmured, his voice raspy with emotion.

"Are you sure?" Margo asked without thinking. Both Dale and Sam stared at her, Sam's brows knitted. "We would be happy to help you over if you're ready," she quickly added.

With one last glance at the tree, he let go and nodded, the thoughtful movement slow. "I'm ready."

Margo took a step back as Sam and the spirit rose from the bench, a light already flickering between Sam's outstretched fingers. Watching Sam open a portal gave Margo a sense of fulfillment she'd never imagined she'd feel, especially triggered by someone else's actions apart from her own. The beautiful tree held a narrow hollow in the center, and it grew as the portal materialized, liquid light manifesting in the doorway.

"Wow," Dale whispered, stepping around the bench, though he could've stepped *through*, to stand before the portal.

"Albert?" He moved to the door, his lower lip trembling but an unmistakable smile upon his lips as he disappeared into the light.

The portal closed and Sam groaned, clutching the arm of the bench. Margo eased a hand over Sam's back knowing the movement would do nothing against the onslaught of nausea from opening the portal. "I thought," Sam began, cut off by a dry heave. "I thought I was done with this crap."

"The older the soul, the harder it is on you to open the portal. Sorry for not giving you a warning."

"Guess our question is answered," Sam muttered, plopping down on the bench with a grunt.

Margo chuckled, still in disbelief. "I'm happy for him. And yeah, I guess you're right—now we know he got what he wanted." And now she knew Sam had grown enough to do this without guidance. She sat beside Sam and searched the fair, hoping to catch a glimpse of the woman who she'd chased but to no avail.

Chapter Ten

A CRISPNESS HUNG in the air as Jackie headed up the short walkway to Lauren's little house, dusk spreading across the sky. After the two had finished the day at the art festival, with Jackie pulling in quite a bit of money for the endeavor, they split up, Jackie going home to store the rest of her art for the next event and Lauren heading home to prepare for the game night. Though it was Jackie's turn to host, Lauren offered, apparently sensing Jackie's dismal mood. She couldn't shake the irritation of Roz's dismissal or lack thereof. The two friends weren't as close as they used to be, with Roz delving into worlds Jackie herself wasn't interested in. The differences built a wedge between them, one only bridged by the years of friendship and shared difficulties of living two separate lives, one normal, one ethereal. While Roz was part Grim, she also worked as an EMT, appearing like the average twentysomething with career aspirations to go back to school after a few years off. Jackie could be herself around Roz without fearing judgment or morbid curiosity.

Well, I can do that with Lauren now, I guess, Jackie thought. *But will she ever really accept my differences?* Roz accepted her without a second thought, though their friendship was incomparable. Jackie had no intention of ever taking blood from Lauren as she had from Roz, and Roz wasn't a human. No, separating the two halves of her life undoubtedly made things easier. Jackie could work, teaching eager students to embrace their creativity while living normally. All she ever wanted was normalcy, which she found with Lauren. Discussing the annoying properties of her ailment weren't normal.

She knocked on the heavy front door with her free hand. Lauren's high-pitched holler to come in made Jackie giggle, and she pushed open the front door, juggling the bags of potato chips in her other hand.

"I brought chips!" she called out.

"Since when do you knock?" Lauren shouted back.

Jackie laughed again as she rounded the corner to the kitchen. "I didn't want to barge in on anything, you know." Ever since her blossoming relationship with Sam, Jackie had given Lauren warning whenever she planned to stop by, lest she interrupt a heated moment, which had happened twice already.

Lauren leaned against the refrigerator, a soft smile on her lips as she typed on her cell phone, oblivious to Jackie walking in.

Her long hair was pulled back in a chic braid, brunette wisps laying against her temples. "Hold on just a second," she said as she continued to type.

Jackie hauled the bags onto the counter and chuckled. "Oh, don't mind me." The scents of cheap junk food wafted from the oven as Jackie passed to grab a beer from the refrigerator.

After about two minutes of Jackie staring Lauren down, she finally glanced up from her phone, a wistful sigh leaving her lips. "Sorry."

Jackie shrugged, simply happy to see her friend happy. "No worries. Is Sam going to make it?"

Lauren held her phone, clutching the gadget close to her chest. "Yes."

"You are *so* happy, it's kind of gross," Jackie said, grinning. "I know it's stupid to ask, but how are you two?"

"Things between us are really, really good," she said, tilting her head back as she sighed, longer this time. "Sam makes me happy." Her head dropped, smile fading. "But I don't want to get hurt again."

Jackie placed her beer on the counter and moved closer to her. "I don't think Sam would ever hurt you, Lauren."

Lauren turned to the cabinet, retrieving a stack of paper plates and placing them on the counter. "I know you're right, and I wish my worries would listen to reason, but..." The oven chimed, and she pulled the greasy party food out. "I don't want another Bethany or Maribel."

"That girl loves you," Jackie insisted, taking both of Lauren's shoulders in her grip. "She also knows I'll mess her up if she crosses you wrong."

Lauren placed the pan on the counter and hugged Jackie tightly. "I know and, God, I love her."

"Good," Jackie said, squeezing her back.

When they let go, Lauren grabbed Jackie's wrist and looked at her. "How about you—are you doing okay? You've been off the last couple days, and I don't like it. Is it because of Margo? She seemed pretty intense this morning, but I just assumed that's how she always is."

Chuckling, Jackie shrugged. "No, not because of Margo," she said, realizing she'd never told Lauren about Roz, not a single thing. She kept Lauren and Roz separate, just as she kept her normal life as separate as she could from her preternatural life. Had she truly kept so much of her life secret from her best friend? And if she had, Jackie wondered how she could consider her as such if she kept so many things from her.

The doorbell rang, cutting their conversation short. Jackie wasn't sure if she was grateful or disappointed. As much as she wanted to share every part of her life with Lauren now that she knew the truth, a strong apprehension reigned in her inclination. Lauren may accept Jackie as an Empusa, but the rest of Jackie's weird life was a whole different story.

Liam and Bonny, a couple who also worked at the high school, entered the kitchen. Bonny placed a tray of store-bought cookies on the counter beside Jackie's chips, engaging in a lively debate with her boyfriend over the science curriculum. Though her mind continued to whirl, worried about Roz, intrigued by Margo, Jackie threw herself into the conversation to add her two cents.

THREE HANDS INTO the game, Jackie felt better. Her cheeks hurt from smiling, her gut sore from laughing, and a warm buzz was briskly settling in the back of her mind after finishing off her second beer as she shuffled the deck of cards. The doorbell rang, halting the deck shuffling, and Jackie lifted her gaze, expecting to see Caleb, the only member of their group of friends missing.

Instead, Sam walked into the living room, looking directly at Lauren and smiling wide, as expected. What wasn't expected was the person who trailed in behind her, brooding in a black leather jacket, blonde hair falling over one eye. Margo kept her head low as she followed Sam to the couch, leaning on the arm of the furniture in lieu of sitting on the cramped space. "Margo, there's space over here," Jackie said, scooting over to the other side of the love seat. Margo shook her head. "How about a beer then?" Jackie stood before she received an answer, padding over to the kitchen.

The beer in the fridge varied, and Jackie peered around, wondering what Margo would want when Margo stepped up close behind her. "I'll take one of those," she said, pointing to a lager. Jackie grabbed it, handed it to Margo, and shut the door. She was so close to Jackie, close enough for Jackie to smell the soft scents of her cologne and body wash.

"I'm glad you decided to come. We've already played a couple rounds of poker, but we were thinking of switching to a different game soon anyway," she laughed but soon regretted her words as the music heightened. *So much for another game.* She glanced back to the living room, catching Lauren as she started a dance with Sam, finding it ironic that she was starting the dance rather than Sam. Bonny and Liam soon hopped up from the couch to dance alongside them.

She turned back to Margo, whose gaze was set on the two couples in the cramped space, dancing to the latest pop song. "I think I'll make myself comfortable on that rug over there and nurse this," Margo said, tilting the beer bottle. She pushed past Jackie, her body brushing Jackie's shoulder as she moved.

Jackie cleared the empty plates off the kitchen island before grabbing herself another beer and heading back to the living room. A heaviness weighed in her chest, stripping her of any longing to join in the laughter of her friends as she usually would. Rather than sitting on the love seat she occupied during their card game, Jackie stepped around the living room, finding Margo in the corner beside Lauren's computer desk, cross-legged on the floor.

Not only did she seem out of place sitting on the colorful rug, but the omnipresent scowl usually adorning her face was subtle. Beer in hand, Jackie headed over to her. Margo stared out at the living room, her fingers tapping in sync with the music pouring from the stereo. Lauren's laughter caused Jackie to look up in time to see Sam dip her during their dance, her mahogany braid brushing the floor before Sam pulled her back up.

She eased herself down on the soft rainbow rug a foot away from Margo. "They're adorable together," Jackie murmured over the music.

"Yeah, they're cute."

In the limited light, Margo's brows weren't poised in the usual tightness; she appeared somewhat relaxed, far from her normal façade. Jackie inched closer to her. "I'm glad you saved her."

Margo remained still, aside from clenching her jaw. Her leather jacket was neatly folded by her feet, her black boots placed strategically beside it. She shifted her weight slightly, stretching her legs out from the folded position they'd been in, causing her jeans to ride up her ankle. "Yeah but don't forget I did do it for self-serving purposes, so don't assume it was for the greater good or something."

Jackie leaned closer, her shoulder bumping into Margo's arm as she tilted her head to catch a glimpse of Margo's eyes. Had she really seen a fire in her gaze a few nights before? "I don't think I believe that."

Margo turned her head then, meeting Jackie's stare. "What do you believe, then?"

"I believe you saved her just to save her." Jackie licked her bottom lip.

A deep chuckle reverberated through Margo's chest. "You think too highly of me, Jacqueline." There. Jackie saw it again, a single spark lighting up Margo's blue irises before disappearing. Along with the mere tendril of fire,

Jackie noticed an unfurling desire, not unlike her own, blossoming in the steady gaze Margo held.

Jackie shrugged and shot her a jaunty smile behind the top of the beer bottle, blaming her buzz for the sudden boldness. "Whatever you say. You didn't have to help me the other night, but you did anyway, without expecting anything in return. I think *you* think too lowly of yourself." She lifted her eyebrow suggestively.

"Everyone is entitled to their own opinion," Margo noted, placing her hands on the floor behind her to anchor herself. Her T-shirt stretched over her breasts, and Jackie's cheeks heated as she found herself staring.

She looked back to the living room in time to catch Sam and Lauren kissing during a commercial on the radio. For someone with such a high confidence level, Margo surprised Jackie with her ease of self-blame—the same someone who offered her blood to Jackie on the verge of bloodlust when she had no reason to, regardless of debt owed. If she had simply wanted to pay her back for asking Brent to save them, she could've done something a lot less risky.

"You know what I think?" Jackie asked, half wondering what Margo would do if she asked to kiss her. Would she turn away, reciting her claims that the bite was just that and nothing more had happened, or would she accept the kiss, perhaps even want more? *Where did that thought come from?*

Margo glanced at her questionably. "What?"

"I think I want to kiss you."

"Oh." Margo blinked, a flash of confusion on her face before she whispered, "I think that'd be okay."

Jackie leaned over, brushing her fingertips over Margo's cheek, and she kissed her. Her lips were as warm and soft as Jackie anticipated, and she threaded her fingers in Margo's hair, the seemingly innocent kiss threatening to steal Jackie's breath. Margo wrapped both arms around Jackie, turning herself to kiss her fully, her tongue tentatively licking Jackie's lips. Jackie sighed into the kiss, brushing her thumb over Margo's cheek. The music around them faded, replaced by Margo's soft breaths and Jackie's own heart beating in her ears.

Abruptly, Margo pulled away, cheeks flushed, flames dancing in her irises once again, proving to Jackie she hadn't imagined it the night she bit her. She'd never seen anything quite like it.

"Margo," she whispered, dropping her hands. "The fire in your eyes is so beautiful." The wisps swirled like embers in a deep hearth, twisting around the darkness of her pupils.

Margo cleared her throat, hesitated, but said nothing. Time seemed to freeze and Jackie, unsure what to do, touched Margo's face again, grazing her cheek as she watched the firelight wane.

"I should go," Margo muttered.

Jackie nodded in understanding even though she really didn't understand. Margo's lips lifted in a shy smile before she turned away and grabbed her jacket and boots. The flames were gone, and the only red left was the flush staining her cheeks.

Sipping her beer on the fuzzy rainbow rug, Jackie watched Margo shrug into her jacket without looking at her. The block was back up, not in the form of tension between them but a palpable spacer. One day, Jackie vowed to herself as Margo walked out the front door of Lauren's house, she would figure out why Margo needed her firm armor. *Yeah, that's as likely as figuring out where the hell Roz is.*

Lauren caught her gaze from across the room, a wicked grin gracing her lips. Before she could berate her with questions, the door opened, and Caleb walked into the living room. Jackie hastily pushed herself from the floor, grateful to have dodged the inevitable questions from her best friend. For now.

Chapter Eleven

MONDAY MORNING CAME swiftly for Jackie, her busy weekend at the art fair still taxing on her brain. She rested back in her chair at the end of the day, lifting her shoulders in bliss as she brought a hot cup of tea to her face, the wonderfully aromatic scents wafting upward.

In her free hand, her thumb hovered over the Send button on the text message she'd written out the night before while pacing her house. She'd been too nervous to reach out to Margo the day before; however, she knew she wanted to figure out if there was something between them, the flicker overwhelming her as she'd gazed at Margo. She'd kissed Jackie back, eagerly.

What Jackie would give to see the firelight swirl in her eyes again...

She sent the text message.

Hey, I was wondering if you weren't busy later this week if you wanted to grab something to eat with me, like dinner.

She figured a text would be harmless, a simple invitation to dinner, but her nerves were getting the best of her. She waited, hoping Margo wouldn't leave her hanging one way or another, busying herself with the menial tasks of cleaning the classroom's paintbrushes and palates. Better to know where they stood, if anywhere, which made Jackie question her own attraction to her. What *did* they really have? Margo returned a favor, allowing Jackie to bite her. Sure, they shared a brief kiss on Lauren's living room floor, brought on by alcohol-induced lowered inhibitions and bravado, but Jackie knew Margo was a solitary individual—she made that very clear by pushing away anyone brave enough to try to make a connection with her. This started before the kiss, Jackie reminded herself, replaying the vivid memories Margo and she shared when she bit her.

After completing her cleaning ritual, she sat at her desk and sipped her tea as she opened another message to Margo.

Okay, maybe dinner sounds too serious. How about super casual coffee?

The last person Jackie dated had made things easy, coming on to her rather than the other way around. She didn't approach others wanting a relationship, or even casual dating. She, like Margo, enjoyed her solitude, surrounded by art, peace, and tranquility. Relationships muddled her serenity and didn't prove much interest to her. She never found herself intrigued by someone enough to want to know more about them. Until Margo.

The door opened with a soft creak, and Jackie raised her head. "Funny meeting you here," Lauren teased from the threshold. "You were suspiciously MIA during lunch, but I knew I'd find you here now." She shouldered her way through the door, playful accusation clear on her face.

Jackie scratched her head and avoided Lauren's gaze. "Yeah, I needed a change of scenery." *Here comes the inquisition.* Guiltily, Jackie had avoided Lauren during both break periods for the day and dined in the teacher's lounge instead of her classroom where she usually ate.

Instead of coming out and asking her about the kiss as expected, Lauren inspected the art pieces Jackie had left strewn over the front two tables, ones she had yet to finish grading. *Maybe she's waiting for me to spill.*

Finally, Lauren cleared her throat. "So, you and the scary Grim Reaper kissed. Who kissed whom?"

Jackie chewed her lip, debating honesty. "I kissed her."

"You kissed her?" Lauren's voice reached a pitch Jackie swore she could've broken glass with. "Why?"

"Why what?"

"Why did you kiss her?"

A sigh left Jackie's lips, and she averted her gaze to the closest window. She wanted to push Margo's barriers, wanted to see the glimmer of flames wave through her blue irises, to bask in the heat of her breath. She offered Lauren a lazy one-shouldered shrug. "I don't know."

When Jackie glanced at her, Lauren's brows were contorted in disbelief. "Since when have you gone around kissing random people?" Her question held only sincerity and curiosity.

She had a point, Jackie knew—it wasn't as though Jackie dated to Lauren's knowledge. The occasional one-night stand always fared better in Jackie's life. No need to divulge in her secrets or find time to fit the person into her world. "I honestly don't know," she said, her voice earnest and quiet. She wasn't sure what it was in Margo that sparked such longing to know *more*. It frightened her.

"Okay," Lauren said, her face softening. As if she could sense Jackie's discomfort, Lauren shifted into a different topic. The unspoken switch in conversation caused Jackie's affection for Lauren to surge, knowing she must've sensed the uncertainty and avoidance in her tone. Work talk was safe, much safer than exploring the reasons Jackie found Margo captivating.

Lauren leaned against Jackie's desk. "Is it rude to ask Sam if she's seen a spirit of someone specific?"

"What do you mean?" Jackie asked, thinking about Bethany, however, she knew Lauren's ex-girlfriend had already passed on as one of Sam's first solo reapings.

She pushed her hair out of her face, suddenly shy. "I asked her about Anthony."

The image of Margo, back against her car, head hung low and cheeks tear-stained, materialized in Jackie's mind. She held a tenderness Jackie didn't think possible until Margo aided her in her own time of need. "She didn't help Anthony, Margo did," Jackie whispered.

"Is..." Lauren stopped, looked around, cleared her throat, and then met Jackie's gaze again. "Did she help Anthony move on? Like, he's gone?"

"Yes, she helped him cross over," Jackie said, her tone melancholy.

"Wow, I'm surprised she could do that. She seems to be a little rough around the edges from what I've heard from Sam," Lauren said.

"I thought she was just an asshole, but," Jackie paused and smiled, one that she knew reached her eyes. "She's actually a cool person."

Lauren's lips lifted in a crooked smile. "You like her." It wasn't a question.

"Yeah, I kind of like her," Jackie admitted. While her honesty came quickly, Jackie continued, "I'm sorry there's so much of my life I've never told you. Some friend I am."

Lauren looked away but a smile quirked her lips. "I do understand why you haven't, but," she paused, turning to face Jackie again, "you can tell me. I won't think you're weird, or crazy, or any of that. You're my best friend. I want to know as much of your life as you're willing to share."

"I don't even know where to begin," Jackie chuckled. And she truly didn't know where to start, other than the topic that seemed to be the least daunting. "Have I ever told you about Ezra?" she asked, knowing the answer would be no. When Lauren shook her head, Jackie offered the truth. "They're my older sibling."

"You have a sibling?" Lauren drew her brows together. "How have I never heard of them before?"

Jackie frowned. "I'm sorry."

Lauren waved her hand. "Don't stop to apologize. Just keep going. Tell me all about Ezra." And Jackie did. She told Lauren how they bickered as children, but were always close, how Ezra could catch glimpses of the future by simple touch, and how, although Ezra worked almost every waking moment, the two made time for each other. Lauren listened intently. With every bit Jackie shared with her, a piece of her mountainous trepidation smoothed. Lauren didn't run, even when Jackie told her Ezra also had to take blood to survive.

Maybe this isn't so bad. I'll toss it at her slowly. The kindness Lauren exhibited teetered on unbelievable, but Jackie knew better; it was genuine and authentic. When the five-minute warning bell rang overhead for the students to catch the late activity buses, Lauren beamed. "I would love to meet them."

Jackie grinned. "I'm sure they'd be more than excited to meet a friend of mine." She went to grab her grading sheet from her desk but halted, her focus waning, her mind awash in dizziness. She brought her hand to her head, closing her eyes to stop the vertigo. Sounds became muffled, muted tones, all silenced by the thrum of blood. She slowed her breathing and gripped her desk. Her own breaths sounded foreign to her—sharp, obscure, primal.

Coppery blood filled her mouth, sprouted incisors piercing her gums. She rested her head on her shoulder and tried to slow her breathing.

When she opened her eyes again, Lauren was staring at her, lips tight. "Are you okay?"

"Yeah," Jackie breathed, shaking the wooziness from her mind. "I think I need a little water." Jackie kept her mouth closed, unwilling to allow Lauren to see her teeth. "You go ahead. I've got to get these projects graded before I leave today."

Lauren gave her a worried appraisal but nodded and said, "Okay. Text me if you want to talk more." With a short wave, she left Jackie's classroom.

Phone in hand, Jackie sent a quick plea to Brent, asking if he had a replacement elixir, thanking Goddess that Ezra would be back from their trip soon. The bloodlust was becoming really, really annoying.

Chapter Twelve

"DUDE, I'M TELLING you, I'll find it," the spirit claimed as he ducked under yet another car in the small junkyard. Grass and moss spilled over the metal, warping around the vehicle, nature reclaiming it. The forecast predicted another storm to emerge in the coming days after their initial nor'easter the night before and Margo's excitement was palpable. She always loved a good storm: watching the branches of radiant light spilling over the darkened ground when lightning struck, wind whispering the world's secrets through cracks in the door as the rain pattered a soft melody on the windowsill. *Maybe the storm will keep me from thinking about Jackie.*

Margo worried if she rolled her eyes any harder, they'd disappear into the back of her skull. She lit another cigarette to pass the time. From where she stood on the ground behind the spirit, Sam chuckled with a slight shake of her head as she made eye contact with Margo. As before, Sam took over the responsibility of aiding Fred in his unfinished business without any help from Margo.

The retired car Margo sat atop was beginning to cause her back discomfort and a thick fog ebbed into the junkyard, causing the dreary morning to become even more so. When she'd left the house a few hours ago to pick Sam up, the sun played peekaboo behind the clouds. But now, it was nowhere to be seen.

The spirits she aided had easy unfinished business revolving around living beings, for the most part. Rarely did she have a spirit who was attached to an item. Something they wouldn't leave behind. In the case of Fred, the wiry-haired fifty-year-old who'd died in a car accident, the worldly possession he couldn't leave without was a simple figurine of a famous football player, which he claimed was still in the vehicle. He'd yet to locate the Post-It-sized glass statue, but Margo wasn't going to stop him in his efforts to find it.

When she left Lauren's house from the stupid game night, Margo went home and sulked, kicking herself in the ass. She wanted to stay; she wanted to go, panicked by her sudden poignant emotions when Jackie kissed her. She wanted to feel Jackie's lips on hers again. Margo rolled her eyes at her own thoughts, lifting her hands to touch her lips as if the action would bring back the sensation. She didn't know if she wanted to see Jackie ever again.

You're lying if you think you can stop yourself from seeing her again. Eventually, she decided to go to bed, lest she be questioned by Luis when he got home from work. How could a kiss make her doubt everything? Her plans were laid out in front of her. Sam was practically ready to do this on her own, giving Margo the opportunity to leave guilt-free. Sam would be spared, hopefully. But, Jackie... She complicated things.

"I had my meeting with Alfonso yesterday," Sam said, wandering over. "He's weird."

Margo found herself smiling. "Yeah, he is. How'd that go?"

"Good, I guess. He asked me a bunch of questions, like how many souls I typically get to cross over, how long it takes me, my success rate," Sam said, shaking her head.

"I'm glad Brent was there with the statistic crap because I didn't know I was supposed to be keeping track of those things. How many Board people are there?"

"Okay, it's kind of complicated. All of us here in America are loosely controlled by thirteen people split by region: Atlantic, Midwest, Eastern, and Pacific, with the latter holding a fourth Board member due to population density. The three Board members we fall under are: Alfonso, Sybil, and Cynthia." She paused, taking her cigarettes from her pocket. "I don't know much about Sybil, but Alfonso is the least pompous asshole of them all. Cynthia is a bitch, though," Margo chuckled as she brought a cigarette to her mouth, lighting the end. "I'm glad you didn't get stuck with her. Did he bug you with anything else?" Margo recalled Alfonso's stance on keeping Sam alive—his main purpose to learn from her existence, what made her revival different than other attempts before blood bonds became illegal.

"No, the meeting was pretty boring. He and Brent talked about the statistics then chatted about some foreign plant I couldn't pronounce if I wanted to."

The spirit's low murmur became a loud grumble. Margo and Sam turned their heads as Fred slid into an open window of a car, though he could've gone through the metal frame itself.

Sam's gaze lifted to hers. "I saw you and Jackie kissing the other night."

Margo cleared her throat, turning her head to stare off in the distance. "You were so absorbed in Lauren. I didn't think you'd notice."

In her periphery, Margo watched a deep flush rise to Sam's brown cheeks. "Yeah, but when you notice your cranky boss making out with a girl, you kind of have to pause what you're doing and make sure your eyes aren't playing tricks on you," Sam chuckled.

"I found it!" the spirit shouted in triumph, saving Margo from the awkward explanation she didn't have. Fred's laughter was verging on maniacal as he withdrew the object from the car, blonde hair bobbing as he danced. He held the treasured item, staring at it in awe as he cradled it.

"Great! So, you're ready to go?" Sam asked.

"Huh? Yeah, sure," Fred answered as he tried to wipe a bit of dirt from the sports icon in his hand.

Sam lifted both hands, light glimmering to life between her fingers as she opened the portal. The air in front of a doorless VW Beetle bowed inward, glowing as it grew to Fred's height. His eyes widened, and he dropped the once-prized figurine, opting to walk through the door without another word in Sam's direction. At times, Margo really wondered about people's unfinished business, what drove these people to refuse to leave this plane of existence. Most made sense to her: missing loved ones, worrying about children, property, businesses, but a fucking football bobblehead?

"Do you enjoy doing this so early in the morning?" Sam asked. Their day began before Fred with a spirit across town who didn't want to miss a chance to see their son get on the school bus one more time. Then, they headed to the junkyard for Fred, leading them into a long search for an insignificant piece of plastic.

Somebody needs their beauty sleep. Margo smirked playfully at her. "You and your precious sleep."

Sam shot her a reproachful glance. "Let me guess—you're going to say we can sleep when we're dead?"

"I wouldn't say that. If you haven't noticed already, even the dead don't sleep." Margo finished her cigarette, stubbing it out on another rundown car before she left the junkyard. "And, stop whining. You're done for the day." She patted her pockets. "I don't have any more charges left, so I've got to stop by Brent's and pick up the next batch of lucky souls. You head home and go back to sleep if you're *that* tired."

Sam pulled her hood over her head, sighing. "I'm not sleeping all that well."

"Nightmares still?" Margo asked, her tone softened.

Sam nodded. "Yeah, the same one every time—me dying."

Margo moved closer to her, wondering if she should offer her a hug or lighten up the conversation with humor. "I'm sorry."

"I have to head to the post office for a shift this morning, but then I'm taking a nap," Sam said, shrugging.

They said goodbye, Sam hopping in her Jeep and leaving before Margo started her MINI Cooper.

Margo's reflection in the rearview mirror stared back at her, deep worry lines between her blonde brows. She tugged the collar of her leather jacket down, stealing a glimpse at her neck. The marks were faded now, faintly discolored against her pale skin, and she ran her thumb over the raised scab. How could someone invade another's head with a simple bite? She chuckled to herself at the question. Her own light conjuring was just as odd. She pulled out of her parking spot and headed toward the bridge.

On the drive to Brent's, she realized there hadn't been a gaze set on her. The eerie sensation had followed her since she helped Brent and Collin in the woods. *Maybe it's because I almost caught up with her the last time.* Why would someone be following her and Sam, watching them open portals? The only time she'd experienced something similar was when she and Luis were teenagers. She intended to tell Brent about the watcher when she went to retrieve the stack of new charges but questioned herself. The last time she saw him, he appeared weighed down, struggling under the stress of countless objectives, and she didn't want to add to his to-do list. Didn't matter anyway—she was prepared to leave in the coming weeks once she was confident in Sam's ability to work on her own.

Brent and Collin lived a few towns over from the island, somewhere around a twenty-minute drive on a good day. The winding gravel driveway bore puddles of deep mud, and she somehow managed to keep her car from careening into the woods.

Collin's truck was the only vehicle in the driveway. The Fae man stood beside a fallen tree, the massive oak inches from his greenhouse. Leaves lay strewn around the gravel, yellow and crimson dotting the grass around the greenhouse. Collin knelt beside the fallen tree, placing his hand gently against the rough bark. His hushed tone, etched with sorrow, spoke in a language Margo didn't recognize. The soft incantation soothed the air around them, stifling the breeze that had previously displaced the leaves on the trees on either side. It was quiet, save the lift of his words as he finished his prayer. He stood and the wind commenced, ruffling his crimson hair, and he tossed an ax on the ground and waved to her, wiping sweat from his red brow with his free hand. "Margo."

"What's up?" she asked as she shut the car door and began toward him.

"The windstorm knocked this poor soul down last night." He crossed his arms over his chest. "I'm grateful it didn't land in the greenhouse. Let me wash up. I'll start some tea."

Margo chuckled to herself. What the hell was up with the tea? At this rate, she'd never get a halfway decent cup of coffee. "Don't worry about it. I just came to grab the job lists for me, Sam, and Luis."

Collin shook his head, still ushering her over with a wave of his hand. "No, I insist." His warm smile convinced her, and she followed him. The path leading to the back of the greenhouse reminded her just how strange the space was. From the outside, the building bore little resemblance to what lay inside, the gigantic space at least three times as large as it appeared from the exterior.

Collin opened the glass door into the greenhouse, and a wall of humidity engulfed Margo's senses. She didn't know there was a second entrance to the massive building but wasn't surprised, and she followed him through the dense foliage. Green-and-orange-leafed plants surrounded the area, thicker than the last time she'd been there a few weeks before. Another new addition included countless butterflies flying through the dense air, their silent flight paths nearly colliding as they passed one another.

"Please, sit," Collin said, gesturing to the table as he moved to the workbench with two hot plates set up. One held a chrome kettle while the other heated a familiar cast-iron cauldron, steam wafting from both.

Margo sat with hesitation and eased back in the wicker chair, placing her arms loosely over the tabletop. Chattering birds in the tree behind her made her chuckle, the tones reminding Margo of an argument. The sweltering heat of the room prompted her to shrug out of her leather jacket, and she lay the garment over her lap.

When she looked down, a butterfly landed daintily upon her hand, tiny legs tickling the tops of her knuckles. Their wings appeared painted, the hues a shade Margo had never seen before; a crimson so red she swore it was real blood staining the powdery wings, and a blue with such depth she thought a ripe berry rather than an insect sat upon her shirt. "What's with the butterflies?"

Collin kept his head bowed over the mess bubbling from the cauldron. "It's mating season."

Two more fluttered down onto the glass table: one emerald and another red. Margo snorted. "Of course, it is." She shook her arm gently until the bug flew away with the others. "So, where's Brent?"

He grabbed the plate beside his setup and tossed the remaining leaves into the mixture. "He had a particular request from a client up north and left early this morning to deliver. I imagine he'll be back some time tomorrow, but he left the lists there on the table." A few sheets of paper were in the middle of the table and she nodded. Once done stirring, he looked up. "How's Samantha?"

She cleared her throat and glanced down at her hands. "She's making a good Grim, just like I said she would. I hope I didn't cause a bunch of bullshit for Brent to have to deal with. I'm sorry if—"

Collin lifted his hand to silence her apology. "You acted on instinct, did you not? I don't expect Brent wants an apology from you. Contrary to what he and I initially thought, you made no mistake."

"How do you figure?" *Instinct.* She hadn't thought when she saved Sam. She just did. A breeze ruffled the bizarre bush to her right, and Margo stifled a shudder.

Normal greenhouses didn't catch gusts of wind unless a window was open, but of course this was no ordinary greenhouse.

Collin blinked at her. "She was worth saving, no?"

Duh. She'd come to that conclusion herself long ago, but part of her wondered if she'd doomed the poor woman with a life she didn't need nor want. Would she do it again? Just as she'd told Sam: yes, she would do it again even with the understanding of what would come. Sam was alive because of her, and rather than feel egotistical about the situation, a sense of cautious pride in saving her surrounded Margo as if it were the one thing she'd done right in her life.

"Yeah." Although she'd answered, Collin continued to stare at her. "She's having some nightmares, though, about her death. I don't know how to help her." Her voice sounded pained to her own ears. Her phone buzzed in the pocket of her leather jacket on her lap, but she ignored it.

He sighed. "From what I've read, she may experience this in the coming months, but it will subside after a while. I'll ask Brent to brew her up a tonic that should help."

"Thanks." Margo tapped her fingers on her thigh, partly wondering what to say next. Though she wanted to inquire about Empusa, to find out if all of them could probe into other's minds by simply biting them, she knew she couldn't ask. The situation in the woods with the portal seemed like a safer conversation. "So, you can go back home now whenever you want?"

He nodded, glancing down as the substance bubbled in the cast-iron. "For the most part, yes." The kettle whistled, the sound muffled by the damp air. He poured two cups and brought them to the table. "Though it is a difficult trip to and from."

Margo took in the dark color of the liquid, breathing in the tangy aroma before sipping the tea. The taste was stronger than the scent, sweet with a spicy aftertaste that left her wanting more. "Why didn't Queen Demelza give you what you wanted?"

"How can I put this? She's not unlike the individuals who oversee you. Her lack of tolerance for anything but pure is ostentatious, and this led to her refusal. She frowns upon individuals such as you and me."

"That's shitty." In Margo's understanding, she thought the asshats in Grim's corporate office were the only ones who had negative feelings toward people like her and Collin—people with mixed blood. "Have you gone to see your family yet?"

Collin smiled again, his face almost quaint. "I haven't seen my mother for such a long time. I was relieved she's doing so well."

"She can't come here?" Margo wrapped her hands around the cup and took another sip, cherishing the spicy beverage.

As he rose, Collin shook his head. "She's far too weak. I have you to thank for giving me the opportunity to see her and my family again. I imagine you realize how important it is for me."

She placed the cup back on the table. "I don't know anything about family, but I'm glad you were able to go see yours."

He studied her for a moment as he settled back behind the table, once more stirring the pot. "No matter where I go, Brent will always be my family, my home." Margo nodded. "You have more family than you realize," he said.

"Yeah, whatever you say." What family? Of course, she had Luis, but Collin's words alluded to more than one singular person.

He said nothing. The silence grew, save the chirping birds from a plant a few yards behind her. Well, Margo wasn't sure she could call it a plant: the leaves were the size of her head, and the stalk grew far higher than she stood.

"Are you doing anything for your birthday?" Collin asked. Her birthday hadn't crossed her mind in the last crazy bit of her life, but she realized the day was only a week out. *Not that it's my real birthday anyway.* The day was a guess, just as most things in her life were. When her family dropped her at the hospital as a small child, the staff and social services *guessed* she was six months old. They *guessed* her birthday. They *guessed* where her family could've been from.

"Nope, no plans."

"I'd love to bake you a cake. We could have a little get together here." Margo tried to hide her grimace. The first, and last time she and Luis ate a cake baked by Collin was years before, and they both experienced the strangest dreams they'd ever had in their lives. Brent claimed the harmless additive in the icing Collin used prompted the fantastical dreams. She would never trust a baked good from either of them again.

"I'll think about it," she lied. She finished off the tea in a few gulps, grabbed the papers from the table, and stood. "I'd better take off then. Thanks for the tea." Margo turned to leave, draping her jacket over her shoulder.

Collin dumped the contents from the pot into the mason jar, the copious liquid solidifying once it hit the surface. "Before you go, could you take this to Jacqueline?

I'd be grateful if you'd go check on her for me. She had a bit of a rough time the other night. Unfortunately, my success in earning dual citizenship was not without consequence, and Brent has found it difficult to acquire necessary ingredients to make the elixir for Jacqueline."

Margo stared at the wide-mouthed jar. Did she really want to see Jackie again? Duh, she did. Was it a good idea? No, probably not. "Why can't you take it?"

A knowing smile crept over Collin's face as he tilted his head, gaze lingering over her neck. "I didn't know you two were so well-acquainted."

Damn it. She popped the collar of her polo. "Not well acquainted. I was returning the favor of her saving my ass. A life for a life," Margo deadpanned.

Vibrant smile still present, Collin pushed the jar across the table toward her. "I'm due for company to arrive any time now to help me with the tree, so I can't leave."

She snatched the jar from the table. "I'll see you around, I guess." She made her way for the back door where she'd come in, tucking her jacket under her arm.

"Your favor was appreciated immensely, I presume," Collin called. "She doesn't take blood from just anyone."

"I'm sure," she said, walking away from him. *So much for never seeing Jackie again.*

SHE DROVE TO Jackie's, her apprehension tinged with excitement.

Margo climbed the staircase slowly, soaking up the lingering warmth from the autumn sun pressing against her back, burning through the fabric of her shirt. Muffled music met her as she reached the porch and stepped up to the beach-weathered red door. Wasn't there something about people who had red doors? Margo couldn't remember the reference. She lifted her hand and knocked gently. The door opened and Jackie stared at her, an expression of surprise on her face as her gaze raked over Margo. "Hi," she said, a slight question in her tone.

Margo smiled awkwardly and held up the heavy mason jar. The liquid moved like gelatin. "I was over at Brent's, and Collin wanted me to bring this by, so, here. Apparently, he thinks I'm his new little delivery boy. This," she said, shoving a jar toward her, "is from him."

Jackie tilted her head, causing her hair to cascade from her shoulder and dangle at her side, but she didn't take the offered jar. Margo glanced down. Jackie's dark leggings were sprinkled with various shades of paint as was the shirt she wore, the bold white letters stating *I need coffee right meow* peppered with green. "Huh, the color is different," Jackie said, drawing Margo's gaze upward.

"Yeah, he said this one is a replacement for the one Brent usually makes you." Margo lifted her head fully and met Jackie's stare, her gaze a vibrant hazel in the late afternoon sunlight spilling over the front porch.

A kettle whistled from within the house, halting their stare down. Shit, Margo could get lost in those eyes.

"Do you want to come in for some coffee or tea?" Jackie said over the shrill cry. Margo nodded and followed Jackie into the living room, which seemed unchanged from the few nights prior. She closed the front door behind her and stepped over to the worktable, eyeing the deep gouges on the surface while Jackie hurried to silence the kettle. The wood had been wounded by something ragged and sharp, and Margo remembered the state Jackie was in before she bit her. Horns had crowned her head, white and pointed, pressing through her tight hair. Although her face had remained the same, her eyes had changed from her dark obsidian to bone white, as pale as the horns shooting from her head. Margo knew she should've been scared, should've been terrified of the monster before her but she hadn't been. She found Jackie beautiful in both forms.

"Which do you want?" Jackie asked, disrupting Margo's memory.

Incense burned on a shelf in the corner of the cluttered living room, the scents wafting in Margo's face as she walked past the smoke. "I could kill for some coffee right now, but whatever you're having is cool," she said. The last time Jackie offered her tea she ended up not getting said tea, and she wondered absently if this time would be a repeat.

She walked around the table, her gaze falling upon a painting secured to the wall. The piece was massive, dark, and dreary, with shaded rain over a street somewhere in the city, maybe even Atlantic City or Philly. A name in the corner scribbled in an animated yellow said Anthony McKinney. Margo sighed and moved away from the painting. "That kid will stick with me for a while," she whispered more to herself than to Jackie.

"He would've gone places, big places I only dreamed of. I hope instant is okay."

When Margo glanced at Jackie to ensure she'd heard her correctly, Jackie held up a canister of instant coffee. "Yeah, that's fine."

Jackie's dark hair was pushed back, tucked behind an ear with more tiny silver hoops than Margo could count. She poured two mugs full of hot water before dumping generous scoops of instant coffee granules. "He was a good kid."

"Yeah," Margo said. She dropped her gaze, trying to find something to keep her from getting caught in Jackie's stare again. Every time she looked at her, she felt the same pull, the eerie tug she experienced when Jackie had bitten her.

She found an odd chair, one that could've been taken right out of the foster home she'd spent two years in as a child. The elderly couple who had the living room set from when they bought their home in 1964. "You've got some interesting furniture," she said as she sat on the chair, the springs protesting loudly with her weight.

Jackie walked over from the small kitchenette with two steaming cups, a coy smile on her lips. "I love antiques. I found that chair in an estate sale up north with my older sibling, Ezra, a few years ago for five bucks. Luckily, we took their truck so we could bring it back the same day. No way was I missing that deal." She handed her a mug, and Margo took it.

Margo lifted an eyebrow, noting the pronoun Jackie used in relation to her sibling. "Their? Is Ezra nonbinary?" She chewed her lip, hoping she hadn't been rude.

"Yes."

"Cool. Figured I'd ask, and I hope that wasn't rude."

She beamed. "No, not at all. Actually, I really appreciate you asking."

Margo wiggled, smiling approvingly. "I have to say this is a comfortable chair even if it's ugly."

"One of my favorites." Jackie sipped her coffee.

She handed Jackie the mason jar. "Here."

"Thanks." Jackie placed her mug on the slight end table beside her and then opened the jar. She scrunched her face, and her body shuddered.

Margo straightened in the chair. "You okay?"

"I'm fine, but oh, my Goddess, this smells worse than the other stuff." She held the elixir away from her face.

Margo stretched out her legs and leaned back in the chair. She was nervous, nervous she'd offer her own blood to Jackie again, something she couldn't risk doing no matter how badly she wanted to feel the closeness again. *Fuck it*, Margo thought, *I can't* not *help her*. "What's the worst that could happen if this one doesn't work?" She rolled up her sleeves to busy her hands.

Jackie swirled the liquid around. *Not as if the substance could even be considered liquid. It looks like pudding.* "I could go into bloodlust and turn into a monster again."

Margo grinned. "I thought you were kind of cute."

"Your sincerity is sweet," Jackie said, rolling her eyes.

Margo *had* been sincere, though she didn't correct Jackie's inaccurate assumption that Margo's words were sarcasm.

Jackie pointed to the tattooed vines swirling up Margo's wrists. "What is your tattoo of?"

Looking down at her arms, Margo was unsure how to explain. "Nothing in particular." When Jackie tilted her head to the side in confusion, Margo continued, "I was a teenager and wanted to feel grounded to something. They're roots." She lifted her arm as she tugged her sleeve up farther, taking in the errant black vines. When she had the tattoo done, she wanted something to ground her, opting to get intricate roots sprawling over her arms as a symbolic way to root herself somewhere, anywhere. The tattoo began at her back as a small seedling, the roots spanning over her shoulders and down her arms. She wanted to show Jackie but thought better of it. Taking her shirt off in front of an Empusa in the midst of bloodlust probably wasn't a good idea.

Jackie smiled. "I think it's beautiful." She drew a sharp breath, a tremble running through the fingers that held the jar.

Without thinking, Margo blurted, "You could always bite me again."

Jackie shifted forward in her seat, her steady gaze on Margo, who sipped her coffee. She could see the want in Jackie's stare, the indecision as she parted her lips and closed them again. "No, this will be fine," she said, glancing back down at the jar in her hand.

When she pulled the mug from her lips, Margo cleared her throat. "I'm serious about the offer."

Jackie pursed her lips, one dark brow lifted. "Are you sure?"

"That's what I said, isn't it?" She wanted Jackie to bite her, to feel her hot breath over her neck once again, to experience the sensation of Jackie pressing into her thoughts and pressing herself against her body. Jackie placed the elixir back on the side table.

"Okay."

Heat rose to Margo's cheeks as Jackie spoke, but she tried to shield her blush with nonchalance. "Cool." She stood from the couch and dusted her jeans off, though no dust had stuck to her; the movement was to wipe the sweat that coated her palms. Margo licked her lips, and unsure what to do with them, clasped her hands tightly behind her back. "Do you want to me sit or…" she trailed off when she noticed Jackie move toward her. Despite her feigned calm, Margo's voice betrayed her normal confidence, tinging her words with a slight quiver. "Where do you want me?"

"You're fine just where you are," Jackie said. She brushed the hair from Margo's neck, the tips of her fingers grazing the skin, sending a shiver down Margo's back. Unlike the last time, Jackie was hornless and her obsidian gaze hauntingly dark. Margo closed her eyes in anticipation, craning her neck.

The air around her face changed, a cautious breath stirring her eyelashes before Jackie kissed her lips softly. "That's not my neck," Margo murmured against Jackie's mouth.

Fingers laced through Margo's hair, pulling her closer. "I know," Jackie whispered.

Margo wrapped her arms around Jackie's waist, relishing in the warmth of her, the taste of her. She wanted to stay there, deep in Jackie's embrace, Jackie flicking her tongue over Margo's lips, hands gripping her sides.

Jackie gasped, pulling away from Margo, breaths coming in ragged. Margo reached for her, unsure what to do. "Jackie?" she murmured.

Jackie rested her head against Margo's shoulder. "I'm okay," she whispered.

Margo ran her hand up and down Jackie's back in a circular motion, unsure how she could help other than offering her blood. Before she could speak, Jackie moved away from her, taking up a spot beside her large art table. She pressed a hand to her head, eyes closed and face unreadable. "Jackie?"

"I'll be okay, but I think you should go." Jackie dropped her hand, a soft smile on her lips. "Maybe we could do dinner or something in the next couple days."

"Sure, yeah, we could do that," Margo said, more than a little disappointed not to be kissing Jackie again, unsure if her disappointment surprised her more than Jackie's response. "Are you sure you're going to be okay?"

Jackie busied herself with the supplies laying on the table. "I'll try that new elixir, and I'm sure I'll be perfect." She hopped up on the table, grabbing a clay chunk from in front of her, and she began to knead the gray substance. "Did you get my text?"

Margo patted her pocket for her phone, embarrassed she hadn't checked it since the morning. "Crap, no I didn't even know you texted me."

"That's okay. Do you like pizza?"

"Who doesn't like pizza?" Margo chuckled.

Attention focused at the task in her hands, Jackie giggled softly. "Okay, let's plan for pizza tomorrow. I'll text you the address of a place with some good pizza."

"Okay." Margo stayed where she was, watching Jackie work. Muscles tightened and flexed, crawling up Jackie's arms as she twisted the clay into formation with ease. A sense of whiplash left Margo feeling uncertain, her curiosity around Jackie growing even more with her dismissal. "Okay, I'll talk to you tomorrow, then," she said eventually as she headed for the door. Jackie shot her a wary grin before Margo stepped outside into the late afternoon.

As she trotted down the stairs, Margo shook her head, wondering what the hell just happened.

Chapter Thirteen

THE SCENTS OF fresh-cut grass greeted Jackie as she climbed out of her car and glanced up at Ezra's little bungalow. Jackie roamed up the walkway, taking in the lingering rosebuds on the bushes below the massive bay window. Ezra's hunched form was visible through the glass, head bent over an extensive blueprint. The table lamplight reflected off Ezra's clean-shaven scalp as their hand moved across the paper, swiping away eraser bits. Working, as always. They hadn't been home from their business trip for twenty-four hours, and they were already elbow deep in more work. Jackie knocked on the door, and upon hearing Ezra call to her, she walked inside.

"Hey, Jackie," Ezra said without diverting their attention from the task at hand.

She closed the door behind her and ambled over to Ezra. "Did you get any sleep on the flight from LA last night?"

Ezra shook their head as they erased another line on the thick paper, dusting the eraser debris to the floor. All too familiar with the expression on their face, Jackie left her sibling alone, not wanting to disturb their flow. Instead, Jackie took in the familiar living room.

The only homey bit to Ezra's residence was the dilapidated holiday cactus on the mantle of their fireplace, the plant having drooped considerably since the last time she'd been over, its shed leaves piled on the hearth below.

She plopped down on the stiff couch, sighing as she settled. Ezra's home was extensive and beautiful, though small. Everything was organized and held a definite minimalistic tightness, a stark difference from Jackie's beach house. Their differences didn't stop there; where Jackie thrived on chaos and clutter, Ezra required organization, tidiness, and order. Jackie couldn't stand the cleanliness. No house pet, no company. Ezra traveled far too often for work to own any critters, which Jackie always found lonely, but it didn't seem to bother them.

Ezra stood, brushing the eraser bits from their gray trousers resolutely before walking over and sitting beside Jackie. They touched her wrist and their warm smile fell. They cleared their throat and fixed a pointed stare at Jackie. "The next time I leave town and you neglect to inform me that you don't have enough of what you need to survive, I'll kick your ass."

She grimaced. "I wouldn't have purposely done that to myself, you know." Their reprimand hadn't come as a surprise; in fact, she expected as much when she texted them before leaving her house that morning, asking for blood. She picked up a massive atlas from the end table beside the couch, no doubt a book only present for decorative purposes, and opened the cover. "This is a big book. Are you planning on traveling more of the world?"

With a tilt of their head, Ezra gave her a pained smile. "I worry about you sometimes, you know? How am I supposed to make sure you're good when you don't communicate with me? When I left, I was under the assumption you had all that you needed."

"I didn't expect my useless cats to let a rat chew up the power cord for my mini fridge, and I hate taking more than I need. I found ways."

"What, the nasty drink you buy off that dude?" Ezra asked, one eyebrow lifted. "You really need to get over your aversion to blood, or you're going to kill yourself."

"No! I went beastly and had someone who offered."

The room was quiet. Ezra blinked at her a few times. Their mouth twisted in a wicked smile. "You went beastly and fed off someone, like a real, living person?"

Jackie continued to thumb through the atlas, pretending to be oblivious to their statement. *Maybe if Ezra thinks I didn't hear them, they'll just drop this.*

Ezra sighed, folding their legs under them. "I'm sorry. I know you have it different than me, but Mom's worried about you."

No such luck, she thought with a long sigh. "When *isn't* she worried about me?" She looked up from the book to see a pained expression fill Ezra's face. Their parents lived in Philadelphia, and regretfully, she hadn't been to see them in a few months; not as though she didn't miss them, but she didn't want a lecture from her mother. "Well, now you can tell her not to worry, but I'm telling you that was a one-time thing. The elixir works just fine, and then I don't have to take more blood than I need, no matter where it comes from." She shrugged, as if this answer would satisfy their curiosity.

Ezra pursed their lips. "But what is it really doing to you?" Jackie couldn't answer their question. The elixir allowed her to live her life the way she wanted without taking blood directly from people. She didn't *want* to know if there were any long-term side effects from it because she didn't have a choice. With Roz being her only source other than donated blood, and the occasions few and far between, Jackie had to do what she needed to in order to survive.

"I don't want to take blood from people who need it more than I do," she said, referring to the donated blood she received from Ezra. With each pint she took, she figured that was one less in storage for humans who needed it if they were in a medical emergency. She couldn't help but feel a strong guilt for taking *any* of it.

"*You* need it to survive, too, so you have no reason to feel that way. You can't go through life only taking blood from Roz."

She knew they had a point, but she shrugged and changed the subject. "I heard from Roz's mom," she said, knowing the diversion would help the conversation fizzle out. "She told me Roz took a position in California. She was surprised I didn't already know."

"Huh?"

Jackie nodded. "Yeah, and her mom had spoken to her just a week before answering me, so she's obviously avoiding us."

Ezra looked at her with skepticism. "That doesn't sound right. Why would she not say anything to us?" Without another word, Ezra disappeared down the hall, muttering under their breath. Jackie waited patiently, glancing back at the map.

Mumbling something inaudible, Ezra hurried back into the living room with their tablet in their hands, furiously scrolling. "I heard from a friend there's something going on with the Grim lately: some shady stuff." They glanced up at her. "Have you heard anything?"

"Not really." Jackie wondered if they meant Brent's meddling in Fae business, helping Collin achieve his dual citizenship, but she didn't want to provide Ezra any information they didn't necessarily need, especially when they didn't particularly like Brent.

Their brow creased and they continued to scroll. "I'll ask around to see if this has anything to do with Roz. I've got a few friends who can keep an eye out for her. Does your little potion friend know anything?"

Jackie rolled her eyes at their comment. "No, he's just as dumbfounded as I am. The weird thing is if she did move to another location, taking up a job with the Grim, she would've had to go through Brent. He would know because he's basically her boss."

Ezra shook their head. "This sounds super fishy. She wouldn't miss Samhain."

"You're right; she wouldn't miss that for anything." The three had celebrated holidays together since they were children and continued the tradition well into adulthood as much as possible.

Though Roz's unpredictable healthcare occupation and Ezra's travel requirements for their business made it nearly impossible for them to come together for every holiday, the three always made time for Samhain. Even after Roz grew apart from Jackie, she held contact with Ezra and never missed their annual gathering.

Jackie's phone chimed, and she pulled it from her pocket. The text was from Margo, confirming the time and address they were supposed to meet later that evening. Jackie ushered Margo out the door the other night for two reasons: she worried how her body would react to the new elixir, and she also didn't want to breach Margo's privacy a second time even though Margo invited Jackie to bite her. Her body ultimately accepted the new drink the same way as the other one, causing her discomfort before relief, but Ezra's question left her worried about the potential harm. What *was* she doing to her body with the elixirs Brent made?

"I'm sure Roz would've told us to leave her alone if that's what she wanted. She wouldn't go through all this trouble to avoid us unless something serious was going on."

"For real." Jackie slipped her phone back in her pocket and nodded. "I'm still irritated. Even if she's in trouble, she should've reached out to one of us." Jackie didn't agree with many of Roz's life choices as of late, and she worried Roz had finally gotten herself tangled in dangers even she couldn't con her way out of.

Ezra dropped their gaze back down to the tablet again, engrossed in whatever the screen showed. Jackie checked the time and noted she needed to get going, or she'd be late to her date with Margo. "Thank you again," Jackie said, gesturing to the canvas bag of blood as she lugged it over her shoulder. "I've got to get going."

"Hot date?" Ezra asked as they lifted their gaze, throwing her a mischievous grin.

Jackie smiled. "Kind of."

AT 5:45 P.M., Jackie pulled her car up to the pizzeria and parked. She picked the restaurant strategically, as it was only a few buildings down from the antique shop she frequented. She dropped off the blood from Ezra into her working refrigerator before she hastily got dressed and hurried off to her date with Margo.

She climbed out of her car and made her way to the pizzeria. Margo stood just inside, head bobbing to inaudible music, her hair swaying with her movements. Jackie smiled to herself as she approached, noting how adorably awkward Margo was when she didn't think anyone was watching.

Margo's head turned as Jackie walked inside, and a large smile replaced her prior blank stare. "You look great," Margo said, the statement more sincere than Jackie imagined it should be.

She glanced down at her wrinkled skirt and band T-shirt questionably. "Well, thanks."

After they got their food, Jackie nudged Margo toward the door. "All right, I've got a nice spot we can eat this." Jackie pushed through the door of the shop and into the crisp evening air. The sun set fully, draping the city in a haunting twilight as they walked away from the pizzeria. The homes lining the semi-residential street were all dim, including the shop itself.

"Where are we going?" Margo asked.

Jackie didn't glance back as she said, "Not far." The antique shop was owned by a friend from art school, Thor, who was built like a grizzly but was as soft as a teddy bear. Most of her antique furniture originated from his shop, save the random finds at garage sales and flea markets. She adored the dusty space so much that Thor provided her with a key in case she needed a fresh setting to yank her from the depths of artist's block. Red brick etched the frame around the double doors and block letters on a small hanging sign stating CLOSED.

"Just follow me." The three-story building, circa somewhere in the early 1900s, stood tall compared to the small pizza place beside it. She led Margo down the path off to the side of the building, and she dug around in her purse until she located the key. Grass peeked through rough cracks in the cement walkway, and little stones scattered as they walked, displaced by their footfalls.

She unlocked the door and grabbed Margo's arm to tug her inside.

"I know people say your criminal record is sealed after you turn eighteen and all," Margo started as they shuffled into the small backroom of the antique shop, "but, I don't want to test that theory out."

Jackie laughed as she shut and relocked the door behind them. "Don't worry, I know the owner, and how would this be breaking and entering when I have a key?" Darkness shrouded the room, but Margo's smirk was still evident. The backroom contained Thor's workshop. Two worktables were shoved against a wall, one weighed down by a cast-iron sewing machine and the other littered with spools of thread and furniture polish. Jackie kept hold of Margo's wrist and navigated them through the room to the staircase off to the left. Although she switched on the light, the bare bulb hanging above barely illuminated the space. With each step, the stairs groaned in protest.

"Jackie, this is verging on a whole new level of creepy I didn't even know existed," Margo voiced as they hit the landing.

She turned then, staring down at Margo. "Says the woman who makes a living helping ghosts to the ethereal plane."

Margo made a noise in the back of her throat, which sounded like stifled laughter, and she nodded. They continued up the stairs until Jackie had to pull her keys out to unlock another door. The little piece of heaven her friend loaned her, a silent space to work out any block that could possibly plague her, stood before the door. The attic space was—not unlike her own home—crowded with a beautiful mismatched assortment of furniture, not all antique.

"This is where you get all your funky furniture from," Margo chortled, the sound so seldom heard coming from her that it caused Jackie to giggle herself.

She placed her greasy plate of pizza on a broken table, shed her coat, and draped it over a dusty mirror next to the table. "Yeah. Thor and I trade stuff back and forth. I find crap at yard sales; he likes to buy storage units. He lets me use this space from time to time if I need a change in scenery from my place."

"Huh." Margo plopped her own plate next to Jackie's before she wandered through the room, trailing her fingers over the suede avocado-green couch straight out of the seventies and then over an intricately carved dining room chair. She pulled her hoodie up over her head, revealing a plain black T-shirt. "There's quite a variety," she chuckled, amusement in her tone. Her blonde hair fell into her face as she inspected the detailed painting displayed on the side of an armoire, framing her sharp jawline. Her dark tattoos spread over her arms, disappearing under her shirt that strained against her breasts as she put her hands in the back pockets of her jeans and leaned back, head tilted to gaze up at the chandelier hanging from the ceiling. Heat bloomed in Jackie's chest, creeping up her neck—heat that had nothing to do with bloodlust. Margo straightened and went over to the oval window overlooking the bay.

"This view is amazing."

Twilight had taken over, and the full moon rose over the water's surface, projecting light into the large window. Moonlight shimmered in Margo's eyes, a dazzling display that sparked a profound desire in Jackie. She needed to draw her. "I have a really odd favor," Jackie said as she moved closer to Margo.

Margo tilted her head back to stare at her. "Okay."

"Could I...uh...could I draw you?"

Margo's tongue snaked out, swiping her bottom lip. "I feel like I've suddenly been transported into a cheesy romance movie, but okay."

"You sure?"

She shrugged. "Yeah, why not? Do you want me over on that thing?" Margo asked playfully pointing to a large chaise lounge. "Or, wait, how about I spread out on the rug?" Without waiting for a reply, Margo crossed the room and stretched out on an ornate rug depicting a lush rainforest. She repositioned, lying on her side, one elbow bent, hand supporting her head, while the other fell in a relaxed pose. Her hair hung over her forehead and her posture held a sense of ease. The moon's rays cast white light over her pale face, illuminating her vibrant eyes. Although she knew Margo's behavior was intended to be facetious, her position proved perfect.

Jackie yanked her sketchpad from her purse, turned the light off, and grabbed a set of charcoal pieces she kept tucked away in a tiny drawer by the window. "I think this will do just fine. Try to be super still."

"You got it, boss." The smirk on Margo's face would suffice. Jackie began her initial sketch, outlining Margo's body, from the stray locks falling into her face, to the curve of her hips, and down to her boots. Keeping to her word, she lay incredibly still, her gaze never leaving Jackie's.

The sketch didn't take very long, the edges rough, and though nearly complete, it seemed to be missing a vital component. Jackie couldn't capture the intensity of Margo's stare. Determination knitting her brows, she rose from the chaise, crossed the room, and stood over Margo. Margo lifted her gaze and Jackie drew a sharp breath when she noticed the red wisps flowing into her eyes, wondering what struck the match in that gaze, a trace of flame curling in the whites of her eyes, faintly, barely perceivable if one didn't know to look. "All done?"

"No. Could you lie on your back for a second?" Jackie requested.

Margo paused before moving. "Uh, sure." When she settled on her back, hands cupped behind her head, Jackie leaned closer with her sketchbook, staring at the dancing fire motes in Margo's eyes, knowing she could never recreate the depth. Regardless, she stepped one leg over Margo and lowered herself to the top of Margo's waist. She squinted, her hand moving over the page as she took in the finer details of Margo's face. She was beautiful, her soft lips full, tiny freckles spread over her cheeks, and her blond lashes were longer than Jackie noted before.

Margo watched her, the rise and fall of her chest slowing. Jackie realized she'd stopped breathing. "I asked you to sit still, but I didn't tell you to stop breathing," she said jokingly.

"What are you doing?" Margo murmured.

"Shading," Jackie said. No humor shone in Margo's eyes.

Margo's mouth opened, as if to say something, but her lips rapidly shut. Jackie stopped drawing, suddenly aware of their contact. In her trance-like need to draw, so focused on the art form of Margo rather than the woman herself, Jackie neglected to acknowledge her attraction. Had she really climbed on top of her? Oh, yeah, she had. *In a skirt, no less.* Jackie let herself get so immersed into the portrait, she hadn't thought about her actions before she'd moved, briefly not taking Margo for what she was: a beautiful woman. A beautiful woman she was sitting on top of—who she'd kissed, who she wanted so much more with. She may have even crossed an unspoken boundary between them. Margo looked up at her, unblinking, with the same fire that raged in her gaze when Jackie had pulled back from biting her previously—the look which held not fear, neither trepidation nor disgust, but fierce longing.

A blush painted Margo's face crimson to match her eyes, and Jackie's own cheeks burned with embarrassment. "I'm sorry," Jackie murmured. When she went to stand, Margo gently grabbed her free hand.

"No worries." Margo said, her voice breathless and heady. No, perhaps Jackie was projecting her own feelings on Margo, as warmth blossomed through the rest of her body. "Can I see?"

"Let me finish." Margo let go, and Jackie quickly rose from her position and moved over to the window for the moonlight. The product seemed as complete as it would get, save an outline with a fine-tipped felt pen. She wanted to gaze down at Margo again; actually, she wanted to climb back on top of her and kiss the smirk off her face. She stared down at the portrait. The sketch was lacking something, and she could pinpoint exactly what it was, too—no matter what she did, Jackie knew she wouldn't be able to capture the beauty in Margo's eyes, the haunting gaze she held, a sadness hidden deeply behind the blue. Maybe her perspective was skewed from her brief trip into Margo's emotions. *And this is a perfect example of why I don't bite people.*

"Done?" Margo asked. She sat on the rug and kicked her legs out.

"I guess." Jackie shrugged as she crossed the room and offered the pad to Margo. "You've got wild eyes. I can't get them right," she said flatly.

A smile played at the edges of Margo's mouth as she stared at the portrait. Slowly, she lifted her gaze to Jackie's, her hair falling away from her face the farther she tilted her head. "This is fucking awesome, and I'm not just blowing sunshine up your ass." They stared at each other for what could've been hours but realistically she knew was more like a minute.

Jackie reached for the pad but instead of giving it to her, Margo took her wrist and urged her down onto the rug. She plopped down beside Margo, giggling. "Do you need another close-up?" She opened her eyes wide, a playful grin on her lips.

Jackie snatched her drawing pad from her and scoffed. "No, you're too complicated to draw. It's as done as it's going to get, my friend."

Margo's smile vanished as she cupped Jackie's cheek in her right hand and pressed a soft kiss upon her lips. Jackie closed her eyes and shuddered a satisfied breath. *Why is this infuriating woman so intriguing?* she wondered as she parted her lips. Margo's tongue caressed her own, and Jackie hoped Margo wouldn't flee during this kiss like their first.

She pushed Margo onto her back, climbing over her as she had when she attempted to draw her face. "Okay, I guess I could go for another close-up."

Margo gripped Jackie's sides. "I've never had someone draw me before. It was interesting."

"You could've fooled me," Jackie murmured, tracing Margo's ear with a finger. "You were the perfect subject."

Margo closed her eyes as if lost in Jackie's touch. "You're talented, Jackie," she whispered. "Like, incredibly."

Black vines peeked from beneath Margo's shirt, and Jackie traced their edges with her fingertips. A soft sigh left Margo, and the noise seemed far too gentle to have come from her. "So, besides reaping souls, what do you do to keep yourself busy? Surely, the stipend alone doesn't support your smoking habit."

"I-uh," Margo stuttered. She cleared her throat and opened her eyes. "I do handyman work here and there under the table."

Jackie smirked and switched to Margo's other ear, caressing the obviously sensitive skin. "What type of stuff do you do?"

Sighing softly, Margo said, "You know, boring stuff like replacing drywall, simple plumbing, and—" She paused again when Jackie tugged gently on her earlobe, exhaling rapidly. "—I've even replaced a couple roofs."

"Your skills sound expansive and varied." Jackie never imagined herself seducing someone with carpentry talk.

"Uh-huh." Clearing her throat a second time, Margo opened her eyes, gaze smoldering. "I'm not licensed though."

Jackie stirred the wispy hair beside Margo's ear, causing Margo to close her eyes again. The expression on her face softened, and she relaxed under Jackie's touch at her neck. "Do you ever think about going to school to get licensed?"

Margo said nothing, but her lips parted in a soft moan as Jackie pulled her hair.

Need ignited in Jackie's gut, and she leaned in to kiss her. What harm could come from expressing her desires? Jackie partook in one-night stands, and if Margo shared her interest, that's all this needed to be. Just because

Jackie longed to dive into Margo's head again didn't mean this had to be more than a fling.

Jackie broke the kiss, panting slightly. "Margo." Margo opened her eyes. "Would it be okay if I touched you? I don't want you to feel pressured or—" Margo cut her off.

"Yes," Margo said on an exhale, gripping Jackie's sides with her palms. Jackie kissed her again, harder, fiercer than before.

Margo drew a sharp breath through her parted lips as Jackie unbuckled Margo's belt and slid her hands on either side of her hips, edging them lower. Their kiss broke, and Margo eyed Jackie, then glanced down at her hands before meeting her stare again. "You don't waste time, do you?"

Answering with a smirk, Jackie kissed her again. Margo's arms encased her in a warm embrace as she reached down and eased Margo's belt loose. Jackie moved down Margo's body, watching as fire coalesced in the whites of Margo's eyes, smoldering in a vivacious exhibition.

She tugged Margo's jeans down, pulling her boxers free along the way. She trailed her fingers up her now bare thighs, never dropping her gaze from Margo's, their eye contact as heated as the fire that burned in Margo's pupils. Her hands met at the apex of Margo's legs, running her fingers through the soft curls. This proved to be too much for Margo, and her head fell back on the rug as the air left her lungs in a long sigh. Jackie moved her hands back to Margo's thighs as she placed a soft kiss above her mound, and she watched Margo attempt to grip the rug, coming up empty-handed.

She crawled back up Margo's body, slipping her hands under her shirt and claiming her lips fiercely. Margo grasped Jackie's thighs as she grazed Jackie's tongue with her own.

"You can bite me, Jackie." Margo spoke with such confidence Jackie couldn't find a shred of trepidation in her statement. She trailed her tongue over the soft crook of Margo's neck and up captured her earlobe between her lips. Margo sighed, pulling Jackie tighter to her. Jackie breathed in the scent of Margo's skin, relishing in the delicate aroma of rain and a hint of musk. She ran her hands further beneath Margo's shirt, teasing the hem of her sports bra. She nibbled Margo's ear, causing the woman under her to squirm and draw a sharp breath. "Bite me," she moaned, her stoic resolve, a crumbled mess on the floor.

"No, I don't want to see anything you don't want me to," Jackie murmured against Margo's parted lips. Margo exhaled through her nose, lashing her tongue out at Jackie's mouth, but Jackie moved away, gazing down at Margo's reddened cheeks before helping her out of her shirt and bra. Jackie traced her finger over the dark swirls of Margo's tattoos, the abstract roots coming together over her shoulders, disappearing behind her. When her lips met Margo's breasts, Margo brought her hands up, nails digging into the skin of Jackie's back. Her heartbeat thrummed through her chest, vibrating against Jackie's mouth as she took a pebbled nipple between her teeth, nibbling gently.

Jackie moved to taunt Margo's stomach, swirling her tongue in the divot under her hip, barely making contact with her mound. "Please," Margo whispered, her voice husky with arousal. Jackie gave in, running her tongue over Margo's center, eliciting a long moan from her.

To witness the rough woman so vulnerable, her chest heaving, back arched, perspiration glistening between her full breasts, arms high over her head, nearly sent Jackie over the edge herself. Margo moaned, fists clenching her own hair as Jackie wavered her tongue over her clit. Hips lifted to meet Jackie's mouth, and Jackie slowed, wanting to prolong the ecstasy. A disgruntled groan resounded from above, and Jackie tried not to giggle. Instead, she quickened her speed, running the length of Margo's slit with her tongue, lingering long enough to elicit a low groan from her.

She slipped a finger into Margo, lashing her tongue over her clit. "Jackie," she breathed, her chest heaving when Jackie glanced up at her. The patch of moonlight now spilled over Margo's naked legs, bathing her in iridescence. "Fuck, Jackie, keep going," Margo moaned, her voice muffled in the crook of her arm.

Jackie slid a second finger into Margo, capturing her flesh between her teeth, flattening her tongue. Margo writhed beneath her, hips bucking, breath hitched. Her breath stopped altogether, lips parted, eyes closed. Fearful, Jackie nearly stopped her action until a moan left Margo on a breathy exhale, her body shuddering, muscles tight.

Margo reached down, urging Jackie to her. Jackie obliged, moving back to settle against Margo's bare chest. Her breath evened to a normal pace, and she kissed Jackie's forehead. Jackie shifted position, hovering over her again. Pulling her skirt up, Jackie pressed her bare thigh against Margo, earning herself a sharp intake of breath. "Can I bite you, Margo?" she murmured against her skin.

"Yes. I want you to." Margo's reply was breathless. Her eyes were closed, hands clutching Jackie's back and lips parted as Jackie pushed her thigh harder against Margo's core. Jackie leaned forward, knotting her fingers in Margo's hair as she brought her mouth to her neck, rocking her thigh. A moan left Margo when Jackie pierced her skin as gently as she could. Margo arched upward, nails digging into Jackie's back through her thin shirt.

When she closed her eyes, Jackie was engulfed by Margo's thoughts, her desires, the budding fervor she held for Jackie, but there was something else, hidden in the deep recesses of her mind. Warmth surrounded her again, but Jackie delved deeper, searching for a hint of what Margo was hiding from her. Darkness, swirling in depths of Margo's subconscious, black rose petals falling in a sharp breeze, gathering on the earthy ground. Jackie pushed forward, searching the void. Malevolence, thick and tenacious. No, that wasn't right. A blue flame flickered to life, illuminating a single frame. Jackie couldn't decipher the scene, too confused by the ambiguity the imagery presented.

She tried harder.

Sparks flared, Margo's body tensed, her arms tightening around Jackie. She moaned, her head tipping to the side, exposing more of her neck to Jackie. A roadblock, a firewall, a stronghold Jackie couldn't burst through, furthered her need to know what Margo was hiding from her.

"Jackie, stop," Margo whispered.

Jackie drew back, wiping the blood from her lower lip as she sat back on the rug as she took in Margo's disheveled state, tufts of blonde hair sticking up and a trail of blood slithering down her neck from Jackie's bite mark. "I'm sorry. Did I hurt you?"

Margo shook her head. Flames licked her irises, stark against the whites of her eyes, and Jackie pretended not to notice. "No, you're good. I just want to touch you."

Jackie didn't believe her. "Why does fire dance in your eyes?"

"Just a Grim thing, I guess," Margo whispered, fingers brushing Jackie's cheek. Jackie ignored the lie, too desperate to feel Margo's mouth on hers again, too focused on the bliss of Margo touching her skin.

She wrapped her arms around Margo's neck and yanked her down on top of her, the pair falling back onto the floor. Margo straddled Jackie's body, kissing her. A need, not the familiar painful pang of bloodlust but a throbbing desire filled Jackie; a hunger she knew only Margo could sate.

Margo stared at her, breathless and still red-cheeked. She touched Jackie's face, running her thumb over her cheek to her bottom lip. More than anything, Jackie wanted to inquire about the darkness, the shadows of which lay within the confines of Margo's thoughts, the firelight in her gaze. Nothing could've prepared Jackie for what she'd sensed the times she'd bitten her, the layers of Margo far deeper than anticipated.

Margo reached around her, Jackie arching to allow Margo to unclasp her bra, throwing it somewhere across the room. Hot lips kissed her neck, and Jackie closed her eyes once more, surrendering to the pleasure. Margo's hands slid up her stomach, over her ribs, cupping her breasts, raking nails over Jackie's abdomen. Her mouth showered her with kisses over her breasts and neck, offering small nips that made Jackie gasp.

Margo bunched Jackie's skirt up, caressing her thighs with her fingertips, drawing nearer to where Jackie longed for her touch. She teased her, grazing her inner thighs, easing her underwear down and out of the way. She returned her fingertips to Jackie's mound, but ignoring where she needed her touch the most. Jackie huffed impatiently, eliciting a chuckle from Margo, the sound pouring warm breath over Jackie's neck.

She opened her eyes, meeting Margo's gaze as Margo slipped two fingers into her, her thumb resting atop Jackie's clit. Jackie dropped her head back, exhaling a throaty moan. The surface of the rug scratched Jackie's back when she flattened again, her breath coming in quicker, rougher. The only sound in the room around them was the soft ticking of an old clock, mingling with the soft sounds of Jackie's sharp inhales. Jackie bit her lower lip, drawing blood as the pleasure engulfed her, muscles tightening throughout her body. Margo continued her movements, Jackie allowing her body to succumb to the weightless sensation in dizzying ecstasy.

"Holy shit," Jackie gasped.

Margo stretched over her body and rested her head on Jackie's shoulder, her breath spreading heat over Jackie's skin. She lifted her gaze and smiled at Jackie, a real smile, not one laced with sarcasm, with deceit or arrogance. Jackie touched her face, running her fingers through Margo's hair. Margo's eyes closed and she sighed. "Does your friend know you seduce women up here with the promise of a portrait?"

Jackie giggled. "No. Somehow I think he'd take my key back." She ran her fingers through Margo's hair, then traced Margo's jawline. Turning her head as she urged Margo to look at her, she whispered, "You're the first to reach that level of artistic achievement."

"Artistic achievement? Where's my award?"

Jackie pressed her lips to Margo's in a tender kiss. When she pulled back, she cupped Margo's cheek. "You're the only woman I'd want to seduce with a portrait."

Margo looked away. "I think our pizza is cold," she muttered, shifting their conversation.

Does she really think I do this often? And then she realized the permanence of her statement, no matter how truthful it was.

Goose bumps broke over Jackie's skin, and with great reluctance, she urged Margo off of her. They both dressed quietly, Jackie catching Margo grinning at her out of her periphery, which in turn made her smile even wider. Maybe she hadn't made Margo as uncomfortable with her comment as she'd thought. They grabbed their cold pizza on their way downstairs, and after Jackie locked up, they walked the dark path back to the sidewalk.

"I haven't been on too many pizza dates before, but I have to say that this one would top my list," Margo said as they reached their cars, placing her plate of pizza on the hood of her car while she fished her pockets for her keys.

Jackie halted her search by wrapping her arms around her. "I have a unique palate." A deep chuckle left Margo, reverberating against her chest as she gripped Jackie to her, filling Jackie with refreshed desire. Margo hadn't let go of her, and when she met Jackie's gaze, the same fire from before clouded her eyes, slightly muted as the red died down. "Please tell me what you are," Jackie pleaded. Margo let her arms fall, and Jackie took the cue, moving away from her.

Margo pulled her keys from her pocket, unlocking her car. "Some things are best left secret, Jackie."

Although she was disappointed, Jackie smiled softly. "Are you ever going to stop being so mysterious?"

Margo shot her a cheeky grin and raised her hands in the air. "You've got to get used to the fact that I am an *enigma.*"

Jackie closed the distance between them, squinting her eyes at Margo. "You really have an inflated ego, don't you?" she murmured before placing a soft kiss on the corner of Margo's mouth.

"I can't argue with your logic."

A GENTLE BREEZE caressed her face, soft and rippling like the ocean that lay beyond the sandy beach. The sand nearly scorched the bare soles of her feet, and the sun poured warmth over her back. Glancing up, Jackie took in the otherworldly hues of the sky, visible brushstrokes lining the silver clouds.

A lucid dream, she realized. Months had passed since she'd experienced one, and the revelation along with the strange recent events of her life left her with a deep foreboding. Glossy water licked the shore, spilling over the sand before receding back. She'd been to this dream beach before, nestling herself under the ever-present warmth from the sun and enjoying the calm. Meditation brought her to the same place.

Serenity. Peace. Tranquility. These qualities kept bringing her back to the only place she could find her balance. She was free from the physical stressors of keeping her beast at bay, holding back the bloodlust associated with her being, and splitting her two lives apart. Nothing bad would come of her here in her safe place, and she didn't have to veil herself in a disguise, depending upon who she was around.

A murder of crows flew overhead before dipping into the ocean. With each wave, they bobbed along with the oddly colored water. Streams of dark blue swirled with gray dappled with white brushstrokes. The painted landscape elicited a smile from Jackie, and she continued her walk down the beach. Puffy white clouds obscured the tangerine-tinged sun, causing thick rays to shimmer over the sand. Oh, how she wanted to paint the scene in front of her, to capture the elegance of the orange-glazed sand or the crows afloat on the water's surface. Light flickered in her line of sight, and she yanked her gaze from the bobbing black birds to the assaulting ray.

Jackie squinted to see where the glint had originated from. None other than Margo the Grim lounged against an overturned lifeguard stand, shaving a piece of driftwood with a thick pocketknife. The sun reflected on the metal surface and shone into Jackie's eyes again as she started toward the enigmatic woman.

The scenario was very similar to when the two women met for the first time in Brent's home. Margo's lip ring had caught a glimmer of light, shining directly in Jackie's eyes. Shortly after that, Margo had accidentally called her a vampire, and upon Jackie correcting her, Margo's response had been rude, leading Jackie to kick her in the leg. She assumed this is where her subconscious conjured the action from.

But this is different, Jackie thought. She'd dreamt of people before but couldn't recall the last time she'd brought someone within her place of serenity. Of course, Margo was Jackie's own doing, her own mental depiction of the Grim, dressed in red flannel pajamas, not that Jackie could ever imagine Margo wearing such an outfit to bed. Margo appeared so out of place but completely where she belonged.

"Hi," Jackie said as she stopped next to the lifeguard stand.

Margo looked up and smiled wide. "Well, isn't this fucking weird?" Her cerulean gaze was the strangest color Jackie had the pleasure to see. Margo's eyes reminded her of a precious stone she found at the beach one day, the vibrant azure kyanite calling to her from beneath the tawny sand. She still had the rock, tucked away in the tiny tin box beside her pillow along with a few other gems. However, a fire shifted alight within the woman's eyes, casting flames in the irises, something Jackie had never witnessed before meeting Margo. Whimsical. The last word Jackie would ever associate with the woman sitting on the ground had become the only descriptor relatively close to defining Margo in that moment.

"Sit with me," Margo offered, scooting over.

Jackie settled beside Margo, who lifted her arm and wrapped it around Jackie. Surprisingly, she found the contact incredibly comforting, and she nestled into Margo's side. This was *definitely* new.

"There's something to be said about the beauty of a crow's shadow," Margo muttered, her voice far off.

Jackie smiled. "What does that mean?"

Turning to face her, Margo offered her a crooked smirk. "I don't know but it sounded good, didn't it? It makes about as much sense as me being here. I feel like I stepped into one of your paintings."

The black bird hopped over, tilting its head to gaze up at Jackie. She held out her hand and the creature jumped onto the presented palm with a flutter of their wings. "I have to admit, I love crows. I think my background is to blame for that. Pretty sure all good Empusae have to love black cats and crows."

Margo chuckled. "I think that's a prerequisite, yeah?" The crow fluttered away.

Sighing, Jackie relaxed against Margo, placing her hand on Margo's thigh, surprised when warmth spread through her from their contact. "Usually when I have these dreams, I'm the only cognitive individual. I mean, besides the occasional talking animal. Why are you here?" Jackie didn't expect an answer because she didn't know why Margo was here. Obviously, the woman beside her wasn't *really* Margo, not in her dreams. The woman next to her was nothing but a figment of her own imagination, no matter how her subconscious rendered the real Margo.

"I don't know." Margo averted her gaze. "I wanted to be with you."

"With me?"

Margo blinked, her lower lip disappearing between her teeth. "Yeah. I don't know what any of this means. Fuck, maybe I'm having an existential crisis." Margo laughed loudly to her own inside joke that Jackie didn't get. "There's just something about you, and I can't figure out what it is. I don't think it's only because of the whole bitey thing, which is amazing, by the way." She smirked, cupping her hand under Jackie's jawline. "You're incredible."

Jackie flung her hair over a shoulder. "You're just addicted to me."

Sincerity passed Margo's face. "Yeah, I think I am. I wanted to text you but thought that would've been too weird." She smirked. "Not that this is any less weird," she said, glancing around at the painted seascape in front of them.

Jackie also gazed out at the water lapping at the shoreline, noting the soft brushstrokes of white foam lingering on the water's edge, the textured grains of sand at her feet. The calming rush of the ocean lolled Jackie into a comfort, one she sought when she came to this spot to be alone, to meditate. To share the intimate location with anyone besides the occasional talking animal was something she wasn't accustomed to.

"Jackie."

She turned to Margo again. "Yeah?"

"We can't be a couple."

A painful pang drenched Jackie's brief serenity. "What are you talking about?"

Margo frowned, her expression uncomfortable. "I have to leave; well, I *might* have to leave the country."

"Why?"

Leaning forward, Margo wrapped her arms around her knees, bunching up her pajama pants. Jackie never imagined witnessing fear on Margo's features, but she couldn't deny the dread marring her expression. "I can't tell you, but I have to leave America. There's so much going on with Corporate, and leaving might be my best option, for everyone's sake."

"You have to leave here?" Jackie whispered. No, she rationalized, this all stemmed from the talk she had with Ezra—the conversation about weird things happening with the Grim. Jackie shook her head, as if to shoo away the weird dream. It didn't work.

Margo peered up at the textured sky as a cotton candy cloud drifted by, her face pensive. "Yeah, maybe. Probably." She lowered her head and looked at Jackie. "If it comes down to it, I won't have a choice, Jackie."

"Yes, you do, there's always a choice. Why can't you just stay?"

"Seriously, you have no idea. That's not your fault; it's mine." She paused, shaking her head, then parting her lips as if to speak again but glanced down at her hands instead. Firelight twinkled in her eyes before she vanished from Jackie's dream completely, a vapor of mist left in her wake. A chill crept into Jackie's being, and she wrapped her own arms around herself as the cloud where Margo sat dissipated.

"I have some sick sense of creativity," she said to the crows meandering in the sand a few feet from her.

One of them bobbed its head at her and winked a black button eye. "I concur," the crow rasped.

Jackie withdrew her flip-flop from her right foot and threw it at the crow, rolling her eyes as she forced herself to wake up.

Chapter Fourteen

THOUGH A DAY had passed since Margo's date with Jackie, Margo's neck still bore the obvious redness of her bite marks. She touched the pink skin in the rearview mirror at a stoplight, smiling to herself. Sex in an awkward attic in the moonlight hadn't been on her list of expectations, but she was so glad it happened. *I guess the dream afterward was just a weird way for me to process the whole night.*

The light turned green, and she drove through the intersection, onward to the next reluctant soul on her list. She'd given Sam her own list of charges in hopes of pushing her a little further, hoping she could manage on her own—she knew Sam could do it, but she was having trouble with her current job. The location Sam gave Margo was on the southern end of the island, where the little summer homes were stacked in neat little rows, cookie-cutter lawns with white picket fences, a dog in each, no doubt.

However, the street in question was in a state of disrepair, the homes boarded, lawns in ruin, but the home where Sam's Jeep was parked in front was the worst. A caved roof topped the house, bare planks jutting out from the various holes, and shingles lay scattered over the brown grass. Margo pulled up behind Sam's Jeep. Sam sat on the curb beside her car, and upon noticing Margo, she lifted her hand in a short wave and stood.

Margo turned her car off and climbed out, lighting a cigarette as she stepped onto the broken curb. Not only did the house sit in disorder, but the neighboring structures were in shambles as well, the home perhaps still in ruins after the super hurricane a few years back.

The thin hoodie Sam wore rippled in the ever-present breeze coming from the bay, ruffling her hair as well. "I think we might have a problem with this one," Sam whispered as she ambled up beside Margo, smoothing her hair against the wind.

A spirit stood with their hands on their hips, positioned toward the skeleton of a house, baseball cap on their head. "Why?" Margo asked.

Sam scratched her head. "You remember the creepy dude on the bridge and the body he wanted us to find?"

Oh, great, Margo thought as she nodded. The spirit Sam referred to was far from pleasant, and his unfinished business involved finding the body of one of his murder victims.

"This situation is kind of the same but will be a whole lot harder. Her name is Shannon."

Just then, the spirit turned. She trudged over, her black work boots quiet over the dead grass instead of crunching as they would've had she still been alive. The frayed cap atop her head left a layer of shadows over her face until she was a few feet away. "Hi there," she said. "Are you the friend she was talking about?"

"Hi, yourself," Margo replied. "I'm Margo, and you're Shannon, right?"

The woman's nod was morose, which lead Margo to question how a movement could hold such strong emotions. "This place is pretty beat up, huh?"

A shrug with the same impact as the nod lifted the woman's shoulders. "Believe it or not, I bought this house for a steal," she snorted. "I thought I could flip the thing for a decent profit."

The house was her unfinished business? Margo knew things were never that simple; there was a depth to the situation she hadn't reached yet. "What stopped you from finishing?"

She took the ball cap off her head then, running her fingers through her shaggy blonde hair. "I was spending so much time out here trying to fix this place up. The property really took a hit during Hurricane Sandy, and I thought I could fix it up, sell it, and my husband and I could move out west. The last night I was here, I was exhausted. I'd been working on getting the roof taken down, and my buddy helped me out for a while until he had to head home for the night." She shook her head, cursing. Pain etched her face, and Margo stayed quiet until the woman gathered her resolve. "I left my toolbox up on the third floor and didn't want to leave without it. Stupid kids in this area will steal anything, so I went up there."

"You fell," Margo said slowly.

Shannon nodded. "I fell through the floor and ended up in the damn basement." She sighed then, a deeply profound noise which provoked a shiver through Margo. "My body is still down there. Nobody ever found me. My husband came around searching for me along with a few of our friends. He thinks I took off."

"Seriously?"

"You don't believe me? Come look for yourself." Shannon turned on her heel and walked back to the house.

Though her comment was made at Shannon's husband thinking she took off—Margo didn't doubt her body remained unfound—Margo followed her to the decrepit building, Sam toddling behind them. The front of the stucco-faced house appeared well-constructed, aside from the obviously splintered roof. They walked through the doorway into what appeared to be a living room, but in lieu of walls, thick plywood held the floor above up. Twenty feet in front of them stood a gaping hole lined with jagged floorboards. Dust motes floated through the soft rays of sun beaming in through the hole in the roof. "The last owners did a number when they realized they were going to lose the house, and then the property sat unoccupied during the storm." Shannon made a *tsk* sound with her tongue as she circled the hole.

"Shannon, what can we do to help?"

She stopped pacing and peered over at Margo. "You can tell my husband I didn't walk out on him—that I've been here the whole time. Our anniversary was last month." She laughed without humor, placing her hands on her hips and looking up through the hole in the roof, sunlight shimmering through her spiritual iridescence. "I ordered the flowers months ago before I forgot—I forgot last year—and when he got them, he thought it was some sick joke, like I sent them from wherever I went to spite him. He needs to know I'm gone, and I still love him."

Crap, Sam was right, thought Margo. *This isn't going to be an easy one.*

Shannon gripped the back of her own neck and sighed. "I've got to get out of here for a second. This is too much." She turned and disappeared down a dark hallway.

Margo dared a glance over the rugged edge of the hole in the floor. Nothing was visible in the shrouded darkness of the lower level. There weren't many options. With the body by the bridge, Sam's excuse of going on a run and happening upon the victim worked but this was completely different. Coming upon a body by happenstance in an abandoned building in the middle of October held far too many chances of them becoming suspicious.

On one hand, they could leave the tortured soul for later, give themselves enough time to come up with a suitable game plan before helping her cross over. Another option would be to call the police, offering an anonymous tip. Margo didn't like this idea. Too many potential holes, too much potential for a murder investigation to be opened. She chewed her lip.

Sam stared at her expectantly, brown gaze uncertain.

"Hold on, I'm thinking," Margo said. Leaving Shannon wasn't an option; this would mean not getting the work done, possibly flagging Sam and Margo when they were under supervision, not to mention Brent, who was their superior. She knew the Board started keeping close tabs on their charges the moment they released them after their meeting, and she didn't want to risk an unfinished job flagging her or Sam.

"An anonymous tip will have to do," she said more to herself than to Sam, deeming this the safest option. She'd done it in the past, usually leaving the scene immediately to keep herself from becoming a suspect. If done carefully, it was a useful tactic for individuals who wouldn't move on if their bodies weren't found. She would've gone that route when she had Sam help the murderer by the bridge during one of Sam's first reapings but she'd already done earlier that week and didn't want to push her luck. Plus, Sam was a new face.

"We call the police and tell them there's a body down here? Don't you think that'll be suspicious?"

Reaching for her pack of cigarettes, Margo snorted. "Yeah, but we won't be here. We can do it from a pay phone as long as there aren't any cameras or people nearby and have a deception up. It'll be a piece of cake. All right," she said, exhaling smoke. "Go tell your new friend, and then we'll go find us a pay phone."

As they scoured the town for a working pay phone, Sam repeatedly informed Margo at each convenience store they stopped that she didn't think pay phones existed anymore. When they finally stumbled upon one at a rundown Wawa, they placed the call, dropped their deception, and got into Margo's car, leaving Sam's in the parking lot. Shannon refused to join them in their search, opting to stay with her body, suspicious of their promise to bring closure to her husband. By the time they drove past the house again in Margo's car to attempt to coax Shannon to come with them, two police cruisers were parked in front of the home, lights flashing. A small crowd had begun to form on the opposite side of the street, concerned neighbors flowing in to gawk at the spectacle. "We need to go back for Shannon, right?" Sam asked as Margo drove.

"We're going to park somewhere discreet, and then we can try to get Shannon to come with us."

"Okay," Sam said.

Two blocks away, they pulled into an alleyway and parked the car before heading in the direction of the house. As they rounded the corner, Margo noticed the crowd had grown double in size already, and she linked her arm with Sam's to keep from separating as they pushed through the people. The red-and-blue lights flashed over the faces of the crowd, casting eerie shadows over the broken asphalt at their feet. Across the street officers scattered around the grassy lawn, placing bright yellow tape from one side of the dilapidated building to the other.

Another vehicle pulled up to the curb. A familiar solid form rose from the driver's side of the unmarked cruiser, her sharp features highlighted in the fall sunlight. The same detective from their incident on the bridge. "Shit," Margo hissed.

Sam stared at her, brows drawn. "What?"

The detective's piercing blue gaze met hers, and Margo was sure this time she recognized her and Sam. "It's the same cop you talked to the day we helped murder man move on. Go," she said, shoving Sam through the crowd, ignoring the disgruntled remarks from the others gathered around. Sam shot her one more glance before obeying and disappearing into the crowd.

Though she knew it was futile, Margo snuck out of the crowd in the opposite direction from Sam. Placing a deception around herself was pointless, especially with so many people around. Humans tended to notice when someone disappeared right in front of them. The detective followed, her footfalls heavy behind Margo. She shoved her hands in the pockets of her jacket and sped up.

"Excuse me," the detective called out.

Margo stopped, steeling herself with a deep breath before she turned around and faced the cop. The same gaze stared at her with a ferocious intensity. Margo fought the shiver threatening to roll over her shoulders and down her spine. "Can I help you?" she asked. As the detective drew closer, Margo noted the familiar features separate from her eyes; the angular point of her nose, her prominent jaw and sharp cheekbones were far too familiar. Margo stifled a gasp.

"You've been following me," Margo whispered.

The detective nodded. "I have." She offered Margo her hand. "Detective O'Sullivan, but I believe we've met before."

Even with a few feet separating them, the power exuded off her like waves jutting off damp rocks and the heat of burning driftwood. *A Selkie.* One of Sam's first jobs happened to be for a murderer longing for his victim's body to be found and none other than Detective O'Sullivan was the one who'd questioned her. Grudgingly, Margo shook her hand. "Why the fuck are you following me?"

Visibly taken aback by Margo's cursing, O'Sullivan blinked rapidly before she answered. "I saw what you did in the woods for the elf halfling."

Collin was an elf. This made sense to Margo, the mysterious plants he tended to in his massive greenhouse, the foreign words he spoke directly to the greenery in his home, just as he had talked to the fallen tree in his backyard before he chopped the log into pieces. "You saw me?" Margo whispered.

"I did. Your power is as intriguing as it is frightening. Djinn aren't very common around here, which caused me to have my doubts. I followed you to see if you'd engage in the light bending again." She paused, turning her head deliberately toward the active police investigation. "You're also the one who turned a human with a blood bond, correct?"

Margo closed her eyes, drawing a sharp breath through her nose. Not only did the Selkie know she was Djinn, she also knew she'd created Sam. "Yeah. That'd be me."

She nodded, pulling a small metal-bound notebook from the pocket of her long coat. "I figured as much when I flashed a smile at her during my line of questioning. I knew she smelled like a Grim."

Margo stifled a shudder at the thought of Sam smelling differently due to how she became a Grim.

"You're quite the rule breaker, aren't you?" The crooked smile on O'Sullivan's face was unnerving.

"So, I've been told," Margo said through gritted teeth. *Fuck, now what?* She'd spent so much time, so much energy protecting the truth, and the woman in front of her had discovered it all with a few encounters.

With a soft click of her pen, O'Sullivan shifted the conversation. "This body? I assume you were the one who called it in?"

"Yeah."

"How long has it been here?"

Margo took her hands from her pockets and crossed her arms over her chest, scowling. "Shannon. She isn't just a body." Though she knew most Fae regarded the human population with distaste, mostly due to the continued decimation of the planet, Margo couldn't allow O'Sullivan to speak about a spirit in that way, even though the Selkie now held two of Margo's biggest secrets. She took a deep breath to calm her tone. "Her name is Shannon, and she said she fell about three or four months ago. There was never a missing person's case opened because her husband thought, and still thinks, she left him."

Undeterred by Margo's reaction, O'Sullivan continued to scribble notes on the pad. "So, there was no foul play involved?"

"Not that I know of."

"And her family hasn't reached out to the police at all?"

Margo shook her head.

O'Sullivan snapped the book shut and stared at Margo. "All right. I'll help you with this one if you agree to a conversation with me afterward."

Margo hoped the conversation didn't revolve around her newly splayed secrets, but she wasn't an idiot. "Deal."

DARKNESS FELL OVER the city in a torrent of slow-moving clouds, draping the streets in an eerie orange as rain took over. Soft droplets pattered against Margo's hood, and she lit a cigarette, her thumb sliding off the wheel a few times before she could get the lighter to flicker to life. After Shannon's body was removed from the treacherous basement of the home, her wallet was found in her back pocket, allowing her identification to be swift. While the rest of the investigation team stayed behind, scouting for clues to foul play that weren't there and determining the cause of death—which was obvious, of course—Margo and Shannon followed O'Sullivan to Shannon's home. Before leaving the area, Margo dropped Sam off at her car, sending her away before following O'Sullivan's unmarked cruiser. Part of Margo knew she should've kept Sam there for the experience, but she was grateful she shooed her away to another restless soul. If O'Sullivan spoke of her Djinn half in front of her, then Sam would know, which added to the already pressing risk of being a product of Margo. Knowledge was dangerous, and Margo had put Sam in enough danger.

Water raced down the gutter of the small cottage on the outskirts of town, spilling into the lush overgrown garden beds. Margo pulled her hood higher over her head, though she knew no one—save O'Sullivan and Shannon—could see her in the dark street with her deception cloaking her. O'Sullivan and her partner stood in front of the door waiting for the occupant to answer after their solid knock. "What if he doesn't believe them?" Shannon whispered beside Margo, worry lines straining her forehead. "He was so mad the night I didn't come home and the days after." Her lower lip trembled, tears in her eyes shimmering in the porch light. "I don't know if he'll believe it's really me."

Before Margo could answer, the front door opened, a figure silhouetted by dim light standing in the threshold. O'Sullivan spoke first, her tone muffled to Margo's ears by the falling rain and their distance. The man shook his head, speaking softly at first, then a single spoken word left him. "No!"

Shannon rushed to him, though he couldn't see her. He fell to his knees, O'Sullivan and her partner comforting him with soft voices. Margo stayed back, leaning against the mailbox as rain thundered over her. The pain was always hard to watch, but Margo couldn't look away as Shannon's husband openly sobbed on the porch. Eventually, O'Sullivan and her partner helped him inside, and Shannon disappeared through the closed front door.

I won't miss this, Margo thought to herself. But wouldn't she? Shannon could now pass on without dwelling, but Margo knew things were never this simple. Though her husband now knew she didn't up and leave him, the devastating pain of losing a spouse wasn't something he could easily rebound from, and Shannon may opt to linger as he waded through the transition of anger to loss.

Dampness spread from Margo's jacket to her skin, and she shivered in the cold. Her phone buzzed in her pocket, and she stole a glimpse as raindrops hit the screen.

Hey, Lady Enigma, got any plans for dinner?

The text from Jackie made her smile momentarily. She stuffed her phone back in her pocket before the device became soaked. When she glanced up, Shannon bounded toward her from the house, face resigned.

"How'd that go?" Margo asked.

Shannon stuck her hands in her back pockets and gazed back up at her home. What used to be her home. "He believes them." Shannon didn't look at Margo, her sight fixed on the house instead. "I don't know which is worse; him thinking I left him or him knowing the truth. At least when he was angry, this didn't hurt so bad."

Margo touched Shannon's back, a wave of sympathy swelling to a lump in her throat. "I'm sorry, Shannon."

Closing her eyes, Shannon nodded, tears spilling down her cheeks. "This is by far more painful than that three-story fall," she said sadly. She turned her head to stare at Margo. "Will I still feel this pain after I cross over?"

Margo tongued her lip ring before clearing the lump from her throat. "I don't know. When you cross over, your fate is your choice. If you choose to feel the pain, it'll follow you, but if you choose to move on, I think it'll diminish." *Or that's what I've heard.* The logistics of how things went after spirits crossed over was lost on Margo aside from what Brent had told her and what she actually listened to.

"Can I go now, please?" Shannon murmured.

"Yes." Power flickered to life in Margo's fingers, casting shadows on the ground from the light forming in her palms. The portal shuddered to life a few feet up the walkway to Shannon's home, luminous light gathering at the edges and gently swaying in the soft breeze.

Shannon took a few steps but paused, twisting back to Margo. "He'll find peace, right?"

"I believe everyone finds peace eventually. Time heals," Margo said, surprised at the softness in her words. As Shannon continued down the path, disappearing into the wavering door to the other plane, Margo wondered if there was any truth in her statement. Did everyone find peace eventually, and if so, did that include her? For the second time in a month, tears streamed down her face after the portal closed. Perhaps she would find peace after she left, when Luis and Sam were both safe from any negative influence bleeding from her.

Margo wiped her face and turned from the house, pissed the tears kept falling even as she lit another cigarette. The front door opened and closed, footfalls hitting the wooden stairs leading from the porch. O'Sullivan and her partner walked down the walkway back to their cruiser, her partner continuing toward the vehicle while O'Sullivan stopped in front of Margo. "Tread carefully, friend. Hold no fear that I'll speak of your secret, but do be cautious who you tell. Though you may trust the elf halfling and his Grim lover, others will not hesitate to disclose the truth. You know what your kind does to people like yourself."

"Yeah, no big surprise there. What did you want to talk to me about?" Tension and fear churned in her gut.

O'Sullivan drew her pale brows together. "I don't have much time." She glanced at her cruiser as her partner climbed in and then looked to Margo again. "Meet me at the 7-Eleven two blocks away in thirty minutes."

Margo bristled. "And why the hell should I trust you? How do I know you aren't setting me up?" *Walk right into a trap? No, thank you.*

O'Sullivan worked her jaw. "If I had the desire to condemn you to such a fate, wouldn't I have done it as soon as I discovered your truth?" The question hung in the dense rainfall.

Margo smothered a shiver. "Fine," she growled.

With a curt nod, O'Sullivan said, "See you soon."

MARGO SAT IN her idling MINI Cooper in the parking lot of the 7-Eleven for thirty-two minutes, smoking her fifth cigarette. Rain pummeled the roof, dampening her cigarette when she drew it back from the crack in the window. *Why the hell am I even here?*

If her curiosity hadn't been piqued when O'Sullivan discovered her split heritage, she would've gotten the fuck out of town that instance. Yeah, and curiosity slaughtered the cat. She needed to know what the Selkie had to say and she proved a valid point: if she wanted to throw Margo to the wolves of Corporate, she would've done so long before. Though, Margo couldn't decipher what was in it for O'Sullivan to tell them. Was there a reward for being a snitch?

Why was O'Sullivan involved in such a situation and, more importantly, why did she care what went on with a different race?

Fifteen minutes later, just as Margo had made the decision to leave, a police cruiser pulled into the parking lot and slowed as it made a circle around her MINI

Cooper. When the vehicle's hood faced the opposite of her own, the driver's window rolled down. O'Sullivan stared at her. Margo lowered her window and peered around her, noting an empty passenger seat.

"I assure you, I'm alone," O'Sullivan said.

"Hm," Margo grumbled as she lit yet another cigarette and waited. The rain continued, blurring her view of the detective.

"Are you aware of what your leaders are doing?" O'Sullivan asked after the bout of silence.

"They're giving all of us kickass bonuses?" Margo deadpanned.

O'Sullivan's face remained impassive. "People are dying as a direct result of their disgusting definition of pure. They're being murdered. Were you aware?"

Margo blew smoke through her window, nearly dropping her cigarette into her lap. "What do you mean?" she snapped without meaning to.

"Your leaders are killing anyone who isn't pure," O'Sullivan said.

A car barreled down the street, splashing water from a puddle into the parking lot like the rough surf on the beach.

Margo couldn't have heard her right. "Wait, what? They don't go killing people just because they aren't full Grim; they decommission them."

O'Sullivan chuckled without humor. "I'm sorry to be the one to tell you this, but there is no *decommissioning.*"

"There's no way." Margo shook her head, thinking about the upcoming hereditary census. Why would O'Sullivan know anything about this? Margo discredited her words. "How do you know for sure? You're not even Grim. Why should I trust your word?" Who the hell did this woman think she was? Selkie or not, police officer or not, she had no right to douse Margo in fear, to accuse the entire Board of murder. But, then again...

Margo stubbed her cigarette out and hid her trembling hands in her lap.

O'Sullivan's eyes narrowed. "I may not be Grim, but I am more of an ally than you realize." Static buzzed over the radio in the cruiser, and O'Sullivan tapped on the small screen in the middle console.

Could she be telling me the truth?

It didn't make sense. It couldn't.

Fae stayed out of the politics of others—they had enough turmoil in their own world to deal with, so why would O'Sullivan be interested in talking over the issues within the Grim? How could Margo trust her? If the situation was any concern to her, then Margo had to assume it involved Fae politics, which she wasn't going to get involved with. She made plenty of trouble for herself as it was.

O'Sullivan lifted her head. "I wish I could continue this conversation but—" A static voice chimed through the center console again and O'Sullivan's lip twitched. "Perhaps another time." She tugged a piece of paper from her pocket and reached out her window toward Margo.

Margo accepted the business card. Instead of the police department's information that Margo expected, only her name and a phone number were etched on the stocky card. Calliope O'Sullivan. The flowing font was elegant, far more elegant than Detective O'Sullivan appeared in their brief encounters, this one included. Raindrops splattered the card before Margo brought it into the car.

"We'll continue this conversation soon," O'Sullivan said. She closed her window and the lights atop her car flared to life before she sped out of the parking lot.

Margo shook her head as she read over the card again. *I fucking hope not.*

Chapter Fifteen

THE GENTLE INDIE music coaxed a soft smile from Jackie as she settled down on the worn leather armchair. Behind the counter, a barista dumped a cup of coffee beans into a grinder, turning the machine on and filling the coffee shop with a delicate mixture of noise. She glanced down at her watch, noting Ezra's tardiness, an unusual situation as Jackie was typically the late one. At 7:30 in the evening, the coffee shop was crowded with students from the high school in numerous study groups, some stopping to say hello to Jackie.

Earlier in the day, Jackie sent Margo a text with the intention of inviting her out for dinner even though they'd just seen each other the night before. When she hadn't heard from Margo, she texted Ezra and asked them out for coffee. Had she made Margo uncomfortable the night at the antique shop? It was possible she'd pushed too hard, asked Margo one too many questions. Or, maybe it was what she had intended the evening to be—a simple one-night stand and nothing more. Margo's behavior hadn't leaned toward splitting ways after their lovely night together, but what did Jackie know, especially with her comment?

Quit overthinking. It's not like I proposed to her. All she'd said was that Margo was the only woman she wanted to draw a portrait of, and she hadn't been lying. Jackie enjoyed drawing the portrait, so much so she'd love the opportunity to have Margo as a model again. In hindsight, it wasn't the smartest word choice while holding each other after a naked tousle on the floor.

She glanced down at her watch, wondering where Ezra was. Her phone skittered across the heavily grooved wooden table in front of her, and she snatched the device before it fell to the floor.

Just got your text. Sorry. I had a rough charge, and I'm soaked to the bone from the rain. What about another time?

A smile lifted the corners of Jackie's mouth as she replied.

What are you doing for dinner tomorrow? I found this awesome recipe for crockpot lasagna, and I'd love it if you'd be my guinea pig.

She swirled her spoon in the mug of coffee, nibbling on the croissant she'd bought with it. The memories of their recent date fluttered to life in her mind, and she smiled to herself. The dream her mind conjured left an odd taste in her mouth, causing her to wonder what her subconscious was trying to tell her. Was she allowing herself to become too caught up in the depth of Margo without thinking of possible consequences? Things were going quite fast between them, and Jackie wasn't sure if she needed to slow down. Maybe her subconscious was voicing a clear warning to her. *Maybe I'm trying to protect myself from her inevitable pushback, to tell myself to be careful and stay guarded.* Her phone buzzed across the table, and she snatched it, grinning. *So much for staying guarded,* she thought cynically.

Did you just use crockpot in the same sentence as lasagna? How the hell does that work?

Jackie's smile turned into a large grin as she typed back.

I saw this recipe on Pinterest that I had to try. Please be my guinea pig? We could have a picnic if it isn't raining. Or I could even snag us a spot up in the attic again.

The bell above the door rang and Jackie looked up from her phone. Ezra wandered over to the counter to order a drink. Jackie's phone buzzed again.

Hmm. Like a real date?

Jackie smiled at the gentle flirtation, chewing her lip.

Was our last date not a real one? And I don't know. Does crockpot lasagna constitute a date to you?

The chair on the other side of the table scooted across the floor, and Jackie looked up as Ezra plopped down, Danish dangling from their lips. "Hey," they said, muffled by the pastry.

"Wow. Look who's Mx. Tardy today. Usually *you're* the one giving *me* crap for being late."

Ezra bit a piece off and shrugged. "I had a few errands to run before I came over. The firm is planning a trip to Seattle," they said, sighing heavily. "This job is incredible, but geez, I'm tired." Ezra yawned wide, as if to further the validity of their statement. Though work was their life, Jackie noted the markings of fatigue darkening the skin beneath Ezra's eyes, weighing their shoulders down, and the haze in their stare. She worried about her sibling as much as Ezra worried about her. "So, I've asked around about the Grim and about Roz. Snagged myself a couple bites."

Jackie inched closer. "Yeah?"

They nodded. "I have." Ezra chewed another piece of Danish off before they spoke again around their mouth full of food. "Now, I expect no judgment from you, but I used to frequent a club, one which holds company of a few unsavory characters."

Jackie's smile widened as she listened.

"One of the last times I was there, I bumped into Roz; well, actually, *she* bumped into *me* while dirty dancing with the bartender. I haven't been there in, like, six months, but I'm still in contact with the owner," they said, gaze downward, attempting to avoid Jackie's. "The thing is, it's one of those revolving location clubs. You know, where they change location every night?"

"Yeah, a pop-up club. I know what you mean."

"Anyway, the owner, Monty, said a Grim by the name of Rosalind started working for his business partner about a month ago." Ezra broke another piece off their pastry and popped it in their mouth. "Super charismatic, charming, and handsome."

"That sure sounds like Roz," Jackie said. Her phone skirted across the table again, and she didn't grab it in time.

Ezra beat her to the phone, grabbing it and looking at the screen. "Oh, my sister has a date with someone named Margo?" Their crooked smile elicited a smile of her own. "Do tell."

"No," she giggled with a shake of her head as she snatched her phone back. "First, we talk about Roz; then, I'll *think* about telling you."

"You're no fun," Ezra sighed dramatically before reaching into their pocket and pulling out a small note pad. "This is where the club will be Friday night. Doors open at seven, but, fair warning, this is a *dark* club. They may not let you in. If worse comes to worst, drop my name, and tell them you're my sister."

Jackie stared down at the note Ezra handed her, their delicate handwriting etching out the name of a street she'd never heard of. She wasn't at all surprised that Roz found her way into a dark club, as she'd gotten herself into demon shenanigans before, but she was slightly shocked to learn Ezra had been to the club. "Oh, and all this time I've only been hitting you up for blood, and I could've been asking you for the ins to the dark clubs around here? Since when does my sibling have all the connections?" she jibed playfully.

The barista called out their name, and Ezra smirked as they stood, shooing her with their hand. "Yeah, yeah, yeah." They walked over to the counter to retrieve their drink.

Honestly, Jackie wasn't sure when Ezra had time to go gallivanting to the shady clubs of the ethereal world. She'd never been to one herself, and the thought was exhilarating but simultaneously terrifying. Had Margo ever been to one? Jackie bit her lower lip and blushed as she thought of Margo, remembering her phone vibrating. She peeked at the text window on the screen.

Sounds like a date to me, though I'm a little weirded out by anything made in a crockpot. Don't judge me too hard if I order pizza.

Jackie sipped her coffee as she replied.

I promise I won't judge as long as you actually eat it before it goes cold this time. How about seven or eight? Send me your address, I even deliver.

After she sent the text, she reread it and blushed, embarrassed at her silly shot at humor.

"Oh, my Goddess, are you *blushing*?" Ezra asked loud enough for the rest of the coffee shop patrons to hear.

Jackie shrank down in her chair, yanking the collar of her sweater in a feeble attempt to cover the red tinge in her cheeks. "Ezra, shut up," she snapped, feeling like a teenager again, her older sibling furthering the embarrassment with a teasing smile as they sat.

"Not until you tell me who this Margo person is. Is this the same someone you left my house in such a hurry for when I just got back into town?" Ezra stared at her, waiting as they brought their paper cup to their mouth.

"She's a friend of mine, and, yes, we met up the other night. So what?"

Ezra rolled their eyes, propping their chin on their knuckles. "Oh, don't you dare skimp on the details."

The playful banter had Jackie sitting straighter, a happy smile on her face. "Okay, she's a little more than a friend," she whispered. "She's a Grim I met by chance. It's a long story. You know my friend Lauren?" Jackie tried to condense the happenings of the last month, sharing as much as she herself could remember. Sam's death, Margo's intervention with the blood bond, Bethany's death, and the subsequent dominos that fell, including her own confession of what she was to Lauren. When she finished, Ezra sipped their coffee in silence.

"I wouldn't say we're dating, but..." she trailed off, unsure if she wanted to tell them the truth. "I think I want to be."

Ezra tilted their head, the only body language, or any language for that matter since Jackie began her explanation.

"She's kind of stoic, doesn't seem to do relationships." Jackie bit her tongue before she let it slip that she'd bitten her, that she'd seen the inner workings of her mind and knew she wasn't just Grim.

"Well, you don't purposely partake in relationships, either, sister, so don't count yourself out until you ask what she wants." Ezra shoved the rest of their pastry in their mouth. When they were finished, they added, "Are you okay if she decides you two won't work, or if she doesn't want to be in a relationship?" Ezra asked gently.

Jackie glanced at her coffee. Was she okay if Margo didn't want to further their relationship, unsure they shared even that? "I think so."

Ezra reached out and took Jackie's hand, and when Jackie looked up, the smile on Ezra's face was larger than Jackie anticipated. "She's cute."

Jackie scoffed, pulling her arm away from them. "What did you see just now?"

Instead of answering, Ezra sipped their coffee, a smug grin on their lips. "Nothing."

"I hate when you do that," she huffed, folding her arms over her chest in defiance. Clearly, Ezra saw something when they touched Jackie, their stubbornness withholding whatever the image was. She'd seen the expression before, the pompous, knowing sparkle in Ezra's gaze. The noises of the coffee shop seemed to engulf them in comfort, Jackie finishing the last of her coffee while Ezra polished off their pastry. After a few minutes, Ezra pulled out their tablet and began working, unsurprising to Jackie. Work was their sanctuary, what kept them grounded, and she always gave them room for it.

"You ready to tell me what you saw yet?"

Ezra pursed their lips. "Damn, she is going to give you a run for your money."

Jackie snorted in agreement. If Ezra didn't want to give her the details of their augury, she wasn't going to push. Inconsistencies in their intuition weren't impossible—quite the opposite in the frequency—and Jackie knew Ezra had grown leery of offering up their premonitions in case the image was incorrect or subject to influence. If they told her the future, she could inexplicitly change it by expecting what was to come.

"Do you want to check out the club with me on Saturday?" Jackie asked, steering the conversation to something less irritating.

Ezra glanced up from their tablet. "I'd love to, but I'm leaving for Seattle tomorrow morning for another conference, but you should probably take someone with you. Maybe that cute blonde you're infatuated with." The smirk on Ezra's face was far too smug.

Jackie kicked Ezra in their shin underneath the table.

Ezra drew a sharp breath, wincing. "Okay, I may have deserved that just a little bit."

"I didn't even kick you that hard," Jackie countered with a grin.

Elbow leaning on the table, Ezra propped their head in their hand and stared at Jackie. "I'm still not telling you."

It took every ounce of Jackie's strength to not kick her sibling again.

Chapter Sixteen

A SOFT RAP at the front door yanked Margo from the show on TV just as she'd taken her jacket from the coat rack to go outside for a smoke. Glancing at her watch, she knew she had a good few hours before Jackie was due to be there. The house still needed to be cleaned, dishes done... *This better not be Jackie, or I'm going to be beyond embarrassed,* she thought as she threw a glance behind her before reaching the door. Luis was still home, and although she loved her brother dearly, she would not put herself in the position where she'd have to deal with him telling obnoxious stories from their youth to a girl she liked before she could tell those stories to Jackie herself.

When she opened the door, Brent stood in the entryway, wearing a strange crooked smile. "What's up, boss?" Margo asked as she moved out of his way.

Brent walked inside and moved toward the kitchen counter without shedding his dark coat. "I've got something for you."

Margo followed him lazily. "More souls to keep company?"

"No, more like something to keep you inconspicuous next week when Corporate has the overhaul planned," Brent said, his words echoing in the small kitchen.

"Cool. What day is it exactly?"

"Monday."

Margo shook her head, laughing crudely. "The day before my birthday? Happy birthday to me." Worry knotted within her as O'Sullivan's warning rang in her head, one she had yet to inform Brent of. Would Corporate kill her if they found out she was Djinn?

"Don't worry, I've crafted something extremely unique to fit this situation," Brent boasted, laying his soft briefcase over the kitchen island. When he withdrew his hand, his fingers were clasped around a vial no larger than a spice jar. "Took me a few days straight to make this, and with the correct stewed tinctures and various ingredients I was able to barter from a few of Collin's associates, I think it's ready." The cheery grin on Brent's face did nothing to make the color of the fluid more appealing.

A strange squelching sounded from the jar as Brent placed it on the countertop, and Margo stared at it. "What the hell is that?"

"This"—Brent said, hovering his palm over the lid—"is one of the most complicated potions I've made in my life."

"Nice. Before you go into the long explanation of how awesome it is, I've got a question for you," Margo said, fishing for the business card from O'Sullivan in the bottom of her jacket pocket. "Do you know her? She saw us in the woods the day we opened the portal." The slight quiver in her voice nearly shattered her nonchalance.

He snatched the card from her hand, scanning the print. "Who saw what?"

"This Detective O'Sullivan saw us open the portal." Margo scratched her head and leaned against the counter. "She knows I'm Djinn, but she told me she wouldn't say anything, not that I believe her. She didn't seem to have any kind feelings toward Corporate."

"Calliope. I know this name, but I can't quite place it. What did she want? She's not human, but do you know what she is?"

Margo stretched her arms over her head to the mask the trembling in her hands. *What the hell is wrong with me?* Usually, Margo had no trouble portraying her give-no-shits attitude, but she found herself struggling. Though, it wasn't every day she had the threat of Corporate killing her. "Ocean City's finest and a Selkie to boot. We had a run-in when Sam first started, but I didn't know she'd noticed Sam wasn't a born Grim until our latest meeting. Oh, and she said the weirdest thing."

Brent watched her, his forehead crinkling.

"She told me that Corporate isn't decommissioning anyone, they're killing them." Clearing her throat, Margo continued. "Is that true?"

"She knows quite a bit." The expression that flashed over Brent's face confirmed her worst fear: O'Sullivan was telling the truth. What did this mean for her? No decommissioning. No bland life afterward.

"Is that what the census is for?"

Brent leaned against the counter, holding his chin in his hand as he contemplated his next words. "Collin and I have had our suspicions."

"Shit." The amount of knowledge the Selkie had was unsettling regardless of her intent to keep the information to herself. "Well, she told me to call her if I wanted to talk more about Corporate. She didn't really give me a straight answer when I asked how she knows about all this but claimed she's an ally. The Fae have enough of their own shit going on, don't they?"

Brent said nothing, chewing his lower lip. Eventually, he held up the card. "Can I keep this?"

Margo shrugged. "Sure. I've got no use for it." She wanted to call the Selkie, to inquire about what was happening, if she knew what the future held but she was also terrified. "She knows about me. She knows about Sam." Margo met Brent's gaze. "What happens if she decides to talk to the wrong people?"

Brent's jaw tightened. "I'll give her a call when we're done here. Hopefully, what I have here will eliminate the concerns we both share."

She nodded. *There I go again, letting him fix my problems.* She stifled the eyeroll intended for herself. She needed a distraction, something to subdue the terror running through her body. "Okay, fine. Back to the jellyfish gizzards you've brought me," she said, pointing her thumb at the jar.

"Yes, right. I found the recipe in a very old, very tattered book, but I think we can safely assume it'll work," he said in a hesitant tone, shoving the card into the front zipper of his briefcase.

"We can *assume* it'll work?"

The pause was long, heightening the lull from the TV. Brent scratched his head before letting out a long sigh. "The potion is designed to mask the genetic markers for your Djinn heritage, but it could damage your genotype."

"Damage. What kind of damage are we talking about here?"

He cleared his throat. "Damage beyond repair."

"What? Okay, you're still not spelling it out for me in simple terms, dude. What's the worst that can happen?" The thought of losing her power over light elicited a shiver over Margo's shoulders.

Brent stared directly at her, a flash of pity crossing his face. "If your body can't handle the degradation of the Djinn DNA, the potion could kill you."

Margo drew a sharp breath and glanced down at the counter. *What kind of shit decision is this?* she wondered crudely. *Either I'm killed by the assholes in Corporate, or I take a potion that could end up killing me anyway.*

"Margo," Brent whispered, touching her wrist. "I've been doing my best to advocate for you, not using your name specifically, of course, but I've been petitioning to stop this insanity before more people are harmed."

Folding her arms over her chest, she glanced up at him. "Any luck?"

He frowned. "No, not yet. My point is, if we can get through this with the aid of the potion, my hope is we'll see the end of this soon. I've made progress, but there are still a handful of Board members who are stubborn and idealistic."

Margo's stomach rolled and sweat prickled the nape of her neck, but she forced herself to take a deep breath. She didn't want to. She'd fought with herself daily since creating Sam, finally coming to a decision—albeit one she still wasn't sure about now—what could she do?

"What if I just leave?" Though she didn't know the exact details on how things ran outside of America, she knew she would be safe anywhere else, where the Grim were overseen but not micromanaged or held to some faux standard. They catalogued their dead but didn't push such restrictions on the Grim.

A deep furrow settled in Brent's brow as he shook his head slowly. "Leaving would be a terrible idea. For one thing, you could never come back, and there's talk of extending Corporate farther than the States to include all North America due to the low success rate with the alternative plan, although I think the way they run things outside our Corporate is much smoother and less traumatic for some spirits. You'd have to go overseas, and who's to say they won't find you there?"

Well, shit, there goes that idea.

"This is insane, Brent."

"I know."

"Why does it matter anyway? I get my shit done. I do the work. I try not to complain too much." The last part was a lie, but Margo said every word with conviction.

"You may have pissed off the Board by creating Sam, but you've begun the conversation, one that's been needed since the initiative passed ten years ago. If you leave…" he trailed off.

"You lose your bargaining chip," Margo snapped. *So, it's not because he actually wants to help me—he needs me for this stupid political battle.* She knew the assumption was unfair, as he'd done so much for her, but she couldn't help the instant mental rebuttal.

"No, you misunderstand. Margo, you are proof that someone with varied heritage can do the job. If they can realize how atrocious these acts are, maybe they'll stop and repeal the initiative."

"No, I get it. So, Monday is the blood test?" she digressed, glancing up at the calendar hanging on the wall before looking at him again.

Brent nodded. "Yes, and your meeting with one of the Board members is coming up. It's an unannounced situation, so we won't know until the day of."

"All right, I'll keep that in mind, and I'll try the potion. And if it doesn't work?"

"It'll work. Like I said before, the potion will degrade the part of your genetic makeup that's linked to your Djinn abilities, which is why it could ultimately harm you."

"Great," Margo muttered.

He touched her arm. "The possibility is very slim. I wouldn't be giving this to you if I thought the risk was too high. Do not take it until I give you the call."

"Okay." She shrugged her arm from under his hand and moved through the kitchen.

He gave her a pained expression before closing his briefcase. "I'll see you next week unless they spring your follow-up over the weekend, which I highly doubt."

"Cool. I hope not." She didn't follow him out. Instead, she picked up the vial, holding it under the light to stare at the pink sludge. Not unlike the elixir she'd brought to Jackie, the liquid could hardly be called as such. More like a gelatinous clump. Margo shuddered before sticking the jar on top of the fridge, far out of Luis's line of sight. Then, she grabbed cleaner and a washcloth from under the kitchen sink and began to clean.

A few minutes later, Luis's bedroom door opened, and his footsteps headed toward her.

"What the hell are you doing?" he asked from the doorway of the kitchen.

Margo cleaned the counter another time, leveling her gaze with the surface to ensure there wasn't a speck of food, not that Jackie would judge the cleanliness of her house. The cleaning was cathartic, easing her stress to a low thud in the back of her head. "What does it look like I'm doing? I'm cleaning."

Walking past her, Luis scoffed and opened the fridge. "Are we having company?"

Margo straightened and ran her fingers through her hair. "Kind of."

"Oh, yeah?" Luis asked, smiling wide.

"Jackie...she's coming over for dinner."

Luis laughed, grabbing Margo's shoulder tightly in his hand. "You can say I told you so if you think it'll make your little heart happy," she said.

Luis smiled wide. "So, does this mean you're staying?"

"What, because I have a date?" Margo chuckled.

Luis shook his head, letting his hand drop from Margo's shoulder. "No, because you're going to try the potion Brent made."

"And I thought you were showering, you nosy eavesdropper. Yeah, I'm going to try the potion." She ran the washcloth over the counter again, hoping the action would stifle her nerves. The apprehension she held toward taking the potion stained her thoughts. "I'm going to trust Brent's creation, and if that potion kills me, I will come back and haunt both of you."

They both erupted in raucous laughter, but within her thoughts, Margo wondered deeply, as she did when faced with death before: what happened when Grim died? Brent never broached the subject in his teachings, expressing to Luis and Margo they didn't need to worry about dying—death didn't come easy to the Grim, and they shouldn't worry when the event was far, far into the future. The whole "we'll cross that bridge when we come to it" attitude that Margo couldn't stand. She wanted to know, especially now with the likelihood of either the potion killing her or Corporate doing it if the potion didn't work.

"But you won't die," Luis said, nudging her with his elbow. "You're too fucking stubborn."

AFTER LUIS LEFT for work and Margo deemed her cleaning job sufficient, she sat on the couch and rested, flipping through the channels to find something to keep her thoughts from drifting to the upcoming census.

The doorbell rang and Margo nearly dropped her water. Placing the glass on the coffee table, she stood and straightened the dark button-up Luis helped her choose before he left for work. She headed to the door, eager to see Jackie's smile.

Jackie greeted her with a vibrant grin, lifting a crockpot. "I brought you real food."

"Nice. I didn't order any pizza," Margo said, moving out of the way. "Come in. Don't mind the mess—it's perpetual."

She directed Jackie through the entryway and into the kitchen, where Jackie plopped the container onto the counter, glancing around. When she took off her coat, the low-cut T-shirt she wore displayed the purple amethyst dangling from her neck, and jeans encased her long legs. "Doesn't seem messy to me. There's tons here, so dig in," she said, removing the lid.

Margo crossed the kitchen and pulled down two bowls. "Is that even a thing—crockpot lasagna?"

"Obviously." Jackie threw her an impish grin, shrugging. "You'll have to let me know what you think."

Together, they plated their own food, and Margo showed Jackie into the living room where they sat on the couch.

Margo took a bite of lasagna and hummed as she chewed. Garlic and cheese filled her senses along with a tang of tomato sauce and a hint of a spice she couldn't recognize. She took another bite, dumbfounded that each spoonful contained perfectly cooked pasta despite being cooked in a crockpot. "Holy shit."

Jackie held her spoon midair. "What?"

"I cannot get over how good this is."

"I'm glad you like it." Jackie chuckled and they both continued to eat.

"How long have you and your brother lived here?" Jackie asked after taking her last bite.

Margo looked around and smiled. "We've been here for a while now, since we moved over from Philly."

"You and Luis didn't grow up in Ocean City?" She tilted her head, surprised.

"No, but we've been here since we got out of the system. This has been home for Luis and me for a long time. He and I have stuck together since we first met."

"Does he do handyman work like you?"

"No, he's a nurse."

"I bet that line of work makes things a little easier for reaping, doesn't it?"

"Hm? Oh, yeah, I guess it does. He enjoys it. If you ask me, you couldn't pay me enough to deal with that many sick people in a given day."

Jackie smiled, the sight eliciting a flutter in Margo's chest. "People say the same thing about being a high school teacher."

"I can only begin to imagine how hard days can be," Margo laughed, placing her bowl on the coffee table. "I'm not too good with kids."

"Well, you got Anthony to cross over, and I'm sure he isn't the only kid you've had to help before. You never give yourself enough credit, Margo."

Margo cleared her throat, smiling before she changed the subject. "Do your parents live close by?" Picking up her bowl again, Margo leaned back against the couch to watch Jackie.

Jackie put a finger up, finishing the bite of food in her mouth. "They live right up in Philadelphia. What about you and Luis—do your parents live near here, or do they live far away?"

Margo scratched her face and studied the dish in her hands. Did she really want to scare Jackie away with her sob story? There were only a few things Margo truly hated in life: death and pity. "Actually, we met in foster care when we were young."

Jackie gave her a sympathetic expression. "That's what you meant by out of the system. Oh, Margo, I'm sorry—"

Margo cut her off, tone soft. "There's nothing to be sorry for. He's my brother, regardless of how it came to be. We were there for each other when no one else was. He's a good guy."

"He sounds like it. How old were you when you met?"

"I was pretty young, probably thirteen, and he was twelve. He got a lot of shit in school for just being who he is."

"A Grim?" Jackie inquired, puzzled.

Margo shook her head, not wanting to out her brother. "No, not that. How about you; is Ezra your only sibling?"

"Yep, just me and Ezra. They have a house up in Northfield, but they're always traveling around the country for work. I never knew an architect would have to travel so much."

Margo nodded as she chewed her food thoughtfully. Their conversation continued on the mundane path. They talked about growing up, school, their first concerts, pets—the pleasantly bland things that made up their lives. Margo laughed when she thought about the normalcy.

Jackie threw her a wide grin. "What's so funny?"

Margo lifted her bowl, shrugging. "This just feels so normal."

"Well, we're kind of normal."

"Jackie, we're anything but normal."

Jackie smiled sheepishly. "Okay, I admit we aren't all that normal, but it's nice to pretend sometimes, isn't it?"

Margo licked her upper lip and nodded. "Yeah, it is." She was just a girl, sitting on her couch with a girl she really, really enjoyed spending time with, like any other twenty-something lesbian. Yes, pretending to be normal was nice, no matter how fleeting.

"Do you ever wish your life could be normal?" Margo asked.

Jackie pinched her lips together, sighing through her nose. Her gaze wavered from Margo's face, concentration furrowing her brow. "I do sometimes. I wonder how my life would've panned out if I weren't an Empusa. I'd probably get bored." She laughed and Margo joined her. When she spoke again, her tone was light, but her face held sincerity. "For so long now, I've been trying to keep some level of normalcy in my life. That's why I use the elixir from Brent, so I can pretend, even for a fleeting moment, I don't need to take blood to survive."

Margo nodded. "I get it."

"But, if I had some plain, boring life, I wouldn't have met you." Jackie pressed a kiss to Margo's cheek. "Do you want some more food before I pack it up?"

Margo shook her head, finishing off her bowl.

When Jackie stood, Margo couldn't stop herself from taking in her lithe form. There was no denying the attraction she'd developed for her. If she was being honest, she'd admit the stirring began far before Jackie fed from her. The slight sway of her hips as she moved to the kitchen captured Margo's attention, but not as much as when Jackie turned and met her stare with a taunting smirk. Margo whipped her head back to the television, her cheeks hot.

She stood and made her way over to the kitchen to find Jackie ladling food into two containers she must've found in the cabinets. "You know, you cooked and brought the food. The least I could do is the damn dishes."

Jackie flashed her a crooked smile, a glimpse of teeth peeking behind her lips. "Don't worry about it." The bangles around her wrists clanked together musically as Jackie took the bowl from Margo and tossed it under the running faucet. Margo watched the sinewy muscles in her arm flex as she placed her own dish on the counter, trying to recall the last time anyone made her feel such a staunch desire. Her tee accentuated her breasts outlined in the light above the sink, and Margo looked away, a touch shameful for staring so blatantly.

The bowl in Jackie's hand fell into the sink, and Margo turned back to her. Jackie clutched her stomach, head bent and face in a deep grimace. "You okay?" Margo whispered, touching Jackie's back.

Blood dripped from Jackie's scalp, mixing with beads of sweat cresting at her hairline, the stark white horns bursting through. "Yeah," Jackie breathed, her state betraying her answer. "I'm sorry. I had no idea this was coming. This shouldn't be happening. I just fed from you two days ago."

Margo turned the faucet off with her free hand while rubbing her palm up and down Jackie's spine. "What's going on?"

"Bloodlust," Jackie whispered. "This must be because of the new elixir...I used to have more warning than this, and if I'd known, I would've fixed the problem before I came over." When Jackie finally lifted her head, her eyes were as white as the popcorn ceiling. "Margo," she murmured, the sound unfurling a desire within Margo that couldn't be put to words. Instead of trying, she took Jackie's hand and led her to the living room.

Jackie's elongated nails scratched Margo's palm, but Margo didn't care. She urged Jackie to her, pulling herself back to hit the hallway wall, leaning into her as Jackie took her face in her hands. Scorching lips met Margo's, a vicious kiss that left her wanting more as Jackie moved to her exposed neck. Jackie pressed her mouth to her neck, piercing her skin with her teeth. Margo didn't try to stifle the moan as it left her, wrapping her arms around Jackie as the wave of pleasure washed over her. The vines of Jackie were firm in her mind, searching, relentless, and Margo surrendered.

Margo remembered the words Jackie spoke to her in the dream—that she was addicted to her—and she wondered if there was truth to her statement. She wanted this as much as Jackie did. The first time had been a debt owed; she didn't owe Jackie anything now. Margo wanted this, the act beyond a debt, and she knew it, just as she had the night in the attic of the antique shop. Margo tightened her grip on Jackie's back, her own breath quickening as Jackie clutched her sides. She let Jackie delve further into her mind, wanting her to see the truth, longing for the secret to be displayed.

Again, the sensation didn't feel invasive but akin to a comforting midsummer breeze stirring the memories deeply hidden within the depths of her mind, exposing the very things Margo sought to hide from the rest of the world. Margo moved her head back, pulling Jackie closer. She wanted to touch her again, taste her once more, invoke the beauty of her euphoria. The thought of Jackie in the midst of ecstasy spread through her mind, and they both moaned. Jackie paused briefly at Margo's neck before she ran her tongue over the small wound.

But...she realized how stupid she was being. Jackie couldn't know. Not yet. Knowledge was power. Power was dangerous, and the last thing she wanted to do was put Jackie in danger.

"Jackie," she whispered. "Jackie, stop."

Jackie pulled back, face full of concern, and well, blood. "Are you okay?" she asked, gasping.

Margo nodded. "Yeah, fine."

Less than a second after she spoke the words aloud, Jackie moved away from her, face stricken. "Are you ever going to tell me what you are?" Jackie asked slowly. "If you aren't ready, I understand, but I'm confused. It's like you want me to know, but you keep pulling away from me."

Margo pushed off the wall with her elbows and strode to the counter, conveying her nonchalance with difficulty. She turned and looked at Jackie, who still appeared concerned, standing in the same spot, arms limp at her sides. "Jackie, when you bit me, what did you see?"

"Not much. You've got a strong mind, and I don't mean to push toward whatever you're hiding from me—it just kind of happens."

She threw her gaze downcast, picking at her cuticles. "Huh."

Crossing the room, Jackie smiled softly. "Are you *ever* going to stop being so mysterious?"

Margo gazed up at the digital clock on the living room wall. "It's getting late, and it's a school night, right?"

Jackie nodded with a sigh. "Yeah, I should probably get going." The unspoken truth in the circumstances left Margo relaxing.

Though Jackie spoke of leaving, she hadn't moved. So, Margo rounded the counter, grabbed her leather jacket, and headed to the balcony door. "I'll be right back."

Too much was going on. All Margo wanted was a second to think through things. Perhaps a second wouldn't suffice, but she thought a little time would help her figure out what she needed to do. She realized, with alarming certainty, she didn't want to leave anymore. Sam didn't need her; she was doing just fine, but Margo couldn't deny she'd grown fond of Jackie.

Okay, more than a little fond, Margo thought, rolling her eyes at herself. And if Jackie's behavior was any indication, the feeling was mutual. They still barely knew each other; their little rendezvous had only been going on for two weeks, how could they know each other? That being said, Margo was closer to Jackie than she did with most people in her life, which she attributed to Jackie's ability to delve into her mind. She may have said she didn't see much in Margo's mind, but Margo knew she had experienced the imagery alongside Jackie.

Margo fished her pack of cigarettes out of her pocket, pausing before she lit one. Jackie had a right to know what she was, but on Margo's terms. Finding out from an accidental peek into her thoughts wasn't how things needed to go, Margo knew, but saying the truth out loud was daunting, given the circumstances that next week brought. What if the potion didn't work, and Corporate discovered she was Djinn? *What if the potion does work, and I die?*

Margo leaned her elbows on the railing of the balcony and fumbled with the pack of cigarettes, startled into nearly dropping the lighter as the sliding glass door opened behind her. "It's beautiful, despite how cold it is," Jackie said behind her, closing the door.

She nodded in agreement as she turned to look at Jackie. "Did you get enough blood?" The question wasn't necessary as the horns that were present on her head had vanished, and her nails back to their usual state, but Margo was unsure what to say.

"Is someone getting addicted to being bitten?" A playfulness taunted the edges of Jackie's lips.

Margo gulped. "Does that sort of thing happen?" Her dream replayed in her mind, but this time she wasn't sure it'd been a dream.

"Oh, yeah, it can. The properties in Empusa saliva can inflict an addiction to the whole process on the victim." Jackie's tone was serious as was her expression. "I'm joking, Margo."

Margo snorted, turning back to face the dark city, hands gripping the railing. "Very funny."

"It's *me* who's addicted to *you*," Jackie murmured. "Margo?"

"Touch me," she breathed. Warmth spanned her sides as Jackie slipped her hands beneath her leather coat, caressing her bare skin under her button-up. Margo closed her eyes, lost in the contact, and when Jackie pressed a hot kiss to her neck, Margo dropped her unlit cigarette. The hands moved forward, skirting the edge of her jeans and grazing the prominence of her hip bones. Jackie trailed her tongue over the crook of Margo's neck as she unbuckled her belt and taunted the skin.

Margo bit her lip and exhaled through her nose as her pants slid down an inch. The desire building all evening had become unbearable, drowning her with need. Jackie tightened her grip on Margo's hips, urging her closer. Jackie's breasts pressed hard against Margo's back as she nibbled her shoulder.

"Jackie," Margo moaned, the sound low and dangerous to her ears.

Jackie stepped around, pushing Margo away from the railing to stand directly in front of her. Her gaze, intoxicating and vibrant in the dull starlight, sent a tingle through Margo, and she bit her lower lip harder. She cupped Jackie's face in her hand, wanting more than anything to have that gaze grace her every day. No, she couldn't think like that. Margo cleared her throat, trailing her thumb across Jackie's jawline. "Beautiful or not, my bedroom is a lot warmer than out here, you know," Margo murmured before Jackie claimed her lips.

"Lead the way, then," she said, her breath hot over Margo's face.

Margo threaded her fingers in Jackie's and tugged her back inside the condo. Her room was far from the state she'd wanted to bring another woman into, but she wasn't going to let that stop her, not when Jackie practically tried to strip her on the damn balcony. Forgoing lights, Margo eased Jackie onto the made bed, thankful she at least did that this morning, positioning her thighs on either side of her. She kissed her, slow and sensual as Jackie slowly unbuttoned Margo's shirt, replacing the material with her hands as it fell down her back.

When Margo leaned back, Jackie smirked at her, running her finger over the sore bite mark on her neck. "I like staking a claim to you," she murmured.

"What, do other Empusae know not to mess with someone you've bitten if they see the bite marks?" Margo found herself sincerely curious.

Jackie leaned forward, capturing Margo's lower lip between her teeth before kissing her deeply. She kissed down Margo's jawline, her exhale loud in Margo's ear. "I'd like to think we're too far and few between for those kinds of things to be a problem, but I like the notion of you being mine." Her words ruffled the wispy hairs on Margo's neck, and Margo moaned from the sensation as well as the statement itself.

"I don't mind being seen as yours," she murmured truthfully.

Jackie ran her hands down her sides, stirring goose bumps along Margo's torso and thighs as she edged closer to her waist.

Pulling away slightly to look down at Jackie, Margo smirked. She reached down to grab Jackie's wrists, gently guiding them up and over Jackie's head. "You may have instigated, but I'm touching you first this time."

A mischievous smile crossed Jackie's face, and she quirked an eyebrow. "Oh, really? Is that what you think?"

"Ye—" Before Margo could finish her words, Jackie yanked her wrists free and wrapped her arms around her, pushed herself up from the bed, and pinned Margo on her back, hands clasping Margo's wrists. She stared down at Margo, appearing quite accomplished, hair falling into her face and tickling Margo's neck. Her penetrating gaze stretched the length of Margo's body, lingering, lavishing.

Jackie wriggled out of her jeans before she completed the job of removing Margo's pants and boxers, throwing them to the floor without hesitation. The pile of clothing on the floor beside the foot of Margo's bed was impressive.

Margo helped Jackie out of her T-shirt and reached around, unclasping her bra. The purple gem dangling loosely from a chain around her neck chilled Margo's naked skin, the sensation one she realized she enjoyed. She touched Jackie's breasts, running her hands over the hardened nipples, cupping them softly. Jackie closed her eyes, letting out another breath before kissing Margo once again, her own hands canvassing Margo's body. Her fingernails scratched gently over Margo's ribs, sending Margo into a short fit of giggles. "And now you're tickling me. Woman, are you just on a teasing strike today?"

"Maybe," Jackie said, dragging her tongue over Margo's neck. Margo closed her eyes, losing her train of thought as Jackie took her earlobe into her mouth.

Soft palms flattened over Margo's stomach, pushing lower until reaching the apex of Margo's legs. She moaned as Jackie parted her lower lips with a deft finger, brushing her tender nerves.

Jackie's fingers grazed Margo's clit and she arched, drawing a breath sharp enough to slice concrete. "Fuck, Jackie," she groaned, grabbing the blankets under her with both fists. Jackie pressed into Margo, her thumb nestling atop her clit, and Margo gasped, eyes shut so tightly she saw sparks behind her lids.

Her hips bucked, meeting Jackie's movements, eyes squeezed shut as pleasure erupted over her, stealing her breath. Jackie circled her thumb over Margo's clit faster, throwing her deeper into euphoria. Lips crashed into hers and Margo could barely focus on the kiss as her body writhed under Jackie. She cried out, louder than she thought possible, as Jackie continued to please her, every single piece of her.

"Wow," Margo muttered against Jackie's mouth as she kissed her. "I wasn't expecting that."

Jackie snorted, pushing back the sweat-dampened hair from Margo's face. "What did you expect?" The look on her face was one of affection, all warmth and soothing ardor, a shocking comparison to anything Margo had seen before. It scared the shit out of her.

As for Jackie's question, Margo wasn't sure. She kissed Jackie again, wrapping her arms around her, not wanting to examine her own feelings. What had she expected? Sex, duh, which is what happened. What she didn't expect was the undeniable connection between them, drawing them nearer, her own feelings for Jackie becoming too powerful to ignore, too massive to tuck away in a linen closet. Still stuck in the heady afterglow, Margo pulled back and stared hard at Jackie. "You're nothing like I expected."

Jackie blinked. Instead of speaking, Jackie lay her head on Margo's chest, finding one of her hands and tightening her fingers around it. Margo breathed in the soft scents of her hair, closing her eyes, wanting the moment to span over the course of her lifetime.

"What exactly did you expect, Margo?"

"I don't really know. You're just," Margo said, stopping as she searched for the right word. Amazing? Incredible? Unflappable? "Your kindness is more than I can handle."

Jackie lifted her head and ran her tongue over her lips before burrowing her face in Margo's neck. "I have no idea what that means." Her lips pressed against Margo's shoulder; soft, dainty kisses that left Margo feeling an overwhelming sense of being cherished, something she'd never experienced before.

Lifting her arms, Margo clutched Jackie to her, not wanting to let go. Their breaths slowed into an even rhythm, and Margo closed her eyes.

"I really should get going," Jackie muttered. "Six o'clock comes quick."

"Oh, right, you have work tomorrow." Margo hoped she hadn't kept Jackie for too long in her selfish need to feel her touch.

Chuckling, Jackie removed herself from Margo and scooted down the bed to the edge. "Yeah, not everyone gets to sleep in and hang out with dead people for a living." She shot her head back as if to make sure she hadn't said anything to hurt Margo's feelings.

Margo smirked, placing her arms under her head. "I take advantage of the scant benefits, like making my own schedule." She didn't want Jackie to leave, part of her wanting to tell her to stay the night with her, but...

Jackie rose from the bed and walked over to the doorway, then searched the wall for the light switch. Before she could find the switch, Margo hopped off the bed, then crossed the room to wrap her arms around Jackie's naked form. She sighed, leaning her head back against Margo's shoulder. Margo kissed her neck, squeezed both breasts in her hands. Jackie moaned, arching against Margo. "Do you have to leave right this second?"

"No, not *right* this second..." Jackie trailed off. Her breath hitched next to Margo's ear, the rest of her sentence lost in incoherent gasps as Margo caressed her nipples.

She took Jackie's earlobe into her mouth, nibbled gently, and let go. "Good. It's my turn now." Margo guided Jackie backward, spinning her until Jackie was poised in front of the bed. "Lie back." Jackie's eyes were heavy lidded, her plump lips parted.

"Okay." She eased onto the bed, legs dangling.

A smirk lifted the corner of Margo's mouth, and she dropped to her knees on the carpet.

"Where'd you go?"

Margo pressed her hand on Jackie's stomach. "Lie back."

Jackie obliged, resting backward.

Starting at Jackie's stomach, Margo drew lazy lines with her fingers over Jackie's skin, grazing her navel. She moved back up to Jackie's breasts, cupping them, nipples hard against her palms. Margo peered up at her just as Jackie brushed Margo's hair from her face, her head lifted enough to make eye contact with her. Margo kissed Jackie's hips, one at a time, and Jackie laced her fingers in Margo's hair, sighing with each kiss. "What are you planning on doing down there?"

"I'm staking a claim to you." Margo bit the prominence of Jackie's right hip, not hard, but enough to earn herself a reaction. Jackie gasped, fisting a handful of Margo's hair. When Margo let go, she looked up at Jackie's flushed face. Jackie craned her neck, blinked at Margo, and smiled, her face awash in desire. The bite mark above Jackie's hip bore pink skin, and Margo kissed the spot. Margo guided Jackie's legs over her shoulders, and Jackie opened for her.

Jackie sighed as Margo lowered her head and kissed Jackie's mound. She brought her tongue through soft curls over Jackie's core, and Jackie's hips jerked at the contact. She ran her tongue over Jackie's clit, savoring the soft whimper that left Jackie's lips with each movement as much as the heady taste of her. Delving further, she took the nub into her mouth, swirling her tongue over it. With featherlight touches, she grazed Jackie's legs, feeling goose bumps raise beneath her palms as she urged Jackie's leg farther apart.

Jackie's fingers tightened in Margo's hair, holding her head in place. Tension built in Jackie's thighs as they pressed against the sides of Margo's head. Her muscles tightened, quivering under Margo's palms.

"Oh, Margo," she moaned, each syllable drawn out and breathy. Margo steadied her pace, eliciting another softer sound from Jackie before her body tensed. Jackie gasped, rocking her hips forward, dropping her hands from Margo's head to grip the bed as she lost herself to the pleasure. Her hips lifted. Her breath hitched. Margo sped her movements up, pressing her tongue hard on Jackie's clit. Jackie's exhale turned into a moan as she slipped into bliss.

"Come up here," Jackie breathed after she recovered. Margo crawled into Jackie's embrace, wrapping her own arms around Jackie's neck, knees on either side of Jackie's hips. Jackie's chest heaved against Margo's, her whispered breath pouring over Margo's shoulder. Jackie sighed, edging closer to Margo so their bodies were flush with each other. They breathed in sync and Margo closed her eyes, basking in the bliss she'd only ever felt from Jackie.

They lay still for a few minutes, so long that Margo wondered if Jackie fell asleep beneath her until she spoke. "You said it was warmer in your room but laying here naked, I'm getting pretty cold."

Margo chuckled, rolling off Jackie. "Well, I don't heat the place enough to hang around in my birthday suit." She rolled onto her side and watched as Jackie climbed out of the bed. "I've got some flannel pajamas you could borrow if you want."

Jackie sat on the edge of the bed. Her hair was draped over her naked shoulder, a few dreads framing her face in the dark room. "Are they red?" she asked, her voice amused.

Margo licked her bottom lip, drawing her brows together in confusion. "Yeah, how'd you guess?"

Recognition shimmered in Jackie's eyes, and she smiled. "Because you were wearing them in a dream I had, though now I'm beginning to wonder if that was a dream at all."

Margo couldn't stop the gasp that left her mouth. The memory of the dream and the scent of Jackie's skin washed over her in painted hues and Margo closed her eyes briefly as if to grasp at the reverie. "No wonder it seemed so real. I knew I couldn't make up something so beautiful in my own head. I don't have a single artistic bone in my body." She chuckled.

Margo tried to recall what she'd said to Jackie during the dream, if she'd told her the truth about herself. When she realized she hadn't, she was relieved and simultaneously disappointed. The room remained quiet. Jackie's gaze set on Margo, a soft smile tugging the corners of her mouth.

"Has that, uh, ever happened to you before?" Margo whispered. Maybe it wasn't a special interaction. Perhaps Jackie had dream visitors every night.

Jackie shook her head, teeth pressed on her lower lip. "That was a first for me."

There goes my assumption. "What does it mean?" Margo mused aloud. Margo never imagined they'd truly shared a dream, a moving, beautiful, transformative dream, but they had.

"I don't know." Jackie placed her hand over Margo's, caressing her thumb over Margo's knuckles, and she simply watched her. "Will you ever tell me what you're so afraid of?"

Margo surprised herself with her answer. "Yes, I will, just, not yet, okay?" Before Jackie's question, Margo hadn't been sure whether she would tell her or not, but now, she knew she needed to. No, Margo *wanted* to tell her, to open herself to Jackie, to embrace the vulnerability of such a release, but she couldn't yet. Not tonight.

Jackie nodded, glancing down. "Thank you," she said as she leaned forward to grab her clothes from the floor.

The honesty in her expression was too much for Margo. She picked a fuzzy off her bedspread, knowing she had to change the subject or she'd possibly blab everything she couldn't. "No. Thank you for some kickass crockpot lasagna. Who can say they've had lasagna baked in a crockpot?"

"A lot of people, actually," Jackie said matter-of-factly, tugging on her jeans.

Margo sat up and climbed out of bed, wrapping her blanket around herself to stave off the chill. "I've got a couple jobs to do with Sam tomorrow, one before she heads into work."

After tugging her T-shirt over her head, Jackie glanced up and smiled. "Yuck, and she works early."

Margo shrugged. "Shouldn't take us very long. She's getting really good."

They walked silently to the front door hand in hand.

When they reached it, Jackie turned, tugging Margo's blanket toward her. Jackie kissed her, her lips lingering on Margo's. "I'll see you later, Margo."

Margo stood in the doorway, shivering in the thin blanket until she watched Jackie climb into her car and drive away.

MARGO NAPPED ON the couch until her alarm woke her an hour before dawn, and she left the house to pick Sam up for their early appointment. Crickets rumbled a low symphony nestled deep in the thinning dune grass sprawled over the hilly sand mounds. Margo lit her cigarette, then blew the initial smoke out into the light winds coming off the water. Leaning against the boardwalk, she perched the cigarette between two fingers and picked her cuticles with her free hand.

Out on the beach, a few feet shy of the water, Sam stood beside a spirit, hands moving sporadically as she spoke. The spirit, a middle-aged woman who had died a few days prior, simply wanted to see one last clear sunrise before she moved on—an easy request—easy-peasy. Margo didn't even need to be there, but she wanted to watch Sam reap one more time. She could leave without guilt, without the worry Sam would fail. Before her evening with Jackie the night before, Margo believed it would be the last time she'd reap with Sam, but she wasn't so certain anymore. Something changed, a paradigm shift, not that she believed in any of that crap.

Leaving had become a crutch heightened to a necessity when Brent told her about the census testing. She couldn't leave now, not when Brent was trying to make something out of her case, to use her as an example. At first, this annoyed her but the more she thought, the more she recognized how much he'd gone out of his way for her. Leaving would be a literal slap in his face, not to mention she wasn't sure where she'd go anyway.

Heat scorched her fingers, so she dropped her cigarette. Seagulls dipped down from the brightening sky, crying out to one another as they got to the sandy ground. *Jackie.* She got under Margo's skin—this was a fact, and Margo was embracing her doubts, her second thoughts. She wanted to stay, she'd admitted to herself as she watched Jackie slip through the front door only four hours before, waving goodbye as she hurried to her car.

Margo lit a second cigarette, determined she'd actually smoke this one instead of wasting it while deep in thought. Feelings stirred in her chest at the thought of Jackie's infectious smile, her easy mirth, the affection swelling in Margo's chest. She tried so hard to allow Jackie to see her truth when she bit her the third time, but she fought herself. The feelings scared Margo more than the thought of Corporate discovering her truth. *The least I can do,* Margo thought as she examined the cherry reddening the end of her cigarette, *is to tell her that I'm part Djinn rather than let her see it in my head before Monday if I even let her drink from me again. I can't have her not knowing in case I do die.*

She sighed and looked up at the horizon. The gray sky shifted into a light burgundy, bleeding through the scant clouds. Sam and the spirit were facing the ocean now, Sam's arms crossed in front of her. Margo pushed off the piling, ambling through the uneven sand toward them. Above all, Margo could give Jackie her honesty minus her modus operandi. Although she trusted Brent, even the slight chance of her dying pushed her into recognizing the need to tell Jackie, and she knew Brent wouldn't tell Jackie if she did die out of respect for her privacy. Her opinion of Brent seemed to waver recently, her leery approach transforming into a strong respect for what he'd done for her.

Orange peeked over the horizon, throwing the clouds into a lively juxtapose in the lightening sky. She pulled her phone from her pocket and opened a new text to Jackie.

Hey, I'm sure you're still sleeping. Do you want to get together for dinner again? This time it's on me. There's a cute little restaurant in Atlantic City I think you'd love.

The sun lifted completely over the water, pitching light over the ocean's surface. The spirit lifted her arms, allowing the sun to wash over her. Sam joined her, hands outstretched to the sky. Margo stayed a few feet back, folding her arms over her chest, proud of how serious Sam took her new identity. Her kindness slated her as being a natural, giving the spirits ease and comfort before embarking on their journey, whereas Margo threw them her usual curt dismissal. At least she'd initiated a blood bond with a competent individual.

I'm glad I finally did something right even if it was an accident.

Chapter Seventeen

RAIN PELTED THE windshield as Jackie steered the car over the bridge toward the back route to Atlantic City. Waves thrashed under the bridge, shaking a glowing buoy side to side a short distance from the beach. Jackie had been surprised and relieved to have a text asking for a third date the morning after their night together at Margo's. Even more so, she was elated when Margo mentioned going to Atlantic City as if they had mental synchronicity. Margo made reservations at a restaurant, and Jackie had asked if they could meet earlier her intention being to drop by the club Ezra told her about. She'd forewarned Margo about the club, her hope of finding information on Roz at the location, and how likely it was they'd leave empty-handed.

Jackie had given Margo the address of the casino parking lot closest to the location of the pop-up dark club, figuring their cars would be far safer in the lot than where the club was located. Night hadn't quite fallen, and the lingering light caused the clouds to take on an unnerving jaundiced glow.

After dinner with Margo on Thursday, Jackie called Brent to tell him his elixir caused the opposite of what it was supposed to do. Her bloodlust came on in less than two days instead of a month like the old one offered. He apologized and promised to make a new one, but she wasn't in a rush to trust his next concoction.

Once in the city, Jackie drove to the northernmost part of the island, the last place Jackie would ever travel during the day let alone at nightfall. An inexpensive parking lot positioned a few blocks from the closest casino seemed the best bet. Jackie pulled into the crowded lot, paying the attendant before finding a spot. Looking around as she stepped out of the car, the area appeared near desolate, striking a bit of fear in her. Ezra wouldn't send her into trouble, she knew, and she swiftly banished the concern. Margo's adorable MINI Cooper was a few rows down as was the woman herself, leaning against her car, cigarette perched between her fingers.

Jackie strolled over, taking a moment to cherish Margo's beauty before approaching her. The rain had eased to a low drizzle, coating the cars with tiny droplets. "Hey."

Margo smiled, stubbing the cigarette out on the bottom of her shoe. "Hey yourself."

"You ready?" Jackie pulled the paper from the pocket of her purse. "I've got the address right here."

As if to look at the paper, Margo moved in close and kissed Jackie on her lips. "Let's check it out."

Though once revered as a city ahead of its time, the one-time fancy resort town, which had a board game with its street names, Atlantic City had become a distant version of itself, hit hard by the recession. The decimation of its stability began far before then. The large casino they parked beside glowed hazily in the evening air, illuminating the darker part of the city as they headed down the street, away from the grandeur. Jackie tightened her sweater around herself and shoved her hands in her pockets, apprehension filling her with unease. *Is this really a good idea? It's not too late to turn around and go have dinner.*

Apparently, Margo sensed her trepidation, sidling up close enough to bump shoulders with Jackie. "So, are you and Roz pretty close?"

"Kind of. She and Ezra are a lot closer than we are, but we all grew up on the same street. I can't tell you how nice it was to have someone my age besides Ezra who didn't fit in with the norm." This was an understatement, of course. Knowing another child who was cognitive of the underworld eased Jackie and Ezra's isolation. They grew close to Roz throughout adolescence and beyond. "Do you know her well?"

Margo sighed, sliding her arm through Jackie's with nonchalance. "We get along all right when we're in the same room, but I hardly know her from the rest of the Grim."

The warmth of Margo's arm against her own was comforting, and Jackie leaned into her slightly. "You don't seem all that connected with your people."

Margo chuckled instead of commenting.

Jackie filled the quiet street with her murmured explanation of Roz's disappearance, the email from her mother, and the continued silence she and Ezra both endured from their friend. Margo listened intently, tightening her linked arm around Jackie's as they continued to walk.

Clustered apartment buildings fought for space on the narrow streets, people lining the small alleyways between the bricks. Jackie stifled a tremor as she read the number of each building, searching for the right one. An upscale, clandestine casino in this place? The area didn't appear to be anything like what Ezra described. Maybe they were wrong; perhaps their friend hadn't seen Roz, or they had, but somewhere completely different.

"We almost there?" Margo whispered as they passed a trio of suspicious-looking individuals, each with their hood shielding their faces.

"I think so."

After passing several structures, they finally stumbled upon the right one. The massive building appeared out of place, its roof reaching for the skyline at least twelve floors while around it lay smaller shambles of homes, worn apartments, and condominiums. Brick crumbled from the face of the structure, chips of red laid strewn over the old flagstone porch, and thick plywood covered the doorway. A divot in the ground led to a smaller, child-sized door below also covered by plywood. Jackie reread the address on the slip of paper and looked back at up the building. "I don't get it—this is the address Ezra wrote down but there's nothing here."

"Seems like a dilapidated apartment building." Margo lit a cigarette, the smoke wafting toward Jackie. "Maybe we should forget about this. I don't think there's anybody in there, and if there is, we don't want their attention."

"No, let me check around the side." Without awaiting an answer from Margo, Jackie hurried down the stairs and walked through the alley to the right of the building. Darkness stretched the length of the space, sparing nothing. She knew walking in the alley wasn't her best idea, but Jackie wanted to make sure there wasn't a side entrance they were missing and knew she wouldn't be satisfied leaving the location unless she checked. Once she finally found Roz, Jackie decided, she'd have to choose whether to hug her until she choked or kick the ever-living shit out of her for disappearing. Maybe she'd do both.

"Uh, Jackie," Margo said from the front of the building. With one last glance at the dark alley, Jackie turned around and joined Margo. The plywood covering the door lay wide open, an imposing woman taller than both of them standing with her arms crossed over her chest and face severe. "Can I help you?" The woman's face was impassive, her jawline sharp, and she was built like the stern of a massive ship.

"Hi, I was wondering if we could get in. I'm looking for—"

She cut Jackie off. "Affiliation?" she asked.

Margo quirked an eyebrow at Jackie.

"My sibling, Ezra; they sent me over here."

Recognition flashed over the guard's eyes, and she nodded. "Ah, come in," she said, opening the metal door. Jackie entered the threshold with hesitation, Margo behind her. A heavy bass poured through the hallway, drenching the space with the promise of loud music.

Fabric hung from the ceilings in turbulent waves, a sea of blues and magenta drifting in the wake of moving bodies. Jackie squinted against the pulsating multicolored lights spilling around the large space as she pushed through the crowd, clutching tightly to Margo's hand.

A long bar spread the length of the room from one wall to the other, and patrons dotted the expansive wooden assembly. Neon lights were strung up, ebbing and flowing in vivacious hues, amalgamating in torrents on the reflective floor. A makeshift dance floor separated Jackie and Margo from the bar. Jackie figured she'd find someone to ask, someone who'd be willing to look at Roz's picture. Better yet, she hoped she'd simply bump into Roz while they wandered around the club but didn't hold high hopes of that possibility. Chaise chairs and couches were scattered on either side of the dance floor, couples and more were draped across them, some human but most not. Jackie breathed in the scents of several creatures: the stagnant scent of a vampire, metallic and dusky, the sharp wild of a wolf shifter, its crushed fern and damp earth smell contrasting heavily to the scents of a pixie, who smelled of fresh fallen snow and peonies.

"Let's ask the bartender," Margo shouted over the swell of music. Jackie nodded and tightened her grip on Margo's hand as they threaded through the maze of tables and chairs. The person in question bobbed their head in their direction, pointing a finger at them to hold tight. After helping another patron, the bartender came over to Margo and Jackie, metal shaker in hand. The dazzling lights highlighted the numerous shades in the bartender's hair, showcasing a beautiful teal and hot pink. They smiled at Margo and Jackie. "What can I get for you two?"

"Actually—" Jackie began, pulling her phone from her purse. She opened the photo of Roz and turned her phone to the bartender. "—have you seen her here? She goes by Roz or sometimes Rosalind."

Their smile fell, replaced by a suspicious expression. "Who's asking?" they snapped.

Jackie glanced at Margo before answering. "I'm Jackie, her cousin," she lied. What the hell was going on? She kept her smile open and innocent, worried Roz had gotten herself into serious trouble.

The bartender gave her a skeptical once-over, their gaze shifting over to Margo briefly before they nodded. "Okay. Hold tight." They finished their task, pouring a drink for another customer before taking off down the bar to the left and disappearing.

Margo leaned in close to Jackie. "Well, that was weird," she muttered. "You aren't really Roz's cousin, are you?"

Jackie turned to her and smiled. "Nope."

Climbing onto one of the barstools, Margo chuckled with a shake of her head. "Great."

Five minutes passed before the bartender came around again, seemingly materializing from the far-right side of the bar. "Okay," they said as they reached Jackie. "Follow me."

Another doubtful look presented on Margo's face, but she hopped off the stool and threaded her fingers in Jackie's before they followed the bartender. The hall was dark, the music muffled to a low thrum behind them. Jackie began to wonder if she should've questioned Ezra more about the club rather than take their word for it and jump into it.

Cracks filled the blank space of the walls on either side, causing Jackie to wonder how stable the structure really was. Margo's hand was warm, comforting in her own, and she squeezed it briefly, thankful Margo agreed to go with her. *Maybe this was a mistake,* she worried. Just as she considered turning to run back out the front door, the bartender stopped, pointing to a cracked door in front of them. "Ozais is right through there." With that, they turned and hurried back down the hall.

Jackie cautiously pushed open the splintered door and entered the room. Much like the rest of the venue, the floor held cracked cement with a distinct scent of rotten wood. In the middle of the room stood a solid desk the size of Jackie's worktable, though it was polished and richly stained. Rather than coming off as an empty room in an abandoned skyrise, the space was comparable to Brent's study. Magnificent bookcases lined the walls, plush armchairs placed neatly beside the rows of books, leaving Jackie to ponder how such a space could be transformed to this level of elegance. A pop-up club with this kind of décor? Jackie tightened her hold on Margo's hand.

The individual behind the desk lifted his head, smiling when his canary-yellow gaze met Jackie's. "Welcome. I'm the proprietor of this establishment, and I heard you had an inquiry," he said, his voice deep, rumbling over the room with an intensity that rattled in Jackie's chest.

"Please, sit." He indicated the two elegant armchairs positioned in front of his desk and sat back in his own chair, amusement upon his face. Jackie stifled the eye roll, not at the man but at what Roz obviously had gotten herself into. Another figure stood a few feet behind Ozais, arms folded over his chest and eerie orange gaze fixed on Jackie and Margo. The scents of wildfire smoke and crisp sulfur drifted toward Jackie as she approached the chair. Demons? She tried to be surprised, though these circumstances weren't at all shocking. Roz didn't know how to leave well enough alone.

Jackie stayed standing, as did Margo. "I didn't request a meeting with you," Jackie began, wringing her hands behind her back. "I'm just looking for my cousin."

He nodded, flicking his gaze to Margo briefly before looking at Jackie again. "Fair enough, but what leads you to believe you'd find this person in my club? As a matter of fact, how did you obtain the locale of this club?"

She creased her brow as she spoke, hesitant to name-drop for the second time. "I'm Ezra's sister."

Recognition lifted his lips into a devilish smile, gleaming razor teeth surfacing, which Jackie would've found somewhat humorous if they weren't in their current situation. "Ah, Ezra. I haven't seen them in some time now." He folded his hands in front of him and smiled. "Who is it you're looking for?"

Not wanting to move too quickly, Jackie took a tentative step forward. "Roz, uh, Rosalind Darab."

The warmth left his face, and he straightened in the chair. "Why are you looking for Ms. Darab?"

"She's my cousin," Jackie said, perpetuating the lie. "I haven't heard from her in almost two months, and I'm really starting to worry. I was told she's been seen here at this club."

He watched her carefully, an uncomfortable silence unfolding. The man behind him moved forward until he placed a hand on Ozais's desk. "She is none of your concern," Ozais said.

The finality in his tone pissed Jackie off. She stepped forward, fuming. "Yes, she is very much my concern. I'm not going to let some guy tell me otherwise. Is she here or not?"

His gaze narrowed, yellow flecks weaving around his irises. "Your cousin belongs to me for the time being." He relaxed back, a satisfied grin gracing his lips. "She signed a contract, and she will fulfill the duties outlined in the agreement."

"She doesn't *belong* to anyone," Jackie yelled, unsure how to process the possible implications of his declaration. His companion moved closer, posture threatening.

Ozais narrowed his gaze at her, fists clenching in front of him. "Stand down, Empusa. She willingly works for me, and she's safe. There isn't a thing you can do unless you want to buy her contract from me."

"How much?" Margo asked, the first words she'd spoken since they entered the sophisticatedly furnished room.

"I assure you, much more than you could possibly afford." He glanced back down at the tablet on his desk, shuffling paperwork in a dismissive manner. "If you'll excuse me, I have a great deal of work to tend to. Leave."

"Please let me at least see her. I want to make sure she's okay."

As if she hadn't spoken at all, Ozais continued with his work, scrolling through the tablet, tapping away on the keyboard. Jackie moved to the desk, placing a hand on the surface, ignoring the watchful gaze of his bodyguard. "Come on, all I want is to see her, to make sure we're talking about the same person before I go on my merry way."

His gaze flashed to her hand on his desk before casually lifting to her stare. Before she could move, searing pain erupted through her hand, and Jackie stumbled backward, thrown into Margo by an unseen force. Margo wrapped an arm around her, pulling her farther from the desk.

"Are you okay?" she murmured.

Jackie stared down at her still throbbing hand, finding her skin untouched.

"I told you to leave," Ozais repeated. He rose from his chair, and his guard stepped closer.

Just as Jackie went to turn to the door, flecks of light fell from the walls, coiling in incandescent puddles on the floor. Margo let go of her, stepping between her and the demon, the light following close behind until it ebbed at her feet like a metallic lake. Telekinesis was one thing she'd expected as potential when interacting with a demon, but this?

"Margo," Jackie whispered. What kind of demon could control light? It seemed counterintuitive. Jackie took a deep breath, tentatively reaching for Margo's arm. "Come on, Margo, I'm sure he's just going to show us out." Margo didn't budge, face poised toward Ozais.

"I don't think you're going anywhere," Ozais said. A wicked grin twisted his lips.

Jackie reached for Margo again, trailing her gaze upward as the sparkling light wrapped around Margo's arms, climbed up her legs, and coated her leather jacket. It seemingly consumed her, stretching as far as her fingertips until she glowed vibrantly in the dull room.

Pain burned in her arm, refreshed and worse than when she had touched his desk. She clutched her arm, horrified as she struggled to find her voice. "Please stop," she whispered.

Ozais's smile only widened as he took in the glow pulsing around Margo. "Or what?" he asked. He gripped the back of his chair, pursing his lips as he tapped his long fingernails against the ornate wood backing. "I'd like to see what happens next." How could a demon have two skills? Jackie gasped as the sear spread up her arm.

The light around Margo grew, nearly blinding Jackie. It filled every crevice in the room, causing her to squint. Power cracked the air like a whip, and Jackie ducked, raising her arms over her head. Margo jutted her arms forward, and the light shuddered as it hit Ozais, knocking him and his guard to the floor. The sickening sound of bone hitting solid concrete resonated throughout the room, bouncing off the walls several times.

Jackie lowered her arms. Margo's chest heaved, and her hands glowed, as if she dipped her fingers in a basin of sunlight. "Margo?"

Ozais chortled madly, drawing Jackie's attention away from Margo just as he pushed himself into a sitting position on the floor. Violet blood trailed down his wrist, dripping to the pale concrete. He breathed deeply, scenting the air with the grace of snake.

"I wonder if Corporate realizes they have a child of blue flame among them? It was my understanding your kind left decades ago," he said, shaking his head in disbelief.

Hands clenched at her sides, Margo's fierceness wavered at the title, a small tremble running over her tight jaw.

A child of blue flame? This is what she's been hiding from me? Jackie wasn't sure what the name entailed, but from the intensity in Margo's continued secrecy, she knew nothing good could come from it.

"Margo," she whispered.

The guard stood, rapidly moving to aid Ozais up, but Ozais dismissed him with the wave of a hand as he pushed himself from the floor. Dusting his dark suit off, Ozais lugged his fallen chair back behind his desk and rested his large hands on the back of it before addressing Jackie. "I could arrange a deal for your cousin's release if your friend here took her spot."

"No," Jackie snapped. She grabbed Margo's arm, shaking her from the strange haze which seemed to muddle her understanding. "Margo, we need to leave," she said sternly. Then, she turned to Ozais. "I'm sorry. We'll leave and you won't see us again."

"As you wish, but my offer still stands if you happen to change your mind or if you ever have any trouble with your superiors," he said. As if nothing happened, Ozais lowered himself into his chair and resumed his work. The guard began toward them.

Jackie urged Margo through the door they'd come in, hurrying down the hall toward the main room of the club. Music continued to boom around them, and Jackie elbowed her way through the crowd, making the distance to the door in a succession of quick strides.

They burst through the entrance and rushed down the stairs, putting as much space between them and the club as quickly as possible. When they were only a block away from the parking lot, Jackie stopped at a streetlight and stared at Margo. "You did that...that thing with the light?"

It was the first time since the incident Jackie glanced at Margo's face, and she wasn't at all surprised to see the familiar flame dancing in the whites of her eyes. "Yeah," Margo said, her tone clipped.

"How?"

The sign switched to walk, and Margo crossed the street, Jackie running to catch up with her. "Margo, please don't ignore me."

Their walk back to the parking lot appeared to take half the time it took them to find the location of the club. Margo rushed through the gate, almost in a run as she made her way to her car. "Margo," Jackie called after her.

Once at her car, Margo whipped around, the fire in her eyes subdued by the irritation. "Would you just leave it alone, Jackie?"

"Excuse me?"

Margo opened her mouth to speak, but she scoffed in lieu of words.

"What the hell happened back there?"

"I've got to go," Margo said as she turned to her driver's side door.

Jackie wanted to grab her wrist, to hold her against her car, to beg her for an explanation, but she observed Margo climb into her car, and when the engine started, Jackie backed away. She watched as her taillights receded into the ebbing fog cloaking the city. All the while, Jackie's mind mulled around the event, replaying the scene within her head over and over again, coming to the same conclusion—Margo was far more than just a Grim. To her knowledge, there was only one creature capable of calling upon light itself, and Jackie had never met one in her life.

Until now.

Chapter Eighteen

MARGO PUSHED INTO the condo, slamming the door behind her. The living room was dark, but both loud music and the sound of cascading water traveled down the hall from Luis's bedroom. She went directly to her room and shut the door. She'd been wrong to think she could stay, wrong to go along with Brent's plan. This was it. She'd put off her departure far too long, and now, she had no choice. How long until Ozais came looking for her, maybe going as far as to use Jackie as bait? *Fuck, now Jackie knows what I am.* Margo didn't say it, nor did Jackie; neither of them had to. Conjuring light wasn't a skill any old individual possessed, demon or otherwise, which was obvious based on Ozais's reaction. If Ozais went to Corporate and told them about her, would Jackie be in harm's way? Would Luis? Had someone followed her to her apartment?

Fatigue plagued her already befuddled mind, but she couldn't rest even though the bed looked appealing and warm, her blankets still ruffled and astray from the night before. Not now. *Cat's outta the bag,* she thought as she yanked her suitcase from deep in her closet. The blue luggage was a far cry from the pink Jansport backpack she'd lived out of most of her childhood and adolescence. She'd burned the thing in a jolly dumpster fire on the outskirts of Philly after running away from her last foster home, and with good reason. Every single thread composing the backpack had remnants of a life she preferred to forget.

Not only did Ozais know, but Jackie and the detective. Margo had no choice. The shower turned off, and Margo heard Luis's singing heighten before he quieted, presumably as he dressed. Margo removed her clothes from the dresser, freed them from their hangers, and emptied her closet as best as she could. She wasn't even sure where she was going; somewhere far from home would do. Maybe things would finally settle for Brent, for Sam. Brent would lose his bargaining chip from Margo, however he still had Sam, and her blood wasn't tainted, as far as Margo knew.

Staying wasn't an option for anyone, especially Luis. If trouble came for her in the form of either Ozais or the Grim, Luis would go down with her, as would Sam and Brent. *Not worth it*, she thought. She dropped to the floor in front of her dresser, tossing her clothes into the open bag without paying much attention to what she grabbed. Detachment settled over her shoulders like a cloak burdened with masked sorrow she couldn't shake off. *Just my luck. I decide to stay and get booted out anyway. Figures.*

Footsteps approached her bedroom, and her door creaked open slowly. Luis cleared his throat, stepping fully into the room. "You staying over at Jackie's tonight?" he asked playfully, though the tremble in his voice betrayed his humor.

Margo continued to shove more clothing into the overflowing suitcase. "No, I'm leaving like I should have weeks ago."

"What?"

Moving to the other side of her room, Margo said nothing as she emptied the dresser.

"You're really leaving." There was no question in Luis's tone, only a poignant resolution, an acceptance of her plans.

She continued to pack her bag, getting up to move on to her nightstand. "Yep."

Somewhere behind her, Luis took a deep breath, paused, and then scoffed loudly. "I don't believe you."

"You don't get it," Margo muttered.

"What about Sam?"

She shrugged without turning toward her brother. "She's a good Grim who doesn't need me. If she needs help, she's got Brent. Maybe Corporate will leave her alone if I'm gone."

"You're leaving, *again*." His voice was detached this time, flat and emotionless.

Margo closed her eyes, a quiet rage budding in her chest, not directed at Luis but the situation that brought her to this position in the first place. She turned and stared at him, her anger diminishing when she saw Luis's wounded face, brows tight as he wrung his hands in the towel in his hands.

"Luis, you don't understand. Things are different this time. I'm not just leaving because I'm scared for myself—other people's lives are at stake because of my dumb ass." Luis continued to stare at her. She shifted back to her belongings, shoving a wad of socks into the already brimming suitcase. "Besides, you were fine the last time; you'll be fine this time."

"*Was* I fine?"

Margo swore she saw tears in his eyes, but she said nothing.

"I distinctly remember feeling like my only family left me."

It was Margo's turn to scoff. She rolled her eyes and sighed. "You had Brent then, and you have him now."

"You are fucking clueless."

She returned to packing. "Just looking out for number one." She reached under the bed to feel for anything she might've forgotten.

She snatched a pair of shoes and tucked them into the heap of clothing, moving to recheck the drawers of her nightstand slowly, unwilling to gaze at her brother's pained face again. "You want to know something, Margo?" Luis asked.

Margo paused, staring at the knob on the drawer, watching Luis in the bronze reflection.

"All those times you've gone on about how egotistical you are in your little self-deprecating rants, I always told you to knock it off, that you aren't as selfish as you believe." He paused and shifted. "But I think this is the first time I actually agree with you."

She watched him leave her room, his footfalls receding far away. He'd be fine, she knew. He wasn't the painfully shy kid she'd fought for, stole toys for, and made up stories for to make him feel stronger about himself—he was tough, confident, and the amazing person she knew he would be, who he'd always been. She was lucky to call him her brother.

On her bed sat the stuffed mongoose, threadbare ears and glossy-black eyes staring at her. He must've thrown the old toy on her bed before leaving her room. She stared back at its beady eyes and swallowed around the lump in her throat. She had the half thought to take the damned toy with her, but she left it as she headed to the door; she had no right to it.

As she wandered down the hall, dragging her heavy suitcase to the kitchen, she wondered if she'd lost him for good. Even if she did see him again, would he forgive her? She shook her head, unable to let herself linger on the possibilities, the reality of her potential demise too strong. No matter how badly she wanted to stay, she couldn't. Luis would eventually understand, after time passed on. She stepped outside, locking the door behind her.

The cloudless sky was blackened, the new moon cloaked in darkness and offering the stars a display they could only dream of in the light-polluted city. Margo tugged her suitcase down the long flight of concrete stairs, the wheels hitting every step with a cacophony of noise that left her feeling mildly satisfied at disrupting their neighbor's quiet evening. She breathed in the crispness of the clear night as she heaved the luggage into the back seat of her tiny car. She didn't have the funds to buy a last-minute plane ticket but maybe she could buy one once she was out of the states. *How long is it going to take me to get to Canada, or would Mexico be faster?* she wondered. Did she want to go north or south? Stay in the country? These questions could be answered once she got on the highway.

She had enough cash to take her where she needed. The last time she'd left, she went straight north but didn't manage to hitchhike farther than the middle of nowhere Kent, New York. Somehow, Collin had tracked her down. They wouldn't be bothered to this time. She'd gotten Brent into enough trouble, caused Luis far too much grief. Things were different now, obviously.

She pulled out of the parking lot of her condo for the last time, glancing through the rearview at the building. She shouldn't have left things the way she did with Luis, but she'd rather have him hate her than talk her out of what had to happen. Like she told him, Luis would be fine, and so would Sam. Things would blow over. But...Margo chewed her lip as she pulled up to the stop sign. If she went right, she'd head onto the main street and, after that, the Ninth Street bridge, taking her directly off the island. If she went left, she'd head to the beach.

Instead of turning right toward the bridge, Margo turned left and headed to the boardwalk. Regardless of which direction she chose when she got onto the highway, she wouldn't see the boardwalk again. One last look wouldn't kill her—it was almost midnight anyway. What was one more hour or so in town?

She pulled into the empty parking lot of the amusement park that was closed for the winter. The night had become at least a few degrees colder on her short drive, and Margo zipped her leather jacket as she climbed out of her car and locked the doors. She climbed the staircase and started a leisurely pace down the walk. The boardwalk was deserted, as she'd expected it to be, and the lamps every few feet were like spectral lighthouses on a sea of wooden planks. Boards ornamented the windows of most of the shops she passed, closed for the season and protected from hurricanes. To her left, the ocean crashed against the sandy beach and rocky jetties, offering her a peaceful ambiance as she walked the boardwalk one last time.

There weren't many options. She couldn't stay, not after what happened at the nightclub, not with the looming threat of Corporate discovering her heritage. Taking the chance of the potion not working and possibly flagging her as different, even a shard of variance, set Sam up for the same end.

Jackie had seen Margo call to the light. The woman deserved an answer at the very least. A vague explanation, anything before Margo disappeared, or she'd be just as bad as Roz. Anything was better than a silent disappearance. Would Jackie put herself in danger again just to find out if Margo was alive or dead?

Before she could stop herself, Margo began to jog down the boardwalk, knowing Jackie's home was only a few short blocks away. Terror coursed through her veins as she drew closer to Jackie's street—afraid she'd tell Jackie what she was, afraid she wouldn't tell her what she was, afraid she'd never see her again.

A frosty haze coated her face as she ran, mixing with the dampness of her own perspiration. She hurried down the ramp and displaced gravel as she continued toward Jackie's house. A lone light shone through the front window of the first floor rather than upstairs. She slowly walked up to the door on the lower level, her breath misting in the air. Muffled music played from within the house, the lyrics inaudible. Margo knocked. The song playing quieted, and the door opened. Jackie's brows furrowed as she took Margo in. "Hey," she said with confusion.

Margo licked her lips, her mouth suddenly dry as she struggled for words. "I wanted to talk before I left."

Jackie's shoulders visibly dropped, but she nodded and opened the door fully. "Come on."

Margo entered the warm first floor of the home, taking in the subtle differences and similarities to the upstairs. The layout was the same—an open space, living room on the left and kitchen off to the right—however, this part of the home had a fully operating kitchen rather than the single hot plate Jackie used to heat her tea kettle and four-cup coffee pot. Steam billowed from the black stove, and Jackie continued toward the kitchen, pulling a pot of boiling water off the stovetop. "Are you hungry?"

Margo realized with shame they hadn't made their eight o'clock reservations at the restaurant. "Nah, I'm okay." She took her gaze off Jackie and walked into the bright living room. The furniture wasn't as absurd as the antiques on the upper floor, a dove-hued loveseat positioned neatly in front of a moderate sized television and a low rising lounge chair pushed against the wall. Margo eased down onto the edge of the loveseat, hoping the conversation would be painless. Maybe Jackie would tell her to get out, making the departure easier for her.

"Were you just in the neighborhood?" Jackie asked as she took the pot of pasta over to the sink. Mist coiled around her when she dumped the contents into a strainer, casting an iridescent light around her.

Margo cleared her throat, dropping her gaze downward. "I needed to go for a walk, get some fresh air or something."

"I don't think you lie very well," Jackie said.

"You sound like my brother."

"What are you really doing here?"

"I *did* need air." She blew a sigh through her nose. "I got stuck in my head."

Jackie moved to the stove and stirred the sauce into a smaller pot. "Stuck in your head?" she repeated, enunciating every word. She left the pasta in the strainer and took her spot at the stove again, giving equal attention to another pot.

This isn't how Margo wanted the conversation to go. How did she want it to go? Right. She didn't *want* to have the conversation where she splayed herself out in front of

Jackie. She wanted to run as fast and as far away as possible before anything could take away everything she loved. "Yeah, you know when you have a horrible song in your head and nothing you listen to can make it go away? All you need is some silence."

Jackie snorted, stirring the pot. "Okay. Well, you might as well stay for dinner seeing as I didn't get the dinner you promised to pay for." Although the words were playful, Jackie's tone was severe.

"Thanks," Margo said, staring at the blank television. What were these petrifying sensations coursing through her, and how could she stifle them? Was this what people meant when they said they had butterflies in their stomach? If so, Margo wanted to withdraw into herself with a flamethrower, so she could burn each butterfly to ashes.

Jackie tilted and Margo caught the whimsical look on her face in her periphery. "Margo, I wanted to ask you a question."

"Yeah?" She met her gaze, chewing the inside of her lip as perspiration tickled her palm and the nape of her neck. Here we go.

"How did you control the light?"

Nope, she couldn't do this. Margo rose from the couch, her cowardice winning. "I can't do this." She couldn't lie to her, not after saving her life, after touching her, kissing her, but she also couldn't tell her what she truly was. Offering that knowledge would lead to a chance at rejection, a rejection Margo couldn't face. *I'm leaving anyway. What difference does it make if she thinks I'm a freak who controls light?*

"You know what I am, and I'm not going to judge you for what you are." Jackie tapped her own chest, a fierceness within her obsidian eyes Margo had yet to witness. "Talk to me."

A minute passed. Two minutes. "I can't," Margo said, her voice cracking with emotion. She bolted from the room and headed to the front door. Cold air washed over her as she stepped onto the porch and lit a cigarette. Her fingers trembled as she brought it to her lips.

"Margo." Jackie's voice was a tentative whisper behind her, sending a chill over her shoulders that had nothing to do with the wind.

Smoke left her mouth as the words tumbled out. "When I was a kid, I had this awesome foster mom. She even adopted me. Well, I don't think the adoption was ever finalized." Margo sighed as she ran a shaky hand through her hair. "She knew I was different before she even took me on. I guess my chart had a nice little warning on it about my abnormality, not that they had a fucking clue what was wrong with me."

Margo put out her unfinished her cigarette, pinching off the cherry before using both hands to grip the railing of Jackie's porch. Margo was thankful Jackie remained silent. "Everything about her was kind. I figured it was too good to be true and was a little shit the first two months she had me in her home because I knew things couldn't stay that good." She chuckled crudely, shaking her head.

Jackie's hand touched her back softly, and Margo forced herself not to recoil from the tender contact. Instead, she continued her memory. "She finally looked at me one day and told me, 'Margo, I'm not letting you go anywhere no matter how bad you think you're behaving. Lighten up, kid.' After that, we were golden. I knocked off the crap, and we got along well. We had a nice routine, and she accepted that I could see ghosts, or at least she never treated me differently because of it. I think back, wondering if she was more than just a human but have no way of knowing."

A gust of wind whipped against the house and Margo shivered, the cold seeping through her jacket. "We can go inside," Jackie whispered. Without a word, she laced her fingers through Margo's and led her through the front door.

Just inside, Margo stopped and continued, an overwhelming need to finish compelling her through the painful memory. "About a year and a half into my stay with her, there was an accident at work. She died." She sniffed, fighting the tears that were already falling as she recalled her foster mom's death. The hardwood floor creaked under Jackie's feet as she moved closer to Margo, wrapping an arm around her. "I lost it. I almost killed my social worker when she told me what happened. The light nearly suffocated her, and I ran away after she came to." A warped cry echoed in the living room, and for a moment, Margo didn't realize it came from her.

"Oh, Margo," Jackie murmured, her arms tight around Margo's back.

Margo accepted the hug, burrowing her face into the warmth of Jackie's neck, and she cried. Her chest heaved, her tears drenched Jackie's T-shirt, but she couldn't halt the onslaught of abhorrent emotions. A sob left her, transcending years, erupting from what felt like a lifetime ago. Jackie ran her hand up and down Margo's back, her soft whispers inaudible but soothing, nonetheless.

When her breathing normalized, Margo moved her face from the crook of Jackie's neck long enough to draw a deep, shaky breath. "She was the first soul I ever helped cross over. It happened so fast, I didn't know what to say or do. The portal just opened, and she left."

Jackie cupped Margo's face, thumbs swiping away the still falling tears. "I can't imagine what you've been through, Margo, and I'm so sorry."

Margo rested her face against Jackie's hand, savoring the tenderness, the warmth, the affection. "All I've ever done is run away from my problems. I ran away from Brent's house when the initiative was passed, terrified Corporate would find out what I am, and they would take away my ability to open portals."

"Is that what you were doing—running away? You don't have to."

Margo shook her head, the movement causing Jackie to drop her hands. "Ozais could've killed you, and all I did was make things worse. He could've hurt you because of my stupid decision and still can." She threw her hands up as if she could dust off the malevolent force flowing through her veins.

"No, you were only protecting me." Jackie took Margo's hands in her own and frowned. "I'd be dead if you hadn't done what you did. Goddess knows I would've stayed until he told me where Roz was." Her dark gaze was full of unfaltering honesty, and Margo's eyes watered again. Jackie's nose flared slightly while they stared at each other, and Margo couldn't look away.

"What are you?" she asked in awe.

Margo dropped her gaze, yanking her hands from Jackie. "I'm half Grim, half Djinn from what Brent and I figure. Djinn are the only kind who can manipulate light the way I do."

"Oh," Jackie said, her tone impassive.

Margo waited patiently, waiting for Jackie to reject her, to tell her to leave, but she knew Jackie wouldn't. "Did you already know?"

Jackie shook her head, the words spilling from her mouth in a rush. "No, well, kind of—after what happened tonight. I just didn't think there were any Djinn in North America anymore, but it makes a lot of sense."

Margo tensed, shifting her weight slightly. "How?"

"I noticed before how electric you are. There's a subtle flicker within you, the deepest burning section of fire right at the base where the flame is blue. That probably sounds so weird, but it's the only way I can describe what I felt when I was in your head. Plus, the whole light conjuring makes a lot of sense, not that I've met another Djinn before."

Margo smiled ruefully. "I guess that's a good description. Djinn are called the people made of smokeless fire."

Jackie smiled and Margo almost swooned, but the gesture turned to a frown as Jackie touched her face again. "I don't see you any less, Margo."

Margo licked her lips. "Only Brent, Collin, and Luis know. The Grim would kill me if they found out, or worse—they would kill Sam."

Jackie shook her head, bringing her other hand to cup both of Margo's cheeks. "I'm not going to tell a soul." She pressed a soft kiss to Margo's lips and pulled back. "You are such a kind person, and I wish you'd get over yourself and accept that as fact, no matter how much you deny it."

Margo leaned her forehead against Jackie's, sighing. "You don't understand," she whispered. "There's so much going on right now. I have to leave to keep everyone safe."

"You're not going anywhere," Jackie murmured.

"But—"

"I'll help you. Whatever needs to be done, I will be there with you, if you'll have me." The pure honesty in Jackie's words hit hard against Margo, and she said nothing, wrapping her arms around her, kissing her, holding her, loving her. She wanted to believe her, desperately. With every cell in her body, she wanted to believe Jackie spoke the truth.

Her stomach growled, disrupting their moment in each other's arms, and Jackie laughed against her parted lips. "Okay, you need to eat something."

Chapter Nineteen

THE MORNING BROUGHT an odd glow to the sand outside, and Jackie stood on her porch, steam wafting from the ceramic mug cupped in both hands. She breathed in the crisp air, closing her eyes as the first tendrils of the sunrise bathed her in warmth. When she awoke, Margo was still asleep, sprawled out on her bed, and it pained Jackie to leave her side, but she needed to work, needed to feel the raw power only creation gave her. Her hands were nimble, workable, ready to sculpt a masterpiece. She took another breath and opened her eyes. The acknowledgment of her feelings for Margo grew like rosebuds in a spring snowfall. She cared about her a lot. A lot more than she'd allowed herself to care for another being besides a family member and that frightened her.

The incident involving Ozais left Margo numbed and fearful. Jackie's opinion—tell Brent. The man had countless resources, some Jackie herself didn't know he possessed, and if anyone could help Margo tread the waters around the situation, he would be the one to ask. Astonishingly, Margo didn't argue. She agreed to consult Brent as soon as she was given the opportunity, holding only a slight amount of hesitation before she explained the second reason why Margo wanted to leave: the census. Jackie didn't like the thought of Margo drinking something that could kill her, and a lump formed in her throat as she thought it over again under the warmth of the morning sun.

The emotional overhaul of the night before left them both exhausted, Margo falling asleep against Jackie on the couch after they'd eaten a quiet dinner of bland pasta in lieu of their planned outing. Jackie still worried about Roz, hoping Ozais hadn't lied to her in stating she was safe. When Margo had drifted into a snoring sleep, Jackie texted Ezra, informing them of what happened at the club. She had yet to receive any word from them. She hoped Ozais hadn't lied about her wellbeing.

A soft creak yanked Jackie's attention back into the present and she looked back as Margo exited the house, coffee cup in hand. "Hi. I didn't see you downstairs, so I assumed you were up here."

"You assumed right," Jackie said. "I hope that coffee is strong enough."

Margo lifted the cup in answer as she stepped over to the railing. She balanced the cup on the ledge as she lit a cigarette.

Seagulls flew past, their noisy chatter rattling off the concrete driveway below. "I've been thinking," Jackie said on the breeze flowing through the air.

Margo tilted her head, a crooked smile on her sleepy face. "Yeah?"

She held onto her calm, easing the words out slowly. "I was wondering if Brent had any other ideas besides the potion he made you to mask your other half." *Something that won't potentially kill you.* She kept her anxiety disguised beneath her faux calm for fear of frightening Margo.

The smile vanished as Margo looked out at the beach. "The way he put it, it's more like the potion will kill that part of me."

"Oh. And there's no other way?"

"Other than me leaving?" Margo shook her head as she took a drag. "No."

When Margo finished her cigarette, they headed inside.

Jackie filled her mug with more coffee before retreating to the table once again. She took the piece of wood and began to scrape the surface, shavings falling to the table in front of her. The block was large, comparable to a loaf of bread—not the largest she'd carved but she was still unsure what she wanted the finished product to be, and this kept her mind off the external dilemma Margo faced. At the moment, the wood piece appeared more like a shoe than anything she'd thought to create. "What's the worst they can do if they find out?"

She peered up to find Margo holding a wooden lighthouse in her hands, a piece Jackie completed a few weeks ago but hadn't decided if she wanted to paint or not. "Well, Brent and I think they'll kill me."

"Oh." *Kill her?* She slid the knife over the wood, dust sprinkling the table as Jackie tucked her legs under herself. Her eyebrows lowered, concentration piquing.

Wandering over to the kitchen, Margo sighed loudly. "Brent thinks the potion will work. I trust him, but he said it could damage my genes or something. I might lose my Djinn abilities, which would fucking suck. I don't know anything about that side of me, but it's still part of me. A huge part." The coffee carafe clinked, liquid filled a cup, and Margo walked back over to the table.

Jackie kept at her work, blowing away the shavings and then carving another slice from the wood. "You don't know anything about your family, like your Djinn family?" A rough outline of a crow sat in her palm, Jackie tilting her head to the side, and then raising the X-ACTO knife once more to carve out a feather.

Margo shook her head. "My parents left me in a rural hospital in the middle of Minnesota at six months old, but my age was just a guess. I don't know either of them. If it weren't for Brent, Luis and I would still be wandering around, reaping ghosts just for shits and giggles. Hmm, now that I think of it, that probably wouldn't be so bad." She took a long sip of her coffee. Her brows furrowed and she glanced at the ceiling absently. "Plus, I've already made Sam's life a living hell. She doesn't have any of the Djinn magic, but if they find out I do, she'll be killed right along with me, or they'll just kill her. I don't know which option is worse. They're both pretty horrible."

Jackie placed the wood on the table and dusted off her lap. "Sam doesn't have any of your Djinn qualities, then?"

"None that I know of. She can't bend light, and that's the only thing I've got from them."

"You need to stop blaming yourself for her situation and start remembering she'd be dead right now if it hadn't been for you." When would she stop seeing her act as one of idiocy rather than compassion?

Margo cracked a smile. "Point taken." She sighed after a long sip. "She's doing a really good job too. She's got a lot more empathy than I do."

Jackie watched her stand and cross the room to the kitchenette before placing her mug in the sink, and Jackie enjoyed the way she moved, the way she looked moving through her art. If anything happened to Margo, Jackie wasn't sure what she would do. She tried to disrupt the sudden onslaught of affection by picking up the wooden piece again, bringing the carving tool to the surface, and scraping without purpose. Never had she developed such distressing affection for another, especially someone so emotionally unavailable, but Jackie knew she'd broken down a barrier, the hardest one yet. And now Margo was worried for her life as she knew it, and rightfully so. Jackie was just as worried.

Jackie scraped the wood again, a furious movement brought on by her frustration. Teach her to let herself become too close to someone.

Margo cleared her throat. "Jackie," she whispered as she walked in front of the table, staring up at her. Her gaze raked over Jackie's body, from her legs crossed beneath herself to her face, and she parted her lips as if to say something.

"I'm almost done with this, and then maybe I can figure out something for breakfast."

Margo reached up, cupping Jackie's face softly. "Jackie, thank you."

"I haven't made breakfast yet." Jackie giggled. "What do you want?" Jackie asked, leaning into the contact with a smile.

"Thank you," Margo repeated.

"For what?"

"Thank you for—" She paused, shrugging. "—being you."

Jackie leaned forward and kissed Margo, dropping the wood on the table to thread her arms around Margo's neck. Warm hands encompassed her back as Margo grabbed her, hugging her firmly. "I can come with you, if you want, when you go see Brent," Jackie murmured. She rested her forehead on Margo's, watching the firelight spark to life in her eyes.

"No, you go teach your class, and I'll let you know how things go with Brent later tonight."

Jackie grinned. "Like a date?"

A deep chuckle rumbled from Margo's chest. "Yes, like a date."

"Margo—"

Before she could continue, Margo's phone rang. She pulled away to answer.

"Yeah? What do you mean?"

Jackie hopped off the table, brushing off the wood chips and dust from her pants before heading to the kitchen for more coffee.

"Got it. Bye." Margo shoved her phone in her back pocket, rolling her eyes. "That was Brent. He's got some stuff he wants to talk about and told me to come over as soon as possible." She drew a shaky breath, apprehension clear on her face. Running her fingers through her hair, she sputtered, "No time like the present to talk to him about all this shit, huh?"

Jackie touched her arm, and Margo looked at her. "Relax. I can cancel my class and come with you, if you want." Jackie wanted Margo to tell her to cancel, to beg her to tag along, just so she'd know Margo was all right.

She shook her head. "No, no, I'll be okay." A smile crested on her face. "Date night tonight still, right?"

"Absolutely." *I sure hope so.*

They kissed, slow and soft before Margo grabbed her jacket and headed out into the day.

BY THE TIME Jackie drove the fifty minutes to Philadelphia to teach her art class, she was no closer to a plan than she was upon leaving her house. She had no stakes in Grim politics, no leverage, nothing to contribute to help save Margo's and Sam's lives. Lively chatter filled the small classroom in front of Jackie. The group of teens she taught once a month in Philadelphia warmed her heart with their gratitude. Since she'd volunteered for the program shortly after graduating from college, she was grateful for the opportunity to give the teens a creative outlet beyond the miniscule programs some schools offered. The lessons weren't much; Jackie brought the supplies—from pastels to pencils, paints and clay—and she let the students vote on what they wanted to work on during her time with them. Most of the kids were in their early teens, a few younger kids coming with an older sibling. This Sunday, they chose a Halloween theme to their lesson, which sent a pang of sadness through Jackie. She and Ezra hadn't spent a Samhain without Roz since they'd met her.

"That's all I've got for you today," Jackie said to the class. "Please take your work with you, and I'll see you next month." The students thanked her as they left the room, one leaving her their drawing of a dragon. She smiled to herself, placing the sheet of paper in her portfolio bag to take home.

The classroom stood empty as Jackie moved around the room, gathering the supplies she'd brought with her before the next class came in. As she meandered to the front of the class, picking a piece of tape from a pastel, a chair scooted across the tile flooring. A figure shifted in her periphery. Jackie turned her head from the desk and gasped. Soot-black hair sweeping over one eye, and a smile dimpled each cheek. Roz. Jackie dropped her bag, shaking her head as she ran over to her friend.

She fought back joyful tears but held her jaw tight. "Roz, I don't know if I should hug you or fucking punch you."

Roz smiled broadly and pushed her black-rimmed glasses up her nose. "How about a hug?" she asked, opening her arms.

Jackie grabbed her in a suffocating hug. "I thought you were dead," Jackie said, her voice muffled on Roz's shoulder. Her normal scent of patchouli oil and lavender was muddled with acrid car exhaust and dirt. "Where the hell have you been?" She pulled back to stare into the face of her friend. Darkness smudged the skin beneath Roz's eyes like weathered coal, far from her normally bright appearance that lit up every room she walked into.

"All over the place." A rough chuckle left Roz, one that sounded more like a bark than laughter.

"You've been missing for two months." She took a step back, crossing her arms over her chest. "Your mother thinks you're in California, and you've been avoiding me, Ezra, and Brent nonstop since you dropped off the planet. I had a demon threaten me because I was trying to find you last night at a creepy club Ezra heard you were hanging around. Where the hell have you been?" Jackie repeated, thankful the room was vacant, the rest of her class having left a few minutes before.

"You really upset Ozais."

Jackie scoffed. "So, you *were* in the building?"

"Yeah, I was." She appeared guilty and turned away, pretending to inspect the large color wheel pinned to the cheap corkboard at the front of the room. For as tired as she looked, her appearance was as pristine as usual. Her pale button-up held no wrinkles and the dark jeans she wore were clean and unrumpled.

Jackie grabbed her arm lightly. "What have you gotten yourself into? Ezra and I have been so worried about you."

"I don't even know where to begin, Jackie."

"Just try."

Roz took a deep breath and sighed heavily. "I got myself a contract with a demon so the Grim wouldn't find me."

Jackie gasped. "Wait, what?"

Roz scrunched her nose. "I didn't know what else to do."

Before Jackie could probe her further, the next scheduled class entered the room, spilling through the tables and chairs.

Jackie ushered Roz over to the desk, where she collected her belongings to make room for the next instructor. The autumn sun pressed over them as they walked across the street to the small park nestled between grimy buildings. Roz glanced from side to side, her pace hurried until she planted herself on the ground under a massive tree. She motioned for Jackie to join her, and she did, lowering herself onto the cold grass.

Roz fished a slip of paper from her back pocket and began to fold it. The seemingly unconscious movement was familiar, one Jackie knew Roz did to calm her omnipresent nerves. Her forehead crinkled in concentration.

"Are you ready to tell me what's going on?" Jackie asked.

"You know how Mam isn't Grim, right? How I'm not full Grim?"

Jackie nodded. While Roz's one mother was half Grim, half human, her second mother was a witch, passing those practical traits down to Roz through years of teaching.

Roz worried her lower lip before she spoke. "The Board called me in for a meeting one day. I wasn't really sure what it was about, but it wasn't like I could just not go. I didn't know they were going to tell me to stop using magic or they'd decommission me."

"Meaning what exactly?" Magic was part of Roz's life from the moment Jackie met her. Asking her not to use it was akin to banishing an entire half of her being. Jackie wished she would've asked Brent more about the politics in the Grim but hadn't, wanting to pretend the world was normal, that she could escape the bizarre ethereal reality, aside from her own basic needs.

"They told me if I didn't stop, they'd decommission me because I'm not pure Grim but, I've never been pure Grim. I wouldn't be able to use magic to begin with if I was. I blew off their warning, lied and said I'd abide by their silly rules, and I did what I wanted instead. So what if they decommissioned me and I couldn't open portals? Their loss, right?" Roz grabbed the back of her neck, turning her attention from Jackie to a passing car.

"What happened?"

"I was so wrong."

"Roz?"

Roz turned her attention to Jackie. "Back in February, I was working a night shift and me and my buddy were called to an unresponsive individual. When we got there, the caller was doing CPR as dispatch requested, and we took over. That's when I recognized her as a Grim. Not just any Grim, but a Grim I've seen before. A Grim my age. One I'd talked to." Roz paused, sighing heavily. "I tried everything to stabilize her on the way to the hospital, but I couldn't."

A cold dread filled Jackie as she listened to Roz's story.

"A few weeks later, I asked one of the ED nurses I'm friends with what happened to her. There was nothing outwardly wrong with her. They couldn't bring her back either, which left a question haunting me relentlessly: What the hell would kill a healthy Grim in her twenties? I wanted to know but it's not like I have access to autopsy records. So, when Corporate called me for a follow-up meeting, I booked a last-minute trip to visit Mom and Mam instead of going."

"You intentionally missed your meeting?"

Roz nodded, her gaze downcast. "I think it really made them mad because when I came back and got off the plane, this macho guy in a suit was waiting for me by baggage claim. I don't even know how he knew where I'd grab my bag but there he was, telling me he was supposed to escort me to another meeting with Corporate."

"Why didn't you call me?"

"I didn't want to worry you or Ezra. It would've been unfair to drag you into something you know nothing about. I lied to the macho Grim dude, ran to the bathroom, and called my friend from the club. All I could think was that Corporate was going to..." she trailed off as she focused on the paper in her hand again, a pained expression pinching her nose. Leaves fell from overhead, wavering in the wind as they fell to the ground around her.

"You were afraid they were going to kill you," Jackie said, finishing Roz's statement for her.

Roz pursed her lips, studying Jackie with what appeared to be suspicion. "How'd you know?"

With a long-drawn-out sigh, Jackie explained Margo's actions, Sam's rebirth as a Grim, and the subsequent consequences of her good deed. When she was finished recounting the events leading up to Margo's current predicament—sans the fact she was half Djinn—Roz covered her mouth with her fingertips, stifling laughter.

"I never would've thought Margo Petrov had the humanity or the smarts to save someone. She seems way too selfish to do anything for anyone but herself. Are you sure we're talking about the same woman?"

With her thoughts on Margo, Jackie couldn't stop her lips from spreading into a large grin. "Yeah, we're talking about the same woman. She told me every single Grim will be tested for their lineage next week. Something about a census," she said, making the statement sound even more ridiculous than it did in her head.

"A census is convenient, as terrifying as it is." A paper bird sat in Roz's palm and ruffled its wings before fluttering away. Jackie sighed as she followed the bird's flight until it disappeared, having not realized how much she missed Roz's simple magic tricks.

"You still haven't answered my question. Where have you been the last two months?"

"Well, I did visit my moms, but when I got back and had the run-in with the Grim guy at the airport, I called Vanessa and asked her what to do. I snuck out of the guy's sight, ditched my phone after Vanessa gave me some directions, and I headed to the city on foot. She lined me up with a contract at the club, and I've been with them ever since."

"The club from last night?" Jackie recalled the contract Ozais had mentioned. *Your cousin belongs to me for the time being. She signed a contract...*

Roz nodded. "The club moves all over the Tristate area, from New York, to Philly and Pittsburg to Atlantic City."

"I could've helped you, Roz. I would've dropped everything to come and get you if I had to." Jackie couldn't stifle her swirling jealously over not being Roz's first choice for help. She could've dealt with Roz calling Ezra over her, but someone else...

Roz avoided her gaze, the swoop of curly bangs falling over her face. "Look, Jackie, you know I trust you—you and Ezra are my best friends—but I was afraid you'd tell Brent." She glanced at Jackie. "Believe me, I wanted to call you and I'm sorry I didn't."

The statement didn't hurt as much as it should've. She knew Brent could be trusted from what Margo had disclosed and her own interactions with him, but Roz couldn't know for sure. She saw him as an authoritative figure, a manager in the chain of command.

"Something big is happening," Roz said, shaking her head as she pushed off the ground and grabbed the sturdy trunk of the tree for stability. "Something bigger than Brent could handle if he isn't in on it. The club was in Allentown last week, and I overheard a conversation during a lull in the music between a Board member and another patron. Apparently, Corporate is planning to kill every single halfling. They're calling it *culling the cur,* so I'm not really surprised about a census, or them cracking down on me being a halfling."

"Oh, my Goddess, Roz. Why haven't you considered at least calling Brent?"

Roz grimaced. "Because, hell, no. How do I know he won't call the Board and wash his hands of me?"

"I don't think he would do that," Jackie said cautiously. Margo explicitly told Jackie the few people who knew about her heritage, one of whom was Brent. Although it would undoubtedly bring Roz slight comfort in knowing she wasn't alone and he could be trusted, Jackie couldn't break Margo's confidence.

Roz ignored her and continued with her story. "The woman was a Board member for the Atlantic section. She literally bragged about how they'll be free from the cur in four months tops."

Jackie stood, shaking her head as she absorbed Roz's words. The pieces began to fall into place, the census, the fear Margo held, why Roz disappeared. Jackie subdued a shiver. If Roz was in trouble, was she safe in the club with Ozais?

"How long is the contract?" Jackie asked. She touched Roz's shoulder.

There was a pause in conversation as a dog walker passed on the sidewalk, Roz watching the person well until they'd crossed the intersection. "Eighteen months."

"That long?"

"Yeah."

"What exactly do you do—tarot readings?"

"No, he actually has me as a bouncer, which is as ridiculous as it sounds. I figured he'd want me to do stuff for his clients to entertain them like sleight of hand crap or parlor tricks, and who better to give that than a charming magician like myself?" Roz asked, waggling her eyebrows. "Instead, I meander around the club, keeping an eye out for shenanigans. He says I'm the perfect person for it because I'm small and nonthreatening but can hold my own. It's not half bad. He comes off as a controlling monster but, for a demon, he's not a bad boss, and I'm safe..." she trailed off.

"You have no freedom?"

Roz bit her lip and shook her head slowly. "I have to follow his club all over the place. Tomorrow, we're heading to Cape May for two nights. Then, we'll be in New York City. Then, off to Atlantic City again." She placed her palm on her cheek and sighed. "I'm exhausted, Jackie."

"Is there any way out of the contract?"

"No, I've looked. The only way I can get out of it is if someone else buys the contract from him, and honestly, that possibility terrifies me. He's assured me that I'm safe, but I do worry one day before the eighteen months are up, he'll sell it to someone else." She picked at the sole of her worn sneakers. "Or time will run out, and I'll be out in the world again with Corporate after me."

"I don't know what to say. You're safe where you are?" Jackie's mind whirled, a fear so thick and noxious, she became lightheaded as it rolled through her.

Roz lifted her shoulder, lips pursed. "As safe as I can be right now. I would've been safer if I stayed in the UK with my moms."

Jackie wrapped her arms around Roz and squeezed her. "I was so damn worried about you."

Sighing, Roz hugged her back tighter than Jackie's hold, and then she let go. "I'm sorry."

Jackie readjusted her bag's shoulder strap, setting a heavy gaze on Roz. "Are you okay, I mean *really* okay?" *Not that she'll tell me the truth anyway.* Jackie not only worried for Roz's physical health, but her mental health as well.

Roz glanced from side to side slowly, purposefully, before she spoke. "I don't know." She met Jackie's stare. "I've got to get back. The only saving grace I have is the club will stop floating around in a month or so." She rolled her eyes. "Ozais says he likes to hunker down for the fall and winter in one location."

She touched Jackie's arm, wincing. Without another word, she crushed Jackie in another, tighter hug, sniffling beside her ear.

"I missed you, Jackie."

After releasing her, Roz darted out of the park and down an alleyway until she vanished in the churning city.

Chapter Twenty

THE FIRST PLACE Margo went after leaving Jackie's was her own apartment. The parking lot was nearly empty and when she noticed Luis's car wasn't among the five parked, she left without so much as getting out of her car. She released a resigned sigh. The words she'd spoken to her brother couldn't be taken back, and she couldn't fathom how badly she'd hurt him by her arrogance. There was no excuse no matter what state of mind she'd been in when she said what she had. How could she have treated him that way?

She lit a cigarette at a stoplight, debating on giving Luis a call. Apologizing to him over the phone seemed too insincere and with the way he—rightfully—stormed out of their apartment the night before, she knew anything but in person would fall flat. *I distinctly remember feeling like my only family left me.* His words burned in her memory, and a pang of guilt forced her to waste a drag. She coughed on smoke and smushed the cigarette out in her astray as the light turned green.

She stole a glance in her rearview mirror, catching a glimpse of her suitcase on the backseat. If she hadn't gone to Jackie's house, she'd be in another city, in another state, perhaps even across the border.

What made her stay?

The draw toward Jackie was undeniable, and it had tugged Margo to her when she thought her mind was made up to leave, to disappear, but it couldn't have been the only reason. Why had Margo chosen to stay? Jackie couldn't help her other than being present for her, offering her support just as Luis and Brent had.

Brent led to her current dilemma.

The call from Brent had been unexpected and Margo didn't know what to expect, as his tone had been calm, almost disinterested when he told her to hurry to his house. When Jackie offered to cancel her class to come with her, Margo had fought the desire to accept her offer but couldn't. She needed to do this on her own, regardless of what Brent's urgency entailed.

The last time she'd seen him, he'd handed her a potion with the potential to kill her. A question resurfaced, and she gripped the steering wheel. Was she just a ploy in his drive to protect the halflings as a whole, or did she matter to him as an individual? Her initial instinct was to assume he wanted her for the sole purpose of proving a point to the Board—she was a decent Grim who happened to be a halfling—but the more she thought about it, she knew it was the latter. He'd brought her and Luis into his home after finding them as teens, housed them, fed them, taught them the basics of their people. She knew Luis regarded Brent and Collin as family, probably nearly as much as he considered her his sister.

Ugh, and now I have to tell Brent I conjured light to fight a demon. She rolled her eyes at herself as she drove over the bridge. Why had she? Oh, yeah, to protect Jackie from getting herself killed. Just as she had saved Sam, Margo had acted on instinct and needed to do anything to protect Jackie.

Jackie was different than anyone Margo had met before and she knew it wasn't solely due to who Jackie was as a person, though this did factor into it. Margo had willingly opened herself to Jackie, offered her own blood to help her, and Margo was still trying to decide why. Margo hadn't been forced to allow Jackie to feed from her, didn't have to help her in any way, but Margo didn't regret her choice to do so because it had been her choice. And, shit, did she feel good afterward, not just because of the bite.

She had after saving Sam. A bubble of pride had swelled within her as it did when she aided Brent in opening the portal for Collin to visit his family. She couldn't hide the fact she enjoyed helping people.

Wow. Go figure helping people makes you feel good. Maybe that's why Brent is helping me. Brent and Collin cared for her, that much was clear, but Margo couldn't understand why when all she'd ever done to them was adamantly push them away. She chose to live her life with a scant sprinkling of people. "Yeah, more like person," she muttered aloud to herself. Luis had been the only constant in her life, the only individual she'd opened up to, and she enjoyed the simplicity of one person, but now...

Margo turned onto Brent's road. Luis wasn't the only one who cared what happened to Margo as discerning as that realization was. Brent cared. Collin cared. Sam cared. Jackie cared. This wasn't the most alarming aspect; she cared for them as well. Her life was far better with them in it. She couldn't just leave, not with Brent going beyond what was necessary to secure her safety and with Jackie disarming her own guarded self to her.

As her car tumbled down the bumpy driveway toward Brent's house, Margo allowed herself to care for them wholly. All of them meant more to her than she ever let herself acknowledge.

Brent stood beside his car, face stoic and jaw tight. Margo pulled up beside him, flashing a wicked smile as she rolled her window down. "What's up, chicken butt?"

His expression didn't waver with her humorous tone. "Come on, we're taking my car."

Margo fumbled with her keys as she turned off her car. "Where?"

"To your meeting with Sybil Chomsky."

"WHY IS THIS meeting with Sybil and not the whole group of holier than thou folks?" Margo pulled her feet down from the dashboard as Brent turned off the highway north. She knew the answer but needed to talk about something, anything to fill the car with sound. From the moment she climbed into Brent's car, he was quiet, reserved even. His unusual silence stirred blatant fear within Margo, but she took the hint, keeping her mouth shut until she couldn't handle it anymore.

Brent kept his gaze set ahead, but Margo noticed his jaw tighten. "She was the one to make the decision—the one who chose to side with Alfonso when they discussed what to do with you and Sam. The meetings are one-on-one, and she's the Board member who has to conduct the follow-ups with you."

The intense set of his jaw, the line carved between his brows, and the overall unease exuding off him left Margo speechless. She couldn't formulate a way to tell him about Ozais, or that Jackie now knew she was part Djinn. How could she when she couldn't decide whether he looked as if he was going to kill someone or he was going to throw up everywhere?

"What is she going to ask?" Margo didn't care about the time of the meeting as long as it didn't ruin her evening with Jackie, which she hoped wouldn't be her last. If it was, she didn't want to be late.

"She will ask a series of questions about your performance—if you're abiding by their rules, keeping yourself from making more assistants, completing your work, etcetera." He stopped the car at a red light and turned to look at her, his dark gaze somber. "I want you to avoid most of the questions, if not all. Let me do the talking, and I will ensure nothing is said out of place."

"Okay." Margo found his warning strange but decided she would heed it, lest she get herself in even more trouble. "You're acting weird, dude." Apprehension whirled in her stomach, turbulent uncertainty gnawing at her insides.

An awkward smile tweaked the corner of his mouth, but he remained quiet.

The squat building sat beside a shopping center, which included a nail salon, dollar store, and a vague check-cashing venue. As late afternoon turned to evening, the parking lot was nearly deserted, save a pristine white Prius and a filthy Toyota truck. Brent parked his car a few spaces from the Prius, which Margo assumed to be Sybil's. Part of her hoped to have the meeting with Alfonso, as he was the only one of the three Board members who didn't want to immediately have her and Sam decommissioned.

Brent cut the engine. He reached in the back seat and withdrew a small canister. "What's that?" Margo questioned as Brent cradled the object in his hands.

"A peace offering," he replied, carefully cradling the canister in his hand after he shrugged his gray satchel over his shoulder.

The two got out of the car.

A door between the nail salon and an out-of-business video store held no name, and paper blocked out the windows. When they reached the unmarked door, Brent pulled it open and ushered Margo inside.

The room greeting them was more of a cramped box, four walls painted an off-white—the color was probably marketed as egg shell or alabaster—and a popcorn ceiling above the single particleboard table in the middle of the room. Sybil Chomsky barely raised her head from the laptop sitting on the table in front of her, her fingers clicking away at the keys. Her ginger hair was held in a tight bun, not a strand out of place around her soft, pale face as she looked up at them temporarily. "Thank you for your punctuality. If you'll just give me a moment." Sybil bent her head back over the computer, squinting.

Brent sat in one of the scattered folding chairs around the table, and Margo plopped down next to him, immediately wanting to leave the moment her back hit the chair. His "peace offering" was suspiciously hidden beneath his chair. Five minutes passed, according to the clock on the wall, ticking loudly in the margin of Margo's hearing, and Sybil finally glanced up. "My apologies. I was finishing up an email. We were lucky to find a venue on such short notice. There was an electrical problem at our normal location, so please pardon the disarray," she said, indicating the blank white walls surrounding them.

Brent nodded. "Of course. Yes, just hoping this will be brief."

"Right. I wanted to conduct this meeting prior to our census this week, so let's begin." Sybil yanked a folder from beneath the now closed laptop and opened it, sifting through the sheets of paper with a pen ready in her hand. "Has she completed all the tasks assigned to her?" Sybil asked without raising her gaze from the folder in her hands.

Brent folded his hands on the table. "Yes, and some. She has become an exemplary Grim in a matter of weeks."

This didn't impress Sybil. Well...her face didn't change from the ever-present disapproving expression as if she had a thumbtack in her shoe. "You aren't partaking in any suspicious activities such as, but not limited to, creating another Grim using a blood bond, breaching confidence by telling humans of our existence, opening portals without intent, insinuating oneself into the politics of another race..."

Margo's jaw dropped as Sybil continued, dumbfounded by the rules she was completely unaware of. When Sybil finally stopped naming off the arbitrary regulations, Margo nodded. "Nope, none of that."

"I can truthfully attest to her following the rules of our people," Brent said. Though Margo knew they'd both broken at least two of those rules—if not more.

"Wonderful. I'm pleased to hear this." She placed the folder down and stared directly at Margo. "Moving on to our next topic of discussion: When is the last time you spoke to or saw Rosalind Darab?"

"Roz? Shit, it's got to be going on two or three months since I saw her."

She turned her attention to Brent, her pointed nose flaring slightly. "And you?"

"I spoke with her roughly two months ago, but you know that." Brent's tone was as unreadable as was his facial expression. A car honked outside followed by a loud voice, but the room remained quiet.

"If either of you know the whereabouts of Rosalind, I strongly advise you to share any information with the

Board. We worry for her safety," she said curtly. "Our meeting is concluded."

Margo stayed in her seat, waiting for Brent's word to move while Sybil gathered the paperwork in front of her. Tension filled the quiet space around the table. "That's it?"

Sybil smiled. "Yes, painless, right?"

Brent made no effort to move, his gaze still fixed on Sybil. "Have you found a new distributor, Sybil?" The relaxed way Brent asked the question caused Margo discomfort, and she shifted in her seat, patting the front pocket of her hoodie for her cigarettes, not that she should smoke one inside, but knowing they were still there would hopefully get her through the rest of the awkward meeting. But the meeting was concluded. The meeting was done; they could leave, and everything would be fine. *What the hell is Brent doing?*

"This is hardly an appropriate topic to bring up around her," Sybil said, gesturing to Margo with a tilt of her head, brows knitted.

"Why are you so interested in Rosalind's whereabouts?" Brent's tone was sharp, but Margo noticed his hands trembling in his lap, the movement revealing what hid beneath this guise. *He's nervous,* she thought curiously.

Deep wrinkles creased Sybil's forehead as she knitted her brows. "The concern is obvious: we fear she may be in harm's way. We only wish to ensure she's alive and well."

"There's no need to lie."

Sybil cocked her head. "Pardon me?"

"The Board's distaste for anyone who deviates from purity is common knowledge, and as the Board just discovered the truth behind Rosalind's heritage, the question of your true intentions is in the forefront of my curiosity."

She sighed loudly, gaze narrowing with impatience. "Individuals with muddled backgrounds have no place with the Grim. This is how it's been since the initiative and how we continue to thrive," she said through gritted teeth.

Margo scoffed. "Seriously?"

Brent twisted his head slowly to her, shooting her a sharp glare before turning his attention back to Sybil. He sat up straighter in his chair now with his attention solely on Sybil. "That's a peculiar way to talk about your own kind." *Own kind?* Margo's eyes widened, and she dropped her head again, afraid she wouldn't be able to contain her words. *What the hell is Brent talking about?*

"You'll have to beg my pardon. We uphold our strict policy with the exception of Ms. Diaz, as you both know," Sybil said, but the unsteadiness of her voice contradicted her statement, making Margo wonder if what Brent said had gotten under her skin.

Brent took his phone from his coat pocket and typed a quick message before he spoke, tucking the device back where he'd retrieved it. "And yourself, no?" He looked up at Sybil, whose lips were a tight line.

"I am not a filthy cur." Instead of sounding fierce, Sybil's voice continued to quiver, as did her lower lip.

Margo's patience evaporated—the slur set her off. Rage burned within her, prompting her heart to race. Fury at Sybil, at the idiots in Corporate who held such sickening ideations. Rage toward her family for leaving her with nothing, no knowledge of her heritage, of what she was destined to do in her life. The light spilling in from the covered windows skittered around on the floor, snaking their way toward Margo. She didn't have control over their movement, her fury clouding her judgment and her ability to care. Her breath quickened as she rolled up the sleeves of her hoodie, ready to fight. "Why do you people hate anyone who doesn't meet your fucked-up sense of purity? You know it's a bunch of garbage—I can tell by the look on your face!"

Brent sighed disapprovingly but said nothing.

Sybil crinkled her nose at Margo. "We have this standard in place to ensure the protection of ourselves and the spirits we vow to assist to the other side. If we let any person with a hint of anything other than Grim background help these spirits, we'd have a mess on our hands."

"That is such bullshit!" Margo jumped up, her chair falling to the floor behind her. Warmth from her rage spread over her face and down her neck, contrasting with the coolness as glowing incandescence flooded around her. "What the fuck is wrong with you? They have as much right to be a Grim as you do—it shouldn't matter how much Grim blood they have. If they can help the spirits that need help, why the hell would you stop them?"

Brent wrapped his hand around Margo's forearm, urging her to sit, but she wrenched her arm free, glaring at him.

She turned back to Sybil. "You're an awful person. You and the rest of those shitheads at Corporate." She was done sitting on the sidelines, allowing Brent to fight her battles for her.

Eyes widened, Sybil shook her head, her mouth opening and closing, the words dying before she could speak them. Margo glanced down at herself. Light coated her fingers in luminescence, drawing lines across her forearms, creating a delicate lattice design overtop her tattoo. The expression on Sybil's face told Margo all she needed to know; Sybil saw her conjure the light. Fear crept into her chest as the realization slammed into Margo.

"What on earth are you?" Sybil asked, her head shaking from side to side.

Brent sat the container he brought with him in the middle of the table. Sybil turned to it suspiciously. "For years, I've allowed you and your colleagues to harass me to join in your fight to find individuals who fell short of your pitiful standard. I've watched you sentence countless Grim to an existence worse than death, if not outright ending their lives simply for being who they are. When you came to me with your own ailment, I was disgusted by the hypocrisy—"

"You don't understand, Brent," Sybil interrupted in a whisper while her gaze lingered on Margo.

Margo watched the altercation with unmasked interest, reaching for her pack of cigarettes despite the strict "No Smoking" sign taped to the door. It didn't matter anymore; Sybil knew what she was. All this time Margo had protected her secret, and she had displayed her power right in front of the person who could call for her death.

No matter how true Margo's words were, Sybil now knew she wasn't full Grim. Her hand shook as she brought the cigarette to her mouth; her anger yet to dissipate, and she wanted nothing more than to berate Sybil further, not that her words would change the Board's decisions, but she sure felt good after speaking her mind. She had nothing to lose now. She dared a glance at the floor, grimacing when she noticed the shining pool at her feet, despite forcing her rage back.

Brent was no longer standing still; he'd begun a slow pace around the table, a predator stalking his prey. Although he was speaking, Margo barely heard his cryptic words. Sybil cowered lower in her seat, gaze now downcast. He rounded the table again, directly behind Sybil as he spoke again, and Margo tried to pay attention despite her fear.

"You kill people—people just like yourself who deviate from the standard—who share traits with other preternatural creatures, and you hide your own heritage." Ash fell to the table as Margo tried to contain her shaking. Tension—no—*magic* hung in the room, hovering low above the table between the three of them, restricting her breath.

Margo cocked her head, unable to stop herself as she asked, "What heritage?"

"Even before the initiative was enacted, you hid the truth very well but not well enough." Brent stopped in front of the chair he previously occupied, hands gripping the back, attention fixed on the terrified woman. He reached for the container on the table. "The entire Board is a disgrace to our kind, but you are especially evil." The conviction in his tone frightened Margo, but she stayed close to him, offering her silent camaraderie in the form of her proximity. Although he exuded ferocity with his attention directed at Sybil, a tremor ran through the arm hovering over the canister, and fear quivered his lower lip.

Margo's skin prickled in goose bumps, her stomach rolling as a cold dread shivered down her spine.

"Brent," Sybil sniveled. Brent slammed his palm down on the canister, causing the container to explode, and Margo covered her mouth. Powder coated the scene in front of her, and she closed her eyes, covering her face with her arms.

Margo opened her eyes.

Dust motes settled on the tabletop, and Sybil was gone. Before Margo could question the disappearance, a furry creature ambled out from behind the table, shaking their head, ruffling their fur-covered face. The creature peered up at Margo with an orange gaze, their dark nose flaring, and twitching whiskers adorning the sides of their face.

"What the fuck?" Margo muttered, stepping backward.

"You could say we discovered the loose links in the chain of command," Brent said, brushing off the dust from his cardigan, unphased by the bobcat sniffing the air. No, not a bobcat, Margo noted. The wild animal was far too large to be a simple bobcat. As the creature took a step toward Margo, their massive paws smacked the carpeted floor with heavy thuds.

"You mean loose link?" she countered.

He snorted. "No, I said links." When Margo said nothing, he continued. "Sybil Chomsky is a lynx shifter." He took a step back as the creature moved forward, lowering their head to the ground. "Well, half-lynx shifter."

She shook her head furiously. "You're fucking with me."

Gaze still set on the animal, Brent reached into his bag and chuckled nervously as he withdrew a peculiar gun. "Nope. You know, puns aren't funny when I have to explain them to you at length."

"Brent!" Margo threw her hands in the air as he lifted the strange gun. "What the hell are you doing?"

He pointed the gun at the lynx and pulled the trigger. A stubby dart flew across the room before hitting the lynx.

The creature's ears flattened on their head as the dart hit them. "The tranquilizer should go into effect any second."

A low growl emanated from the lynx's mouth as they edged closer to Brent, teeth displayed in a wicked snarl.

"I didn't expect her to be so volatile during our meeting—she's usually more docile," Brent said as he dug deeper in the satchel.

"She?"

Holy shit, he isn't kidding. The lynx is Sybil, Margo realized with shocking clarity. Just as Brent opened his mouth to answer Margo, the animal crouched, her growl heightening as her body tensed. The lynx-Sybil sprang from the floor, catapulting through the room before slamming into Brent. Margo acted, immediately forcing the light around her to the lynx. Brent fell to the ground, and a vicious growl erupted from the lynx as Margo surrounded Sybil with light. Harnessing the light still quivering at her feet, Margo threw the animal across the room, the weight of the impact shattering the chair Sybil once occupied before Brent dispersed the powder. Sweat dripped on Margo's forehead from exertion, and she swiped at her dampened bangs as she switched her attention to Brent.

Deep rips splayed open the polo beneath his cardigan, and red seeped through the holes. He held up his hand as Margo crouched next to him to look closer at the wounds. "I'm all right," Brent said. "Is she okay?"

The animal lay on her side, eyes closed but a steady rise and fall lifted her fur-covered chest. "I think so." Margo helped him to his feet, glancing behind her. "What the fuck did you do to her?"

"A simple powder to initiate her shift. I intended to fully tranquilize her before she got any closer, but it seems the loading dose didn't suffice as it should've." Brent breathed, pointing a shaky hand to the gun.

A door at the back of the small space opened, one Margo hadn't noticed when they'd first entered, and Collin stepped through, lugging a large bag over his shoulder. He took in the room, looking from Brent to the animal on the ground back to Margo.

"Brent, you're bleeding. What happened?" The bag dropped to the floor, and he hurried to Brent's side.

"I'm okay." Brent grimaced as he held his chest, the wound oozing slightly. "The tranquilizer did nothing. I adjusted the dosage per weight but perhaps I miscalculated," he said, nodding toward the gun on the floor next to his satchel.

"How did you manage to...?" Collin trailed off.

"I didn't do anything," Brent said and jabbed his thumb in Margo's direction. "Margo. If she hadn't been here, Sybil would've mauled me."

She licked her lips, unsure what to say with both Brent and Collin staring at her.

"Thank you," Collin whispered.

Before she could comment, Brent pushed himself from the ground, and Collin aided him the rest of the way up to stand. "Just get Sybil out of here before she wakes up. The plan is the same. You've got the backup tranquilizer in your car?"

"Yes."

"Good. Get her out of here."

Hesitation flashed over Collin's face, but he nodded. "Okay."

Brent grabbed Margo's wrist and tugged her out the door before she could watch Collin lug the unconscious animal into the giant burlap bag he'd brought. The afternoon sun bore down on the parking lot, but a crisp autumn breeze flattened Margo's hair against her face as she hurried along with Brent. They reached the car, and Margo pulled her arm from Brent's hand. "Brent, just stop for a second and explain what the fuck is going on." She pointed to his blood-stained shirt, and though the bleeding appeared to have slowed, the wounds were painful to look at. "You need to see a doctor."

"We don't have time for this. Get in the car."

"At least let me drive."

Reluctantly, Brent handed her the keys and climbed into the passenger seat as Margo got into the driver's side. When Margo started the car, she glanced over at Brent. "Where are we going?"

"The highway," he said, reaching behind him into the backseat.

Margo drove out of the parking lot and headed toward the highway.

Brent lugged a small first-aid kit from the floor, heaving it into his lap. A sigh, one which spoke of exhaustive planning, left Brent as he leaned his head against the window, and Margo realized the seemingly disastrous meeting hadn't been an accident. "Lucky I brought this just in case."

Margo chortled, shaking her head as she tried to figure out the madness that had just ensued. "So...so, all that—you planned this whole thing?"

Digging through the bag, Brent sighed. "We caused the 'electrical problem' at their office, also preparing this location for their use by installing a camera to capture her shifting. I knew this was their backup office from a previous issue that arose."

"You and Collin?" Margo glanced over at him.

"Yes."

She turned her attention back to the road. "What happens to Sybil?" she asked, still dumbfounded that the creature who attacked Brent was Sybil.

"Let's just say she won't be going back to the Grim any time soon," he said, drawing a sharp breath.

Margo shot him a sideway glance. "You okay?"

"I will be." He pointed to a lane a mile ahead of them as he yanked a pack of gauze from the bag. "Turn at this exit here."

Sighing in relief, Margo nodded. If Sybil wasn't able to get back to Corporate, then perhaps Margo would be safe. The offramp sign told Margo they were heading the opposite direction of Brent's house and not even close to her place. "Where are we going?"

The bleeding on his chest had ceased, the dried blood causing his polo to stick to his skin. He pulled his shirt up and set to work patching the wounds with thick gauze, taping it off before answering her, "I've got a pit stop before I go home."

Margo continued on the road, following Brent's directions as he told her where to go. Up ahead stood the Atlantic City airport and Margo was confused when Brent told her to keep going. Her first thought was they were picking someone up—perhaps Roz had finally decided to come back from her disappearance, though the timing was bizarre. No, *everything* was bizarre. When Brent told her to turn into the departure lane, Margo tensed. "Brent. Why are we here?"

She stopped in front of a budget airline where two people stood behind a baggage kiosk. They watched the car expectantly, and Margo looked away, switching on the hazard lights. "What are we doing here?"

Brent twisted in his seat, a deep crease in his brows. "Collin believes this may start a war. I find the only fair thing to do is to give you an out." Brent reached forward, withdrawing a thick envelope from the glove box. He met her gaze and frowned. "Things didn't go according to plan, and there is no proper way to thank you for saving my life," he said, handing her the envelope.

Margo opened it. Inside was a printed flight itinerary with Margo's name on it. A one-way ticket to—of all places—Iceland. "I don't understand."

"As selfish as this is, I needed you here to have our meeting with Sybil, so I could get the plan in motion. She wouldn't have stayed long enough in the meeting for me to toss the powder at her. I needed to catch her off guard."

Margo glared at him, pursing her lips. "So, I could've left all along?"

He nodded.

"Is there anything else I should know that you've been lying to me about?"

Sighing, Brent nodded again. "Collin's trip to Jael wasn't solely for him to be granted citizenship again."

Margo leaned back, baffled and livid. "Why the hell couldn't you just tell me the truth from the start, instead of using me this whole fucking time?"

"There was a certain way we had to do this to keep things quiet." He brought his hand to his forehead. "None of that matters. You have the opportunity to start new somewhere else far, far from here in a very discreet location. Once Corporate discovers Sybil is missing, chances are they'll do a full investigation, which will halt their planned census tomorrow, but eventually they will conduct it."

"Of course, it matters! You lied to me this whole time when you could've told me what was going on, what you guys had planned. I could've fucking helped. I could've at least been a little less worried about getting myself and Sam killed."

"You're right." Brent swallowed, his downcast gaze hanging in shame. "I'm sorry."

The hazard lights clicked like a metronome as they sat in silence.

"If you hadn't been there with me, I may not have made it out. I've never seen Sybil shift before, and I poorly miscalculated how she would react in her lynx form." Brent's tone was whispered but hung heavily between them.

"I acted on instinct and returned the favor. You saved Sam and I."

Brent looked down at his hands. "You already returned that favor by helping me open the portal for Collin."

"Yeah, a favor you lied about."

"I'm sorry."

"So, what's the real reason behind opening the portal?" She'd been tricked into believing it was for Collin, a reason she'd held close to her heart as if she aided Collin in seeing his family again.

"In part, we didn't lie about Collin longing to reconnect with his family—that was a positive side effect—but initially, we needed to speak with Jael to see if he would assist in what could be a war with Corporate."

A war? Margo looked away, settling her gaze on the airport instead of on Brent. He could've told her the whole time, but she realized it was her fault he hadn't been truthful. Did her average behavior lead Brent to believe she'd ever help him with such a matter unless forced? No, of course not. She didn't give many people the warm fuzzies, nor did she go out of her way to help anyone, so why would he tell her?

I did this to myself, damnit. She glanced at the paperwork on her lap while running her fingers through her hair. "I can leave, and I'll have no consequences?"

"No," Brent said, his voice forlorn. "None at all. You'll be safe."

She had a choice, one that shouldn't require much thought on her part, but Margo found herself torn, uncertain. When she looked up again, Brent was watching her. "You have every right to hate me for what I did."

Though she knew he was right, and she *was* angry with him, she didn't hate him. She couldn't leave, not now, not without the people who mattered to her. *Fuck it.* She smiled despite the situation, regardless that she could've left weeks ago, could've avoided this, could've been forewarned. She spoke her mind, standing up for not only her, but for Sam and other partial Grims out there. She wouldn't miss the opportunity to be part of whatever Brent and Collin were planning. She tossed the papers behind her, and they fluttered to the back seat. "I'm not going anywhere. Let's fuck up their world."

Chapter Twenty-One

CHILLED AIR PRESSED against Margo's back as she unlocked the front door and pushed into the condo. The day began with a handful of reluctant spirits whose unfinished business didn't take Margo long to conclude, but all she wanted to do was have a beer and sleep for a week after the insanity during her meeting with Sybil. Though the epic incident on Sunday ended very boringly, the two days following the revelation about Sybil Chomsky's blatant hypocrisy were exhausting.

Brent took Margo back to his house, claiming she couldn't speak to Luis or Jackie since the situation had to stay quiet until the proper authorities interviewed her. Monday morning, bright and early before Margo could even think of pouring her first cup of coffee, she headed home from Brent's in anticipation of a guest. A representative from Corporate paid Margo a visit, just as Brent said they would, asking a multitude of questions regarding her meeting with Sybil. As instructed by Brent, Margo claimed she went to the agreed location. Yes, she was aware of the sudden change in venue. No, Sybil never made it to the meeting. Margo kept her composure while the man questioned her, throwing her sarcasm around like confetti to add to her nonchalant attitude, wishing Brent were there to buffer the awkward encounter. After the thirtieth question, the man left, seemingly satisfied with her story, which of course aligned perfectly with the story he received from Brent.

Sybil Chomsky was still actively listed as missing, but Brent assured Margo she was safe, whatever that meant. After Sybil's audacity in commenting on the *cur* living among the Grim, Margo couldn't care less if she was still alive. To hold such judgment toward others when she hid her own bloodline deemed her useless in Margo's eyes. She couldn't fathom someone bringing harm to others with the amount of hypocrisy Sybil spewed. If it were up to Margo, she would've taken the video of Sybil shifting straight to the asshats at the main office in New York, but Brent claimed all good things came in time.

Margo warned Brent about Ozais, the possibility of him spreading what she was in the community, a lone Djinn in the U.S., but Brent told her not to worry. She wanted to tell Luis why she left, that she feared he would face some type of retaliation for her interaction with the demon. Keeping to her word, Margo said nothing to Luis or Jackie. Brent told her they'd know eventually, to keep a low profile, and he would take care of the rest. And Margo trusted his word.

The darkness of the condo welcomed her, and she flipped on a light before closing the door. The low murmur of a television met her, and she looked around. Luis's shoes sat by the couch, a glass of water dripping condensation onto the table. They hadn't spoken since the night Margo meant to leave, but when she went to her room the day before, Vincent the mongoose wasn't on her bed anymore.

"Hey, sis." Margo turned to the voice, finding Luis standing in the hallway, shrugging into a coat.

"Hey."

They stared at each other for a long moment, Margo unsure what to say, unsure if there was anything she could say to relay the guilt possessing her. "Luis, I—"

"Brent's expecting us," he said, cutting off her attempted apology.

"Okay."

Luis walked to the living room without another word and turned the television off before slipping his sneakers on. He walked to the front door, head down as he passed Margo.

Margo exhaled through her nose, zipped up her jacket, and followed Luis.

They were silent as they strolled down to the parking lot. "I may be a few minutes late. I have to stop for gas," she said.

"No worries. Just ride with me."

After getting in the car, Margo tried to revive her apology. The cold attitude Luis threw at her was expected and warranted but stung, nonetheless. She couldn't expect him to forgive and forget the way she treated him as she packed to leave for good just a few days ago without any regard to his feelings.

As Luis turned onto the main road, Margo lost her nerve, peering out the passenger window instead of trying to apologize again. Tension blanketed them, broken only by the soft music playing. Margo picked at her fingers, wanting to apologize, wanting to know what Luis knew, and if he understood why she wanted to leave.

Luis switched through the radio with his free hand as he stopped at stoplight after the bridge. "Did you hear that story on the news?" Luis asked, breaking their silence.

"No, what else could be going on?" Margo thrummed her fingers on the passenger door, hoping for no more news. No news was good news. She was becoming quite wary of anything newsworthy.

A smile crinkled the corner of his eyes. "A bear tried to attack a mongoose and that little fucker took the bear down all on his own."

"Oh? Tiny but tough as nails, right?" Margo grinned at the story she'd made up for him years and years ago.

He glanced over at her, smiling broadly. "They may be small, but they're mighty and fierce."

The atmosphere in the car calmed, her guilt-burdened tension slipping away. "I'm sorry for being such a selfish asshat."

Passing lights flashed over his face, showcasing the seriousness in his demeanor as he spoke. "Don't. If anything, you should be apologizing for not telling me what was going on."

Margo sighed. "I know I should've, but I didn't want to drop all this drama on you when you've got your own things going on."

Luis tilted his head back in a wary gesture before directing his attention back to the road. "You're *supposed* to burden your bullshit drama on your siblings."

They made the drive to Brent's quicker than Margo anticipated, their banter easing her nerves and bringing her a comfortable familiarity she didn't know she needed desperately. The porchlight usually illuminating the winding walkway to the house was dimmed, and Margo squinted as Luis pulled up beside Brent's SUV. "So, did Brent say what he wanted us over here for?" Margo asked as she climbed out of the passenger seat, slamming the door shut.

Luis offered her a lazy shrug. "Not much other than to talk about the impending doom of our whole system."

"Cool." Margo rolled her eyes at her brother's ambiguity. "This is really a big deal, isn't it?" She followed him up the path, kicking loose stones from the sidewalk.

"Pretty much. I still can't believe Sybil is a lynx shifter. Who would've guessed?"

Margo shook her head, scaling the stairs to the porch in two steps. "Not me. Did he tell you everything?"

"Pretty much."

When she reached to knock, the front door opened wide, firing a sickening unease through Margo's belly. "Hello?"

Darkness cloaked the normally bright foyer, a small fire burning in the hearth providing scant lighting. She stepped inside, holding a hand back to keep Luis from following in case danger lurked within the home. "Hello?" she repeated.

Lights flared on, causing Margo to throw her arm over her face. "Surprise!" announced a disharmony of voices.

"Happy birthday!" someone chimed, and then another person echoed.

Margo pulled her arm from over her face and allowed her eyes to adjust. Sam stood beside Jackie, both holding strings attached to vibrant balloons drifting toward the ceiling, cheesy grins on their faces. Brent and Collin stood with a banner, etched with a celebratory statement. "Happy birthday, sis," Luis said, nudging her with his elbow.

"You motherfuckers," Margo said, but she smirked despite her words. "You were in on this?"

Luis shot her a sheepish smile. "Hell yeah, I was."

Butting into their space, Collin hugged Margo tightly, telling her about the cake he made for her in the kitchen, trading off to let Brent squeeze her. When they moved, Margo took in the state of the space. Streamers bowed from the ceiling of the foyer, various hues and shades, and music drifted from the stereo. *A damn birthday party, after all that happened?* Margo shook her head.

"All right, now that you've all thoroughly scared the crap out of me, let me go smoke, and then I might let you sing happy birthday to me."

When Margo turned, Jackie was already opening the front door. "Care if I join you?"

"Since when do you smoke?" Margo teased.

They stepped out onto the porch and closed the door behind them. Jackie looked out into the night sky, her face sculpted beauty in the light of the moon.

Margo patted her pocket but stopped herself from retrieving a cigarette. "I'm sorry I didn't tell you more about what was going on," Margo said in earnest. She looked over at Jackie, smiling when their gazes met. The only words they'd spoken to each other since Saturday were a handful of texts, Jackie letting her know she'd spoken to Brent, and she'd visit her when things calmed down.

Jackie turned to her. "Brent told me everything."

Margo tilted her head to the side. "Everything?"

Jackie nodded. "I told him about the situation with Ozais, and it would seem we don't have to worry about him saying anything to Corporate."

A coyote howled in the distance, and Margo gazed out into the woods, nodding. Music from inside rose an octave, the sound muffled behind the solid oak door.

"I saw Roz."

Margo faced her again. "She's all right?"

"Yes. She's got a contract with Ozais; he wasn't lying about that, and he's protecting her from Corporate. She also told me Corporate has been hunting her down since they discovered she's been using magic regularly. She also seems to think that Corporate is using the census to find any Grim who deviates from their standard."

"To kill them?"

Jackie's nod was solemn. This wasn't fair to her; she wasn't even Grim. All she strived to achieve was a life of normalcy, and Margo had done nothing but complicate almost every aspect. She had to give Jackie a way out before things became even more complicated in her world.

"Look, Jackie, if you want to bail from this...from me because of the cluster that's revolving around me and the rest of us, I wouldn't hold—"

Jackie's fingers pressed hard against Margo's lips, her obsidian gaze pointed. "I am not bailing from anything, Margo Petrov, so shut it." She removed her fingers and replaced them with her lips, the kiss fierce, leaving Margo dizzy. Margo threaded her arms around Jackie's waist, wanting nothing more than to stay in this very position forever. "Whatever goes down," Jackie whispered, her lips warm on Margo's forehead, "I'll be sure to stick around to be the annoying reminder not to get yourself killed."

Margo chuckled, clutching tighter to Jackie, pleading with her eyes not to let go of the tears welling beneath her lids, but they slipped down her cheeks anyway.

The front door opened abruptly. "You two coming in here?" Luis asked, head poking through the small gap in the threshold. "Collin is getting antsy about cutting the cake, something about the filling staying good."

"If I were you, I'd skip the cake," Margo murmured to Jackie.

With great reluctance, Margo untangled her arms from Jackie, who in turn snatched her hand as they headed back into the boisterous environment of the house. Someone had turned the music up, and the sound washed over them as they closed the front door.

Margo located Brent in the living room, walking toward the hallway. "I'll be right back," she whispered to Jackie before following him.

The brightly lit kitchen had Margo squinting again. Brent rushed over to a drawer next to the stove, digging through the contents with vigor. A large cake strewn with obnoxious blue and green sat on the counter, the colors exploding on the white frosting. *Happy Birthday, Margo* was sprawled over the top in red, and Margo chuckled. "Nice cake."

Brent paused his rummaging to look at her. "Yeah, uh, Collin made you one, but let's just say it had an unfortunate end."

Chuckling, Margo shook her head, not wanting to know the story on Collin's cake. Instead, she asked, "Any news?"

Brent resumed his fumbling through the drawer, tossing random items onto the countertops in his search. "Nothing yet. They've called off the census testing for now until they've found Sybil, just as I anticipated. Not sure how long the respite will last." He picked up a withered piece of cardboard, inspecting the trash before throwing it. "How can I not find one single cake candle? We've got ritual candles, wax for parcel sealings, tapers, votives, tealights, but not one birthday candle?"

The testing was canceled. Margo smiled, leaning against the refrigerator as a weight lifted from her shoulders. A thought occurred to her. "If you guys recorded her shifting, why not take the tape to Corporate?"

Brent rose, shutting the junk drawer without putting the junk back. "Because Calliope has a plan in place that I think will be foolproof. Taking the tape to Corporate could potentially work in our favor; however, they could simply destroy the evidence, as well as Sybil herself, once they find her. Pretend the whole thing didn't happen."

"Calliope, the detective?"

"Yes, we've been collaborating, and I have to say she's a very resourceful person." O'Sullivan had a plan? Margo wasn't sure she completely trusted the Selkie, but at this point, she didn't think there was a choice in the matter. "Did Jackie tell you about Roz?"

"Yeah. What're we going to do?"

Brent sighed. "We have a plan involving Sybil. I only hope she'll cooperate."

"Where is Sybil, anyway?"

Brent hesitated, lifting a brow. "She's in a safe place where she can make the decision."

"And if she doesn't?"

A wary smile crept across Brent's face, but before he could speak, Collin entered the kitchen triumphantly holding two worn stick candles.

"Here!" he exclaimed, poking them into the top of the sheet cake beside the stove.

Handing Collin a lighter, Brent began the horrendous birthday anthem, and Margo ran for the living room, but they followed, getting louder. Once around the corner and in sight, Sam, Luis, and Jackie chimed in to the song, and Margo plopped onto the couch, her cheeks burning as they all sang to her.

Once finished, they all clapped, and Margo grinned, still shaking her head. "You guys are too much." Collin placed the cake on the coffee table, grumbling that *his* cake was far better. He couldn't understand how it ended up falling on the floor. But he was so thankful Brent thought to have another just in case while Brent smirked behind him. After everyone had a slice of the store-bought cake, Margo took a small bite of her own before placing it on the table.

Brent stayed standing, a hand resting on his hip. "I'm not sure how many of you know about this," he began, his voice reverberating off the foyer walls. "Corporate is determined to remove every single half—or less—blooded Grim. Now, our first assumption was they would only decommission these individuals, but this was a lie. They plan to kill them. We have to stop them."

Jackie settled next to Margo as Brent continued.

"This isn't going to be easy nor a guaranteed success, but we have no other choice. What they're doing is wrong by anyone's standards. I have a meeting to discuss this with a colleague and Prince Jael. My hope is we can build an allegiance with them. We can't do this alone." He clasped his hands together, his smile forced. "Now, who is willing to help?"

Sam lifted her hand, a shadow of doubt cloaking her face. "Uh, I'll help, however I can."

"Yeah, me too." Luis tipped his beer bottle in Brent's direction. "I want my sister to stay alive and any other Grim who is just a little different."

"You know I'm in," Collin said from beside him.

Brent nodded, his gaze landing on Margo.

Jackie cleared her throat. "I'm helping whether you want me to or not."

"Do I have a choice?" Margo asked. Brent blinked at her, unamused. "Have you lost your sense of sarcasm? Jesus, Brent, of course, I'm going to help."

Brent shot her a smirk. "Wonderful."

Margo picked up her cake again as the stereo was turned up, and the tension diminished throughout the room. She looked around, taking in the faces of the people surrounding her. Sam knocked back a beer, chatting animatedly with Luis by the flickering fireplace, both laughing raucously. The events preceding this moment told Margo things would get worse before they got any better, forcing her to believe this reprieve would be her last for a while. As if sensing the dilemma bouncing around in Margo's mind, Jackie interlaced her fingers in Margo's and squeezed. Margo turned her head to catch Jackie's mouth tilting into a beautiful smile, the corners of her eyes crinkling. "You okay?"

Despite the madness flooding their people, regardless of the mystery cloaking their future and uncertainty in the coming days, Margo found comfort in being surrounded by the ones she called family. She smiled, leaning in to press a kiss to Jackie's soft lips. When she pulled back, she whispered, "Yeah, I think I am."

Acknowledgements

Gigantic thank you to my editor, Barb, for loving my characters—especially Margo—as much as I do. Serious gratitude to my friend, Eddie, for staying with me through the countless false starts with this one and listening to me rant and rave about my elusive characters.

Thank you so much to Natasha for creating yet another incredible cover. It's gorgeous!

Huge thank you to my other half, Les, for not giving me the side-eye every time I stayed up well into the early-morning hours writing this, and for always being supportive, even when I'm rambling about random story tidbits. And thank you to Brittany for the incredible last-minute feedback that truly helped this story along.

About the Author

Jodi Hutchins is a healthcare professional by day and fanatical writer by night. Along with taking entirely too many photos of their four cats, they drink coffee strong enough to hold up a spoon, pretend to harbor an artistic talent, bake more things than they can possibly eat, and hike with their spouse and children as often as they can despite the near-omnipresent rain of Western Washington.

Email: jodi.hutchins.author@gmail.com

Twitter:@HutchinsJodi

Other books by this author

Yule Love Her

The Grim Assistant

Also Available from NineStar Press

Connect with NineStar Press

www.ninestarpress.com

www.facebook.com/ninestarpress

www.facebook.com/groups/NineStarNiche

www.twitter.com/ninestarpress

www.tumblr.com/blog/ninestarpress